Cassandra
Singing

Books by David Madden

Fiction

THE BEAUTIFUL GREED

CASSANDRA SINGING

Nonfiction

WRIGHT MORRIS

TOUGH GUY WRITERS OF THE THIRTIES
    (*editor*)

PROLETARIAN WRITERS OF THE
    THIRTIES (*editor*)

THE POETIC IMAGE IN SIX GENRES

Cassandra
Singing

a novel by
David Madden

CROWN PUBLISHERS, INC., NEW YORK

© 1969 BY DAVID MADDEN
LIBRARY OF CONGRESS CATALOG CARD NUMBER: 75–89872
MANUFACTURED IN THE UNITED STATES OF AMERICA
PUBLISHED SIMULTANEOUSLY IN CANADA BY
GENERAL PUBLISHING COMPANY LIMITED

To my Grandmother,
who told me stories

Cassandra
Singing

CHAPTER

I

THE BACKFIRING OF A MOTORCYCLE AS IT ROARED OVER THE LOOSE planks of the swinging bridge opened Lone's eyes. Through melting frost on the windowpane, he looked down the hollow and saw Boyd jounce off the bridge onto the highway in front of an overloaded coal truck.

From the kitchen came the ringing clatter of a stove lid. Looking up past the catalpa tree, Lone watched Coot, followed by the snaking line of hounds, trudge up the ridge behind the barn, shotgun riding his shoulder.

Lone turned his head and gazed at the silence of the house: a swath of cold pallid sunlight lying across the foot of Cassie's bed. Behind her closed eyes was she awake or asleep, he wondered. His gloved hand, curled under his chin, reminded him that he had slept in his clothes. The other hand, bare, its glove clutched between his legs, lay outside the quilt Momma or Cassie had thrown over him in the night. The mouth of one boot looked up at him from the floor. Sensing that Cassie was awake, he shut his eyes and kept still.

Barely loud enough for a person beside her to hear, Cassie

said, "Lone, you didn't even tell me where all you and Boyd
went last night," making him feel like an eavesdropper.

The acid of sleep in his mouth, he dozed. The morning chill
penetrated even the leather jacket and the corduroy pants.

In the doorway, Momma coughed, and Lone kept his eyes
shut. "I'll swa'an, sleepin' in that old motorsickle getup agin." A
floorboard near his cot creaked. Lone smelled her. He waited,
expecting her to shake his shoulder. Was she wearing the torn
slip or the starched green uniform?

"Momma! Momma! I had the awfullest dream!"

"Now, Cassie! Don't you start us all off this mornin' with
one a your blamed nightmares hangin' over us."

"Nearly chewed me to rags and molasses! Coot's ol'
hounds! Chasin' me roun' 'n' roun' that ol' buckeye tree outsyonder and the buckeyes was people's eyes! Double cross my
heart to die."

"Blamed if I've *ever* heard the likes of the dreams and
nightmares *you're* always havin'!"

"Sometimes it ain't the dreams that's so bad . . ."

"I tell thee, it's got so a body cain't hardly believe a word
you utter."

"Then I'll just keep my trap shut."

"And nothin' that ol' doctor says explains a thing. 'Children
with chronic rheumatic fever often tends' "—faking sleep, Lone
enjoyed the way Momma mocked the doctor—" 'to have highly
unusual imaginations.' Junk!" Momma turned and, bracing her
legs against the cot, looked for a sign of Coot out the window.
"Soon's your Uncle Virgil comes home I'm havin' him turn you
over to the Holy Physician."

"What do faith-healers know about *me?* Even God don't
care nothin' 'bout hangin' round no sickroom."

Momma turned so suddenly her leg mashed Lone's hand
against the steel frame of the cot. "Cassie McDaniel! If I ever
hear such talk agin from that mouth of yours—!" Stepping
toward Cassie, she stumbled over the boot. "Honestly, that boy
burns up all his time on that contraption."

"Well, you know what happens when he stays home."

"I don't know no such." She kicked the boot—it skidded across the floor, whopped the wall. " 'Less it's the way his sister and his daddy torment him. You stuff one silly question after another into his head, and the songs you *won't* stop singin', and the weird things you try to tell him 'bout the Saharie Desert and the North Pole"—two magazines slapped together—"that you get out of this trash!"

"They's somethin' about trash that thrills a body's soul!" The magazines slid into a row of Cassie's medicine bottles. Lone remembered yellow *National Geographics* drying in the scorching sun, scattered over the tar-paper roof of the condemned house at the mouth of the hollow where the Poor Fork of the Cumberland River deposited them, roaring south, flooding Harmon four springs ago. "Well, Momma, I cain't get out and *go* like Lone can."

"That's it, start another day by layin' back and givin' up."

"I'm just gonna lay here like a mummy in one a them pyramids."

"Well, if pyramids are packed with junk, this room sure qualifies."

"One a these days I'll have me a good spell that won't quit, and I'll go off with some gypsies, all over creation, just a-wanderin' and a-lookin' . . ."

"Well, 'fore you light out, take your six o'clock syrup." As Momma turned, the hem of her slip grazed Lone's ungloved hand, and she shook his shoulder. "Lone, honey, wake up. Time to jump up, honey." She tapped his skull with her finger. "Honey, come on now." He stirred. "I said, git up from there!"

Rolling over on his stomach, Lone stuck his rump into the air and clutched his pillow. "What time is it? What day? What country? What a goddamn stupid way to live!"

Momma slapped his rump. "Shut up your cussin', you no-'count hoodlum!"

"I'm gittin' up. I don't know why." On his heels, he stretched his body elaborately, yawning up and down a musical scale. Suddenly, he gave Momma a comic grin, but seeing her ribs through the rent in her slip, he turned to look at Cassie.

Giggling, she was burying her head in her pillow, sticking up her rump. "She learnin' to be a mole?"

Momma smiled and watched Cassie wiggle her rump, her thin, ragged nightgown draped over curved, sharp bones and caught between her buttocks. Her long, blond hair obscuring her face, she sat up, slowly turned on her knees, twisting the sheet, preserving the track of the movement. Embarrassed to watch Cassie playact in front of Momma, Lone lit the stub of a cigarette he found in the hubcap he used as an ashtray. "I'm blind! I'm blind!" Cassie wove her head slowly left and right, her long, bony fingers groping through the darkness she conjured. "I see nothin' but the Great Northern Lights and I hear ever' sound in the world at once. By the beard of Allah, now that I, their leader, am struck blind by the black spirits, who will lead my tribe across the desert to the oasis?"

On his knees, head bowed, spewing smoke, Lone ignored Cassie. Standing in the morning light before the oval mirror above the dresser, Momma threw back her head, her soft hands lifted, spread her coal-black hair over her wrists, then let it spill down her back, her strong brown neck bent back above the creamy sheen of her slip, and with a reverse flick of her wrists, she brought the hairnet up over her head and forward, puffing the pompadour.

Giggling, Cassie parted her long hair and blinked at Lone's blank stare.

To avoid the hurt look in her pale green eyes, Lone turned abruptly to the window. "Dang, look at that frost!"

"It's a freak frost!" The backs of her hands lifting her long hair, Cassie imitated Momma's morning gesture with the net.

"Good thing I pitched that tarp over my 'sickle last night."

"You could barely pitch your*self* on that cot." Lone knew that Momma was only working herself up to say more later.

Vigorously scratching his head with the gloved hand, Lone began hopping around in the one boot, feeling Cassie watch him as he looked for the missing boot.

"This frost's apt to kill off the 'simmons. Like me to put up some preserves 'fore it's too late?"

"On hot biscuits!"

"With pickles!" Cassie crossed her eyes and wiggled her nose.

"Hush!" Momma snapped her fingers, pointed one at Cassie.

"Where the hell's my cotton-pickin' other boot at?" Lone on his knees looked under the big brass bed.

"Well, I tell you." Cassie bounced up and down on the mattress, shaking dust loose. "When I woke up, they was this one-legged cowboy limpin' out the door . . ."

"Lone, honey, do your momma a favor and don't disgrace me by wearin' that motorsickle rig to school agin."

"Man, oh, man, I smell coffee boilin'!"

"Pourin' hot, I reckon." Going down the hall to the kitchen, she said, "That Coot don't even wait for his coffee no more."

"Worries the holy hell out a me . . ." Lone muttered. He hobbled around the room. "Hey, whistle britches, you seen my other boot?" He sat on the edge of his cot, about to give up. Cassie pulled the boot from under the quilts and held it out to him. "What— What in the name of fire was it doin' under there?"

"Wearin' it. My foot was cold."

"Just one of 'em?"

"*Of* course. Any law says they both gotta be cold at the same time?"

Lone pulled on the boot and stood up. "Good thing I got over that fever when I'uz little. Be—light-headed as you by now."

"Don't . . ." Cassie reached for her guitar, cradled it in her arms, and, staring into the box, began to strum. "Drunker'n forty hells on that medicine," she once told him, "it feels like skin," and ever since, the gray guitar seemed like a living thing. "If it was left up to me, we wouldn't *be* so different."

"Honey, I'uz just kiddin'. One way, that bed, this room— it's better. I wouldn't want you out in Harmon—cleanin' up a filthy old *ho*tel, like Momma . . ."

"Would it really get *on* you, Lone?"

"Girl, don't put me under the bright lights this early." He glanced out the window, trying to catch a glimpse of Coot on the ridge.

At his back, shifting from one bony hip to the other, setting the springs to jigging, Cassie tried to make the damp pages of *Look* crackle, to turn him from the window. She spent most of the daylight and waking night at the only window in the room, but she didn't need a window to look out. Her eyes at the window, glassy as the pane itself, she often seemed to stare into the room. Her back to the window, she likely gazed at something outside.

Until he crossed the swinging bridge, he could not begin to escape her, for if he turned from the junk in the yard—the rimed, red shell of an old-timey gas pump, leaning against the outhouse that Coot had painted green halfway up from the ground, its glass dome cracked, coal dust griming its white globe with the red Texaco star, its hose and nozzle flung out like a snake reaching for the jungle of kudzu vines that had begun to invade the clearing, and the busted car seat under the white ash, the baby buggy, its ribbed frame stripped of the blue canvas hood, the frayed ropes and rusty chains dangling from the buckeye tree, the coal truck steering wheel hanging from a limb high in the catalpa tree—he would see a room crammed with the junk they had scavenged together when he was little and that she now collected alone, from the riverbanks when the floods receded, from Gran'daddy Stonecipher's junkyard, from the streets of Harmon where she wandered, burning up the energy of her good spells—the big merry-go-round horse, its red nostrils flaring the way Cassie's did when she got excited, its two upraised forefeet broken off, its colors faded by sunlight burning through the window glass, its bridle rotten, and the flock of alarm clocks that hung from hooks in the ceiling on long strings that she sometimes got going all at once but were all run down now, and the old records nailed to the clapboard wall next to the kitchen that was left exposed when the bedroom was added to the old house the year Lone was born, and the highway sign warning of a curve that the flood took, and another warning of

DEER CROSSING, and the Royal Crown bottles littering the floor, and the peacock feathers, and the photographs tacked to the walls, and the blue speckled night pot he emptied for her every morning in the outhouse, and the surveyor's tripod that the engineers for the new highway left in the yard when they went to lunch, and the rifle that drops flakes of rust if you touch it. And now with a speed only her high voice could imitate, she was writing in the margins of *Look*.

Lone tried to scrawl his name in the melting frost on the pane but the sun had warmed the glass. Often the messages Cassie wrote on the pane in the morning wept in the noon sun. Through the moisture, he looked at the rusty tractor parked at the edge of the crude road on the crest of the ridge. Turning from the window, he took out the makings and began to roll a cigarette.

Cassie stood up in the bed, the patchwork quilt drooping from her head, behind her the faded poster of *Gone With the Wind*, relic of last year when he was an usher at the Majestic. When Cassie lifted and spread her arms, she obscured Rhett Butler carrying Scarlett O'Hara up the wide stairs. Peeking out of the tent she had made, Cassie said, "Hey, Paleface, come on in off the prairie."

"Rollin' my own like a cowboy?" Lone laughed, spilling some. "Boyd learned it in the Marines and taught *me* how."

"Smokin' ain't all. Taught you how to ride a 'sickle, how to stay out late, how to drink Falstaff. All *I* get taught from my homebound teacher is long division, parts of speech, and when Napoleon met his Waterloo." Letting the quilt drop, she reached for her guitar.

"Be meetin' mine 'fore long, if I don't live right."

"You never told me what happened last night. Just staggered to your cot, leaned over, dropped, and sank—like into that creek water you smelled of."

"I ain't been in no creek, that thing runs with filth, girl!"

"Yeah, but the flow's clean."

"Aw, hush it, you get me all turned around." He tossed an

empty matchbook at her feet—"Don't say I never give you nothin' "—and took a giant step toward the door.

"Lone, whoa a minute."

He slapped the bottom railing of her bed. "Honey, will you quit houndin' me?"

"Sister, leave him alone!" Momma thumped the iron on the stove in the kitchen. "Your brother's gotta git off to school."

"I just wondered. What does that X mark on your boot stand for? Looks like somebody made it with their finger."

Embarrassed, Lone smiled, remembering Gypsy's moist mouth, the tip of her tongue when she licked her finger and, while Boyd's back was turned, made the mark, her secret sign that she would meet him in the silo after Boyd had gone home. "That's for big boys to know and little girls to find out when they get married."

"Foot fire!" she strummed. "Go on, *turn* your back on me. I'll use my imagination."

"Be more'n anything *I* could ever say—or do."

"I bet I'd know a few things if I started night prowlin' again."

"You too old for that. 'Sides, that good spell you had last spring'll *do* you awhile yet."

"When you all was still, I'd creeeeeep out in the dark and go in and out of ever' house up the holler." As she crawled around on the bed, he noticed that it had become smaller because she had grown almost as tall as he was, but stayed as skinny as ever. "Set in their livin' room and look at the moonlight over ever'thing. Slip in their kitchen, and I could hear the mice stop chompin'. And even sneak in their bedrooms and the windows would be open and the curtain blowin' out over the bed and draggin' over their feet. . . ."

Seeing that in bright morning light chilled Lone. "You ain't leavin' that raft, girl." Lone shoved out his foot, shook the springs.

"Raft, huh? You better keep a eye on me, 'cause if I ever learn to *swim* a stroke—" She swayed on the mattress that seemed afloat, her nipples rippling the thin mauve gown.

"You hush, Cassie! And keep that damn nightgown up over your shoulder! You ain't no little girl no more!"

"Cain't prove it by *me!*" Her voice lashed out at him as he walked quickly down the hall toward the kitchen: "Damn it to hell!"

Momma was pouring coffee. "Why don't you get her a new nightgown?" He sat at the round oak table before the steaming cup, across from Momma. "Ain't fit. And that slip *you* wear ain't decent, neither."

"Why, I never think about such things, honey. Ain't like they's a lot of grown men around allatime. And Coot, he just—"

"Well, when it comes over you I'm old enough to be drafted, send up a flare. Oh, skip it!"

Just as Lone took the first scalding sip of coffee, Cassie began to sing: "Come all ye fair 'n' tender ladies. . . ."

Lone stuck a broom straw through the cookstove vent, lit the cigarette he had rolled. Staring over each other's shoulders, Lone and Momma drank silently awhile. The ironing board, a padded plank, rested on the back of a blue straight chair and the edge of the table at Momma's elbow. The smell of steamed, freshly ironed starched cotton came across the table from the green uniform Momma had put on.

A shotgun blast boomed on the ridge, rumbled down among the outbuildings, shook the windowpanes over the sink. Lone and Momma looked toward the window, then at each other, their hands gripping the hot cups. Then Momma took another sip, and Cassie sang again:

> "I wisht I was some little sparrow,
>   And I had wings and I could fly. . . ."

"Hope he missed."

"Don't make fun a your daddy." Momma tucked loose strands of hair into the net.

"Didn't you say one a the big dogs over on the L & N offered to let him work on the tracks agin?"

"He did, he did. Coot just give him one a his looks and

turned his back on him and staggered into the barn and squatted down in the middle of his congregation a dogs." Closing her eyes, she shook her head.

"Youn' man, ne'er cast your eye on beauty,
For beauty is a thing that will decay."

Lone stared into the black coffee that no longer warmed his face.

"I've seen many a fair and a bright sunny mornin'
Turn into a dark and deludinous day."

"Is that radio on?" Lone asked casually, seeing the light behind the station band.

"I'uz lettin' it warm up." She stood up and turned the dial on the table model that set on top of the warmer of the cookstove.

". . . for I'm bringin' you the good news of salvation this mornin' and the bad news of damnation." Recognizing Uncle Virgil's voice, Lone, surprised, excited, started to speak, but Momma put a finger to her lips to shush him, then pressed the finger on his shoulder. "And I mean to speak it plain, honey, they ain't no salvation without Calvary, for there'll come a day, there'll come a day, bless Jesus—maybe before the hour is up— so the time is now, the time is now. There was a time when I wasn't worthy to breathe His name, bless God, but, honey, come the day I looked on Calvary, and drunk the blood of His broken body, for I knew, I knew I had come into condemnation without Him, and by the spirit of the livin' Christ, I was transformed into His likeness. Oh, I'm glad this morning it'll work. Just one look—thank God. If you're sick of soul, I've got the remedy for you—the only thing, bless God, that'll satisfy the longin' of your soul. Look to Calvary's rugged mountains and believe on Him, step over the rock of ages into paradise, let that glorious power that's rooted in God work a change in your body, a body without no sin, never be no pain, for after a while, praise God, it'll be washed pure in the blood. One glimpse of Calvary, honey, one glimpse of Cal . . ." Organ music drowned out Virgil's voice, but Lone suddenly saw his face: the hollow eye sockets and cloudy eyes, dark brown like Momma's, but a face more like Cassie's and Lone's, with sharp cheekbones and a curved thin mouth, for he, too, had had rheumatic fever when he was little, and languishing three years in a Japanese prison camp had broken him down all over again.

"You have been listening to Virgil Stonecipher, guest evangelist on the 'Morning Worship Hour' . . . from La Follette, Tennessee."

"Oh, shoot! that blamed"—Momma snapped the dial— "clock! I thought he was just comin' on."

"Uncle Virgil's in La Follette?"

"Sure as the world."

"Then maybe he's comin' home 'fore long. I'd sure love to see him."

In the doorway, Cassie struck up:

> "There is power, power,
> Wonder-workin' power
> In the blood, in the blood. . . ."

"Save it, Cassie." Without turning to look at Cassie, Momma stared at Lone: "You reckon he'd love to see *you?*"

"Why not? Didn't he always say I—"

"—could charm the marks off a snake." Cassie struck a chord.

"That you'd make—hush, Cassie"—Momma flapped her hand at Cassie, still not turning—"a better preacher than he ever thought of bein'?"

"Oh." Lone stared into his coffee cup. "I hope he *don't* come back for awhile yet."

"Well, I'll tell you one thing." She turned to Cassie, the movement of her wide hips making the starched uniform hiss. "You get off these cold floors. . . . Lone, it'd break his heart to see you on that 'sickle, runnin' with the lowest trash in Harmon.

They ain't a razor-cut difference between Boyd Weaver and the way Virgil roared around 'fore he went to the war. And I wouldn't doubt if Boyd don't run moon like Virgil done."

"Ha!" Cassie strummed a raucous chord.

"Quit that horsin' around, Cassie!" Lone wished again she would pay attention to the way her nightgown kept slipping down over her shoulder.

"Maybe if *Boyd* spent some time in a Jap prison camp—"

"Momma, Boyd's got nothin' to do with this."

"Then who keeps you up after midnight, drinkin' rotgut and ramblin' around till you're so run down you couldn't chase a three-legged hound dog, much less a two-legged boy that wants that athletic scholarship bad as *you* do? You almost as thin as Cassie."

"Don't worry, Momma, I got till spring to get in shape for the track meets. I know how much that atheletic scholarship means to you."

"Well, don't it mean the same to you?"

"College seems far away as the North Pole, till you or Uncle Virgil get to talkin' about it . . . I just hope he waits a while to come home."

"It'll only be to see you. They ain't no future in *me* for him. Or Harmon. 'Cause ever since he left home, he ain't gone nowhere but *up* in religion. It's you he's after. What you gonna say to him? Because he might come walkin' crost that swingin' bridge before dark."

"How *you* know?"

" 'Cause I wrote him."

"Momma, that was a dirty thing to do to me."

"It was Virgil got you down on your knees in the Square that Saturday night, so I'm hopin' he can be the one to make you park that blamed motorsickle in Daddy's junkyard."

"Momma, if you could just see what that motorsickle means to me . . ."

"All Harmon can see what it's *doin'* to you. Lone, Lone, I never know from one day to the next what you're gonna pull. The way you talk lately, the way you race all over creation with that Boyd Weaver, up and down ever' dangerous highway in the county—tryin' your levelest to get yourself killed. Oh, I tell thee, I'd love to slap that Boyd Weaver from one end of Harmon County to the other! And if you live long enough, you'll end up like your daddy. Farmin's the only thing that man ever knowed, cared about, or could do at all. Me and your Uncle Virgil see more in the future for you than scratchin' around, tryin' to force a stalk of corn out a soil that give up the ghost long long before you'uz ever born."

"I know, Momma, I know."

"Then act like it!"

"One way you could keep your motorsickle and satisfy Momma and Uncle Virgil, too"—Cassie stood almost behind the stove to keep out of Momma's reach—"is to do what we always dreamed of doin'—roam the mountains and sing for Jesus."

"If it ain't speed on the highway steerin' you wrong"— Momma slapped the table—"it's the wild talk pourin' out of that child's mouth!"

"Ramblin' over the hills of Kentucky and Tennessee and West Virginia in the hurtin' cold and fryin' heat." Cassie picked out a steady thrum-thrum-thrum on the gray guitar as though trying to give herself a background as in a cowboy movie. "Just me and Lone, roarin' from town to town on that motorsickle, him preachin' and me singin' spirituals ever'where we go. 'Power in the Blood'!"

"You quit dreamin' up stuff for you and Lone to do. He's got a future a his own to follow."

"Remember how Virgil used to innerduce us? 'Brothers and Sisters, I want you to look at these young'uns! Skin and bones and eyes like green-eyed cats and hair like lions. Perfect twins—'cept Cassie was born three years late. And if you don't believe me when I say they can sing the birds out of the trees, let your own ears be my witness!' " Watching Momma get up, Cassie backed toward the door, the guitar before her like a shield. "Set my cheeks afire to hear him brag on us."

"Git in that bed 'fore I jump you." Cassie whirled around,

and went down the hallway, whang-whanging the guitar. "Hatefullest little hellion ever I saw."

"Maybe ever'body'd be better off if I'd just run that motorsickle in the Cumberland River, and me go with it to the bottom."

Suddenly Momma crossed her arms over her face and began to cry, walking about the room, bent over. "Oh, Lone, honey, stop it! Don't say another word! A boy with maybe a college education waitin' for him that would stand up to his Momma and talk like that . . ."

> "Black Mountain, Black Mountain,
> We're a-comin', Black Mountain."

The wall between the kitchen and the bedroom couldn't distort Cassie's high, piercing voice and the shriek of the guitar strings.

Annoyed, embarrassed, sorry for having provoked Momma's tears, Lone got up and walked around the table, his hands in his pockets, unable to do or say anything to comfort her. "Cassie, will you for pity sakes cut it out!" Then he realized that she had already stopped. "Momma, please don't cry. Time to get on to work in a few d'recklies. Listen, I'll leave the 'sickle at home and walk over the bridge to the *ho*tel with you."

Her back toward him, Lone stood close to her, looking down at the soft coils of her black hair forced into the net. Between two fingers he caught a piece of lint, remembering the feeling in his wrists when he pulled the big snaggle-toothed white comb through her thick hair as she sat on the edge of the bed where he and Cassie both lay sick, her face young, as in the soft, oval-shaped picture of her on the console radio in Gran'daddy Stonecipher's living room. "You got lint in your hair. . . ."

"Lone . . ." She turned, dropping her arms, and looked up into his eyes. He let the tiny strand of cotton drift from between his fingers. His heart began to thud, and he turned abruptly half-aside, thrusting his hands into his pockets again. Blood seemed to beat in his hands. When he turned again, tears glistened in her eyes and her full mouth was moist. Fear crossed her face, and she stepped back awkwardly on the broken linoleum. But then she moved slowly, very close to Lone as he pulled his hands tensely out of his pockets. He was shut away with her in a small, warm place.

His fingertips grazed her bare arms just below the short sleeves of the starched uniform when he heard a foot strike the side of the house on the back porch.

LONE AND MOMMA STEPPED QUICKLY APART AND LOOKED AWAY from Coot, who stood in the open doorway, the shotgun resting across his shoulder, a bleeding rabbit dangling from his fist. Cassie stood in the hall doorway, the mauve nightgown hanging over her thin body like a sheath of gauze, her hands in front of her, fingertips touching.

Unshaven, railroad cap crooked on his head, brogans streaking the floor with red clay, Coot limped across the room, his right shoulder slumped lower than usual, and Lone knew that he must be feeling sad and mean.

"*There* he is," said Lone, in a tone of mock indignation, trying to create good humor. "Man that let the air out of my tires the other mornin'."

"Lord's sake, what's that danglin' from your hand, Coot," said Momma, going along with Lone, "a rabbit?"

" 'Bout time," said Cassie, looking at Lone and Momma. "You've fired off every mornin' for the last ten years and ain't hit nothin' yet."

Standing still, Coot squinted his bloodshot eyes at them.

"Looks like I've stirred up a nest a smart alecks," said Coot. "Way it happened, these two rabbits come up where I'uz restin', and one was peekin' into the barrel while the other was fiddlin' with the trigger."

They laughed, slapping each other, pushing at Coot.

"Want me to skin him up?" said Momma. "Be good for supper tonight."

As he walked about the kitchen, wiping his hands inside his back pockets, Lone felt Coot's eyes on him.

"But Lone don't eat no rabbit, do you, Lone?"

"Why sure, good buddy. I go ape over rabbit." He held a glass under the faucet and began to pump.

Coot pitched the rabbit onto the table, upsetting the coffee cups. Lone turned and they all watched coffee drip off the round edge.

"No, but you'll sure as hell squash 'em on the highway for no reason, with that murder machine. Feed for the everlastin' flies, huh?"

"Now, Coot honey, don't you all start this mornin'!" Momma put her hand over her mouth, her eyes pleading.

Coot rared back and the coffee dripped on the muzzle of the shotgun. " 'Start'? Start what? They ain't nothin' *to* start 'twinxt *us*. Is they, Lone? We mind our own business, don't we? Why, if they *was* anything to start, we would a started it back in April when the ground was ripe, wouldn't we, Lone? But here it is harvesttime at Black Mountain and ever'where else, and that sudden frost outsyonder's all we got to show."

"Well, I'm showin' you my hand. Come on, shake, good buddy. Don't go away mad."

"I ain't goin' *no* damn place."

Cassie stepped up to one side of them and stuck her scrawny arm between them. "First one spits over my hand wins."

Coot didn't laugh. He just looked at them. "All right, you damn heatherns, *make* fun." Then he looked hard at Lone.

As Lone stared into Coot's green eyes, he realized for the first time that he had grown as tall as his father.

"Coot, you all worked up over somethin', and you tryin' to provoke *me*."

"It's provokin' as hell to *me* to watch you ride that over-grown tricycle around. Out there's *good land*—and you jist ride away from it. After Virgil left, I thought it was gonna be okay agin. Me and you cleared and sowed the land. Then Boyd Weaver come on that motorsickle, and you neglected that land and the rains warshed it down, and it ended up another summer of just dabblin'. That frost on the window brung it all back to me."

"All spring long not two words from you, but come fall you run at the mouth day and night—accusin' *me*, every damn year."

"I knew it!" said Momma. "I knew it the very minute you come through that door!"

"Was it my fault you let the farm go to the dogs after scrapin' all those years to buy it? The corn left to die and the plow left to rust? Say!"

"A man with a broke foot cain't run a farm without his young'uns in there he'pin'!"

"Farm! What a place for a farm! Right on the edge of Harmon, where every cloud of poison from burnin' slag heaps can sift down on the plants, where the spring floods can dump tons of mud on the fields and back up all the trash from the river onto our front porch . . ."

"Well," said Cassie, "least I get to see *somethin'* of this world."

"You all argue like you got forever before you, when they're about to run that turnpike right through this kitchen." Momma stirred up the fire in the cookstove, clattering the lid. "Less'n a month, this house'll be nothin' but kindlin' in ever' stove in Harmon."

Lone turned away from Coot.

Through the windows over the sink, Lone saw above the barn the rain-cut rivulets in the slab of dirt the bulldozers had already spread over the side of the ridge.

"Yeah. Turnpike, so they can plant crosses where the cars wreck," said Coot, taking short steps, making sudden turns between the table and the sink. "And so you can take the money they give us and move us to some housin' project. Don't start that."

"You all needn't worry 'bout me," said Lone. "I ain't so sure I'll even *be* in the big city of Harmon when *next* spring comes. I just might take a notion to get on that old 'sickle of mine and head straight for the South Pole."

"That's your *sister* talkin'."

"I ain't said a word."

"Get back to bed, girl, and see if you cain't dream us all into paradise before dark."

"Cain't never tell what I might do." Lone stopped and stared at the wall. "Come back some day in my old age and set a iceberg smack-dab on old Coot's grave. How'd that look, Momma, 'stead of the monument he ain't gonna get?" Lone turned away from Coot's blinking stare.

"It'd be me under it beside him, don't forget, son. We may not behave no more toward one another like two people made one in the sight a God, but we are." Momma pressed the tips of her fingers against the fleshy lids of her large eyes. "Now let's just hush this wild talk. I swa'an, I just don't know what's come over you all lately!"

"The valley of the shadow of death," said Cassie. "Didn't it ever come over you?"

"Coot," said Momma. "You better get those old shoes off—you'll come flat of your back certain as daylight."

"My heart bleeds," Lone muttered, "ice water."

"Lone," said Momma, in a loud whisper, "it's God's commandment a son love and honor his daddy."

"I wish to God he'd give me cause. He tries to forget the way he acted towards me when Cassie and me *both* laid sick in that bed . . . callin' me a sissie and a coward, sayin' I wasn't no credit to him, and me so weak with the rheumatic fever I couldn't see light. Didn't I feel low enough it was me took Cassie out in that snow and . . ."

"When in this world are you going to stop blamin' your-self?"

"Ever' fall it comes over me agin . . ."

"Nobody *made* you to strike out for Black Mountain, lookin' for your gran'paw."

"They wouldn't a gone in the first place if you hadn't come back that fall cryin' about how your own daddy wouldn't even speak to you," said Momma.

"Oh, Momma, I've heard this stuff a thousand times," said Lone.

"Old man McDaniel's as much to blame as you, Lone. You was just so scared to see your daddy go down so fast after that trip, you wanted to go get his daddy and bring him to Harmon."

"If it hadn't snowed . . ." said Cassie.

"Why ain't you in bed?"

"Let her alone," said Coot.

Then Momma turned to Lone. "Son, you just don't know what that old man's done to us *all* without even comin' near us. All those years Coot tried to make a farm to please his daddy, and then that hateful thing just went in the house when he saw who it was comin' up the path."

"Well, you needn't git on that," said Coot.

"You," she said, turning on Coot, "ain't never done a single thing in all your life without it somehow aimed to please your daddy. And knowin' how the old man hates the very sight of you."

"It's not Gran'paw's fault, Momma!" Lone wanted to keep Gran'paw separate from Coot and Momma, and even from Cassie.

"You don't know a thing about him—never even seen him."

"We used to dream up stuff about him all the time," said Cassie. "Want to hear my best song about him?"

"Least he stays up on Black Mountain," said Lone, "where he don't bother and he ain't bothered." Lone knew that Gran'paw lived in a cove at the foot of Big Black Mountain, but he always thought of him as standing on the top—highest point in Kentucky—five thousand feet above Harmon.

"And I hope he *never* shows his face up this holler. I don't want my children even to lay eyes on that old devil."

"I can see him just as plain," said Cassie.

"Now, woman, I told you to keep your mouth *off* my daddy!"

"Just watch how you talk to Momma, Coot!"

"And *you* keep your tongue in the back of your mouth!"

"Cain't you all hush!" Behind the stove, Cassie hugged her guitar.

"Oh, how I wish Virgil'd stop tryin' to save the world and come home where he's needed," said Momma. "Cain't we forgive and forgit?"

"I'll worry about forgivin' after I've forgot," said Lone.

"I'm sick of you turnin' your back on me." Coot nudged Lone's back pockets with the wet muzzle of the shotgun. Lone flinched, jerked away.

Coot leaned the shotgun against the table and fished for something in his pocket. He thrust it toward Lone's face. The thick hands could still intimidate Lone, for his own hands were no larger than Momma's. "Know what that is?" Lone turned his back and held on to the pump handle. "That's a corn husker." Lone glanced over his shoulder. What Coot slipped over his finger looked like a rooster's spur. "Found it in the barn. No corn though. Anybody ask how come?"

"Who's gonna clean up this mess you made? Not Momma!"

"What you say, boy? You say somethin' to your father?" Lone stared into Coot's eyes. "Take them hands out your pockets and answer me, you no-'count little hoodlum!"

"All right, you damned malingerin' drunk! You stop tormentin' me, you stop throwin' off on Momma, and you clean up your nasty mess, or I'll knock the livin' hell out of you!"

Drawing back his fist, Lone flinched even before Coot lashed out and the corn husker slashed his cheek.

Lone shoved him against the table, and Coot rolled off with the gun, the ironing board dropped, and the iron slid down on top of him. Lying on the floor, Coot groped for the gun and raised the muzzle. Confused by his own action, he waved the muzzle awkwardly up and down, trying to pretend he hadn't aimed it at all.

"Were—you about to—*point* that thing at me?"

"You dared to—?" Momma's face turned red. "Git out of this house—Git out!"

"I god, Lone, I god, I god—" Astonishment made his gaunt face go slack.

"I said, git out, and don't you ever set foot over that sill agin!"

"Cassie, you think I would do a thing like that?"

"You weren't about to do no such thing, Coot." Cassie was in the middle of the room now, the neck of her guitar in front of her face.

"Ask Cassie, Lone. You think I would turn a gun on my own . . . ?"

Coot's thin, dry lips and the gray stubble on his chin evoked a tenderness in Lone that he knew no way to express. Hurt, dazed, he stared at Coot a moment, then walked out slowly.

"Lone, honey, please"—Momma's voice followed him down the hall—"for your momma's sake, leave that 'sickle in the yard! Don't you leave this room, Cassie!" Lone heard the slap of Cassie's bare feet in the hall behind him. "You just make him worse."

Lone's motorcycle was braced between two persimmon trees. When he was a child they sprang up side by side close together, forming a V, like legs sticking up in the air. The bark, composed of chunky rectangles, made Cassie see alligators on foggy mornings. But the glossy oval leaves were gentle. Lone slung the gray tarpaulin onto the ground and mounted the red motorcycle. The rubber handgrips were cold. Cassie ran across the steaming grass where the frost was melting in the level morning sun.

"Git in out of this cold, Cassie, with them bare feet!" *That long walk in the October snow twelve years ago. Only as far as Coxton before Kyle pulled off the highway in a patrol car in front of them and said, "That ain't the road to heaven, honey."*

Cassie pulled at his arm. "Where you runnin' off to, Lone?"

"I'm not runnin'. I'm gonna go off very slow, and I would appreciate it if you would very kindly and very slowly turn loose. Sometimes I feel like a bell rope from people hangin' on my arm."

Taking her hand away, Cassie pushed hair back from her eyes. "That's pretty good, Lone. Pretty good. Except maybe people wouldn't hang on your arm so much if they didn't hope the bell would ring one time. Ever think of that?"

"No. But I'm goin' somewhere where I can."

"To Gran'paw's?" Shocked, he saw the possibility so clearly in her eyes, he felt as though he was on Black Mountain now.

He wanted to reach the curve of his arm out and scoop her up and take her with him to paradise. Show her what she had never seen in pictures.

Gently, Lone pushed her away from the motorcycle. "One a these days, you're gonna pull on my arm, and the bell will toll. That's when I'll take you with me." Placing his feet firmly against the trunks of the persimmon trees, he pulled backward on the handlebars, forcing the motorcycle to roll backward, out of the V, and then he kicked at the starter rapidly, turning with quick twists of his wrists the handgrips, feeding the gas until he felt the power rise up in the machine like rage, between his legs, into his fingers on the grips, and then out of its shuddering into jolting forward motion, slowly down the path toward the swinging bridge.

"Lone! Lone!" Momma stood on the front porch. "Please, Son, don't! For your momma's sake!" The motor, backfiring, cut off her screaming.

His legs hugged the stuttering life of the motor, embracing the speed that blurred the trees. Propelled by anger and hate, he inhaled the acrid fumes, the wet raw chill of early morning, sucking it in violently. His eyes began to water, blurring his vision. Wishing he had remembered his goggles, he saw the green haze of a willow ahead, but the whips stung his face before he could duck. Turning off the path between a birch and a white oak, he slurred down the ragged bank, littered with debris dumped by the eleven families in the hollow, and rode over flat rocks that thrust ahead like deep steps down the bed of the shallow creek. As he jolted down toward the bridge, windows on the right, struck by the morning sun, flashed between the trunks of poplars, hickories, cedars. He glanced at Boyd's shack on a bank above the creek. He passed the new church being built for Virgil and the tent where Momma attended services meanwhile, three nights a week, and then the path dipped down and crossed the stream, and he climbed it and mounted the ramp to the swinging bridge.

Below the bluff on which the bridge was anchored curved the river. Then along the double set of L & N tracks stretched coal gondolas, a mile in both directions. The whopping of the tires over the loose boards and the sway and swing of the suspension bridge that he felt in the pit of his belly released in him a wild desire to race through Harmon and climb the Cumberland Mountains and go to Black Mountain. Over the highway he would wind, and off the highway onto a dirt road, and somebody would tell him the way to Ishmael McDaniel's place, and he would park under a blighted chestnut tree and climb a steep path beside a stream up the deepest hollow in the mountain and, with the morning shadows still on the hillsides, see a thin ribbon of blue smoke and frost on the window, the crystals still hard. It would be like Coot coming home after all those ruined years, and, with one strong embrace, Lone would be back in the time before the first railroad forced its way into eastern Kentucky, the first mine shaft penetrated the earth, the first macadam led the way out of the thousands of hollows into the towns.

Feeling the hard smoothness of the highway, he approached the deserted coal tipple where he always met Boyd after school. Lone speeded up, staring at the yellow line.

Passing the gray, deserted coal camp houses at the city limits, Lone began to climb into the mountains. High enough to see the town below, he didn't look back, and as he rose above ponds of mist toward the sunlight on the pine trees, he felt his burdens drop away: Cassie and her songs and her questions and her pale green, penetrating eyes—Momma and her pleading look of hope—and Coot and his forlorn look of reproach—Virgil and his voice of salvation and doom. But the feeling that someone was following him, catching up with him, made him look back suddenly, as he took the turn at a hairpin curve, expecting to see Boyd on his black Harley-Davidson, his goggles flashing sunlight. But the highway was bare, and he almost lost control. Slowing, he turned and coasted back down into the town. He would hunt Boyd and they would ride from Harmon to hell and back.

CHAPTER

3

PINES GREW THICKLY IN FRONT OF BOYD'S HOUSE, KEEPING OUT the sun. Brown needles and cones covered the yard and the small, square porch. Planks lay over the two broken steps, and until the days turned crisp at dusk, a ragged black slip stuffed under the door kept it open. In the living room, oil stains and jabbing scars on the soft floor showed where Boyd parked his motorcycle. Glass lay on the floor and outside in the tall grass that reached almost to the window locks. Wind down the flue had blown the reddish ashes and the soft soot, fanned it out across the floor. A child's rocking chair lay on its side, the straw seat gutted, as though someone in a fit had rammed his foot through it. Across the mildewed, rose-patterned wallpaper waved stains of urine.

In Mrs. Weaver's bedroom, where Boyd now slept, wallpaper hung down in buckles from the ceiling and stuck out like enormous dried plants from the wall, exposing gray plaster where sleek cockroaches darted. Boyd's lumpy mattress lay on the floor beside the window, four black holes testifying to the times when Boyd had fallen asleep with a cigarillo in his hand. In the middle, a mustard-brown army blanket lay, like something strangled. The breeze blew a stink through the screen where Boyd got up and stood in the night to piss into the creek below. Scattered over the floor were the romance magazines Boyd's mother had left behind, the faces on the covers mud-smeared from his boots. One lay open, its insides ripped out. In the closet hung a housedress buttoned up crookedly, a black brassiere, a white slip stained yellow, ripped down the side seam—and a sundress dangled by one strap. Under a thick layer of dust, old Kotex boxes lay on the floor. A contraceptive, slung against the wall, stuck, decaying. Photographs of Boyd in dress uniform and his letters from Parris Island lay among the debris on the floor.

Lone turned to go, but he had stepped in something and a letter stuck to his foot. He tried to scuff it off, but finally had to pick at it. "Dear Momma," he read, aloud, through the brown streaks, "How's my best girl? I hope they're sending you my checks okay." The writing was very poor. Lone let it flutter to the floor, and then he began to cry, at first dryly, from deep in his chest, and then, leaning against the wall in the kitchen, seeing through the window the dead rosebushes in the garden where Mrs. Weaver had grown the prettiest white roses in Harmon, he wept without restraint.

Lucidly seeing the objects in the room—the yellow sink full of garbage, a skin of mold on the drainboard, the vivid V crack in the window, the faded, gashed linoleum, the gaping black flue that had drooled a soot-and-rainwater stain, the punctures in the linoleum where the cookstove had sat, the hairy gray light cord with a broken bulb, the green spoon tilted against the white baseboard—Lone remembered Boyd's homecoming.

Walking down the wide path one Sunday morning last April, in the first sunlight after days of spring rain, Lone had watched a black motorcyle with a rider dressed in black emerge from the arch the kudzu vines made, hanging from the boughs of sycamores on each side of the path to Boyd's house. Flashes of sunlight seemed to buzz around him like wasps, glancing off the steel, the glass, the white leather seat, the handle grips, the tasseled trimmings, the goggles under the white-billed cap. The motorcycle passed the tent where Virgil was preaching and came up the hill path and was lost for a moment, the steady throb of the motor tuned down a little. Then he was suddenly up over the rise and pressing to a stop right in front of Lone, who stepped aside, afraid he would be run down. With one smooth movement, the rider slipped his goggles up over the bill of the cap, and it was Boyd on a new Harley-Davidson, back from Korea.

"They *dis*charged me," he said, " 'cause my momma needed me."

Lone was the first to know he'd lied, and nobody knew the truth. Because when Boyd had turned off the creek path and parked in front of his house, calling to his mother, *this* ruin was what he walked in on. Now that she had left, Boyd's nearest kin was twenty miles away, in Cumberland.

About to turn off the path to go into the tent, Lone heard him again, coming back down along the creek from the head of the hollow where he had been showing off. This time he aimed, straight as an arrow, at Lone. From behind the tarred telephone pole, Lone saw the tears glistening under the black rubber rims of the goggles that returned the wink from the glass insulators as Boyd sped past the poles and the slack wires.

Boyd had lived here, without light, in the last cold nights of early spring, burning, piece by piece, any part of the house he could jerk loose. Fighting anybody in Harmon who dared look cross-eyed at his outfit. And he'd bought the white silk scarf to taunt somebody into calling him a sissy. Nobody had.

Lone couldn't keep his eyes off Boyd, the very image of Virgil before Virgil went to war. Lone went where he hoped Boyd would be. He lapped up Boyd's indifference and cynicism as if it satisfied a craving he hadn't known he had. From the first sight of the motorcycle, his desire to ride made blood throb in his head. Then one morning in May on the highway in front of the coal tipple, Boyd scooted up to make room for Lone on his buddy seat.

A month later, they had found a wrecked motorcycle in Gran'daddy Stonecipher's junkyard, and Boyd had ended up at the supper table the evenings they spent working on it in the front yard under the leafbudding persimmon trees. Momma hated the sight of Boyd. Coot kept quiet. But he was the one who had told Boyd how he might make himself a little money—running "moon."

At his back, Lone heard the rats in the walls squeaking and scurrying.

As he walked toward the front door, he remembered a night a few weeks ago when he and Boyd had sat on the front porch eating Concord grapes they had swiped from a grocery store. "Son, it's high time you lost that cherry of yours." And he said he knew a place in Hazard.

Boyd turned up a steep street in Hazard where the long front porches of seven houses dropped down like steps from the top of the hill. Women's voices called to them from a porch near the top. Lone, slowed by the climb, scanned the porches and listened. Before he fully realized what the voices were saying, he felt a burning thrill.

"Hey, Boyd, who's that you got with you down there?"

"Harmon's number one cocksman." Boyd put his arms around Lone's shoulders.

Lone had broken free, turned, and coasted back down into Hazard, the high, piercing, almost singing laughter of the women, one voice louder than the rest, hovering above him in the air. During the long ride back to Harmon, he had ached with shame.

"Let's hit it, McDaniel! Come on, Lone Ranger, you're on the clock!" P. O. Fletcher stood inside the white circle on the basketball court with a stopwatch in his hand. The gym class sat in the bleachers, elbows propped on their knees, chins cupped in their hands, watching. The second turn had winded him, as P.O. could plainly see—he was going to make Lone run down like an alarm on a clock. In the streets below, the band marched soggily in the rain, tooting and pounding and squeaking "Columbia, the

Gem of the Ocean." Across the street wreckers ripped at some of the oldest houses in Harmon to make a clearing for the new highway. Each time Lone passed the open doors, his gaze fell on an exposed wall, red as an inflamed gum, where an old overcoat hung next to a door that opened on the sky. P.O. wanted the boys to see, when Lone finally bent over, his hands on his knees, panting, what he was worth to the school as a runner next spring. Last spring on the track he had showed what P.O., his arm around Lone's shoulder, had been pleased to call "promise." Every time he passed him during gym period, P.O. would give Lone a buddy-boy pat on the butt. Now he stood, khaki legs solidly apart, one fist on his fat hip, the other hand holding the watch, his massive arms brown from Florida beaches below the white sleeves of his T-shirt.

"Your time is about up, slue-foot! You better hustle if you gonna beat the record set by the world's fastest turtle."

"Huh huh huh huh huh huh huh huh huh" was all Lone could say. Well, to hell with it. He didn't care anything about running next spring.

Approaching the outside door, Lone saw a garbage truck start to pull away. Passing the door as some cabbage leaves bounced over the tailgate, Lone saw Boyd, who had stopped for the truck, step toward the open door. From that room this morning, he had emerged spotless, sleek and pressed. Except for the white scarf around his neck, and his olive skin, black covered him—black cap, black hair, black leather jacket, black denim, black boots.

P.O. slowly pivoted on his heels as Lone made another turn. "Come on, Christmas. Easter's just around the corner." Lone passed the bleachers, heading straight toward the open door, an inspiration. P.O. would have just enough time to see Boyd standing in the door, arms braced against the inside frame, one foot aslant the other, before he saw Lone run straight through it, Boyd stepping aside, and on out into the yard where the bicycles were parked. Laughter from the bleachers followed Lone out into the yard.

"All right, on the double, hit the showers!"

When Lone came back to the door, P.O. was there, looking at Boyd. "My God, two of a kind—the Lone Ranger and Zorro." Lone stood just outside, his hands on his hips, huffing and puffing. Boyd leaned in the doorway, smiling at P.O. "Who *you* lookin' for, Weaver? That fagged-out nothin' behind you? Hell, take him. He ain't worth nothin' to us. Look at him. Looks like he's been screwed to death by a elephant." Boyd looked at Lone and snickered, then looked at P.O. "Anybody sticks to you's bound to turn rotten sooner or later. Reckon the marines knew a rotten apple when they saw one. I can imagine what they did to you at Parris Island. We had a few just like you when *I* was in boot. They give you a scrubbin' party with barracks brushes? Or did they throw a blanket over you in the night and let you have it?" Boyd stopped smiling and straightened up. "If I was *you*, I'd keep leanin' till I was finally told to get the hell off the premises, Weaver. McDaniels, get in that shower!"

Lone caught his breath enough to say, "I was lookin' for you this mornin', Boyd."

Staring at P.O., Boyd said, "Just stopped by to see *you*, son."

"If I had my way, they'd take all you dropouts and drop you in the Cumberland River—below the city, so you won't pollute our drinkin' water."

Boyd smiled again, his thumbs hooked in the back pockets of his pants. "Can I say one thing, Mr. Fletcher?"

"Say it."

"I think you jealous of us because on our 'sickles we doin' the next thing to what you did in the marines, son. Tryin' to get ourselves killed. You missed *your* chance, and now you begrudge us ours."

"If this wasn't school property I'd laugh—then kick your ass around this schoolyard."

"Welcome to kick it, if you want the law all over you."

Down his neck into the white curve of his collar, P.O.

turned red. "Don't provoke me, Weaver. Get in that shower, McDaniels!"

Boyd knew when to stop. Smiling, he did a smart about-face out the doorway into the yard, came to attention, and called cadence as he marched away: "Hut, two, three, hut, two, three, hut, two, three. . . . Eat shit, Fletcher!" he yelled from the curb, where the black Harley-Davidson leaned arrogantly.

Lone stepped into the locker room full of naked bodies, pink from action and steam. Shucking off his shorts, he heard the motorcycle roar down the hill. The boys looked at him as if to say, you really pulled a hot one, Lone. He smiled, jerked off his tennis shoes and socks, and took a step past a stack of wire baskets into the shower room where nozzles ran hard, collecting steam that almost took his breath in the same instant that he heard a noise like a pistol shot and felt a sting on his buttock like a wasp.

Turning, he saw P.O. just outside the shower-room entrance, a sopping-wet white towel dangling at his side, a weak smile on his tan face, as though he had just realized he shouldn't have done it. And he shouldn't have. Lone lunged at him, tripping on the high sill.

P.O.'s arm slammed down on Lone's shoulder next to his neck. Stunned, Lone fell back against the lockers. His spine struck the edge of a bench where wire baskets were stacked, and his body collapsed limply, half on the floor, half across the bench, ensnared in the baskets. P.O. crouched over him, his arms spread for some terrible embrace, his stubby fingers splaying into claws, clenching into fists. Crawling backwards on his forearms and buttocks, Lone kicked and jerked his feet free of the wire snare.

"You better stay where you are, McDaniels. If you get up I won't be able to control myself."

"Kiss my ass!" said Lone, rising to his feet in a sudden thrust of energy. He grabbed a metal lunch box from one of the boys and cocked it over his shoulder, waiting for P.O. to move closer.

P.O. kicked the baskets out of his way and moved within range, poised for reaction. Lone swung. A loud whoosh through the air. P.O. ducked. His arms pulled back by the force of the finished swing, Lone couldn't resist P.O.'s plunge, so quick he didn't see the lowered bald head before it struck him in the stomach, pinning him against the sharp edge of a locker, knocked tilted against the wall.

P.O.'s arms closed around Lone's waist. Lone pummeled his back with his fists, weakly. Then his body, broken at the waist, arms and legs dangling, was rising above the benches and the baskets scattered over the wet, footprinted floor. The nausea in his stomach sent spurts of color through his head, filling the room. He was on the floor suddenly, flat on his back, breathing in short, painful gusts. P.O.'s thick body loomed over him. A sharp weight impaled him to the floor, crushed his chest. Blurred, P.O.'s face, teeth clenched, eyes blazing, hovered just above Lone's.

Many faces clustered together against the wall, where beads of moisture slipped down the glistening tile.

"I say kick him out—all the way out." P.O., standing in the middle of the principal's office, swung his thick arm past Lone toward the tall windows. Lone looked out and saw the wrecking crane swing the lead ball through the drizzling rain toward the wall just as the black overcoat dropped from its hook, as if ducking the blow that ripped through the red wallpaper of the exposed bedroom.

"Now, now, Mr. Fletcher." Gray ash streaks on his vest, as if he'd swatted moths, Mr. Deaderick sat behind his desk, tapping the tips of his fingers together, rocking back and forth in his swivel chair. *Probably sits that way on the commode, too.* Rain dripped on the window ledge from a tree, where a roll of toilet paper someone had tossed out the latrine window hung tangled, the tail end fluttering. Lone tried to hypnotize himself with the white flutter, but Deaderick's deep voice penetrated. "Lone, what do *you* have to say?"

"Nothin'."

"You're actin' like a kid who's about to throw his life away." Mr. Deaderick looked directly at Lone but pouches of flesh concealed his eyes.

"Well, ain't it mine to throw?"

Lone opened his notebook and began to sketch a motorcycle.

"You think it's just *you*, don't you?"

"I don't owe nobody a damn thing, do I?"

"You think that what you do, what you are, concerns you alone, don't you?"

"Well, don't it?" Lone drew the seat of the motorcycle.

"Look at me."

"I see you okay."

"One of the first things I heard when I got back from the Baptist retreat was that Lone McDaniel was gettin' his kicks ridin' a motorcycle."

"I like to ride."

"You used to like other things, too."

"A lot of things used to be. You're just like my sister. Always talkin' about what used to be. Why can't they leave me alone?"

"Who is *they?*"

"You—mark one."

"I haven't said a word to you since last spring at the track meet when you won that race."

Lone didn't like what was happening to his friendship with Mr. Deaderick, and he hated the way it was going to end.

"Give up on me, huh?"

"You heard that, didn't you, Mr. Deaderick?" said Fletcher. "Carbon copy of that Weaver scum. If I had my way—"

Paper fluttered in the tree. Rain dripped on the sill, and Lone imagined the throbbing pain in Cassie's bones.

"What're you drawin'?"

"My 'sickle."

"Do you still draw—the way you used to?"

"Sometimes, I guess."

"I heard your Uncle Virgil on the radio this morning. Close by. That streak still *in* you?"

"Haven't thought a hell of a lot about it. Besides. I'm up for a physical soon. Be hackin' my way through the jungle. Happy Hallowe'en."

Mr. Deaderick looked at him as though he thought the look was all it would take.

Fletcher's bald head, still red from the fight, made Lone think of a boil the first morning it shows up. The streamer of toilet paper appeared to flutter out of P.O.'s ear—then it broke from the bare branches of the tulip tree and soared toward the low clouds, underslung with the soot and smoke of Harmon coal stoves and slag heaps.

"Lone, it's a—"

"Cryin' shame."

"Waste."

"You people've had a hold on me long enough. Turn loose."

"Then you could ride, ride, ride, and nobody'd flash the red on you."

"Nobody?"

"Listen, what's tormentin' you, boy? It's not hate. I can see that. Maybe it's love. I once heard your Uncle Virgil preach that too much love can kill a person. Is that true?"

"How would *I* know?" Lone began to feel that the voice of Mr. Deaderick, who was once a preacher, was put-on compared with Uncle Virgil's.

"Point is, are you tryin' to find out? This is what your uncle would ask, you know." He paused to let that soak in. Lone, his pencil still, kept quiet. He looked at George Washington, hanging above Deaderick, steam as from a pot rising up to his neck.

Deaderick and P.O. talked awhile as though Lone weren't in the room.

"He's too young to get work." Very slowly, Lone blacked the body of the motorcycle, the soft pencil staining the butt of his palm. "Expulsion's pretty final, Mr. Fletcher." Lone was aware of Deaderick in his swivel chair: patty-cake, patty-cake, bob-and-sink, bob-and-sink. "We'd just be dumpin' him on the community."

"Know what'll make a man of him? Few years in the marines."

Blackening the handlegrips on the motorcycle, Lone said, "Well, least Uncle Sam wants me, don't he?"

"Lone," said Mr. Deaderick, "don't be like so many kids in eastern Kentucky. They join the army for glory and gory, and it wears off in boot camp like a spit shine. Don't fall for a pointed finger and its promises. With a sports scholarship—"

"He knows that, sir. Throws it in our face."

Lone sat very still, staring at the motorcycle's body until he heard gas gurgle in the tank. "Got something throwed in *my* face while ago, too, and it wasn't a scholarship."

"I *told* you he was a smart aleck." P.O. pointed at Lone as if he were a target.

"Don't say *was!*" Lone sat up straight. "You didn't kill me. I'm right here, you bastard."

"What's the matter with you, Lone?" Mr. Deaderick leaned forward, squinting, drawing tight the slack pouches under his eyes. "I really wonder what's happened to you."

"It never hurts to wonder."

"Well, I'm wonderin' what you have to offer this school." The lead in Lone's pencil was down to the wood. "Perhaps, Mr. Fletcher, if we got his mother in here—"

"Perhaps if you just went to hell, Mr. Deaderick, you'd *do* better."

"Lone McDaniel, I wash my hands of you. You're expelled."

"Mr. Deaderick," said Lone, softly closing his notebook, blotting out the motorcycle, the black body wheelless, like a streamlined roach, "I thank you."

"Get out." Deaderick shuffled papers on his desk, red-faced. "Go on, hit the road. Enough's enough."

"Kick 'im out, kick 'im out, kick 'im out!" Lone sing-songed, and, remembering, too late, his mother, for whom this school was a temple of hope, slammed the door.

CHAPTER

4

LONE TURNED OFF THE PATH, OVER THE RUTTED SWATCH OF DIRT and ashes, and thrusting the motorcycle between the persimmon trees, he stopped, shut off the motor, sat back in the saddle. The last vibration of the motor absorbed, he swung his leg over and his feet received the shock. He had moved on the wind through Harmon and over the swinging bridge—the ground felt dead. He stood still, staring at a shriveled yellow persimmon that dangled above the bill of his cap.

Looking out the window behind the swing chains, Cassie knelt on his cot. Her breath, clouding the pane, obscured her face, but her hair was a golden shimmer around it. A thin film of dust his motorcycle raised, coming and going. Her hair another film behind the pane, fine-spun silk she claimed she wove herself. At the window when he left. At the window when he returned. *She always seems like the night, even in the morning.* A keyhole to the city. Moving her face to a clear section, she looked at him, silently called, "Lone," and the vapor on the window stained her face again.

Suddenly, Coot's three hounds exploded through the

sagged-open door of the outhouse, rattling it, making it sway like a caboose, and stirred a coil of dust around themselves just outside the door, their teeth glistening with saliva. Then from the tall, narrow shack, Coot emerged, very slowly. His back to Lone, he shut the door, slowly, as though buttoning his fly. Poised between stepping off and standing still, he remained a moment at the door, his hand flat against it, holding it shut, one loop of his overalls hanging limply from his shoulder—and in that instant, Coot, the striped railroad cap; the overalls, bone-blue, a husk; the blue shirt, a paler, thinner husk under the twisted straps, behind the bib; the shoes, rooted to the ground; and the dogs, rigid, mouths open, enringed in their own growling, and the motionless dust, were caught in a photograph. Until the hand fell from the soft wood and dangled at his side. Until the foot rose, and the statue moved, setting the dogs off into a surging of brown hair and glaring eyes down the slope, bounding over the rain gulleys, the stumps and rocks toward Lone, waiting for the move he had learned not to make. Lone froze. But the bill of his cap had set a cluster of persimmons swinging, blotting and revealing the golden haze at the window. Around and around him and the persimmon trees the dogs whirled. In the corner of Lone's eye, Coot stopped trudging up the hill toward the barn, pivoted on his heels in the soft path, flicked his head aside to spit, and watched. Once, Lone ran when they set upon him in this way. They had caught him, blocked the front door, without even touching him, only streaking his trousers with saliva, like snail tracks.

Coot on the slope broke again the statue stance, raised his arm, flapped his hand, and yelled in a monotonous voice meant only for them, "Git away from him! Barn, you flea factories!" A tone of having told them twenty times already. They caught his voice on the air, followed the echo, and whined and crawled around his legs.

Lone leaped into the air and came down with a persimmon in his hand to throw after the dogs, but it squashed rotten, and the spoiled juice leaked out of his grip, down the inside of his wrist, into the sleeve of his jacket. Coot walked with a limp, giving a little shake as if trying to kick off a vine that got stuck to his bad foot. Years ago, somebody on the repair crew as lackadaisical as himself had dropped a rail on it. Elbows pumping, his hands in his pockets, he climbed past the willow, where the plow, as if lynched, hung from a low limb, pulled up to keep it from rusting, and up to the barn door. Then only his forearm and hand, holding the door open until they were all in, then pulling it to, shook slightly and was still.

Lone walked to the steps, anticipated, then felt, the sway of the lower one. Cassie had turned from the window, the stain of her breath dissolving on the glass.

"Lone."

He was not ready for her voice. He stopped on the sill. "Don't—"

"Where you been?" The rain had made her long hair straggly, moist and curly at her temples and in front of her ears. The sun on the window behind her turned her small, thin ears red. When she got down off the cot and moved into the shadows cast by the junk in the room, her ears turned pale and bloodless.

"South Pole."

"Does it hurt where Coot cut your face?" She knelt at the foot of the bed. The springs rasped—the sill creaked when he shifted his weight.

"It thobs a little." He didn't look at her. He lay back on the cot, closing his eyes. The hum of the motor dead, his body was limp. Pull the string of questions tight. Then cut it. "Ridin' in the mountains."

"To Gran'paw's?" Lone imagined her nostrils, quivering with excitement.

"No."

"Alone?"

"Yeah." No, she rode behind him on the buddy seat. Her thin arms hugged his ribs, her hair flicked the corners of his mouth. Cassie sighed, quietly, half-satisfied.

She turned on her knees on the edge of the bed and waited,

her open mouth a fountain, questions trembling at the lip. "What happened in the country?"

"Nothin'. It's just the country. Let me sleep."

He dozed. Then his eyes snapped open. His cap on her head, the goggles burnished with sunlight, she stood in Virgil's old army overcoat, the tail spread fanlike around her on the floor, and held out to him a letter, the other hand rising, as he blinked, to a salute. "Special delivery."

"What's that?" He took it and opened it. The U.S. Army ordered him to appear for a physical examination.

"I got a foolproof way to fox 'em," Cassie said. "Strike out for India on that motorsickle."

"When did *this* come?"

"Yesterday. I forgot. Does it mean they gonna send you to Asia?" Even through the goggles, he saw fear in her eyes.

"Maybe."

"It's a mistake, it's a mistake, it's a—" she said, grabbing the letter, wadding it into her mouth.

"I can't sleep around you." He started for the door.

"Stay in here with me, in our room, Lone. I'll be still."

He reached for the guitar where it leaned against the oak dresser and placed it in her hands and guided her gently onto the big bed. "Here, honey, sing yourself a homemade song. Real soft."

She got onto the bed and leaned against the bottom rail and hugged the guitar to her as though it were a doll, shook her head slowly four or five times to swing her hair away from the strings, and looked up at him. "Okay, *leave* me on this deserted island, but if you find my bones picked clean, don't act surprised."

In the dark attic, he walked on the narrow shelf of boards that Coot had nailed over the beams. Coot's old hats that had hung on wooden pegs in the hall, now hung on loose nails in the roofing. Lone lay down on the canvas cot, crossed his ankles, tucked his hands under his armpits.

Cassie's voice, singing, woke him. Still dozing, he listened.

"Hangman, hangman, slack up your rope,
    O slack it for a while;
I looked down yonder, I seen Maw coming
She's walked for a many long mile.

O Maw, say, Maw, have you brung me any gold?
Any gold to pay my fee?
Or have you walked these many long miles
To see me on the hangin' tree?

No, son, no, son, ain't brung you no gold,
No gold for to pay your fee,
And I have walked these many long miles
To see you on the hangin' tree."

Through the little grilled attic ventilator, eye-level where he lay, he saw Boyd walk in the clear, bright sunlight down the path from the barn, his body sectioned by the horizontal vent slats.

Cassie sang another verse, naming "Paw" instead of "Maw," and another with "friend," and then "O love, true love," and ended with one Lone wasn't prepared for.

"Yes, brother, yes, brother, I've brung you gold,
    Some gold to pay your fee,
And we will go to the mountains far,
And we will happy be."

He thought he'd been half-awake, half-dreaming, until he heard Boyd's voice distinctly in the room below.

"I bet if I was your manager, I could make a million dollars. You'd really tear *up* that Grand Ol' Opry, son."

Lone slipped off the cot onto the shelf and fitted his eye over the hole where Coot's foot slipped and cracked the plaster last night. The quilts covered Cassie's head. Boyd stood directly under the hole at the foot of the bed.

"No fear, Cassie, doctor examined me the other day. Said,

'Boyd, you can celebrate—you only got seven diseases left.' I says, 'Doc, cure me of the one that turns Cassie McDaniel against me, and I'll be content.' I *hear* you *laughin'* under there." The quilts quivered, the pale colors nibbled along the contours of her body. Then she peeled them down to her waist, wiggled back toward the head of the bed, and propped herself up on the three lumpy pillows.

Now that the sun had come out, burnishing the brass bed, making the studs on Boyd's jacket glitter, Cassie had loaded her fingers and wrists and neck with rings, necklaces, bracelets, dog tags Lone and she had collected and kept in a miner's black lunch box and a black violin case, along with a French harp, Shawnee arrowheads, a police whistle, a railroad spike, pipes, false teeth, an air hose nozzle, eyeglasses, the skull of a hawk, a light switch, a doll's eyes, a roll of movie tickets, spyglasses, and maybe a few things he had forgotten.

"You better sneak *out* the way you snuck *in*."

"Let's me and you both sneak out and ride to Kingdom Come. Be back 'fore bedtime."

"It's always *my* bedtime."

You better get the hell out of our room, Boyd, Lone told him silently.

He saw Boyd sail a new motorcycle cap over the bedrail into Cassie's lap. "Try *that* on. Promised Lone I'd make him a present of one." She put it on, giving the shiny bill a neat little pull to get it set on her head, a perfect fit. "Kindly put you in the mood?"

"Yeah, but thanks anyhow—Lone's gonna take me ridin' up on Black Mountain next time one a my good spells comes along."

"How long since the last time?"

"Longest yet—'bout a year."

"All that time in the same room!"

"I got ways of gettin' out without liftin' a bone. Seems like Coot works half the junk of Harmon into our yard, and the stuff people's always carryin' in—keeps me in touch with all kinds of folks. But *that's* the best way." She pointed at the stacks of boxes stuffed with magazines and papers on each side of the bed against the wall. Her library of scraps.

"Well, I hated to ask, but it always did prey on my mind what was in—"

"I got the world packed in them boxes. Magazines full of pictures of ever' kind a people and ever' kind a place. No need to even open them *National Geographics.* Shut my eyes and all the Greek ruins and ever'thing just flash right up on that screen inside my head." Continuous showing. Waking was only a changing of reels. "Momma says that proves I ain't right."

"Beats me how a girl with no more than a fourth-grade education can outread somebody that dropped out in the eighth."

"Not ever'body's my brand of maniac. Sometimes I want to live way back in the times when they built those temples in Mexico and cut your heart out on the altar, and sometimes I just want to be like any girl that goes to high school a year or two, gets a job in a café, and marries some ol' boy that drives a coal truck, and fills the holler with a gang a kids. I just daydream all the time 'bout bein' different people."

"Me?"

"A time or two. But mostly like Lone—be free and not think about anything, forget ever'thing, not give a—damn for nothin'. Not have to be somebody that's made up of ever'thing and ever'body I ever heard of or knew. Out a this bed, outs-yonder in the streets of Harmon, livin' my own life and nobody else's. But you know what scares me sometimes?"

"What?"

"That even if all those things I remember do hurt, somehow all those old memories are beautiful in a funny way . . . and I write in the margins of *Life* and *Look* and *Time* and *Official Detective,* anywheres they's room. . . . Might someday," she said, spreading her arms, curved slightly, "take to these walls . . ."

"What you do, just make up stuff in your head?"

"Shoot fire, when Lone goes out ridin' with you, I just slip on his goggles and hold on tight."

"Yeah, I sold him that thing at a loss to me, 'specially since I helped him get the parts and put the thing back on wheels for him."

"Oh, well, if you do what folks claim you do, you must be filthy with money."

"I just *did* what folks claim I do." He waved a green check over the quilts. "That's your daddy's whole government check —a month's supply of good old white lightnin'."

"Well, before you started robbin' him, somebody else did. I reckon you used *your* government check to buy that motor-sickle when they kicked you out of the United States Marines."

"Who says I was kicked—?"

"Everybody up the holler that ain't deaf and dumb."

"Don't you know a lie when you hear it? Hell, I tore *up* that damned Marine Corps, son."

"Whether you was kicked out or not, I guess they figure you're the kind that would be. They remember your daddy."

"Well, they got more to remember than *I* have. All I remember is fillin' his empty duffel bag with toys one mornin' while him and Momma was still in bed." Boyd backed into Coot's wicker rocker. He removed his cap, and the sight of his stiff black hair springing up slightly, like tough grass when you lift your hand from leaning on it, made Lone remember that Boyd's mother's black hair and Momma's came from the same Indian wife about a century ago, for they were third cousins. Boyd sniffed the bowl of his cap and stuck it on his knee.

"You mize well still be *in*, wearin' that uniform—except now you look more like Zorro, and ridin' that brand new Harley-Davidson motorsickle. Now, that was a sight ain't no-body gonna forget soon. The day you come ridin' home on that coal-black Harley-Davidson—that white seat and white leather trimmin' takin' the sunlight so pretty! Make your heart jump."

"And *jealous!* I had to beat me up a few people that first week 'fore they'd leave me alone. Makin' observations about my

clothes! Hell, son, drive right on by them peons—they step aside
for somethin' they respect. Me and Lone's gonna work on that
little red fire engine of his, give her a slick coat of red paint, till
she can scorch the highway good as me—go like greased lightnin'. Ain't nothin' sweeter than two honchos leanin' into them
steep, hairpin curves on up in the Cumberland Mountains,
coastin' through the night. By yourself it don't feel the same—
more'n two, it's a loud-mouthed gang. Good to have a girl lay
up against you when you open her up, though. Seventy miles an
hour of wind in your face and ninety pounds of flesh on your
back."

"You hush! Folks say that Gypsy's about a wild one."

"The way *you* like to sing about different stuff, why, if
you ever *took* a ride, I bet you'd make up a song about it that
wouldn't quit."

"Someday I'm gonna stop singin' and start dancin'. But
seems like Lone has a big enough time for both of us."

The smell of moldy plaster stung Lone's nostrils.

"Saddest thing I know of is the sight of you pinned to that
mattress, like a moth that, if it ever got a little sun, would be the
most beautiful thing ever flew."

"Dr. Boatwright says chronic rheumatic fever don't last
forever. You just have to fight the fool thing. Lone did. After
that trek in the snow when me and Lone'uz tryin' to get to
Black Mountain, we both come down with a sore throat, and we
was both put out of commission for four years, then Lone threw
it off somehow and left me behind in this ol' tomb."

"You don't *look* too sick."

"Talk to my bones, mister. When the air turns cold and the
ground gets damp, I commence to hurt. The pain comes and
goes, and when it comes, it rambles like a drunk, from joint to
joint, from my wrist to my knee, to my fingers, to my backbone—leap here then yonder, like it's tryin' to find a place to
settle down, like it's a livin' thing with a life of its own."

*Sometimes your bones burn, and it's a wonder you don't
catch fire and go up in smoke,* thought Lone.

"I get so stiff in my bones I feel like a chair or a tree, so I just go ahead and play like I really *am* a chair, mostly I like bein' a tree. Like Lone's persimmon trees outsyonder, two trunks feedin' off one set of roots. You know how it sounds when you sit down in that old wicker rocker, well, sometimes I hear the same racket all through my bones."

And that's how it feels, *too.*

"I get stomachaches that make me feel like my whole body and even my mind is packed into a tiny ball of thobbin' pain. Sometimes my nose runs blood like you turned on a faucet."

And you get nervous and can't make your hands and feet do what you want 'em to do—they just let fly on their own sometimes.

"Sometimes, my skin peels like a snake, and I just coil up in a pile of skin and bones and feel like givin' up. And that medicine the doctor gives me makes me feel the way Coot looks, so I guess I'm drunk, and I hear myself talk—like my body's in the kitchen, listenin' to my voice in here. I see wild things, and even the guitar feels like skin. Sometimes I don't feel sick exactly, just mean and cranky and draggy, and my skin turns whiter'n a lily."

And you get these little knobs on your backbone and your elbows.

"Doctor says I got Still's disease. Hell, if you ask me, I got Cassie's disease. Says it runs in families. But he claims Momma and them's *makin'* a invalid out of me by not watchin' after me when my good spells come along. Doctor says only thing can cure me now is for ever'body in the house to be real good to each other and not fuss all the time. It tears me up. Says it ain't took over my heart yet, but if I don't get out of this bed, it might, and it could kill me. 'I know I'm scarin' you,' he says, 'but that's what I mean to do.' But from the times I been out, I'd rather be in—shut up in this pyramid, rummagin' through the bones of ol' Mister Tut. When I do get out and roam Harmon, people always try to tell me ever' thing that happens to them—and I get scared—like I know stuff about them even *they* don't know. And then I try to tell Lone or somebody and they—"

"Tell *me*. Let it pour, son."

"Some things I can talk to you straighter than anybody, but—"

"Hell, pack off your troubles on God."

"Who you think packed 'em off on *me?*"

"Hell, if Sanny Claus was to take off that red suit and slip on a sheet, don't you reckon he could pass for God?"

"Sometimes I wonder."

"My gran'maw used to say religion's a comfort when you get older, but it sure is hell on us young'uns."

"It's a wonder God don't burn you to a crisp, with a flash of lightnin'."

"Out ridin' by myself the other night, I got to wonderin' how come you hardly ever mention God."

"Maybe he hardly ever mentions *me*. But we play a lot together."

"Play a lot?"

"Hide and seek. He seems to get a bigger kick out of it than I do, anymore. When I was little I used to go to sleep talkin' to God. And I guess Uncle Virgil stirred me up deep as he did all the rest a the family. Wasn't that first year he was back the damnedest Harmon ever went through?"

"Cassie! You want me to reach for the P & G soap?"

"I even read the Bible all the way through once. Skipped the parts that read like a telephone book—read it, too, once. Understood about enough to wad a shotgun, I reckon—Bible, I mean. And I used to go to Sunday school, the times I felt good, and one time I got saved when a whole bunch of 'em went to the railin', singin' 'Jesus, Lover of My Soul.' Me and Lone'd just come from seein' *The Return of Frankenstein* at the Majestic, and we had to run across that swingin' bridge in the black dark. That was before Uncle Virgil come home from that Jap prison camp and started preachin' there. But you know what really got me about religion?"

"You gonna get God teed off at us."

"You ought not to turn the faucet if you don't want to get splattered. See, I believed in Sanny Claus till I was ten years old and Lone did, too, even if he *was* more'n twelve. You can laugh, but I always got Sanny Claus mixed up in my mind with God, 'cause you know, you ask both of 'em for the same things, almost. And then when it comes to beards, Gran'paw McDaniel kindly confuses it more. Well, I remember we went to that Sanny Claus parade years ago. The biggest that ever was. Momma was ringin' the Salvation Army bell up in front of the Gold Sun Café, and me and Lone stood by the box so she could watch over us. And here it come down the street toward the railroad crossin' where we was standin', holdin' hands, and so excited I nearly wet my panties. Well, when Sanny Claus—"

"Hey, *I* remember *this* one."

"—come down on his float, he was just wavin' to beat the band and throwin' kisses somethin' awful and bouncin' jolly, and it was just like God come from the South Pole with all his little helpers."

"When all of a sudden—"

"When all of a sudden, he just keeled over and rolled off the float and busted his head on the railroad tracks like it was a cantaloupe. Deader'n four o'clock." They paused to look at him, and Lone saw him, too. "How could God let such things happen, Boyd?"

"Well, I been told and told and told not to question the ways of God, Cassie."

"Well, if I ever see Him that's the first thing I'll ask Him, whether he likes it or not."

"You tickle the fool out of me, son." Boyd slapped his hands and leapt out of the rocker and did a dance-walk around the room.

"Only time religion ever gets me's when I pick out the gospel on my guitar. You know what I dream of?"

"I'd be afraid to guess."

"Don't talk so smart, now."

"Didn't mean to. Just seems like my voice gets all over people."

"Of me and Lone roamin' the Cumberlands on that motor-sickle, called on a singin' ministry for Jesus. Just a guitar and a tambourine and the rags on our backs. And whenever the spirit moves us, we just stop and start singin'. You don't need no college degree to preach Jesus crucified."

Lone's eye hurt from the strain of watching. The smell of old plaster almost took his breath.

Boyd sat on the edge of Lone's cot and pulled out a cigarillo.

"Boyd, don't you ever let on to Lone you come in here when he's gone."

"Why, Lone thinks I'm Jesus Christ. He wouldn't—"

"Maybe he's got you mixed up with somebody else."

"Besides, you ain't gonna tell him. You *like* to see me come through that door."

"You want to know what I really like about you?"

"Yeah, what?"

"Not a goddamn thing."

"Well, ain't that good enough reason to want me around? Why you think I run with Lone so much?"

"I reckon you're like me. You love him."

Boyd jumped up, then sat down again. "You think so, huh? Is that what you think? Well, he's sure a saint, ain't he? Yeah, that's right, Cassie. We all love Saint Lone. I bet even the Marine Corps would love him . . ."

"Remember how people used to talk about him bein' the prettiest, lovin'est creature that ever took breath?"

"I always noticed, no matter what he did, people loved him, and no matter what people did to him, he loved them. He loves to forgive. I don't get it, son."

"And now they say he don't love nobody but himself."

"I don't know the person that don't resent ever' breath *I* take."

"Well, he loves *ever*'body—even Coot. Don't try to get him to admit it, though. But love don't seem to be enough—or maybe it's too much. It pitches people off bridges and the top story of *ho*tels and gives 'em the gas in closed garages. It worries me. Too much love can kill a body."

"Then can hate keep him alive?" Boyd sat still a moment on the edge of the rocker, then scooted back and began to rock, making the wicker sound like dry twigs catching fire. "Hey, son, you the very image of Lone in that cap, and he ain't even had it on yet."

"Then you and Virgil see eye to eye on one thing anyhow, 'cause he used to call us twins."

"Don't set it straight. Cock it a little and spit through your teeth."

"Say, how come you always wear that sissy white scarf?"

"This? Why to show ever'body I'm really a virgin, pure as the sheets in the Monday wash."

"You better watch your mouth, Boyd Weaver!"

"Naw, when I race my 'sickle at the speedway in Middlesboro, I wear it to keep from comin' in last."

"To do *what*?"

He began to rock as though he were riding. "Just imagine how silly I'd look comin' in last, this ol' white silk scarf flutterin' in the wind. I *got* to place third, at least."

"Let *me* wear it sometime."

"Hell with *some*time."

Boyd got up and bent over the bottom rail toward Cassie where she sat in the middle of a whirl of quilts, and the contrast of his olive skin and black clothes moving closer to her pale yellow hair and blanched skin made Lone catch his breath, inhale dust, and he had to stifle a sneeze as Boyd dangled the pearl-white scarf, almost touching her cheek.

"Go flutter that thing *out*side."

"I was just gonna tie it around your neck for you."

"Don't touch me, Boyd."

"I can't help it if I got the leprosy."

He tossed it over the rail, his feelings hurt. But when she covered her face with it and with one finger pulled it down below her eye and said, "Ever been to India?"

Boyd laughed. "Son, you tickle the fool out of me."

"Now get gone, 'cause Lone's liable to wake up in a few d'recklies."

Lone flinched, hearing his own special phrase come from Cassie's mouth.

"Wake up?"

"In the attic takin' a nap."

"Oh."

"Don't worry. He was bone-weary."

"Who looks worried? I'm goin'. But I cain't go without a song in me."

"I got just the one for you." She took the guitar into her arms. "Folks, I'd like to dedicate this number to Boyd Weaver, the Cumberland's most lovable—snake in the grass.

"Go 'way from my window, go 'way from my door,
Go 'way, 'way, 'way from my bedside,
And bother me no more, and bother me no more."

As she sang, Boyd was backing out of the bedroom, giggling.

"Boyd!"

He skipped back into the room and up to the bed, grinning expectantly. Cassie flung the scarf around his neck and pulled his face close to hers, and Lone, thinking she was about to kiss Boyd, felt a momentary shock before she said, in a tense, almost vicious, dead-serious whisper, "Don't you *ever hurt* my brother."

The scarf dangling around his neck, Boyd left the bedroom, the steel taps on his boots clacking.

The sight of Lone in the doorway where Boyd had just stood, the sound of the motorcycle still in the hollow, disturbed Cassie.

"Boyd come by and said to tell you to come to the tipple." Shadows under her jaws emphasized her long neck—strange after looking at her from above.

"Cassie, don't trifle with me. I heard you all. You woke me up."

"He just likes to say hello to me. Most of the time he just comes to the window."

"Listen! You listenin'? I don't want him sniffin' around you when you're by yourself."

"I thought he was your buddy?"

"Well, maybe I need to talk to him." Lone went out into the hall, clenching and unclenching his fists.

In the kitchen, he ate a fried bologna sandwich and some cold pork and beans and drank a glass of aching-cold pump water. He offered Cassie some beans on a plate. "No, thanks," she said, "I'd only be feedin' the germs that's killin' me."

"You seen that old bicycle pants-clip I used to have?"

"In that Campbell soup box somewheres."

Lone rooted in the bulging cardboard box, stirring up the odor of merging seasons that lingered in old clothes. His finger-tips touched something soft and furry. Green fungus swelled up out of the church-key incision in a beer can he had stuck down the side.

"Let me smell," Cassie said, putting out her hand.

He threw it on the bed. She closed her eyes and sniffed it, and he turned away, not wanting to see the hollows go deeper, the blue veins on her eyelids.

"You sure love to smell corruption, don't you? Hey, where's that new cap Boyd left for me?"

"You don't need it, do you?"

"You sure don't need it."

"I think it got misplaced under the bed some way."

Sinking to his hands and knees, he half crawled under the bed, but the bedstead scraped his spine and he couldn't reach it. He went down flat on his belly, and, stretching out in the dust and orange peelings and prune seeds that she had thrown under the springs, pinched hold of the hard new bill and cracked his skull coming up.

CHAPTER

5

AS LONE'S MOTOR COUGHED AND SNEEZED INTO SILENCE, FINE COAL dust raining from the chutes of the tipple stopped. Dead but still warm, the motor seemed eager to lunge back to life. His red motorcycle lessened the darkness. The river gargled in some rocks behind the abandoned tipple. Silence poured into the empty coal bin. Smoke from the exhaust thinned out around his ankles. Lone's eyes adjusted from green moonlight outside to the dark inside. Sideways on the seat of his motorcycle, solid black against a softer black, Boyd leaned against the planks, his booted feet resting on the silver exhaust pipe. His cap shadowed his face. When he moved, moonlight through the spaces between the boards leapt among the silver studs on his jacket. A frayed veil of smoke hovered around his mouth.

Gypsy rose slowly from the buddy seat behind Boyd, pinched her yellow slacks away from her sweating buttocks, and sat again. Lone cracked his knuckles, aware of the tips of Gypsy's fingers resting lightly on the soft flesh above Boyd's hips as Lone's had before he got his own motorcycle.

Lone, sitting still in the saddle, felt himself part of the

picture he saw: a cave drawing, not yet discovered by the men shown digging in Cassie's *National Geographics*.

Sounds from the highway, muffled by the wood, hovered faintly about the tipple.

Stepping away from his 'cycle, Boyd scratched his back against the edge of a loose plank, then walked the width of the bin and blotted out the beam of moonlight that shot through a knothole, and unzipped his pants. Lone felt himself listening with Gypsy to the steady stream that struck the soft coal dust on the ground below. When he and Boyd were alone, there was something impressive about Boyd's exhibition, especially from high places, but with Gypsy there, Lone was embarrassed. A moment of silence, then Lone heard the river run low over rocks behind the tipple.

Gypsy pivoted slowly around on the leather seat and rested her feet on the back fender, her legs spread, the buckle of her belt flashing in Lone's eyes where he sat astride his 'cycle, springing delicately on his saddle.

Pointing his finger below Gypsy's buckle, cocking back his thumb, Boyd said softly, "Bang! Got me a beaver!"

Gypsy's voice was slightly louder: "You shot it. Stuff it."

Lone dismounted and walked around, coming back to slap the tassels of leather strips that hung from the grips.

They were quiet again. The river creaked like the swing on the front porch.

"Boyd," said Gypsy, "you bust that jar goin' over the ditch?"

"Lordy, lordy, lordy, young'un, don't even talk that way." He pulled the jar from under his jacket and passed it to her. She swigged, Boyd swigged, then Lone swigged, remembering Gypsy's breath one night, redolent of Grapette, her tongue purple by streetlight.

"Loan me your comb, Boyd."

"Loan you my knife, hack off a few feet of that hair. Ridin' 'long, all of a sudden, switches me right in the mouth—spittin' hair sixty miles an hour."

"Loan me your comb, Lone."

Lone handed her his comb. Lone imagined a strand of his blond hair, mingled with all that black. Gypsy began to comb out her hair.

"Hair like that," said Boyd, "you *may* turn out to be my sister, girl."

"I ain't no Indian. I'm pure Armenian, mister. Daddy *and* Momma. 'Shoved off boat, shoved on train,' " she said, deepening her voice, imitating her daddy, " 'wake up Kentucky, big hole in ground. Man say, Dig, you crazy Mexican.' My daddy ain't never got over it."

"Shut up and comb."

"When we gonna git us another hideout?" asked Gypsy. "This ol' coal dust 'bout to black up my lungs."

"No need to worry, son. That highway's gonna take this old tipple and that café across the pike and the icehouse and that old fillin' station, and the damned state's gonna ream out our holler and Lone's farm and shoot a four-laner over the river and right through this tipple."

"You mean where we're sittin' is where that new highway's gonna shoot?"

"I wants to bless you," said Boyd. Gypsy leapt off Boyd's motorcycle and looked both ways. "How 'bout that, Lone? Us racing up and down a four-lane highway, side by side?"

"I keep tryin' to picture it in my mind." Vague images formed and moved, unsettling him. He leaned against the wall. Coal dust flaked off.

"Wish they'd run over that school."

"You hush talk like that around Lone, Gypsy. He loves school."

"No, I just hate to hurt the people that *want* me to love school."

"Be like Boyd," said Gypsy. "Drop the hell out."

"It's a long drop for me—and hurt other people even more."

"Ain't nobody gives a shit if mangy ol' Boyd drops right on *down* to hell."

"You ain't got a Uncle Virgil and a momma . . ."

"Go ahead, son, say it. A momma that don't act like the rot end of womankind."

"I didn't mean—"

"You love to be a preacher," asked Gypsy, "like your Uncle Virgil on the radio this morning?"

"Well, sometimes I think I ought to live better."

"You talk one way," said Boyd, "but you ride with *me*, by God."

"Yeah, right out a school."

"*Let* 'em expel you."

"They did."

"Today?"

"Yeah."

"It'll kill your momma," said Gypsy.

"Who all's ready to ride to Mexico with me?" Boyd and Gypsy laughed. Through the cracks and knotholes, Lone saw the lights of Harmon, and, high above the rest, the hotel's neon red.

"Yeah, but it ain't funny. They kick me out, and I'm like you, Boyd, I don't give a damn. But who it hurts is Momma and my uncle."

"You left somebody out."

"Who?"

"Kyle?" Gypsy giggled. She had combed her hair into one smooth black strand.

"No. Cassie."

"Let's *leave* her out, Boyd."

"But come to think, she'll celebrate you gettin' kicked out of school. Means you can ride more. From sun*up* to sun*down*. And her on that buddy seat *with* you."

"Why, it'd wear her out just to loop her leg over the seat," said Gypsy. She stuck Lone's comb in her hair and tied a green ribbon around the long strand of her fluffed pony tail. Wings fluttered in the little sycamore that had grown up in the slag heap.

"Boyd, don't come around the house when Cassie's by herself anymore."

"I was only lookin' for you."

"No, you wasn't."

"Don't be so touchy, son. I said three words to her."

"No, you didn't. I don't want you around my sister. Ain't none of us fit to breathe the same air."

"If it wasn't so corny, I'd get mad at you, good buddy."

"Let's drop it—'fore *I* get mad."

"At your own brother? Ain't we been like brothers? Ain't we?" Boyd put his arm around Lone's shoulder.

"Yeah, I reckon." Lone wanted to shrug Boyd's arm off.

"Then that makes Cassie my sister. What's wrong with somebody bein' around his own sister?"

Gypsy laughed suggestively.

"Knock it off, Boyd."

"What's you worried about? Ain't you her favorite brother? You the only one gets to sleep in the same room with her. *I* don't."

Lone backed out from under Boyd's arm and swung his fist at his face in the dark, and missed. A flash of white popped like a whip. As the scarf snapped before his face, Lone dodged and stepped back.

"Come on, Lone. You ain't afraid of a little silk, are you?"

"I know a lot of boys in this town who *are*," said Gypsy. "You all better quit 'fore you get mad."

Lone turned in a tight circle as Boyd pranced around the bin—black against black in the gray light, and white, fluttering. Boyd feigned a move toward Lone every few steps, slapping one boot in the dust, raising a little cloud, snapping the silk scarf at him.

"Don't worry, Lone," said Gypsy. "I think he just wants to dance."

"All right, Boyd. I'm sorry I swung at you. Now you know how I feel, so let's—"

The silk tassels stung Lone's lips, and as his hand went to his mouth, another popped at the corner of his left eye. In a rage, Lone rushed loosely at Boyd. But the darkness favored Boyd, and the moonlight revealed Lone. Suddenly the scarf was around Lone's neck, pulled tight, and Boyd was on top of him, his knee in his back.

"Turn 'im loose," said Gypsy.

"You done riskin' your life, Lone?"

"You gonna watch your mouth about Cassie?"

"You still be my little brother if I turn you loose?"

"I'm willing to forgive and forget." He felt guilty himself for bringing Boyd to the house, exposing Cassie to his dark charm.

The silk slipped gently along his throat. Boyd dangled one end of the scarf within Lone's reach. Lone took hold, and Boyd pulled him up. Grains of coal trickled down Lone's back.

"You didn't seem to *try* very hard," said Boyd.

"I don't blame you."

"For what?"

Lone wanted to confess to Boyd about his meetings with Gypsy in the silo. But the pain in his throat made him feel a little less guilty. "Nothin'."

"Saint Lone, you're one for 'Strange but True,' ain't he, Gypsy?"

"You two set a good example for Cain and Abel."

"When did they drag *you* to church?"

"It gets in like coal dust in your lungs." She coughed like an old miner.

Boyd reached over his shoulder and struck a match on a plank and lit his cigarillo again.

"Got a spare?" Lone asked.

"Pocketful a 'ducks' is all I got. Raided the ashtrays in the Gold Sun Café. I need to cash a check. Here. One of *mine*." Boyd offered Lone the stub of a cigarillo.

Lone put it in his mouth—maybe the very one Boyd had smoked at the foot of Cassie's bed. *Virgil giving him a stick of Juicy Fruit that first year he broke free of the bed, and he took it out of his own mouth and Cassie chewed it two days.* Boyd leaned forward, Lone leaned toward him. Dark skin in the cigar-light, as Boyd's pulsed and Lone's caught fire. Close, Boyd had an odd smell that even the tobacco fumes and coal dust didn't stifle.

Gypsy threw up her arms. "Let's grease some lightnin', hombres!"

"Tryin' to say let's do somethin' real wild-ass crazy tonight?"

"Let's eat breakfast in Mexico!" yelled Lone.

"Yeah, yeah, yeah. More fun, more people kilt!" Giggling, Gypsy bounced on Boyd's buddy seat, working herself up, obviously aware that even in the dim light, Lone and Boyd could see her breasts move. Boyd looped his scarf over Gypsy's neck and pulled her lips against his and deliberately exaggerated the noise of the kiss.

Lone and Boyd turned their 'cycles, passing each other, and aimed them at the open end of the bin. Lone reached into his jacket for his goggles—but Cassie was wearing them. Boyd pushed his goggles down over his eyes, and Lone watched his foot. Then Boyd kicked his motor into power and uproar, sparking Lone. Gypsy put her arms around Boyd's waist, and Lone felt the hug himself.

Boyd led Lone down the ramp and over the leveled slag heap, and their lights danced across the black trunks of trees that hovered over the highway as they came to a gravel-scattering halt. Lone, waiting, felt their motors idling. Boyd's goggles flashed light. Seeing an opening in the stream of cars and coal trucks, Boyd shot out in front of a Trailways bus. They didn't look back as the horn blared. They sped through the tunnel of black tree limbs, like briars, that the projected highway had doomed.

"Here comes the Hellhounds!" they yelled.

"Out the way, you sonsofbitches!"

"Let's practice up for Hallowe'en, hombres!" They laughed ghoulishly. Head lowered, feeling like a bullet aimed at a target, Lone surrendered his will to the motorcycle and realized with a constriction in his stomach how good he felt. He brushed a fleck of dirt from his eye and cursed. Cassie, sitting at the window, wearing his goggles, looking down along the creek out of the hollow where she could see the lights and hear the motors gunning. Without his goggles, Lone knew that soon everything would be submerged under an oily blur. Car lights on the highway made red-painted letters high on a rock pulse like a neon sign: JESUS COMES TOMORROW.

Having ripped though Harmon in one long tear, Boyd led Lone back to the highway and off, over the swinging bridge, past the revival tent that had been raised by the creek while Uncle Virgil's new church was under construction. In the moment of passing, looking between two upflung and fastened tent flaps, Lone saw a light glare suddenly into the dark: Momma in a brown dress standing on tiptoe, one arm stiffly reaching up, fingers still pinching onto the light cord, the other arm held out at her side for balance, her black hair free of the net, her legs slender and strong.

Most of the lights on the hills and along the hollows were out when they slowed at a railroad crossing and rode down the tracks between the rails, taking it so slow Lone felt each tie as the wheels bumped over them. With nerves open to the chill air, and bones aching, the creeping pace felt good, a pause before they ripped loose one last rag of hell before the roll home alone.

Boyd led Lone up the winding, narrow, curving path that veered to the right of the house and climbed the ridge. Lone kept his eyes on the dark tower of the crumbling silo through the trees, looming on the crest of the ridge, hoping Gypsy would make an X in the dust on the toe of his boot to let him know that she would meet him in the silo after they broke up to go home. Trying not to look at the light in the bedroom window, where Cassie sat watching the black figures, blended with their machines, climb against the sky on the spine of the ridge. He tried to shut off Coot's dogs' barking as he, Boyd, and Gypsy rose above the barn. Low branches scratched them as they climbed the steep path. The moon glowed behind a sooty screen of kudzu vines on the horizon.

Before he let the motorcycle roll down the path that he couldn't see in the dark, Lone glanced up at the stars, needle points in the hard sky, and looked out over Harmon at the lights going out, over the hollows strung among the hills, and the colored lights of uptown that looked like the smoldering brush fires that would start to break out any day now in the dry timber.

To Cassie, he thought, the stars must be like the lights she sees from her window: the swarming constellations of lights below, lying in clusters among the hills of Harmon. In the designs of the lights, she saw the boundaries of neighborhoods where she had walked every street, during the few months in her life she had not been bedfast.

Tonight Lone was *it* in their nightly daredevil good-night to the day of speed. As he poised to drop down the mountainside, he saw Gypsy, a dark shape in the bower where the vines shut out the moonlight, lean down from her seat beside Boyd, and Lone felt the pressure of her finger on the toe of his boot, felt it scrawl the X in the dust, sending a shock of excitement through his body. Then Lone let the 'cycle roll, as though he were being poured into the dark.

CHAPTER

6

LONE LEANED THE MOTORCYCLE AGAINST A BIRCH SAPLING AND LET it lean. Gypsy stood between him and the silo, waiting. In the clearing, the moon cast their shadows, curving, on the wall. Their legs made a soft, steely rattle in the thread-thin, dry grass as they walked. Where the ridge rose steeply behind the silo, lightning had knocked down a sycamore tree. Staring into its top branches that crowned the tower and formed a trellis for kudzu vines, spilling lushly down the walls, Lone listened carefully to the sounds of motors on the highway far below to make certain Boyd had parked his motorcycle and gone to bed. He had a strange feeling that Boyd knew about these meetings and would slip up the ridge some night and cut their throats as they lay in the silo.

A few rocks in the grass showing by moonlight were the only trace of the narrow, rocky road that once rose from the barn door and circled the silo. Now a cluster of high tall blackberry vines blocked the road at the edge of the yard behind the barn. Ferns, bushes, and long nodding sedge grass hugged the pale yellow concrete tower. Through briars and saplings,

Lone saw the barn and the house, both half-eclipsed by the slope of the hill. From the bedroom window, a warm, orange light glowed upon the ground. The tar-paper roof of the coalhouse glistened.

Gypsy leaned against the cool concrete near the low, narrow entrance. The little tongue shapes of leaves from a lush bush lapped her face, her shoulders, and her yellow slacks below the knees. They darkened her eyes until a breeze stirred the bush, and light grazed her moist lips gently. The motorcycle crackling behind him as it cooled, Lone walked very slowly toward her. He wanted to be inside, shut in, hidden away with her. Quiet, soft, wrapped in the blanket they kept hidden inside.

Gypsy's arms rose, moved slowly behind her head. She untied the ribbon and took his comb from her hair, and shook her head gently. Her mouth slightly open, she began to comb.

He thrust his fingers into her hair above her ears as she pulled the comb through it. Her hand moved faster and faster, and as he leaned forward to put his mouth on hers, the teeth of the comb glittered in the moonlight, three tiny sparks flew out of the black luxuriance, and he inhaled the fragrance. In the instant before his face eclipsed it, he saw the light glow in her eyes. Her full lips were almost hot. Suddenly, she shot her tongue into his mouth and the thrill vibrated through his body. The tips of their tongues flicked at each other. Her arms held him tightly as they leaned against the round wall. He let his hand move gently down her side, his wristbone scraping slightly against the curve of the wall where it fit into the hollow of her back. His hand lay on her buttock, cool and smooth through her yellow rayon slacks, style of the forties, that the Salvation Army had sent after the flood last spring.

Afloat in moonlight, he looked over her shoulder into the dim silo. The teeth of the comb fastened and pulled through his own hair. It soothed the ache that had started when she made the X mark on his boot at the top of the ridge path.

"Let's go in." The loose legs of her slacks made a sound like her whispering voice as they rubbed against the concrete toward the entrance.

Running her arm through his unzipped brown jacket and around his waist, she pulled him after her sideways through the opening. Wings fluttered suddenly over their heads. A bird rose from a vine that grew through a crack in the cement. As it flew out the top of the silo through an opening in the branches of the fallen sycamore and the vines, light glowed through the thin membranes of the wings, outlining the bones, and Lone knew it was a bat. The moon hung in a dark blue sky directly over the silo. The straw he had spread late in the summer rustled under their feet. Nestling sounds blended together as they knelt.

Gypsy sat back on her heels, flicked her hair, long as Cassie's, back with her wrists and shook her head, her eyes half-closed, her mouth open.

Lone leaned against the wall, and worked a handful of straw with his fingers, listened to it rasp, listened to Gypsy breathe.

"You're pure, one of the few."

"What's pure about me?"

"I don't know. You have a certain look about you that gets me. You come through the door of that flood-ruint shack by the bridge that mornin' sweepin' a cloud of dust before you and stood in the sunlight after six days of dark. You looked to be the purest creature ever breathed. And . . . Oh, I don't know, honey. . . ."

"Why do you like to think about me bein' pure?"

"Ever'thing's so nasty, I like to know somethin' is clean. That I can touch it and coal dust won't come off on my fingers."

"If I was pure as you wanted me to be, you reckon God would've let me out the gate?" Lone laughed. She moved on her hands and knees toward him. Moonlight caught her breasts where the collar of her blue rayon blouse made a V. A black shadow cleft them. "Pure. Blamed if that ain't a funny idea."

"You are, aren't you? You swear Boyd never touched you? I mean never . . ."

She pulled away from him and looked at him until she saw he meant it. "I swear I never give him none." She moved very slowly and quietly over the straw in the dark until her strong body lay against him. Her arms, soft, warm, went around his neck, and her mouth overwhelmed him, as his fingertips rippled up and down her silky ribs.

"Lone?"

"Huh?"

"I like to be pure for you, honey, but—couldn't I still be if we—? What would be wrong if—? As long as I love you, Lone. Lone?"

"Do you really want it?"

"Well, it would be just us. We'd be pure together."

"Do you ever think about it, honey?"

"At night in that dark ol' shack, I hear the water drip in the pan under the icebox and the coals in the grate slip and fall and sparkle, I get to thinkin' how good—Oh, Lone, I love you, honey, and I want to. I want to do it with *you*."

"All these girls round here are just hurtin' for a ride," said Boyd. *"Few smacks on that buddy seat and they hurtin' for something else."* Watching him on the motorcycle, imagining him with the girls he told about, seeing him with Gypsy hugged up to his back, Lone had been in awe of Boyd. Now he reached around Gypsy's hips and felt under the planks for the blanket.

In the house below, Cassie was singing. Faintly, the melody floated up the slope and wavered in the round dark. She sat at the window, the pale light behind her, the moonlight on the pane in front of her, the gray guitar in her arms, the nightgown hanging loosely over her skinny body, her long blond hair shimmering at the edges. Her eyes shut. Her head tilted on her long neck where blue veins, thick as on the backs of a miner's hands, pulsed.

Through the leather jacket and his brown corduroy pants, he felt a warm, trembling body. Not Gypsy. A body. The legs kicking off the blanket as he tried to spread it over them. Her hand moved up his leg, hot and quivering. His fingers fumbled between the silky collar of her blouse and felt hot, soft flesh.

With a sudden rush of straw, she rose and nervously clawed

at the snaps of her slacks. Her fingernails clicked. The slacks were tight at her hips. Watching her, Lone began to undress. She let the slacks drop, lie over her feet and the straw. The light pouring over her like milk through the round top of the silo and her body standing like a soft white vase, she stood over him, naked, and he lay on the straw, on his clothes, the jacket studs rubbing hard into his naked flesh.

"What was that?" said Lone.

"What?"

"That sound."

"What sound?"

"Somebody out there."

"Ain't nobody likely to be . . ."

"Listen!"

"*What?*"

"Well. . . ."

Coot's dogs barked over the hill. Momma on the back porch at the icebox, getting something out, or putting something back. This was another time, some other place. Far away where she would never know what he was doing with the body that loomed above him and then seemed to fall over, slowly, upon him.

Then he lay upon her, hair sharp like straw cutting into his stomach. His mouth found her nipple and he began, slowly, to suck. A strange, overwhelming, aching peace suffused his body. She moaned. Thrashed. Heaved.

"Don't. Lone, that hurts. Let's do it. Please don't, don't do that. Do it to me."

Her hand caught him between his legs and she tried to make it go in. He wanted to, but he didn't help her. He wanted to plug her mouth with his tongue, to stop her from saying the things that scalded his cheeks, but he could not leave her breast.

A while later, they lay side by side, not touching. He smelled the sour damp straw that lay against the wall of the silo. She breathed deeply, sucking up jerking sighs. His head throbbed painfully. He wanted to ask Boyd to forgive him.

Cassie still sang, low, and Coot somewhere near the barn answered her, yelling to her, then he sang the same song, then one it reminded him of, trying to get her to sing with him. "I've had as much as I can take," Momma yelled. The back door slammed.

Gypsy laid her hand gently on his hip. "Why didn't you like it, Lone?"

"I did."

"No. You didn't. I could tell. You like suckin' my—"

"Let's don't talk about it."

"We wouldn't have to, if we'd really done it."

"It'll be better next time. My head hurts. I feel like crackin' it against the wall would soothe it."

"It's sore where you sucked too hard. Look in the moonlight how red it turned."

"Shut up talkin' that way."

"Lone, what's the matter with you?"

"What ain't?" She patted his hip, letting him know she would be quiet. His mouth was dry. "How come no—nothin' came out?"

She giggled. "They ain't nothin' till the baby's born. And I hope you knocked me up sky-high."

"I said quit talkin' like that, Gypsy."

"But it makes me feel good to talk about it. I love to, Lone. I want to all the time. I wish we was married so we could do it from sun*up* till sun*down*." Her fingers felt around between his legs and she took it in her hands as though it were a bird that trembled inward, tensely, upon itself, that might suddenly burst into flight. "Enjoy it, honey. Enjoy *me*. All the time."

Lone stood up and began pulling on his trousers. "It's late. I better sneak you back home before your daddy has the law lookin' under every rock in Harmon."

"Ha! He'd be lookin' for a baby, if I know him. So they could draw another check. My daddy thinks he's better'n anybody else up the holler because he can draw total disability off that cracked hip he got in Blue Diamond. And Momma'd love to see me draggin' around with a little bastard on *my* hip so she could have a case more a Pepsi Colas a week. I come from high-class people."

Gypsy rose and stretched her arms and one leg and then the other leg, and then threw back her hair with her wrists.

"Don't do that!" said Lone viciously.

"What?" Bewildered, she stood frozen in the pale light, her hands in the black liquid of her hair, her eyes and mouth wide.

"Nothin'. Put your clothes on, honey."

"Hold still. You got a vine leaf on your jacket."

He turned to let her pluck it off. Turning back, he saw it just as she screamed: a snakeskin, the rattlers attached.

"Hurry and get dressed."

"You ought to feel good," she said, stuffing her blue blouse with spadelike thrusts into the top of the yellow slacks. "Just think. You got my cherry tonight. I feel like I just got rid of a hangnail."

"Damn it! Shut up!" Lone coughed to stifle a sob. "How come you started talkin' that way tonight? You—" Zipping up his jacket, he saw something printed on the wall. The leaves of the vines growing out of the wall cast licking shadows over it. He struck a match on the wall and read it: FUCK CASSIE MAC-DANIEL. THE MARK OF ZORRO.

Lone quietly rolled the 'cycle down the path, past the barn, past the outhouse, and shoved it between the persimmon trees. He hoped he could walk into the house on cotton and drift off to sleep, but a light burned bright orange on the shade at Momma's window, and where it didn't meet the sill, Lone saw her bent over a chest of drawers in her torn slip. He wanted to tell her about getting expelled before *they* got to her, but dread turned him away from the steps. A weaker light shone in his and Cassie's room, and he knew she was at the window.

Something moved among the vines in the woods on the path below the house. "Boyd?" Lone whispered. He felt he was being watched, not just by Cassie at the window. Maybe it was

Coot. Most likely it was a raccoon or a possum. Lone got back on the motorcycle and rode it down the path, coasting. Willow whips rippled gently over his face and shoulders.

In a level field near the swinging bridge, the flaps of Virgil's tent were up. Moonlight and mist from the river made the tent seem to float. Before leaving on his evangelical march across the South, Virgil had bought an army surplus tent in Cincinnati. Poled up and pegged down now at the mouth of the hollow, it had flapped in the May wind before the flood like one of the prehistoric reptile birds in Cassie's *National Geographics*. It seemed unable to decide whether it should flatten itself against the ground or let the wind lift it and sling it into West Virginia. The flaps slapped the men who wrestled with the tent, waltzing them into each other, trying to control the beating wings of the demonic angel. As he struggled with the tent, Lone had seen the wind pluck, sheet by sheet, his notebook clean, only the steel rings glistening in the sudden rain, and then hurl his *Our Government* text, then his *Exploring American History*, then his *Life and Literature* texts, up into the trees and over the river and the railroad, the pages fluttering high above the smoldering slag heap.

Now Lone's wheels rumbled over four planks that bridged the creek and went over the crushed grass where wheelbarrows hauling cinder blocks for Virgil's new church had passed back and forth, and he parked on the strewn sawdust where the ropes were drawn taut and pegged. Through a rip in the sooted screen of clouds the moon shone on the tent and on the three-foot-high walls of the new church.

Lone reached into one of his saddlebags and took out the jar of 'shine Boyd had given him. Between two sycamores, he sat on the bare bank of the creek and swigged from the jar as he pulled off his clothes. Glancing toward the tent to see if the motorcycle still leaned on its stand in the soft dirt, he waded into the shallow creek and rubbed the water over his skin and scraped his hands together. Sitting on the sandy bed of the creek in cold water up to his navel, he rubbed vigorously between his legs. To get her off. To erase this time. And the next time, the right time, would be as though it had never happened. "You got a memory like a butterfly," Cassie often told him.

On his hands and knees, he crawled very slowly out of the creek, up the sloping bank. He stood up and hugged the smaller sycamore, no thicker than Gypsy's waist, and let the breeze dry him. Shivering, he stared into the darkness of the tent and remembered Uncle Virgil the night he came home from the prison camp, the way he looked, naked. Momma had awakened Lone to tell him that Virgil had appeared without warning on the porch of Gran'daddy's house. She had walked across town to nurse Gran'momma, who was bad sick and had already lived beyond expectation. "I'll be dead 'fore they turn him loose," she kept saying. Momma had just opened the front door to come on back home, and there stood Virgil. "He was always like that, drunk or sober," said Momma. "Be laughin' and kiddin' ever'body, and let you turn around one time, he'd be gone, gone for a week or a month, maybe, and then he'd slip up behind you at the kitchen sink and start ticklin' you. Only this time, he looked like a ghost." Lone was eleven, still bedridden most of the time, and feverish that night. "I'm goin' to see Virgil," he said, crawling out of the brass bed. "Don't you wake that poor man up. He's asleep. Come all the way from Washington on a bus." But Lone started looking for his clothes, and when Momma hid them, he started out naked, and Coot had to hold him, and he fought and bit till Momma wrapped him up in two sweaters and Coot put a miner's helmet, the lamp lit, on his head, and Cassie screamed to go, too. "I took you out in the cold *one* time, girl."

Lone rattled the fence to the junkyard and nobody came, so he climbed it and hurt his foot jumping down on the other side. The house was dark, but he went on in, the miner's light bouncing over the walls, and searched for Virgil. Gran'momma moaned in one of the rooms, her head flung back, her chin sticking up, obscuring the rest of her face. In another room, Gran'daddy rolled over and snorted in the light, and Virgil lay sleeping in another room.

Lone sat on the bed, afraid of the strange-looking man with

the covers up to his chin, but knowing it was Virgil, he turned out the miner's lamp, took off the hard black hat, and lay back on the bed beside him, breathing so loudly from the long, hard walk down the hollow, across the swinging bridge, and along the highway to the other side of Harmon that he woke Virgil.

"Lone?"

Out of all the people he might have waked up to find lying beside him—Lone was so surprised he couldn't answer. Without waiting for an answer, Virgil started telling Lone what had happened to him in the Japanese prison camp.

"That sniper's bullet hit my metal-plated New Testament or I'd be dead tonight. But the Lord saved me so I could save myself, and 'fore it was over, I helped other boys."

After awhile, Virgil pulled the quilt out from under Lone and spread it over him, then went on talking, telling the same story three times, until there was enough dawn light in the room to see his face again. When he got up to get the New Testament he was naked, and he looked like one of those Jews Lone had seen in newsreels, liberated from the camps in Germany. But as he came back toward the bed, the pocket-sized Testament in his long hand, a gleam of metal against his white skin, he smiled, showing the four yellow, crooked teeth he had left from a three-year living death, and it was the same sweet smile he had the day he went, a smile that made everything possible. As he had stood bent over, naked, in some jungle hut each morning, that cocky grin, head tilted sideways, one eyebrow raised, the other squinted in a half-frown, must have been the first thing the other prisoners saw and it must have made them mad at him and happy at the same time—just as it had affected everybody in Harmon. His head was shaved, but in a few months he had the big blond wave at the front again. He showed Lone where the bullet had dented the metal.

"In the beginnin' was the Word, and *that's* the Word Jesus sent me. Time. So I took it, and I'm goin' to earn however much I got left. Startin' with you. I'm gettin' dressed now. I want you to stay in that bed until you make up your mind to get well. And when you're ready, call me, and I'll come."

When he was dressed, he looked like his old self, except for the hollow eyes. On the second morning, Lone called Virgil.

As he pulled on his clothes, he knew that to wash in that creek was stupid. Strip-mining scum and sewage flushed from houses all down the hollow flowed through here. Boyd pissed into the creek behind his house, and the creek pissed out of the hollow into the river, and the river ran piss. Lone wasn't clean. Strictly clean. But he *felt* clean.

CHAPTER

7

STILL FEELING THE EFFECT OF THE WHITE LIGHTNIN', LONE RODE the 'cycle partway up the hollow, then cut off the motor and pushed. Surely, they were all fast asleep now, and he could sneak in, and maybe he would wake up with a cold heart—tell Momma that he had been expelled. Or maybe he would wake up before she did, sneak out again, and roar away and go, this time finally go, to Black Mountain and hunt for Gran'paw. He was so worn out when he reached the yard that he lost his grip, the tires slid on the dewy grass, and he let the motorcycle slur and fall. The rear wheel pinned him to the grass from ankle to knee. He let it lie, let the pain throb. From the black shapes of persimmons and the oval leaves, drops of dew fell on his face, clinked on the fender. Evening clouds had thinned and passed, the stars were hard and clear, and he felt summer go out of him and out of the earth in one moment. It would be autumn in the morning.

He turned his head in the damp grass, and the glow of the weak light in the room he shared with Cassie fell across the porch. The light meter on the wall beside the mailbox whirred and clicked like a pistol cocking. Within reach, a tire hung from a chain. He gave it a little shove and watched it swing. He listened. No sounds came from the house. Only the tick of dewdrops on the fender that cut into his leg and the click of steel as the motor cooled.

Struggling out from under the motorcycle, he stood up and limped into the road, trying to jar feeling back into his numb leg. The leaves of the kudzu vines that crawled thickly over the side of the ridge and hunched over the trees hissed in the wind like lizards. Feeling the pain come back, he limped into the grass toward the porch, letting the motorcycle lie. It was over. The night of speed, when he turned the earth with his handlebars. He'd have to go in. And listen.

On the bottom step, Lone glanced over at Momma's window. The yellow shade was drawn within a foot of the sill—the cord and finger-loop swung slightly. As though she had jerked it down a minute ago. Lone started up, but stopped as she passed the window in her pink slip. Along her ribs, wear and wash had pulled the rayon thin. He felt ashamed. Before quitting at the movie theater, he should have bought her a strong new slip instead of the butterfly brooch. The butterfly had been intended to soothe her when she smelled the moonshine on his breath.

She sat on the bed, sideways, her head tilted back as she brushed her long, black hair. She closed her eyes very softly. And sighed. He felt the weariness of her body in his own.

When Lone's foot landed noiselessly on the next step, Momma looked up. Her finger suddenly at her lips, her other hand made a warning for him to go back into the yard. He listened. Coot's feet thudded upon the worn boards of the back porch. He heard the fumbled opening of the screen, the rattle of the knob in the wooden door, the jarring of the wood when the door stuck, the sudden opening and banging against the kitchen wall, the slam of the screen door, then the opening again. "Out, you mangy— Out! I said, git!" The screen slammed again. "Quit tormentin' me. Cain't I go nowhere 'thout'n a pack of dogs droolin' all over my heels? Strike for the barn where y'b'long!" When he shoved the door shut, the house shook till Lone felt vibrations faintly in his boots. Then a swaying silence. "I gotta see my young'un . . ." Coughing, mumbling, he moved across the kitchen, a sudden sharp scrape as he stumbled over a chair.

On the porch, Lone put his hand into the mailbox. A sediment of rust in the bottom. Then he remembered that Cassie had already delivered the notice from the draft board that he had looked for every day since his birthday in June. Sniffing the rank flakes on his fingertips, he went to the wall and moved carefully toward the window, avoiding the swing chains. Last night, he had stumbled up to the attic, as though climbing a washboard, and awakened Coot out of a deep sleep to tell him the barn was afire. A friendly joke. One that made Coot stomping mad. This morning, things had been said. Things not easily taken back. Lone saw the corn husker coming at his face again and looked down into the muzzle of the shotgun.

Putting his ear to the clapboards, he felt the inevitability of return. Coot's shoulders bumped and scraped the wall as he staggered down the hallway. He whispered so loudly that the dogs in the backyard probably heard him. "Cassie? Cassie, you awake, child? Hit's you' daddy, honey. Wanna come in and set a spell and talk awhile."

Lone glanced through the window. The blanket wrapped tightly around her, Cassie sat at the foot of the bed, her back against the faintly damp wall, her green, feverish eyes wide open. As the door opened, the rusty hinges whining, she fell, turning as she tipped, and landed dead-weight on the bed, twisted in the covers, her back to the door, her face toward the bottom rail and the only window.

"Hey, puny, wake the hell up. Look. Brung you somethin'. Flood warshed it up on the riverbank." Coot turned and, seeming to display it to Lone, waved a boat paddle back and forth as if it were a flag. "Says to myself, now who in the world would 'preciate somethin' like that? Cassie, I said. Hey, look! Ain't you gonna look?" He jerked on the string tied from the bottom railing to the brass chain on the ceiling light. Dark. Pulled it again. Light. Dark. Light. Dark. "Don't you like lightnin'?" Light. Dark. "Ah, horseshit." He walked around in the dark in his fitful way, limping, shaking his bum foot, but there was junk everywhere he turned, and he barked his shins on the arm of the wicker rocking chair. He fell into it, pushed back the miner's helmet, the lamp burning, and the rocking hummed through the wood where Lone had pressed his ear as Coot worked up and held a slow and steady tempo. "Now you know I never meant to *hurt* that young'un." As Coot rocked, the helmet, set down lightly on his big ears, wobbled, and its light swooped up and down over Cassie's bed, from the brass bottom rail up over the quilts and Cassie's hair, to the ornate headboard, up the wall, back over the ceiling. "This here ol' rockin' chair's"—slap!—"the only thing I got out a the Cove. Momma give it me, said, 'Son, this here's your'n when I've crossed over to glory, for when your heart is sad and lonely. . . .' I know you awake, you little dickens. Come on. Sang me a song. 'Down in the valley, the valley so low, hang your head over, hear that wind blow.' She'd sing that'n while we shucked corn on the back porch in the shade of Black Mountain."

"I know . . ." Cassie murmured into the quilt.

Lone imagined Momma sitting on the edge of her bed, trying to keep still. The light meter whirred above his head.

"I got many regrets for the things warn't good in my life, but one thing I couldn't he'p. I regret you didn't know my momma, Cassie."

"I know . . ."

"She— You know how she died, honey?" Each telling as if for the first time. "They run electric wires into the Cove when you was just a dishrag in heaven. She warshed her long, silky ha'r. Good ol' mountain-made soap. Come all the way down to her ankles like a waterfall of silver. And her with only a raggedy lavender slip on and standin' in a pool of water in the kitchen. I know he blames *me*. And him sittin' there readin' out loud out of Kings and lookin' up to see her standin' there so small, an' her silver ha'r clingin' wet to her ankles and around her tiny ears, and smilin' at me. Then he whispered, 'Go fetch the new ha'r-drier,' we bought in Whitesburg. Me, I was plumb thrilled 'cause it was from me *and* Daddy to her on her birthday. I handed it to her and went and put the plug in, so excited I nearly wet my pants, even if I was more'n thirteen years old, and then ever'thing got real still and I heard my heart a-thompin' and that little click sound, like somebody suckin' at a holler tooth, and the first thing I saw was a flash like lightnin' ballin' through the room, and the shock of it hit her weak heart."

"I know. . . ."

From the edge of the yard, like the rings of a whirlpool, a long silence moved in around them. Below, the spread of lights over the hills of Harmon swarmed and clustered.

". . . jerked out all the wires and chopped down the telephone poles, and when the electric folks come around, he told 'em, 'Shoot on back to hell from whur you come!' I regret you didn't know my daddy, too, child."

"Way you talk, I get a glimpse of him at least once a day."

"Someday, maybe, we'll all be back in the Cove, all of us with my daddy and grow things agin and love the mountains and ever'thing be right . . ."

A hoarse insuck of air as he twisted the lid off a jar. In the back yard, one of the dogs barked. On the front porch, Lone glanced through the window again: Coot's mud-dripping brogans rested on the heels in a swath of moonlight. Lone knelt in the cramped space between the swing and the wall, spread his arms, laid his palms flat against the rough boards, and rested his chin on the sill at the corner of the window. His eyes on Coot's feet, he heard the lid rasp round loosely, too quick for even Coot to have taken a swallow.

"Honey, I done resolved to never drink no more. That's all they is to it. I been the grief of my family. I god, I god, I god, I'm a sinner so bad even the devil won't claim me. Ain't no good to a single solitary soul in this world. Sometimes I think even my dogs is just waitin' fer me to croak so's they can dig me up and tear me apart, and hide my bones in some slag heap.

"And her, what does *she* know? Raised and borned in the city and got city streets instead of veins, and *ce*ment fer flesh, and rayroad fer bones. Ho, Charlotte! you gonna tip off the edge of that bed and crack open the top of your head d'reckly!

"What am *I* doin' hy'ere? I know he blames me fer that,

too. But wasn't it Daddy's gift as much as mine?" On the back porch, the dogs whined and scratched on the screen, wanting to be with Coot. "By God, someday, I'll shoot them dogs that lick my hands all day. I'll spit on this house, and I'll leave her in the Square at the Gold Sun Café where I found her. And I'll take my children up on Black Mountain, and, and, and. . . ."

The windowpane cold, soothing his cut cheek, Lone listened to the insuck of the jar lid again, then Coot's brogans lifted stiffly as he drank, showing a mud stain on the floor under his heels, and the lid rasped on again. "Don't God know I'd never hurt that boy?" One of the hounds came around the edge of the front porch, as if tiptoeing, hoping Coot would come out the front door. Seeing Lone, he crouched instantly, growled, backed up a few feet, turned, and slunk back around the way he came. "Oh, me, oh, my, let's quit this o'mopin' aroun', Cassie girl. Whur's that blame gittar a your'n? Lemme peck on that thing a while. Just 'cause it was your birthday present from Lone's no sign you cain't let it go a minute." Coot rose to a crouch and moved his head from side to side like a rooster's, looking for the guitar in the moonlight.

Cassie rose just enough to get leverage to reach out and pluck the guitar from the head of Lone's cot, then she pushed it across the bed toward Coot. Still crouched, Coot reached and grabbed it, staggered backward, and fell again into the rocking chair. He cradled the guitar in his arms, the moonlight slithering along the strings, and licked his thumb. "Sing a song with some life in it." And he began to strum. "Kinda rusty, folks, but just you let me git started and I kin outsing 'bout anybody. Lemme see now. . . . Uhp, here we go!" The tempo he tapped on the floor with the heel of his boot vibrated in the glass against Lone's cheekbone. Cassie set the bed springs to rocking as Coot plunged:

> "I went to see my Susie,
> She met me at the door,
> Shoes and stockin's in her hand,
> And her feet all over the floor."

Behind Lone, the front screen wheened open. Over his shoulder, he saw Momma, frowning, biting her lip at the sound of the screen. Barefoot, in her slip, the tear at her ribs.

"Whoooooooeeeeeeeee!" yelled Coot, seeing what he sang.

Lone rose, lost his balance, staggered backward on the porch, and as he turned, the wall stopped him at the front door.

> "I went to see my sweetheart,
> She met me in her nighty,
> She walked b'tween me and the light—"

Stepping past Momma into the hall, Lone remembered Cassie standing with the light behind her in the thin-as-gauze night-dress she claimed she found while rooting in a mummy's tomb on the Nile.

> "Oh, good gosh-a-mighty!
> Whoooooooeeeeeeeee!"

Cassie lifted her head to grin at Coot, the fingernails of one hand pressed against her teeth, and saw Lone as he slipped past the door. He followed Momma into her room and pushed the door almost to.

"I may been a good singer in my time, but I bet you got a nice song you itchin' to sing, ain't you now, girl?" Coot lugged himself up out of the rocking chair. "Will you, fer your ol' no-'count daddy?"

Cassie began to strum.

"What—?" Lone started as though a sweat bee had stung him, and Momma took her moist warm hand from his neck. "What makes him hang around her like that?" she whispered. "Seems like ever' time you and him fusses, he goes to her."

Lone watched her place a sleeping pill on the tip of her tongue, take a swallow from a glass, gag, spit the pill out in her hand. "Foul-tastin'." She handed the glass to Lone and made a sign for him to get her some fresh water. Standing beside him at the slightly open door, she moved her mouth soundlessly: "Be quiet as you go."

While Cassie sang, Lone stepped softly into the hall. He went to the kitchen, filled the glass, and crept back up the hall to the doorway of his room.

"I'm as free a little bird as I can be,
  I'm as free a little bird as I can be,
  Sittin' on a hillside and I'm weepin' all the day,
  For I'm as free a little bird as I can be.
  I'll never build my nest on the ground,
  I'll never build my nest on the ground.
  I'll build my nest in a high oak tree,
  Where the bad boys'll never tear it down."

" 'Down in the valley, the valley so low.' " Saddened by Cassie's singing, Coot rocked slowly.

Lone slumped against dahlia wallpaper. From her door, Momma motioned to him. He went in and stood behind the door and sipped the water. It soothed his dry throat as though *he* had sung all day.

" 'Hang your head over, hear the wind blow.' Sing another sad one, Cassie. Sad folks sings purdiest. Sing a sad'n 'bout Lone. . . ."

Lone heard Cassie lie down again, a slow-motion rerun, he imagined, of the first fall, turning her face toward the moon again.

"You play like you asleep, but you hear even more'n I say. You hear what I *don't* say, too. Tomorrow you'll sing about it when ever'body's gone. Charlotte's sweepin' out the *ho*tel, Lone's in school, and Coot's on the ridge with the hounds, and only you and the flies are home, and the cockroaches listen and clap their hands, 'cause they know what *you* know. That they'll inherit this house one fine day. . . ." Coot untwisted the lid of the Mason jar, slurped, and let out his breath in a gust. Momma lay back on the bed, the springs whining. Lone turned just as she flung her arm over her eyes in the dark. Looking across the hall again, Lone saw Coot at the foot of Cassie's bed, leaning over the bottom railing, lifting a long strand of her hair. Lone felt a faint pull in his own scalp. "Soft, soft, Godawful soft. . . . Clap their hands and listen and wait . . . rollin' over and over in the foggy, foggy soot, down in the valley of death." As Coot shuffled backward toward the hallway, Lone closed Momma's door, only a sliver of space showing him the room across the hall where Coot's body blotted and revealed the light through the window, Cassie huddled on the bed.

Sensing Coot about to turn, Lone shut the door, feeling the iron click in his palm. Coot's footsteps paused outside, and Lone heard his breathing. Momma listened on the bed, Cassie listened from across the hall, staring at the moon, and Lone put his ear to the door and heard Coot's knuckles strike on the other side, softly. Muffled by the door, sounding as though it came out of the wood, Coot's voice: "Charlotte, Charlotte, I'm comin' in to you!" His laugh rumbled against the flesh of Lone's ear. "What's you a-feared of? I know he's in yonder, and you got him fenced in your arms to pertect him. Call on the Lord. He'll pertect you. You pray enough, you sing and scream and rave in His tent enough, and jingle His tambourine with *ho*tel money enough. Who am I to buck Him, with you and your goodness and all your wallerin' holy-rollers on His side? Huh? Say? Lone!"

Startled, Lone jerked his head away from the door, and turned so abruptly the water sloshed out of the glass and streaked down his fly. Momma rose, her eyes staring straight into his face, until she sat up on the bed and focused beyond him at the door.

"Lone!" Coot laughed and slapped and stroked the door. "No fear, I'm sleepin' in the attic tonight. Good-night, good-night, ladies, I have to leave you now." He stumbled down the hallway. Knocking over chairs in the kitchen, he climbed the stairs to the attic. "Burrrrrr! Hit's turnin' cold as a witch's tit!"

When he hit the steps, he sounded like a big man.

"I look to see his foot come right through that ceilin'," said Momma, whispering with the huskiness of half-sleep. Seeing that, Lone laughed. Momma bounced and moved along the edge of the bed to her night table and tapped another sleeping pill out of the bottle. She swallowed one and dashed some water after it. "I don't even listen to him when he gets that way. Poor ol' man. Mumble, mumble."

"Since when did *you* take to *pills?*"

"Since *you* took to that *contraption!*" She slammed the box of pills on the loose-jointed night table and they popped out like jumping beans. Lone slumped to his knees, and Momma turned on the light and bent over, and they picked them up. "You're the only healthy one left. Be thankful."

Lone stood up. Pulling Momma up with one hand, he handed her the box with the other.

"You know what I sniffed when we were down there on our hands and knees, don't you?" Momma looked into his eyes.

"Just a few dabs . . ."

"Virgil Stonecipher before he went to the war."

"Then no need to worry. Look how *he* turned out."

"You stayin' away from that Boyd Weaver, ain't you? Say! Boyd can cause you a world of grief. And that Gypsy he runs with. Comes of pure trash that lives off the welfare."

"Well, no need to act proud, Momma. Nobody looks up to *us.*"

"Now you weren't with him tonight, were you?"

"I'm tired, Momma. I been ridin' from Harmon to hell and back since daybreak. Gotta sleep *some*time." He gazed at the wrinkles on the edge of Momma's bed where she had sat.

"Lower your voice. Want him to come trouncin' down them stairs?"

"My bones are creakin', I'm so tired . . ."

"Well, if you'd treat this house like it was more than a flophouse between one strange city and another you'd—"

"Reckon I've turned out a hoodlum to most people, but maybe if I lit out for the South Pole . . ."

"You can't take a step without that Boyd Weaver, and he'd

stick in Harmon the rest of his life if he thought it'd torment me."

"Aw, Momma, people throw off on Boyd like he's some snake the flood washed up. What you expect of somebody that come from a momma like Mrs. Weaver? And with less of a daddy than I've got. Least Coot never deserted us."

"I don't care. Even if I was Mavis Weaver I wouldn't claim that boy."

"If she was *my* momma, I wouldn't claim *her*. Now he's passed twenty-one, she's got no use for him. Can't claim him on that relief check she used to get from the government. I reckon he turns to me like I'uz his little brother or somethin'."

"I reckon it was your big brother put that stink on your breath."

"Momma, I swore I'd never bring the smell of it in your house, and I'm sorry. I hoped to sneak by you."

"Well, hop in bed and sleep it off."

"Any place to lay my head . . ."

"Lord knows, I'll no sooner put mine down than the alarm clock'll wring it off. And I got to get you off to school to boot. Lord, if I could just get my mind off my worries . . ."

"Be like *me*. Forget."

She patted his leather sleeve with one hand and pulled the light chain with the other. The brass clinking against the globe, she said, "Night, night, honey, sleep tight."

Then he remembered that for almost half an hour, listening to Coot, he *had* forgotten. With the school doors shut to him, his future and Momma's future were past.

He groped for his mother's hand in the dark, about to speak, but "forgive me" caught in his throat like a sharp popcorn hull. And she had turned to the bed. It whined under her. He crossed the hall to the bedroom, where Cassie lay. Wide-awake.

He slapped his cap over a nail beside the window and unzipped his jacket, a loud rasp. Taking off the jacket and throwing it over the dead console radio in the corner, he felt like a stripper, knowing that in her mind, Cassie picked it up and slipped it over her own thin shoulders. He unzipped his pants and flung them over the foot of the cot, the buckle clanking against the metal frame. He sat heavily on the edge. Her face was toward him, her lids closed, but her eyes were wide open on the picture of him in her mind. He sat very still a few moments, sighing deeply, then, grunting, pulled the boots off and set them neatly, side by side, at the head of the cot.

A motorcycle rumbled on the bridge, revved loud as it climbed the path. The light bounced over Lone, swinging his shadow along the wall, bending it over the ceiling. The light paused a moment, aimed straight through the window, casting a shadow of the swing chains, two overlapping triangles suspended by two lengths, on the dahlia-patterned wall. As he turned to glance through the window, the light swung out of the room. *Everybody else crawlin' into bed; old Boyd still chasin' his tail.* Then the headlight dipped over the hill.

He crawled in under the covers, and too weary to reach up and pull down the shade, threw his arm over his eyes to keep out the moonlight.

Across the hall Momma coughed. She had gotten up quietly and opened her door again. Listening from beginning to end to the complex ritual of Momma's preparations for bed was one of the things he missed, now that he seldom came home early anymore: in the kitchen, the iron thumping on the padded board as she pressed her green cotton uniform; Momma walking in her shoes, then suddenly in her bare feet; if he listened without breathing, the sound of her comb striking sparks as she pulled it through her black hair—a little grunt when she snagged it on a piece of lint. Momma coughed again and turned over in bed.

Lone waited for Cassie to speak. She lay in the big bed in his clothes, the past churning up in her like flowers that she would lay over him until the fumes put him to sleep. He turned his head from the window, where leaves lay curled on the sill, toward the bed and his eyes met Cassie's unlidded, glazed stare. "Lone, honey, you remember . . .?" No, he didn't. And he didn't want to. But he kept his mouth shut.

". . . the times when me and you would sit in our favorite wrecked car in the junkyard, eatin' blackberries off the vines that grew through the fence till our teeth and lips turned from blue to black, and we'd kiss the windshield to see it stain . . . ? Oh, and 'member, honey, how it got so cold sometimes we'd put our tongues on the brass railin' of the bed and to break loose took the skin off . . . ? I just remembered those pictures in *National Geographic*s of the valley of ten thousand smokes in Alaska where we always wanted to go. . . ." Cassie sat on the down end of a seesaw on the elementary school playground, watching him sharpen his pencil at the window, where the American flag fluttered halfway up the pole. . . . "Remember that summer I had such a long good spell and I roamed every inch of Harmon, and Coot turned up missin' and it was me found him? Over in that deserted coal camp and he was layin' in a dark room full of old miners, drunk and dead to the world, and they'd stripped him and were playin' poker for who got his clothes, and talkin' about him like he was the sweetest old boy they ever come across. . . . And he'd be drunk and Momma'd get fed up and start whinin', and you and me'd go up to the silo and play house in the moldy hay.

"And that old nailed-up church in the coal camp. Remember how we'd play preacher? Me in that ol' rotten pulpit, pourin' it on, but when you stood up there and I sat on one of the benches, 'Let us pray' was all you could think to say. . . . And Momma used to tie one end of a rope to your overalls and the other to the clothesline to break you of the habit of strayin' down to the bridge. And one blowin' hard March day when I was one, Uncle Virgil showed up at the front door with you, naked at his side. Found you down on the railroad, the print of the track still on your butt." Just as Lone himself had told it to her, again and again years ago. He remembered waking from a nap on the big bed with Cassie, and Momma's, Coot's, Gran'daddy's, and Kyle's voices came through the window off the front porch. Uncle Virgil sat in the porch swing alone, drunk, clicking a pistol, and they all interrupted themselves as they talked to tell him either to stop doing that or get off the porch, and then he went out into the yard, and the clicking came from farther away, and Kyle said, "You gonna break Lone's swing down, Virgil." Made of a tire from the T-model Virgil wrecked the year before, running moonshine. "And hide and seek, and you and me'd be curled up in the silo and Virgil's voice came up the slope from the barn door: 'Here I come, ready or not!' "

What made her remember these things tonight? What reminded her? That, as much as *what* she remembered, made him shiver. He lit a cigarillo. Instead of letting her frighten him with the past, he would thrill her with the present. Let his own voice and a cigarillo dope him to sleep. First, he let her finish. "Yeah, I remember . . . Did you hear us tonight?"

"Momma said you ripped by the revival tent to torment her. I can always tell your motor from Boyd's. When you all stop quick, you make black marks on the *ce*ment in my mind, and the tires smoke when they scream around curves, and people look out their windows, frownin', cussin', some of 'em laughin'. I hear you shoot onto the highway and through a tunnel of oaks, and the moon leaks silver coins on the black macadam, and you all race between ghostly fences, that yellow stripe rippin' between you, and horses grazin' lift their faces, them lonely eyes, and cold, drippin' noses, and stare at the blurry speed and the smoke, and they stamp the frozen ground and whinny, the noise makes 'em so nervous. Then it commences to snow."

"You got it all mixed up. Ain't been no snow yet, and we didn't go out to the country." But tomorrow, he would have to slow down and try to separate what *she* had told *him* from what he was now going to tell *her*.

"Tell me about it, Lone." Hearing her sit up in bed, he turned over on his stomach, rose on his elbows, and looked at her. Through the dust-streaked silica of his goggles, her eyes looked at him.

"Give me them goggles, Cassie. I needed them damn things all night."

"Tell me, and I'll give 'em back."

"You stole 'em from me!"

"I never. They slipped outa your jacket, and I just didn't tell you."

"Hand 'em over."

"Tell it. *Ever*'thing."

"Now, Cassie." Across the hall, Momma was wide-awake, straining to hear every word. "You let your brother get some sleep."

Knowing he wouldn't be let alone to sleep until he had told her, Lone turned over on his back again and stared through the window at the moon in the buckeye tree. A pack of dogs that roamed the mountains barked, crossing the highway.

"We met in the tipple."

"Boyd and Gypsy waitin' . . ."

"Yeah."

"And Gypsy had on them yellow slacks and . . ."

"Don't you start that now, Cassie. Hush it. A green ribbon tied around her hair, sets off hair blacker'n any gypsy."

"Don't need to tell *me*. I'uz the one told *you* what to call her."

"You must of told Boyd, too, then, 'cause it was him made it stick. Anyway, Boyd had a jar. That bootlegger never turns him loose without tuckin' one in his saddlebags. We killed it, then lit a rag for the Square."

"And Gypsy's breath on your neck, and her arms tight around your chest."

"Boyd's! She's Boyd's girl. And if you don't stop runnin' your mouth—"

"It's buttoned."

"We tore up Harmon awhile, and passed the police station a couple of times, Ol' Uncle Kyle sittin' by the window on the corner, under that red and white metal awnin' they stuck up this summer, and he kept leanin' over and looking out at us, you know . . ."

"With that clean-scrubbed, red look about him, and enough starch in his white shirt to prop up a . . ."

"You gonna hush? . . . We'd pass and he'd lean out and look between the heads of whoever'd be sitting on that bench they got under the window.

"Then we was just easin' along when we saw this big Trailways bus comin'. It gets so you can sense when the driver's sleepy. The bus moves like a fat woman gettin' up in the night to go down the hall to pee. A sleepy driver makes 'off the wall' more fun, but three times as foolish. Comin' in at eleven o'clock by the bank clock, goin' down to Knoxville.

"See, it swings far to the left, almost scrapes the telephone pole, then swings toward the alley, just misses another pole, with me and Boyd on its flank like catfish 'longside a whale. And I bet the driver in those few seconds feels a sharp tingle in his thighs from his own timin', enterin' a alley that's too narrow anyway, where he has to time it right on the hair or he won't make it."

"It always looks like he's goin' too fast anyway."

"And if other towns are like Harmon for gettin' into the terminal, those guys must have stomachs like leather by now, livin' through that by schedule. Red gashes on the wall from where they *do* miss. And when they's only six feet of space between the door side of the bus and the edge of the wall, I gun for the openin' ahead of Boyd, and the high bumper scrapes my left leg and the wall rakes the skin off my jacket, but I shoot through, down the alley ahead of the bus, my headlight bouncin' over the baggage dock, and some guy bendin' over a flock a suitcases looks up and drops his mouth open."

"Will you all quit that whisperin' in yonder, Cassie? That boy has to git up for school in the mornin'.'"

"It's me talkin', Momma. We'll hush." Lone waited until he felt Momma's sleep was part of the silence.

"Then we scorched the highway out of Harmon."

"And somebody jerks awake and looks between the sill and the shade and sees your taillights fade in the dark."

"Easin' along again, when suddenly it's Indians chasin' some cowboys in Technicolor. We scattered gravel against the legs of this boy in white overalls that stands beside the ticket booth, and as we ripped along the side of the corrugated tin walls, we struck out with the taps on our boots and set up a rumble that must of sounded like thunder up *here*. A pond full of brass frogs give a horn concert, kindly background music, as we weaved in and among the cars and loudspeaker posts. Boyd sped straight at a man tryin' to squeeze out, the post blockin' his door. We rode in one door and out the other of the projection booth where the operator was lettin' in the sweet night air. We was on the highway again before the Indians had run the cowboys into an ambush in a dead-end canyon.

"In Loyall, we stopped at a fillin' station to pump some air in my tires. Boyd yelled, 'Great God, it's Kyle!' and struck up his motor. 'Gypsy, get out a that ladies' room!' Ol' Boyd'd run from Kyle's shadow—he'uz in that bunch Kyle beat up just for the hell of it in that roadhouse he raided back in July. Give Kyle the least taste of blood and he— Well, anyway. . . . Over the hill come his black and white cruiser, and it swooped across the highway, tires just a-squealin' it. I flung the air hose, kicked up my stand, struck up my motor, and yelled: 'Let's have us a race, hombres!'

"But Kyle's aerial lashed the air like a whip, the headlights bounced over us and blinded us, and his patrol car blocked our way. He flung open the door, the top of the car peeled off his hat when he plunged at us. That big fat lummox slaps one hand on the fender and vaults over in front of the car, just as I'm curvin' away to keep from crashin' into his grille. I saw Kyle's arm raised high, a light flash on the steel tip of the blackjack, but didn't even see Kyle come down with it—caught me on the collarbone—and didn't even feel it until I'd sputtered around on the gravel and shot out on the highway. The pain stabbed me in the neck, and I saw I was goin' the wrong direction, and swerved, but too quick, and passed Kyle again. He was at the edge of the station gravel, pointin' his finger like a marksman aimin' to kill. Yells, 'You're headed straight for the goddamn electric chair, Lone McDaniel! Your momma's gonna hear about this, you little son of a bitch!' That's when I *should* a run him down.

"Boyd was close behind, so we greased lightnin' on over to

the other side of Loyall and turned off into a carnival and hid our 'sickles behind the lion's cage.

"We gave Kyle time to give up on us, then we walked into the crowd. Target shot a while, batted a few, rode the Silver Streak that a guy we know and's afraid of Boyd let us ride free till we got almost sick, and at the Dodg'ems we jumped from one car to another, tryin' to run down the ticket man when he told us to stop, and most of the people got out over by the fence and the narrow runway, so we had the pit to ourselves, but it didn't feel right. . . . And then we threw baseballs at the red gadget that dunks the pretty girl in the bikini, but she was cross-eyed and spoiled your aim.

"Then we hung around the skatin' rink. Didn't skate. Just stood behind the green wooden barrier and watched, drinkin' Orange Crush. No place like a skatin' rink—the music like merry-go-round music and the smell of the floor like a bunch of parked, idlin' motorsickles, and the all kinds of looks on their faces, travelin' that floor, waltzin' backwards and swingin' into dips and spinnin' and pumpin' up speed again. We always stay quiet and still in there, and watch all the good ones till they get tired. Gypsy kept sayin', 'Oh, looky,' at girls walkin' by with long-stemmed roses in their hand, and she kept after Boyd to win her one until we come to where they were, and it was a fat man guessin' weight, and Gypsy he got wrong. But, 'Oh, shoot fire,' she says, 'it's just paper,' and Boyd tossed it into an empty Ferris wheel seat as it rose above us.

"Then we looked for the motorsickle stunt riders. Found 'em by the high wire fence, next to Margo the Snake Girl's tent. It's just a big barrel-like contraption with steps leadin' up to a circle walkway where you can look down into the pit at the motorsickles goin' around and around and around. On the platform outside, a young barker was givin' it hell, and a cyclist sat on his 'sickle, gunnin' the motor to whip up your interest, drownin' out the whole midway with that muffler, bangin' it off like a shotgun. We collected right below the front wheel, lookin' up at him. He sighted straight between the handlebars over the crowd's heads at nothin'. So we played like we was above it all, too, and listened to the barker. He was good. Pulled 'em away from the Snake Girl and the freak show and even the girlie show, over to Lightnin' Bill, lookin' ever' person in the crowd right in the eye.

"Then Lightnin' Bill got up and went inside, through a little door in the side of the barrel, and we were first in line for tickets. We walked around the outside rail and looked out over the carnival at the rides and shows and people all churned up. I wanted to be around a place like that all the time. I wanted to be down there in that pit, walkin' around or just sittin', waitin' for my partner to finish."

"Let me be the headless girl." Cassie made a musical sound deep in her throat, imitating the background music for a monster movie. "We could run off together."

"Hush. The people crowded around this thick wire fence, waitin' for 'em to get goin'. Then from the loudspeaker right over my head, the barker said, 'Okay, folks, it's time now to place the act on the wall.'

"The motors roared up out of the pit, and the people stepped back a little. I squeezed through and pressed up against the wire.

"Lightnin' Bill had on a brown leather flier's helmet, a purple silk shirt, and black, puff-legged ridin' pants and light brown knee boots. He looked up nonchalantly at the people like he didn't give a damn while he got as much noise as he could out of his 'sickle in that hollow barrel before he let it roll. 'Keep your eye on Lightnin' Bill, folks. He's the newest sensation in the profession. The midway offers no spectacle to equal what you're about to see.' A tall, skinny guy with a moustache and buck teeth went out the side door and shut it. Lightnin' Bill took it slow at first, like he was trying to pick which street to take at a intersection. But the only way to go was up and around, since, with the door shut, 'out' was part of the wall. He was alone. And the way he pulled down his goggles and rubbed his wrists, wrapped in leather, that seemed to be how he wanted it. Then he started up the wall, goin' till he was parallel to the floor, comin' up at the white line. The women screamed bloody murder, and that seemed to be part of what the rider felt. He put his hands behind his head. He rode sidesaddle. He stood up, and stuck straight out from the side of the barrel. Then Lightnin' Bill folded his arms and put his feet up on the handlebars. Had us all playin' statues, we was so hypnotized. One girl stayed leanin' over the edge. Only her eyes moved. Right with the motorsickle. A long-stemmed crepe-paper rose droopin' in her hand. Her mouth open, awed by it, and I saw she had a cavity between her two front teeth, but she had the prettiest hair.

"Then the other guy did his act, and when it was over, Lightnin' Bill walked around on the wooden mats with a hand mike and asked for donations for the special fund, because the work's dangerous. I pitched down a quarter and Boyd said, 'Can't you read?' and I looked at the sign he was pointin' to: DO NOT THROW FOREIGN OBJECTS INTO THE PIT WHILE MOTORSICKLE IS IN MOTION. I laughed and watched Boyd toss somethin' down. Lightnin' Bill went over to it, but when he saw it was a penny, he stepped over it like it was a puddle.

"As we came down the stairs, the barker asked us how we liked the show.

" 'Hell,' says Boyd, '*any*body can do *that* stuff. But what I love to hear is *you*, talkin' over that mike, son. Reckon could *I* try it?'

" 'Hell, man, cut loose.' The barker handed Boyd the mike and stepped back."

Coot dropped a jar on the floor of the attic and it rolled and clanked across the ceiling between the rafters over Lone's head like a Coke bottle in the picture show. "Lord, Lord, Lord," said Momma, in a long sigh. Coot rolled out of bed on the narrow shelf that was nailed over the plaster and rotten laths, and started staggering from one rafter to another. His foot missed and plaster rained down on Lone and Cassie.

"Coot McDaniel," yelled Momma, "you want a bring this house down on us?"

His mumbling echoed in the attic.

"Cut it out up there, Coot!" Lone yelled, trying to make it sound friendly.

"Hop back in your bed, Coot," yelled Cassie. "You dropped half the ceilin' on mine."

"You people quit tormentin' me and go back to sleep!" Coot yelled. Then he collapsed on the cot again and it got quiet.

"So me and Gypsy stood in the crowd and watched Boyd clown it up. But *he* was good, too. Cain't nobody say he don't look the part. Lightnin' Bill stayed inside, and the buck-toothed rider came out of the barrel, countin' the change in his hand, and sat out front, revvin' his motor. Then he went in, and the girl with the cavity and the paper rose was first in the ticket line.

"The show started up again. You could tell Boyd loved the sound of it when he said, 'And now, folks, we're gonna place the act on the wall.' Lightnin' Bill had already begun when we went back up to watch him.

"Just as we got up to the railin', I saw that girl toss the rose into the barrel. Later, she said she got the idea from a bullfight movie and thought she'd try it. Said she liked Lightnin' Bill's looks. Well, the way he looked when they pulled the motor-sickle off him was like a panther had been let in. They spread his scarf over his face."

Lone heard Momma's bare feet on the sill. "Do I have to beg you all?" Lone and Cassie looked at her, then Lone rolled over and pulled the covers over his head. "I've stood this ever' night since that motorsickle come. Now keep them traps shut!" She came in and Lone heard her coax Cassie to the head of the bed and tuck her in. Tight. Then she closed their door, and, faintly, hers.

Lone was almost asleep when Cassie spoke in his ear, her breath hot. "Then what?" Wrapped in the quilt, she had squatted on the floor at the head of the cot, her hip against his boots, her ear on a level with his mouth if he turned.

He turned and whispered into her ear, her wispy blond hair tickling his nose and mouth, "That's all, Cassie. *All I'm tellin' you.*" He snubbed the cigarillo in the motorcycle hubcap he used as an ashtray. "And please don't bring it up tomorrow. Forgit it."

"Then why'd you tell me?"

"Night, night, Cassie."

"I heard you all above the house little while ago—doin' stunts."

"I said, 'night, night,' little sister."

"Night, night, Lone. Sleep tight, don't let the bedbugs bite." She kissed him under his ear and went back to her bed, and he pulled the blanket up to his eyes.

A coal train passed below the swinging bridge. They listened together. Lone inhaled deeply. It came out in a long shudder. Then he was dead to the world. No dreams. Ever, anymore. A blank. Like the tar-paper roof of the coalhouse in the moonlight where beads of dew were forming.

CHAPTER

8

LONE FACED CORBIN STONECIPHER'S JUNKYARD. GOOD PAY FOR scrap. The lop-jawed gate of iron and wire hung open. A black-cindered, rutted driveway led into the debris. Smoke rolled tightly out of an iron pipe chimney on the roof of a narrow, leaning shack inside the gate. On a billboard above the shack, morning glare bleached a Lucky Strike poster almost white. From the lamppost dangled a new globe. The rock-shattered pieces of the old one lay on the ground. Gran'daddy blamed Boyd. In the middle of the junkyard, a white picket fence surrounded Gran'daddy's house. Stripped mimosa trees, their trunks freshly painted white, and a runty, feather-branched coffee tree stood in front of the green house, and late roses withered on trellises that framed the front porch. Next to the faded ice card, a Gold Star Mother flag found in a load of junk hung in the window. Gran'momma never understood that it was only for boys killed in action. After she died, Gran'daddy let it hang, vague reminder of Gran'momma herself.

Walking toward a block-long, ten-foot-high stack of grimy

batteries, Lone raised dust that coated his boots. Beyond the batteries, a crane dipped its head.

Gran'daddy Stonecipher was lowering a blue Buick, dripping dust. Six feet from a pile of cars, he let it fall and crash on top of a pug-nosed milk truck. The door on the driver's side swung open. The steering wheel shaft rammed into the back of the front seat. Something sparked it, and smoke, then fire, rose from the heap.

The door in the cab of the crane swung open, and Gran'daddy Stonecipher jumped the six feet to the ground. Wiping his hands on his coveralls, smeared with sweat, grease, oil, and grit, he looked at Lone from under a tight-fitting cap, the bill coned like that of a duck.

"See that shaft? Went straight as hell right through his speedin' guts." Through the veil of smoke, Lone saw a blotch of blood on the upholstery. Straw and springs bulged out of the gashed leather. "Had to blowtorch him out. Didn't hurt none, though, 'cause he was already shovelin' coal in hell."

Gran'daddy leaned against the stack of batteries, one short arm flung behind his back, the other out stiff, as if to keep the batteries from falling on him. The light flickering up his chest and over his grimy face, he watched the car burn. On the charred scrap heap, it could smolder for days without spreading.

"You at it early, ain't you?"

"Early for Christians," said Gran'daddy, squinting up at Lone, the bright morning sun making his wrinkled eyelids quiver, "late for hoodlums."

"Say, Gran'daddy, how 'bout my 'sickle?"

"You cain't have *my* 'sickle."

"Now, you better not've touched my *'sickle*."

"Gonna touch it a couple a times with a sledge hammer d'reckly." Since he had grown taller than Gran'daddy, Lone was usually embarrassed to stand close to him, but now he *wanted* to look down on him. "Damn it, where'd you hide it?"

"Talk like that'll get your face slapped for you. Yonder it hangs—over your shoulder."

Lone turned, looking up. Its hook snagged in the spokes, a black crane held the motorcycle high. Above a cluster of wrecked and rusted motorcycles, Lone's bright red one looked vivid. Lynched, but still alive.

"You ain't gonna bury *my* 'sickle in this graveyard!"

"Cain't you tell when somebody's tryin' to take care of you? You and that son of a whore you run with wrecked twelve dollars' worth of damage in that drive-in movie last night. Now your Uncle Kyle could a forced the money out of you, but he wanted to hurt and help you at the same time."

"So he slipped up in the yard last night and stole my 'sickle right from under my window." Lone reached in his jacket pocket and held out seven one-dollar bills and a five. "Now ease it down."

Gran'daddy pulled his cap down over his eyes. "You just have to keep tryin', don't you?"

"What?"

He cocked back his cap, showing thin, pale yellow hair going gray. "You want me to have to haul it in off the highway?"

"What else do you pray for?"

"God don't need to be asked. He's got it down in the Book for soon."

"Well, turn loose of it, if you're so sure you'll get it back."

"Look at that Buick burn. Labor Day they'll be twenty or thirty drug in here from the Pikeville, Hazard, Cumberland, Lexington highways. I'm sure of *that*, son."

"I ain't your son. Kyle's your son—Harmon's public enemy cop number one."

"Yeah, your daddy's done cut a path for you. You'll end up hittin' the same bottle, staggerin' into hell, 'stead of leadin' a few to heaven like you promised your Uncle Virgil."

"Don't you know any words 'sides hell?"

"Yeah. Perdition. Drift back to church one Sunday, and you'll hear it."

"Preachin' never did *you* no good. Kyle's the one that takes after you."

"Still want that face of yours slapped?"

Lone stared a moment into Gran'daddy's face. Grit had worked into every pore in his skin, but his keen blue eyes gave his face a clean, open look. When he bugged them and pinched his mouth, as he did now, Lone had to look down. He looked at the splayed-open hands that had manhandled every scrap of junk inside the fence. "All I want's my 'sickle."

"Take it. I'll wait. I'll pick it up off the highway some early mornin'. . . . It all ends up here!" Stomping three times with the same foot, he raised dust, a violent blend of soot, dirt, and rust. "The good Lord had somethin' on His mind when He stuck my junkyard in the middle of Harmon. And who you reckon got that new superhighway routed through your house, but made it miss my junkyard? Someday I'll junk this whole town. And you with it, trash of the family that you are." He looked at Lone as if he saw some picture of the future. "Else you overcome the devil in you, and throw off that Boyd Weaver that's took hold of you and turned you deaf to the callin' your Uncle Virgil prophesied."

He seized Lone's hand and swung him around behind the stack of batteries. As Lone opened his mouth to curse him, the Buick's gas tank exploded. Flames shooshed up, curled above the stack. A vomit of black smoke thinned around the neck of the crane. As they stepped around the corner to view the wreckage, Lone eased his hand out of Gran'daddy's.

". . . like salvation, son. A way. A way to see. And seein' will do it. See man in the muck, then see Christ on Calvary. I drop 'em just right on purpose to get that. I want 'em to burn, to show anybody standin' around how it ought to end. They come in hy'ere, son, the blood still wet—if it was a fire already, the skin burned into the *up*holstery. You want to know what that does? Makes a man see."

Lone turned to avoid his eyes, but it was with Gran'daddy's lucid blue eyes that he saw the mounds of wrecked cars. "If anybody was to ask you what man has come to, you show him this. Gather it all in and pile it all up and hammer it all down and ship it all out—feel like you're cleanin' up the corruption that makes this Godforsaken town run. Well, it runs, now don't it? Runs itself out, runs itself down, runs itself into a innersection right when another one's doing the same on white lightnin'.

"This town cain't wreck its old self quick enough, to be able to put up new buildin's that will wreck easier and sooner, later on, so it can put out superhighways for vacatin' town as fast as possible, some for everyday use and a special one for the night of the bomb. And when they dig us all up, there'll be the history of Harmon inside these gates, layer by layer.

"You see that God don't mean it to be, or how come he'd let it end here? Work alongside your gran'daddy, son, see Harmon from the dregs up, and you'll see it don't take no church to do God's work in. They got me a deacon in the Second Pentecostal Church, but that's for Virgil, for the day he decides to stop wanderin' from pulpit to pulpit. Right *hy'ere's my* altar, and— Stop!" Like a traffic cop, he put out his arm, and Lone stopped up against it. With his other arm, he swept the yard. "—And all around here is my burnt offerin'." Then he laughed. "They's somethin' about seven o'clock in the blamed mornin'. . . ." He let his arm fall around Lone's shoulder, and they commenced to walk. Lone let it lie, soothed by the redolence of Beechnut chewing tobacco that Gran'daddy had carried since Lone could remember.

Lone had it on his tongue to ask him, "But ain't they no love in it?" when Gran'daddy gave his shoulder a pat, and that was his answer: Lone.

Gran'daddy climbed into the cab of the crane and, with squeaks and clanks that put Lone's teeth on edge, eased the motorcycle down until its hind wheel touched the soft black dirt. As Lone pulled the hook out of the bent spokes, the motorcycle's full weight sank in his arms, pulling him to his knees.

"Now, I don't want your money, Lone. If you can work in that picture show all summer just to save up a hundred dollars to buy a wrecked motorsickle, you can work off that twelve dollars to get it back. I don't want to eat into your school time, 'cause I know your momma and Virgil got your future mapped out on that high school diploma. Your momma talks about you turnin' out a doctor and healin' your poor little sister of the rheumatic fever, but I'm sayin', this place'll make a preacher out a you. Start in tomorrow, Lone. On Saturdays, a dollar a time, till you grow to love it. You know, look at it one way, they's somethin' about junk that rests a body's soul."

"Gran'daddy, I tell you, I be glad to work off what I owe you, but tomorrow—"

"Forgit it."

"Now, don't take it that way . . ."

"Take it, hell. You take it. Take it on out of here." Pulling down hard on the bill of his cap, he turned in the powdery dust. "Pass on what filth the sewers of this town has cut loose in you," he said, walking toward the open cab door of the crane.

Lone slapped into a swarm of gnats with the back of his hand, swung his leg over the motorcycle and mounted. As he passed through the gates of the junkyard, he remembered the climax of Uncle Virgil's Easter sermon of two years ago, a climax that came an hour after the tent was empty: "Thank God for your sins. You don't see God but in sin. Seek the devil, Lone. God ain't never far from the devil. Man lives a life of pure piety is a damned heretic."

From the bank, Lone, astride his motorcycle, returned the green gaze of the toy semaphore that stood on its silver stalk at the end of the trestle, high above the wide stand of corn in the valley. Climbing the cliff rocks made the semaphore grow larger, and when he reached it, the green blinked off with a rusty clack, the red blinked on. As he stood on the trestle astraddle the ties, his motorcycle, winking red in the sunshine on the bank, looked like a toy, the tall grass nodding around the wheels. The rails ticked in the heat, as the motorcycle would be ticking, cooling by the river. A soft breeze coming down through the pines on the ridge rumpled over his bare back and between his legs. He inhaled, mingling the smell of tar on the timbers and of iron and of the river with the odor of raw trees and corn. Birds rose raggedly out of the trees below and smoothed into a covey that spread high over the trestle. Sucking in a deep breath, he rose on the balls of his feet, and dove from the rail into the Cumberland River. As the moving water rose to meet him, his motorcycle, flinging its curving arms into the buzzing heat, keeled over in the grass.

His hands out stiff kept him from "rooting." Crouching on the sloping riverbed a moment, rocked by the muffled boom when the passing of the train over the trestle shocked the cold water, he shot up hard into the sun, the breeze sudden on his head, and yelled. But the train whistle shrieked louder, and when he turned, the ridge sucked in the caboose.

He swam until he tired, then floated, looking up at how high the trestle was now that he had dived from its fenceless edge. The sun striking straight into his eyes, the trestle was a caterpillar wavering in the heat.

Wading to the bank, he grasped a root shaped like the handle of a milk can and plucked himself from the river. The sun and the breeze struck him, and the film of mud began to dry immediately. The 'cycle lay on its side in the high tangled grass, taking the sun. Along the barbed-wire fence, the corn was drying up. He lay down beside the 'cycle and shut his eyes. Imagining someone slipping up on him in the grass where most of the summer insects were dead, he felt a shiver as if cold fingertips lightly grazed his ribs. Opening his eyes, he looked up at the green semaphore. The underbellies of leaves shimmered in the light wind. The red clay caked and cracked on his skin and his scalp drew up tight, and sunlight glinted off the fine sand that had come out of the river on his body.

Again he closed his eyes, turned over sideways, and put his cheek against the warm body of the 'cycle, the fingertips of one hand stroking the smooth leather saddle, the other plucking the spokes of the wheel. The 'cycle had sunk into the tough grass. Gasoline gurgled in his ear. As if standing on the trestle he saw himself, lying in the grass, lean and blond, snuggled jaybird up to a motorcycle, and laughed softly. Then he remembered the stunt rider lying with his motorcycle at the bottom of the barrel, and he shuddered, chilled in the bright sunlight.

He rode all afternoon, without stopping. Getaway fast. Gut-sucking fast. Then swerving slow. Dawdling slow. Almost falling slow. And earth-blurring fast again, among the Cumberland Mountains.

Then, from the mountain above Harmon, he saw the town's highest building and the letters painted six feet tall around its crown: WORK, THINK, BUY COAL.

As he felt the swinging bridge respond, his body tensed against the high note on a violin that Cassie said could make a bridge collapse.

CHAPTER

9

SHUTTING OFF THE MOTOR, LONE GLIDED INTO THE YARD, AND LET the persimmon trees stop the 'cycle. He took a package from a saddlebag and shoved it inside his jacket. If Momma didn't know when she came home tonight that he had been expelled he would have to tell her. The soft bottoms of overripe fruit bounced on his head as he walked through the low branches, not ducking, the morning ride still humming in him.

Hearing Coot and Cassie as he climbed the four steps to the porch, Lone sneaked over to the window. Kneeling now in the evening light between the swing and the wall as he had knelt in the moonlight yesterday, he felt a blending of the two days, a continuation of the harmony he had felt, spying on Cassie and Coot last night. Running wild with Boyd and Gypsy had helped him cut loose from the tangle of feelings that kept him bound to Momma, and Coot, and Cassie, and Virgil, and he dreaded coming back to them. Sneaking up on them seemed to ease the shock of return. But he had often ended up spying, as if he was a thief waiting for the people in the house to go to bed so he could loot the rooms and gaze upon the sleeping bodies as he pilfered.

Pressing his ear against the rough wood, he felt a strange joy, and realized now why he had lingered over these moments of spying. Then he would shun Cassie, Momma, and Coot, going straight to bed, dropping into a deep sleep, shedding all memory of the ride, of lying in the silo with Gypsy, of spying at a loving distance on people he was afraid to love or hate freely.

Through a corner of the window, Lone saw Cassie, sitting in bed, wearing his goggles, the quilt over her jacked-up legs. The old-fashioned, round-domed, table-model radio upside down between her legs, she used the bottom for support as she wrote on a brown paper sack. Lone moved along the sill enough to see the doorway, where Coot stood in the hall, facing the kitchen, balancing a large Lucky Strike box on his head with one hand, holding a pair of dress shoes in the other. Sitting or lying idle, Coot and Cassie moved more than most people working. On the box, overflowing with junk, was the old green-and-red Lucky Strike insignia that Coot said came out of the Depression years. Cassie's voice had caught Coot and transfixed him in mid-stride—Lone knew the feeling—and now she let him go.

Cassie must have wandered into the yard, because the dogs had chewed the red pencil she used. Probably the red No. 3 he had used in school last spring. The words so faint in her weak hand, she probably couldn't read them. Looking at her, he wanted to stroke the sharp, aching bones of her shoulders with his fingertips. The odd ways she moved her hand as she wrote and slid one foot down and up slightly under the quilt made Lone wonder whether she was aware that he knelt outside. The strange thrill of spying that he had felt many times before but had not understood until today made his heart beat even faster. Cassie spent her life looking out on Harmon through their bedroom window, and now Lone was on the other side of that keyhole, looking in. A good view, a view that forced him to his knees.

Imitating cowboys when they wanted to pick somebody off, Lone sidled around the house, hugging the wall, and stopped at the corner to listen. Coot climbed the stairs to the attic. Lone grabbed the railing and swung onto the back porch and went in through the open door. He pulled the white box containing the new slip out of his jacket and put it on a chair and shoved the chair up close to the round table.

On the stove was a skillet of fried apples. He forked a bite and, chewing, went into the dark hallway, tapping his steel ring against the faded dahlias on the wallpaper until he reached Momma's door. He heard Coot's foot hit the top step in the attic, and wondering what Coot was up to, he turned the white porcelain knob, smooth cold. A creak as the door opened. "That you, Coot?" Cassie asked. The pale light from their bedroom fell across the hall and upon Momma's bed. *Damn her, she knows it's not.* The mystery of the bedroom darkness and his ignorance of Momma's simple, everyday, but secret moments met him at the door where he stood, warm and uncertain, rocking slowly on the sill. The blue chenille spread he had bought her for Mother's Day at a roadside stand on the highway was tight across the mattress, the hawk in the center stretched thin like a butterfly under glass. Her green uniform, starched stiff, pressed smooth as tin, hung from the shade cord fingerloop, the shade at half mast. He imagined the rayon slip he had bought her today sliding over her soft body, the wide hips, the narrow, bowed shoulders.

At the bedroom door again, Coot said, "What's that you writin' at such a trot, puny? Ever' word I say, I bet." Cassie didn't answer. "Now I told you and been tellin' you all day yesterday and all day today, I never aimed to hurt that boy. . . . Hey, lookie here what I found! Family Bible—goes back to Scotland. Now don't look at me that way. I may's well move out—we been same as divorced the last ten years. She sleeps on her side the bed, I sleep on mine, and Big Black Mountain runs between us. I'uz about to get in the habit a sleepin' in the attic, anyway, and so all I'm doing is finishin' it, draggin' my stuff up there. . . . Lookie there. Found that pipe. Now, look at it! From you and Lone that first Christmas you was both in that bed, tightropin' the edge of the grave. . . . Now that boy, he surely knows I wasn't about to— He ain't forgive me for yesterday morning, has he? Jumped out of bed this morning and got gone like he couldn't endure the sight of me. Don't God know I love that boy?"

"You don't have to *tell* God," she said, looking up at him through the streaked goggles. "But maybe Lone'd like to hear it sometime."

"And lookie here at this." The bedsprings creaked and popped. "Tells your fortune. Sniff. Still smells of strawberry ice cream." She sniffed deeply enough to make the paper stick to her nostrils a moment. "That sure is a flood of writin'. 'Then me and Gran'paw walked out toward the fields where the mornin' sun soaked up the mist, and I went to hoein' while he trimmed the tobacco. And then I got started tellin' him about Cassie and—' That ain't *you*. That's Lone talkin'."

"What's the difference? Hey, ain't that Gran'paw you got in your other hand?"

"Found it, too, up in the attic. Remember how we looked for it that rainy afternoon? Your momma must a hid it one time. Too dark up there for *me* to get any good out of it. *You* want to hang it up?"

"Oh, thanks, Coot! He looks wonderful. I'll hang him right over my head. . . . Looks like you just tore a picture right out of the Bible. . . ." From the window, Lone saw only the rough wooden back of the frame, but the picture itself was clear in his mind: the long white hair and beard, black eyes powerful, staring into the camera as if staring down a gunman, the mouth closed, as if permanently, the cheeks hollow but the skin smooth. Now, more than thirty years later, Gran'paw's skin would be like the grain in the wooden backing of his photograph. Lone wanted to ask Coot how old Gran'paw would be now. He wanted him to be a hundred, but still strong enough to plow and harvest a crop, to chop a pile of wood, and track through snow after wildcats that threatened his stock. "Nobody said you wasn't wanted, you know," Cassie told Coot.

"I don't want myself." The springs shuddered. "I may be a low-down drunkard, but you know, I bet I got a heart in me *some* damn place."

Cassie loudly jabbed a period on the paper. "That's what it says here!"

"Well, me and the dogs got things to do."

"What, for cryin' out loud?"

"Reckon we'll go down and watch the coal gondolas go by."

Lone swallowed, but the sweet taste of the apples lingered in his mouth. He thirsted for cold cistern water. After Coot had gone out the back door, Lone closed the door to Momma's room, his hand lingering on the knob that now felt soft.

He knew he would not get past the open door of their room.

"Lone?"

"Where's Momma at?" He stayed in the hall, out of sight, walking around and around.

"Getting revived in that tent down yonder."

"You needn't talk so smart about it." Now, he broke loose and walked on toward the kitchen.

"What you doin'?" Cassie's voice, echoing down the hall, could penetrate rock and ice.

In the middle of the dim kitchen, Lone stood knee-deep in the twilight that fell through the window. His cheek brushed against the light cord. He didn't want light. He grabbed the pump handle.

He drank one glassful, then filled it again, set it on the table, opened the oven, and reached for the plate, but the smell of food that usually made his mouth water suddenly turned his stomach. He sat at the table, very still, and watched the darkness mop up the stain of light on the linoleum.

"Lone, come on in."

He looked at the wall. No walls stood between them.

"Any word from Uncle Virgil?" Lone asked, showing himself in the doorway.

"I don't know. What happened all day?"

"You with nothin' to do all day long but waller in bed? Don't you know a damn thing about what's goin' on in this house?"

She let him drop his own answer into the silence. Before it got too loud, he spoke. "What do you know except what you dream? You got it made and don't know it."

"Like to know what I'd *rather* be doin'?"

She knelt at the foot of her bed, looking over his cot out the window she had opened. Her nostrils flared. He caught it, too. Fall and summer. Coming and going. The smell of musty quilts mingling with the air. In a few weeks, the smell of dry trees burning on the mountain slopes. Leaning against the bottom railing, the brass rubbed bright in the middle where people talking to Cassie pressed their bellies, bending over toward her, Lone placed his hands on a slight chill in the brass.

"Wanna see somethin'?" She pinched hold of his jacket sleeve.

"I reckon." She pulled him over to the window above his cot. The sill was worn smooth gray from her leaning there.

"Watch the ridge eclipse the sun when it sinks."

She kept tight hold, and Lone hated to hurt her by pulling loose. Kneeling on his hard cot at the sill, he pressed his head against the window frame. "Don't they look like you'd took a handful of cotton and stretched it thin across the sun?" Until she said that they were just clouds. "Together, the sun and the clouds, don't they put you in mind of that picture in *Life?*"

"Which one?"

"Blown-up pictures of the sun flingin' off whirls of smoke. Remember?"

"No."

"Foot fire, Lone, the only thing you ever remember is to forget. You got the memory of a butterfly. Nail yourself right there till I get it." Getting off the cot, she held on to him to balance herself. Looking out the window at his motorcycle, caught between the persimmon trees, he listened to her scratch around and dig deep into a knee-high Oxydol box among the magazines, some of which he'd brought her himself. She had written in all the margins, and covered the backs of bills, and filled Tarzan and Blue Horse composition books with scrawls that no one except Lone could read. She wouldn't have to root in the other boxes or pick among the other junk. She knew exactly where everything was.

If she dragged the picture out, she'd get started on something in the margin that reminded her of something else. "No need, Cassie. I can see it okay the way you said." All that stuff was alive. Cut into it at any point and it bled for hours.

She came back beside him on the cot. A sickening odor in the room made his head feel light. "Ever notice how the sun, when it gets awful near the trees, the ridge turns into a huge cockroach and sucks the sun out of the sky?" Now she was trying to draw him in, focus his eyes on something from her own head, hold him with a picture he wouldn't shut his eyes to. Whatever came through the window fell on her green, fever-glazed eyes the way the light fell now on his polished hubcaps. But in her head she saw clearly everything she said and did, and more than she told.

"And pretty soon the leaves'll shrivel and fall, the fires'll come, and all over the hills it'll be like people's left a skillet of grease smoking on the stove, and then the snow's gonna come pourin' down all over creation and load the trees and roofs and coal cars and pack the creek and the river with ice." Cassie's voice got shrill, and Lone wondered how anybody could muster the breath to talk that fast and high. "And then it'll all thaw and it'll rain rain rain and come roarin' like a wild Indian down out a the Pine Mountains and flood us all over agin, and come summer you can walk in the dry, rocky riverbed, and even *I* could jump the river."

"I gotta go, Cassie."

"You just got here."

"They ain't nothin' to do here."

"Let's us just sit and talk a while."

"Gypsy and Boyd's waitin' for me."

"They won't run off without you."

"It's too still around here. I gotta—"

"Just look at the sunlight till it's all out, and the radio tower light comes on, Lone. With me. It won't hurt. Then you go on, and me with you. See how pale the light lies where you're gonna ride when it's dark? That quick shower that come awhile ago cleared it off sharp and blue. Mist thin as a razor blade edgin' around. All the hills of Harmon spread out, and if it was five minutes ago we could see just barely, 'way yonder, Big Black Mountain." What good was it to have eyes if he couldn't see for himself the very things he had first pointed out to her years ago? "And right now the last light's fallin' where lightnin' struck open the roof of the barn and stabs the damp ground at Coot's feet where he's sittin' on that railroad tie and the dark gettin' thick around his head while he holds a fruit jar a white lightnin', burnin' to the bottom, and behind him the brass of that busted statue a Jesus I found in Gran'paw Stonecipher's junkyard grows cold as a well-digger's do-lolly. One of Coot's hounds curled up, skin and bones, flashin' its tail into the spears of light like a grandfather's clock strokin'. And the light falls on the flaps of the revival tent down yonder and the sawdust and the stray spikes a grass, and swipin' across the backs of benches on the back row, the light lays a stripe on Momma's neck while she waits for the healin' to commence. She don't feel the cool light, just the tiredness seepin' out a her back even on that hard bench. And then, and then the sun dies, and hangs like a cap on a hook behind the ridge while the moon takes over, and the spokes a your wheels are a swarm a needles cuttin' through the moonlight on the highway. And, know what? Looks like your goggles are painted over soft silver."

As if rising from the bottom of the river, spurting breath, Lone said, "I got expelled from school yesterday."

"Tell it, Lone, tell it!"

He told her.

"It'll kill Momma," she said.

"I dread the look on her face."

"I tried all day long to make up a song, but couldn't think of even a startin' word. Day like this makes me want just to sing one that don't make sense." She strummed up. "One a daddy's. Okay, go, but listen first."

Maybe they *all* made sense, but most of them bewildered

Lone. "You sing all day long, you wear out your voice, Cassie."
But he wanted her to sing so he could go.

"I rode a big horse that was called a gray mare,
  Gray mane and tail and gray stripes down his back,
  There weren't a hair on him but what was called black.

She stood so still, she threw me to the dirt,
She tore my hide and bruised my shirt.
From saddle to stirrup I mounted again,
And on my ten toes I rode over the plain."

As she sang, he began to know what the odor was—Cassie's
blood, warm, tainted blood.

"I bought me a quart to drive gladness away,
  To stifle the dirt for it rained the whole day.

Sat down on a hot, cold frozen stone,
Ten thousand stood around me, yet I was alone.
I took my heart in my hand to keep my head warm.
Ten thousand got drownded that never was born."

Lone made it to the door, step by step. She watched him with
the song's rhythm, pulled at him with the words.

"I'll sing it again if you beg hard enough."

The dogs barked from somewhere up near the barn. Then
they barked closer to the front yard.

"Them dogs better not come *near* me, Coot!" Kyle's voice.

"Come here, you moron hounds! Wanna git the *po*lice
rabies?" Lone glanced out the window. Coot stood on the path,
the miner's hat tilted on his head, the lamp burning in the
evening light.

Lone started backing out of the room. "Tell Kyle I beat
him to the draw—hung myself." He turned in the hall and went
into Momma's room and pushed the door almost shut as Cassie
took up a book, sucked in a deep breath.

Kyle knocked at the front door. "Open this door, Lone!"

"Come in, Kyle," Cassie yelled. "It's unlocked."

Kyle burst through the door and stomped to a halt on the sill of the bedroom. "Where's Lone?"

"Hangin' from the swingin' bridge."

"Sorry I missed him as I come over. I would've throwed rocks at him."

"Daddy told me Lone come for his 'sickle. Parked outs-yonder, now where's *he* at?"

"Hidin' in the silo."

Squatting beside Momma's chest of drawers, Lone heard Kyle stomping down the hall, the floor rumbling under his bearish weight. Kyle stepped into Momma's room a little way, then backed out.

"Well, way I feel, I'd rather not run into that boy. Mainly, I come to see your momma. Me and her's gonna have to *do* somethin' about that boy. They kicked him out a school yesterday. Okay, *don't* look at me. . . . Why ain't you locked in, young'un?"

"Locks don't stop *some* people."

"What's you readin' about?"

"Sex!"

"Let me see that filthy book!"

"It's okay. My homebound teacher give it to me so's I wouldn't get stung by the bees nor crapped on by the birds."

"You need your mouth scrubbed out with P and G soap, girl."

"I thought *po*lice used the electric chair."

"Cassie McDaniel, you got a mean streak in you that's come blazin' out ever since Lone took up that 'sickle. Why do you and Lone torment me? . . . Sometimes I think he's ashamed of his Uncle Kyle, of this uniform."

Cassie rose and sat in the middle of the bed. "Don't be silly, now. Lone's always loved you."

"Bull. . . . But, by God, he's a sweet young'un 'neath all that show he copies off Boyd Weaver. Picked up that cocky walk. Why don't he act nicer to me?"

"Nobody but me knows why he acts like he does."

"I reckon you do," said Kyle, looking straight at Cassie over the bottom rail.

Staring at Kyle's massive back through the crack in the door, Lone remembered him on furlough telling him good-bye in the front yard before he went overseas. Kyle had caught him by the zipper of his fuzzy blue sweater and looked him straight in the eye. "Honey, I wish I had some of the love that people has put into you." He had zipped it up to Lone's neck and slapped him lightly, but sharp enough to sting.

"I started to break down and bring you a bunch of funny books them guys at the jail has read to death, but from the truckload you've added since I was here last time, any *more* books and people'll be tryin' to take out a library card."

"Well, I've got so I don't get sunk too deep in the Phantom and Sheena of the Jungle much anymore."

"I wish I had some of Virgil's credit in heaven, so my prayers would count. Hell, I'd pray you right out of that bed. It grieves my very bones to see a little fifteen-year-old girl pinned to that mattress."

"Sometimes, when Coot's drunk, he puts the blame on Lone for infectin' me with the fever, but I ain't never looked at it that way. It ain't bein' sick that's so bad. It's the way people look at me—me flat on my back, lookin' up over that rail. They look down, and what they see—so sad and hopeless."

Staring at Kyle's back, Lone realized suddenly that Cassie wasn't really talking to Kyle, that she wasn't really talking to Coot before, nor yesterday afternoon to Boyd. They were just telephone poles holding up the wires that carried questions and messages to Lone. Was that why, he wondered, he loved to play this game of hide-and-seek?

"But, listen," said Kyle, "from what you're growin' underneath that gown, you stay away from the leery-eyed men when you do get out. I *know*."

Still sitting up, Cassie pulled the quilt up over her head, and leaned back against the rails. Under the tented quilt she giggled.

"This the hardest bed ever I sat on. How does Lone stand

to sleep in it? Not that I ain't slept on worse. Slept in a barn on a pile a horse manure one time in Sicily just to keep from freezin' to death."

Cassie let the quilt drop and propped up some pillows, prepared to listen. Sleepy-eyed in the darkness of Momma's bedroom, Lone felt like a little boy, snuggled up beside Cassie on the big bed, looking at Kyle over the bottom rail.

"I ever tell you about that girl they made me shoot?"

"Well. . . ."

"Oh, hell, I can see by your eyes."

"That girl that was stranglin' soldiers with piano wire?"

"Just hush. It's bad enough when *I* get started. And I ain't even *had* a sip."

"Tell it. Tell about them spreadin' her out against the wall and the captain give you an order to shoot her and you cut her in half with a machine gun."

"I didn't come here to be tormented."

"It's just a story you told me a hundred times yourself."

"That's different. And it ain't just a story. It's real. I shouldn't tell you stuff like that, anyhow. Throwin' off *my* troubles on *you.*"

"I like to listen to you, Uncle Kyle. Ain't got nothin' about myself to tell anybody. I just like to listen to ever'body else. You, and Lone, and Coot, and Momma, and Gran'daddy, and Uncle Virgil even, and Boyd, and Lone."

"Don't throw *me* in with *that* gang."

"Ain't no way I can cut 'em loose from each other."

"Cassie, honey, this family's rotten, skin to core. Includin' your Uncle Kyle."

They kept talking, and Lone lay down on Momma's bed and let the darkness hug up to him, and dreaded telling her. With Kyle to rub it in, he'd need the new slip to soothe her. Spying and listening made his head hurt and his eyes throb, but Cassie's and Kyle's talk made him feel sad and good at the same time.

"I could do with a good cold glass of buttermilk," said Kyle. "And wish for cornbread." Lone heard Kyle go down the hall to the kitchen.

He wanted to go out and call Coot in and see Momma coming over the hill, and great God! some miracle to cause Gran'paw McDaniel to show up at the door, too. And have them all in the house together and the radio going, all the lights on, supper cooking, and the men sitting around, smoking, and the dogs calm on the porches, front and back. Then he realized that that was what Uncle Virgil had it in his power to do.

On impulse, Lone sprang up from the bed and opened the door. As he stepped over the sill into the hall, the feeling formed in words: *I want to git somethin' good started.*

At the end of the hall, in the kitchen light that hurt his eyes, Lone saw Kyle, standing beside the oak table, raise a glass of buttermilk to his lips, the fingertips of the other hand pressed stiffly on the round table rim; his coat swung open, the shirt a harsh white glare, the rich leather of the polished holster belt gleaming. Lone knew Kyle had crumbled yesterday's cold cornbread into the glass, dashed some pepper after it, and had stirred it daintily with a table knife. A mouthful bulged his pink cheeks, a tiny trickle squirting out of the corner of his mouth under pressure. He loved to slop a mouthful from cheek to cheek before he gulped. Bending his head far back, rising slightly on his toes, he jerked up and down on the upturned glass to make the last chunks of cornbread slide into his mouth, but before Kyle brought the glass down, Lone stepped across the hall, not seeing, but knowing, the look of lulled contentment as Kyle patted his potbelly and licked the buttermilk moustache from under his nose, fleshy like Gran'daddy's.

"He's still here," said Cassie, the gray guitar in her arms again.

"I know it."

"Is that Lone I hear?" Kyle belched.

"It's me, Kyle."

No light came from the grate, and the windows were almost dark. Lone braced himself against the bottom railing of the big bed. Light from the kitchen threw Kyle's shadow down the hall ahead of him, and then he filled the doorway, a mean look on his dark face. He had always been heavier than

Gran'daddy, but he had put on so much fat since he came home from Europe that he looked more like a Mexican bad guy in a movie than a man whose great-grandmother was a full-blooded Shawnee. "I stopped by to let you thank me for that favor I done you."

"I 'preciate you doin' it, Kyle," said Lone, in a friendly tone, "but I thought I'd put it off awhile."

"Till Daddy has to haul it in on a wrecker?"

"I'm just tryin' to picture you sneakin' up to my persimmon tree 'fore daylight and pushin' that 'sickle on your tiptoes down to the bridge," said Lone, smiling, hoping Kyle would take it in a spirit of horseplay.

"I rode it over and out to the junkyard," said Kyle, taking Lone's cue. But then he slapped his hands against the doorjamb. "But if I'd knowed *then* what I know now, I'd throwed *you* in after it."

"I'm going to finally tell Momma myself when she gets home. But listen, Kyle, why don't I call Coot in here and when Momma comes, let's all of us have some supper together and maybe listen to Amos 'n' Andy or something . . ."

"They cut them *off* the radio, boy. . . ." Kyle couldn't believe his ears. And it seemed to Lone as though someone else had just spoken through his own mouth.

"They're just commencin' to sing. She won't be home for a while yet. Reckon I'll just sack out on your cot, Lone, till she comes."

"I told you I was gonna tell her."

"Okay, I believe you, but she'll need somebody to comfort her."

"I reckon I can do that, too."

"You cain't comfort nobody no more, boy."

"Honey, you wanna pull that nightgown up over your shoulder?"

"All you can do is order your little sick sister around."

"No need to talk hateful, Uncle Kyle. I—"

"You overcome the devil in you, boy! *Then* be surprised if I talk hateful."

"I wish she'd come on, so we can get it over with."

"Anybody want to request a lullaby?" said Cassie, strumming.

"You better wish you was down there *with* her—or *instead* of her, since you the one that needs it, 'cause if Harmon's got a saint in it, it's Charlotte. I don't care what they say about Virgil."

"Revival! Don't people ever get sick of gettin' revived! Sometimes I wish I was still sick with you, Cassie."

"Sick—that's just what I git, lately, ever' time I run into you, boy." Kyle lay back on Lone's cot, wiggling to keep from lying on his revolver.

As Lone went down the hall, he heard metal rattle on the sill. "Never could sleep with a gun in my back."

Lone went outside, ducked the Indian cigars dangling from the catalpa tree and went inside the outhouse and sat in the black dark on the smooth wood between the two holes.

Through spaces between the boards, Lone saw Kyle's patrol car parked on the highway side of the swinging bridge. He watched a curtain of rain climb the hollow and blow against the house and heard it hit the roof of the outhouse.

Shortly, he heard Coot come down the path, pass the door of the outhouse, and go into the kitchen.

When he heard Momma's feet on the cinders at the edge of the front yard, he peered through a crack and watched her step off the path past the motorcycle under the persimmon trees, leaning against the stiff wind that twirled some leaves off the buckeye tree and rippled through her ratty fur collar, showing the knuckly bone. He remembered the time she hugged him in front of the picture show and the wind stung the place on his cheek where she had kissed him, and she put a dime in his cold hand to see *Tarzan,* and as she crossed the street to the hotel, the wind rippled the hem of her tacky green coat. Inside the outhouse, Lone waited awhile. He was in no hurry to go in.

The tent lights down in the hollow still burned. Slipping up onto the back porch again, he wondered if something was wrong.

As Lone stepped into the dark kitchen, Momma pulled the light chain and jumped, startled to see him in the doorway. Barefoot, in the frayed slip, she carried a soiled, wrinkled green uniform over one arm, about to wash it. The brass chain clinked against the naked bulb that shed a harsh light on the raindrops sparkling in her hair.

He took the white box from the chair he had shoved up to the table.

"Mother's Day present."

"But this isn't . . ."

"Mother's Day is when you stop in your tracks and—" He handed her the box, red ribbons around two corners. Her hair smelled of the fine rain.

She sat down at the table. Careful not to crush the ribbon, she opened the box. "If that ain't the loveliest thing ever I laid eyes on, honey, I tell thee."

Lone and Momma heard Cassie at the same moment and turned to see her standing in the doorway.

"What you doin' out of bed?"

"What you all talkin' about?"

"Get back in that bed, sister."

"Just let me *sit* with you all. I won't breathe a word."

"We'll put it in a milk bottle," Lone said, going over to her, "and give it to you in the mornin'."

"Did you tell her yet?"

"Tell me what?"

Making a warning face, Lone touched Cassie's arm, and she went back down the hall toward the light that came from their room.

Momma unfolded the slip and held it up. Then she began to cry.

"What's the matter?"

"It's one size too small."

"Well, don't cry about that. They'll let you—"

"I'm *not* cryin' about that." She hugged the slip soft glowing white against the dingy white of her old one, against her full breasts, and Coot's feet hit the attic stairs. He opened the door and leaned in, one foot on the bottom step, the other on the next one up, bracing himself at the doorjamb with one hand, holding the knob with the other. He didn't seem very drunk, though the miner's helmet, the headlight smashed now, tilted over one ear.

Momma turned to him. "What were you doin' up *there?*"

"I'm homesteadin' in the attic, for I want you to be free of me."

"You can move to the barn for all I care, but either one, you'll freeze your fanny off."

"Well, ain't it mine to freeze?"

"I don't care, Coot. Now, listen, me and Lone's talkin'." Turned in her chair, she looked at Coot the way someone does who expects you to leave.

Lone got up.

"Where *you* goin'?"

"No place." He went out on the porch.

"That sudden rain turned it chilly," Momma said. "Come in. I'll get us a wood fire roarin' and some coffee brewin'."

Lone didn't say anything. Up around the barn door, the dogs moved restlessly.

"Lone?"

"Okay, Momma." He went back in. Coot still leaned in the attic doorway, staring at them. Momma stirred up the fire. Her hair hung down over her narrow shoulders, free of the net.

"Don't let *me* butt in," Coot said.

"Go to bed."

Coot stepped down into the kitchen, sat at the table, ran his hand over the slip. "Christmas in September?"

"Now don't start, Coot," said Momma. Coot looked at Lone and opened his mouth. "Don't you say word *one* to that boy, Coot. Be still."

"Ain't a man's home his castle?"

Momma slammed the stove lid and turned, her arms folded, her dark eyes glaring. "Coot: Git up and git out!"

Coot looked over his shoulder at her and saw cause to get up and go out and sit on the back porch steps.

Lone watched Momma set the coffeepot between the two front eyes, red around the rims.

"Why ain't you down there singin'? They ain't let out yet."

"I left early because I just had a feelin' you'd be home, waitin' for me."

"They called you?"

"Who?" She picked up the slip and looked at the lacework around the top.

"Oh, God." Lone turned from her. He wanted to jump onto the 'cycle and become a spurt of quicksilver over a smooth, winding road to Black Mountain.

"What's wrong, honey?"

"I feel rotten givin' you that slip."

"For the Lord's sake, why?"

"Because it'll seem like I'm just—Momma, Kyle's gonna tell you anyway, so *I* may as well. I know what it means to you for me to graduate, but . . ."

"What?"

"Well, you know P. O. Fletcher—teaches phys ed?"

"Who?"

"Well, the point is, he hit me."

She sat back and looked at him, her eyes hard. "He—*hit* you?"

"Yeah."

"What for?"

"For not thankin' him for poppin' me on the—hind end with a wet towel. So I—"

"Oh, Lone, you didn't hit your *tea*-cher!"

"Well, you want them guys over there to *beat* on me?"

"No, but—"

"So they—kicked me out of school. For good."

She slapped her hands on the table and got up, looking up over her shoulder at the ceiling. She went to the back door and shut it tight.

"Lone . . ." said Cassie, through the wall.

He watched Momma. She bent over, trying not to cry.

"Please don't, Momma."

"Lone, you don't know, you just don't know how this hurts me."

"I know, Momma," he said, looking up at the light bulb where gnats had burned themselves out.

"How far away was that black snake Boyd Weaver?"

"Huh?"

"Before you commenced to run with *him*, you never had no trouble with *no*body, except Coot. Now, you *tell* me. Was Boyd hangin' around somewhere?"

"Well, he just stopped by the door of the gym to tell me somethin' and—"

"Just like I thought." She folded the slip very carefully, laid it in the box, pressed the lid over it, sat down, and clasped her hands on top of the box. "Set down, Lone." He sat down. "Now tell me ever'thing that happened. I'll need to know when I go to see the principal tomorrow mornin'."

"You ain't *goin'* to see that principal."

"Oh, but I cer-tain-ly *am!* He cain't deprive my son of the only education in the family."

"I won't *let* you go up there. You'll end up beggin'."

"Then I'll end up beggin'. On my knees! You want Virgil to come home and—"

"You will not beg for me." The sheen of light on her slip made him see more clearly the tear along her ribs. He got up. "I'd rather work in the mines till doomsday."

"*Set down!*"

"No."

"Set down, Lone," said Coot, from the porch steps, through the shut door.

"Shut up, Coot!"

"Lone? What's the matter?" said Cassie, coming into the kitchen.

Suddenly, Kyle dangled in the doorway, his face soft with sleep, creases from Lone's quilts on one plump cheek. "They kicked him out a school, Charlotte," said Kyle gently, but with an I-told-you-so tone.

Momma didn't see him, didn't hear him. She looked straight at Lone. "Lone, you're tearin' me up tonight!" She got up and reached for him. "Sit down."

"You better do like she says, Lone," Coot yelled from the porch. "She's got us *all* by the balls!"

"You can all go to hell!" Lone flung wide his arms, then swung his fist viciously into the air.

"Somebody call a bootlegger?" Virgil yelled down the hall from the front porch where Momma had left the door open.

Momma looked at Lone a moment, then ran to the doorway, knocking Kyle off balance: "Virgil, you ol' devil, you hush!" Kyle followed her.

"Pay me quick, the law's on my tail!" Virgil's voice echoed down the hall.

"You git in here!" Her voice quivering, Momma was about to cry with joy.

CHAPTER

10

"NOW, HE DON'T WANT HALF A ASIA HANGIN' ON HIS NECK," SAID Gran'daddy, out on the porch.

"Where's that little preacher? All right, Lone, don't make me come lookin' for you, boy." Virgil showed in the doorway, jerking his belt through the loops of his pants with a flourish. "There he is, hidin' in the kitchen. Know what happened to the moneychangers, don't you?"

He walked toward Lone, a black hat pulled down aslant his face like a gangster, his arms spread wide. As Virgil hugged him, Lone saw Gran'daddy Stonecipher in the doorway, wearing his Sunday suit, his arms full of groceries, Kyle and Momma crowding behind him.

"You sure been gone a long time, Uncle Virgil."

"Long enough for you to turn into a little hellion? And where's that puny little deadbeat, Cassie?" His old grin looked strange, good to see, but different.

Kyle and Momma stepped aside to let Virgil charge through the doorway, then they turned and, Lone with them, followed Virgil into the bedroom, his belt snapping, the coattails of his unbuttoned, double-breasted blue suit swinging.

Cassie stuck her head out of the covers. "They don't feed me right, Uncle Virgil, and they give me three whippin's a day."

"Good. Good. Make a man of you. Where's that drunken farmer?"

"I'm closer to heaven than *you* are!" yelled Coot from the kitchen.

"Virgil, that man pointed a shotgun at his son yesterday mornin'." Momma stood in the doorway, Kyle and Gran'daddy behind her in the hall.

"Now that ain't nothin' to fool about. Has the white lightnin' finally struck his brain?" The suit made Virgil look as though he had filled out a little around the waist.

"I reckon it was over the same thing that got you back here, Uncle Virgil," said Lone. "Ridin' with Boyd on that motorsickle turned Coot against me worse'n ever."

"And I'm here to testify," said Gran'daddy, coming into the bedroom, "that that boy's raced hisself into the fires of hell since you been gone."

"And don't think it won't hold up in court." Kyle stood on the sill, filling the doorway.

"You all just let up on that," said Momma. "We gonna all be at the table together d'reckly. Daddy's brought the makin's of a feast."

"I'm lookin' at a girl that won't turn loose a the devil," said Virgil, looping and buckling his belt. Lone saw that Virgil no longer *needed* a belt to keep his pants from hanging loose on his hips.

Cassie hid under the covers.

"Now don't you trifle with your uncle, Cassie," said Momma. "We all know you're dyin' to throw off that sickness for good."

"I've come from five months of healin' the afflicted in body and soul. If I cain't heal my own niece, I better shut my Bible and sew up my mouth." Virgil's skin, usually sallow, was tan, and his face looked less stark. "Now, Cassie, before I left, you just wasn't ready. If you lack the will, the Lord won't work in you. You ready to try agin?"

"Now wait, Cassie," said Momma. "Don't answer yet. Think. What would *Jesus* have you answer your Uncle Virgil? What would *Jesus* have you answer your Uncle Virgil?"

"Well, He ain't breathed a *word* to me."

Virgil stood at the foot of the bed, slowly buttoning his coat, looking straight at Cassie. "I've thought about this, Cassie, ever since I went away last spring." She wiggled backward to lean against the pillows at the head of the bed. She put one hand on her hip, and gave him what *she* thought a gaze was.

"Now, Cassie." Momma pointed a warning finger at her.

"You all stand at the foot of the bed and think on Jesus." Virgil kept staring at Cassie. His eyes seemed to have more life in them, but the sockets were still dark. "Reckon she's not used to *people*, much less the Holy Ghost. You've had a lot of pain, ain't you, honey?"

"Yes."

"You know who put that pain in your body?"

"Oh, the devil, I reckon."

"No. God. God wanted you to suffer."

He stood still a few moments, then went around the bed to the side, Cassie's eyes following him, trying to get him back in focus.

"Why?" she asked timidly.

"You've had rheumatic fever most of your life. Your body burns up, then it turns cold. Your joints ache like a toothache sometimes, and sometimes your limbs are so light they don't seem like they're part *of* you, do they? Is that right?" Cassie nodded, rubbing her hands over her arms, looking at him. "Now, I said God put that awful pain in you, didn't I?" She nodded, and as he leaned over and reached, her hands met his at the edge of the bed. "Now you've got to have faith that the same God who put that fever in your body can evict it. Do you believe that?"

"My folks never did believe in faith-healers atall." They all turned, except Virgil. Lone saw Coot in the doorway, a leaning tower of filth, wearing the miner's helmet, its lamp smashed. Kyle sat on the cot.

"Don't call me a faith-healer, Coot." Virgil's green eyes still looked into Cassie's. "Jesus just uses me the way he uses that dirt outsyonder."

"Well, if you'd turn loose a Lone's soul, maybe *he'd* use that dirt outsyonder."

"Why, Coot," said Kyle, trying to see Coot through the junk cluttering the room, "this here's condemned land, and this old house—the least spark'd send it up in a blaze."

"Nobody sent for no cops."

"Let them bulldozers work on *you* awhile."

"Nobody sent for you, either, Coot," said Momma. "Why don't you go off somewhere and keep still!"

"I won't be ordered around in my own house. I may sleep in the attic, but till they aim them bulldozers next month, I *own* ever' splinter!" He turned at the sound of the front screen opening. "Well, walk in, sal-*va*-tion."

Boyd appeared in the doorway, jangling keys, grinning.

"What *you* doin' here, Boyd Weaver?" said Momma. "Since when do you just walk in where you ain't welcome?"

"Just returnin' the man's keys, ma'am." Boyd tossed them to Virgil, who missed them. Cassie picked them up off the bed and handed them to Virgil. "Rides like a storm cloud, preacher."

"Nobody but Virgil would trust Boyd Weaver with his Cadillac," said Gran'daddy.

Through the window, Lone could scarcely see the white Cadillac across the bridge, and by its glow in the twilight, Gran'daddy's red and white wrecker, that appeared to be towing the car, the wrecker's large wooden buffer next to the rear bumper of Kyle's police car. On the bridge, too narrow for a car, was parked Boyd's black 'cycle, as though escorting the Cadillac and the wrecker.

"You want *me* to route you back where you come from?" Kyle stood up and shifted his weight, making the room feel more crowded. Lone looked at the revolver on the windowsill behind Kyle.

"You've raked enough torment over us without us havin' to look at your face." Momma was so close to Boyd, she had to keep herself from slapping him. Lone wished she would leave the room and put her dress on.

"Ain't nobody any need of such trash as you," said Gran'daddy.

"You kickin' me out, Lone? You goin' back to your momma now?"

"Let me throw him out, one piece at a time." Kyle's empty holster looked strange.

"You gonna take to shakin' that old tambourine again, Lone?"

"Well, he ain't gonna make a whiskey runner like you!" Coot sneered at Boyd.

"What about a whiskey-*head* like you?"

"I'm thinkin' of becomin' a nun!" shouted Cassie, draped in the quilt.

"You come here to deliver whiskey, didn't you?" asked Kyle. He reached out and slapped Boyd on the left buttock, expecting to feel a bottle. "Who you run for?"

"Okay, I don't hang around where I ain't wanted."

The look on Lone's face when he saw Gypsy in the doorway turned them all toward her.

"I knocked, but nobody come to the door," she said. "Boyd here?"

"Now, I won't have this goin' on, a night like this," said Momma. "Gypsy, you ain't welcome. Lone's uncle's home now, and we're—"

"Please, Momma," said Lone, "don't talk to her in that tone." Seeing Momma and Gypsy standing close to each other in the crowded room made Lone feel strange.

"Well if we're gonna have a busload of strangers buttin' in . . ." said Gran'daddy.

"I'm gonna fill that patrol car d'reckly," said Kyle, buttoning his coat and flexing his shoulders, giving his balls a quick rake, to stress his seriousness.

Glaring, Momma pointed her finger rapidly at each of them. "This fussin's about to ruin Virgil's homecomin'!"

Aware that Virgil had stayed behind them all, leaning back against the foot of the bed, Cassie on her knees just behind him, one hand on his shoulder, the other on the rail, Lone watched Virgil take one step forward, pulling the New Testament out of his coat the way mobsters in the movies go slowly for their rods. The metal covers caught the light.

"You know what this is, Charlotte?"

"The Bible."

"You know what this is, Boyd?"

"The Bible."

"What's that in my hand, Sister Gypsy?"

"It's the Bible."

"Say it, Coot. Don't you close them eyes!"

"Bible."

"Kyle?"

"The Bible."

"Daddy, say it."

"Hit's the Bible, son."

He turned. "You recognize it, Cassie?"

"The Bible, Uncle Virgil."

Virgil paused, looked into the eyes of each person separately. "No!" His voice went soft. "It ain't nothin'—it's only a *thing* till one a you opens it."

As Virgil looked at them, each in turn avoided his eyes, but he stared at them until they all began to make spontaneous gestures toward the Bible. But Lone moved more quickly and opened it. "The word and the will a God. Do you all see that red print?" Lone started to take his hand away. "No, don't jerk that hand away. Now read His first words on the page, Brother Boyd."

" 'I thirst.' "

"It's open on the blood of Christ. Coot, place your hand over Lone's."

Coot stepped forward and put his hand over Lone's. The

reek of whiskey made Lone suck for breath. Virgil looked at Momma. She stepped forward and put her hand over Coot's. Virgil looked at Boyd. He stepped forward and put his hand over Momma's. Momma jerked her hand away. "That's Christ's blood in his hand, Charlotte. You too good to touch it? Even if he had leprosy, you wouldn't be good enough, if they's a drop of hate in your body. You cain't trifle with the Lord!" Momma put her hand over Boyd's. Virgil looked at Cassie. She leaned over the bedrail and put her hand over Momma's. Then Virgil looked at Gypsy, then at Kyle, then at Gran'daddy Stonecipher, and they slowly put their hands on the others. "Praise Jesus! Now raise your other hands, witness the blood, and take a hold on heaven." They raised their other hands. "Now all I know about religion is what I know personally. And I know I was once the most filthy-mouthed man in Harmon. Fightin', women, and whiskey was all I knew. I used to raise hell outside every tent meetin' I come across—pokin' fun. But I tell you, honey, you cain't fool with the Lord. Them that's loudest in blasphemy, oftentimes ends up loudest in givin' testimony. You're listenin' to a man that's been through it. One day I looked to Calvary, honey, and by the spirit of God I was transformed into His likeness. Just one look. But right there's where the hell starts, honey." They all looked at him, waiting for the next word. "And I know ain't a single person here that's pure. Now if you ain't got love in your heart this minute, you cain't get within a million light-years of heaven, honey. Can you say, Praise Jesus?"

"Praise Jesus!" they said, in harmony.

"Shut your eyes." Lone shut his eyes. "Keep your hands up on heaven. Look toward Calvary. Don't look at *me*, Brother Boyd. Nobody askin' you all to hang by your hands, nailed to any cross. Somebody else does it for you ever' breath you take. Least you can do is let the blood of His love flow through your bodies. Feel how warm?" Lone felt upon his body the murmurs of testimony. "Feel the burnin' flesh and the burnin' word, brandin' your souls with love and forgiveness? Oh, Jesus, purge us of the sin of hate with Thy blood."

"Praise Jesus, sweet Jesus," said Momma, and Lone saw her falling on her back in the tent last spring, raising her quivering arms, jerking her legs, rocking on her hips, screaming, and he had draped his ragged mackinaw over her legs.

"Now, Cassie, do you believe what I said awhile ago?" Lone opened his eyes as Virgil took the Bible suddenly from their hands and pressed it flat against Cassie's breasts. In the moment before his attention became fixed, along with the eyes of everyone else in the room, upon the Bible and Cassie's face, Lone saw tears glistening on Boyd's dark hard cheeks. "That's why God favored you with that pain, so that you could take Jesus in and let *it* go. But Jesus is not going to take up a dwellin' in no reluctant house. Do you believe, honey?" Cassie nodded. "Praise Jesus!" Momma screamed, brimming over with the Holy Ghost. "Now, honey, just hold your arms up, hold 'em up, I'm gonna let go and you hold 'em up. Praise Jesus. Now look up at the ceilin' and put your mind on Jesus and your heart in Jordan, on Jesus, you hear me, in Jordan. Keep them arms up now." Suddenly, he took hold of her wrists. "*Fever*, come out of this girl's body. *Fe-ver*, I command you to leave the body of this little girl!" Virgil's hand slapped against Cassie's forehead. "*Fever*, in the name of Christ our Saviour, I order you to *leave* this child's body. In the name of *Jesus*! Heal!" He bounced on his heels, one hand gripping her wrist tightly, the other clamped over her forehead, pushing her head back, her long yellow hair shaking behind her, dewberries of sweat on her temples. "Heal! My God, you got the spirit of the *Holy* Ghost in you, girl."

"Oh, wonderful Jesus!" Momma bit her thumbs and hunched her shoulders.

"I can see it in your eyes. No, don't look at me. Close them eyes."

"Do what he says, Cassie," said Momma.

"Hush! Force that fever out, Lord! It's afflicted her long enough." His hand gripping her forehead, jolting her frail body, he yelled, "Heal! Heal! Heal!" Cassie fell back, writhing in joy, her eyes shut tight, her nightgown high above her knees. Reaching down, Lone flapped the quilt over her legs.

"Oh, there's power, power," Cassie began to sing, rolling back and forth, blurring herself in Lone's eyes, and Virgil took it up, smiling, his teeth white and strange. "Wonder-workin' power in the blood—"

Everyone took it up, "—of the Lamb."

"There is power, power,
Wonder-workin' power,
In the precious blood of the Lamb."

Cassie began to calm, still singing in a piercing voice.

"Would you be free of your burden of sin?
There's power in the blood.
Would you o'er Satan a victory win?
There's wonderful power in the blood."

Momma took the tambourine off a hook on the wall and Lone reached across Boyd and Gypsy for it and began to bang it, while everyone clapped. Kyle got the gray guitar and handed it to Cassie, who sat up and clapped and bounced on the mattress and sang. Lone looked around the room as he sang, high above the rest, knowing that they all looked at him, remembering how he used to soar above the congregation only a few years ago.

"Oh, there's power, power, wonder-workin' power
In the blood of the Lamb.
There is power, power,
Wonder-workin' power in the precious blood of the Lamb."

They finished, holding hands.
"Now, Charlotte, do you love Coot?"
"Yes."
"Do you love Boyd?"
"Yes, Virgil."
"Coot, hug your son." Coot and Lone hugged, the tam-

bourine still vibrating in Lone's wrist. "Now shake hands with your brothers, praise Jesus." Everyone was sweating and joyfully out of breath, but Virgil's skin was dry, as if all his labor had come from somewhere else.

"And let's feast together—like in the days of the evangelists. Christian love starts right at the table with the givin' of thanks."

"Well, I reckon I better be goin'," said Boyd, backing out.

"Charlotte . . ." Virgil gave Momma a look.

"Boyd," said Momma, "I can put another leaf in the table for you—and Gypsy."

"Well, I'd sure love to *be* with you all." Boyd turned his head shyly, taking off his cap, letting his stiff black hair spring up slowly.

"I just come to tell Boyd somethin'," Gypsy was so timid she seemed strange.

"Well, stay and talk to us *all*," said Gran'daddy.

"It'll be a while yet." Momma noticed Lone looking at her, and crossed her arms over her chest. "So much excitement, I didn't realize— Let me jerk on a dress—I was just gettin' out a my uniform when Virgil come in the door."

"I'll race down to the house and clean up." Boyd backed out of the bedroom. It impressed Lone to imagine Boyd's being able to go into that room in the back of the ruined house and come out clean.

"I been on the road all night." Virgil walked wearily toward Cassie's bed. "If I'm to preach tomorrow, I better lay down."

Cassie got up and smoothed out the quilts. "If you can stand the smell of a lifetime of *me* . . ."

"Wasn't I born in it myself?" Virgil unbuttoned his double-breasted coat, flung it open, and lay down on the bed. "You got a dress?"

"Somewhere."

"Then get in it."

"Yes, sir." She dug into a drawer and with a summer dress over her arm, Cassie crossed the hall into Momma's room.

Kyle went on out. Gran'daddy followed him, saying, "How you like Virgil's new teeth?"

"Well, I'll be damned," said Kyle.

Coot backed up to let Gypsy out, and then he followed.

Momma came back in, wearing a soft blue rayon dress, her best, and pulled the shade half down. "He always likes it dark."

Lone stood at the foot of the bed, looking down at Virgil, who crossed his arms and closed his eyes as Momma pulled off his shoes. Lone smelled his feet.

"What you lookin' at, Lone?" Virgil didn't open his eyes.

"You."

"That's what I come to show you."

Momma rose from setting his shoes down softly, and she and Lone looked at Virgil.

"You go on, Charlotte. I want to talk to Lone a minute." Momma moved toward the door like a sleepwalker. "Turn it off." Reaching back, she pulled the string tied to the brass rail and went out.

Just as Gypsy backed into the swing between Kyle and Gran'daddy, she looked into the bedroom below the window, and Kyle set the swing going, his empty holster like a mouth, open in awe. The revolver still lay in the dull light on the windowsill beside Lone's cot.

They all looked different now. For a moment Lone felt the certainty that there had been this night, this one night, and that after the house had become a curve of asphalt where the traffic would take its toll, this good night would have happened, for no bulldozers could touch it. "It's a strange sight."

"Set by me."

Lone felt for the edge of the bed and sat down. Cassie appeared on the porch in a red cotton dress, skin-tight, that she had outgrown, and sat on the porch railing.

Virgil's hollow eyes watched her, too, through the space between the shade and the sill. "She faked it."

"Huh?"

"Forget it. Reach in my breast pocket, Lone." Lone felt

over Virgil's bony chest until he found the lapels of the coat, and he took out the small metal-covered New Testament, his fingertips touching the place where the sniper's bullet had struck.

Lone sat still on the edge of the bed, feeling no need to speak, comfortable, content in the silence of the room, separated from the voices on the porch, the creaking of the swing, Momma cooking in the kitchen.

"This power you got is real, Uncle Virgil. I want to be like you. Because I've had people come to *me*, too. They all want me to be somethin' great."

"I know. I know. But listen, are you worth a damn to start with?"

"What?"

"Are you?"

"No."

"You got to do somethin' about that first, don't you?"

"When Momma told me she sent for you, I was worried because I ain't been livin' much of a life since you been gone, but now you're here. . . . The only trouble is, they want it to happen overnight."

"Maybe you ain't hit bottom yet. Maybe you need to git out and try and fail and fail again."

"I thought you was supposed to bring the *good* news." Lone smiled loud enough for Virgil to hear him.

"Listen, Lone, they's been in this world only one perfect man, and folks couldn't wait till they desecrated Him. They nailed Him up, spit on Him, called Him ever' name under the sun, and the last breath he took was spoke in love for them that tormented Him. You don't have to be that perfect. Look at what you are *now*. Hell, honey, you got so far to go before you're perfect, you ain't in no danger."

"Well, I want to promise you, Uncle Virgil—"

"Don't promise me nothin', Lone. Your life is *your* business, not mine. Maybe not even God's."

"But don't you want me to—?"

"To take up where I leave off? That's what I always

preached to you, ain't it? But what do *you* want, Lone? I know what your momma wants of you, and your sister, and Kyle, and Daddy, and even Boyd, but what do *you* want?"

"I want to be able to do what *you* just did. Create harmony in the middle of hell."

"But what if the hell stays right inside *you?* Lone, a man's lucky to love *one* person before he dies: himself. That's only human. But the real miracle comes when he can love his neighbor as himself. Christ loved all men—He could do it because He was God. That's what it takes. Maybe to love *two* persons more than yourself is blasphemy. The saints didn't love the multitudes. They loved Jesus and for His sake they *served* the multitudes." He sighed, deeply. "But son, they's more to livin' in this world than a preacher can tell you. I got one last sermon, shortest ever preached." Lone started to speak. "Not now. Ask questions later. Go git me a glass of good ol' cold pump water, will you, son?"

Momma had a fire roaring in the kitchen stove, and she had spread all the groceries out over the table. The light in the kitchen looked warm and sweet on her blue dress, and she smiled when he came to the sink where she was pumping water into a pot.

"I got on your slip, honey."

Lone kissed her temple. "He wants a glass of cold water."

Momma reached up in the cupboard and took down a glass. "You'll have to *work* that pump. The cistern's low." She held the glass under the faucet, and Lone used both hands to pump. As the water began to drip and Lone anticipated the gush, Virgil screamed through the thin walls, "Lone!" A cry of horror and help.

The gush of water knocked the glass out of Momma's hand and the fragments struck the front of Lone's shirt. A gunshot rattled the window over the sink. He ran to the room and smelled powder. And as he kissed his uncle, he smelled the blood, and the muzzle of Kyle's service revolver burned his cheek.

CHAPTER

II

AIMING HIS 'CYCLE BETWEEN THE PERSIMMON TREES, THE trunks looking like two alligators, Lone miscalculated and, as the motorcycle pulled him over, his foot slipped in rotten persimmons and mud. Boyd leaned over him, grabbed the points of his leather collar, and pulled him up. Giggling low and slapping each other on their leather jackets, shushing each other, they unbuckled their bulky saddlebags and slung them around their necks.

All the windows were dark.

They staggered over the rain-wet grass to the porch steps, their shoulders bumping, the saddlebags flopping around their necks. "Gotta tell, gotta tell—ol' Cassie allllll a-*bout* it."

"Yeah, good buddy, ever' damn *thing!*"

"Be quiet as you go," said Lone. "They're all 'sleep."

"I feel like a thief in the night."

Boyd bumped the swing and set it creaking. Together, they stilled it, their fingers tangling. When they turned to the window again, reaching out to raise it, Cassie, wearing the goggles and the new cap Boyd had given Lone, looked out at them, putting her finger to her lips.

As Boyd eased the window up, all three winced at the squeaking. "Don't stir up Coot agin," said Cassie. "He's ravin' and roarin' drunk, and been cryin' like a woman."

Cassie backed off Lone's cot, and Boyd crawled into the bedroom, Lone after him. A rasping of leather on the sill. Their suppressed giggling like a nervous hissing.

As Lone knelt on the edge of his cot, it seemed to drop into the same deep darkness he had plunged into on his 'cycle. Afraid, he leaned back against the wall. Boyd sat beside him at the head of the cot.

"You all look like two cowboy Sanny Clauses—them bags around your necks."

"Have some diced pineapple, son," said Boyd, and tossed a can into Cassie's lap as she settled in the middle of the cot, her back to the window where the moon was bright.

"You all drunker'n forty hells."

"Drunker'n a wal—a wal—waltzin' piss ant. What my sister needs is a good five-cent cigar." Lone tossed a fistful of dry White Owl cigars into her lap.

"The suckers are on *me.*" Boyd flipped five onto the quilt.

"Be my guest. Mars bar and a Milky Way."

Cassie pressed her fists against her mouth to keep giggles from bubbling out loud.

"Have a box of thumbtacks."

"And a Eveready flashlight." Lone shot the beam into her face. Behind her, he saw the big brass bed, the mattress rolled and tied, half the rusty springs exposed. He tossed the flashlight into her lap.

"Mercy me, where you all been, Lone?"

"Where all *ain't* we been?" Boyd bowed, letting his saddlebags slip over his neck onto the cot.

"This cot's warm as a oven."

"I been layin' here listenin' for *you.* This rain's killin' me."

"I found him in a gully," said Boyd, "with his motorsickle wrapped around his neck."

Cassie shot the light into Lone's face, and gasped. He remembered the lump on his forehead, and the cut on his cheek Coot made and that the wreck opened up again.

"Don't worry. He can't feel a thing. I slapped his face till his eyes opened, then poured a gallon a white lightnin' down him. We been rootin' up hell ever' since. Ain't we, good buddy?"

"Yeah. Bo—uh, uh, somebody—take this *off* me?" He felt Cassie's hands on his neck, and she lifted the heavy saddlebags and pulled them over his head as he tipped forward into her lap. She helped him pull himself up, and he leaned against the wall again.

"Where *was* he, Boyd?"

"Windin' up into Black Mountain."

"Gran'paw McDaniel . . . Gran'paw McDaniel, Cassie. . . . I—"

"You struck out to find *him?*"

"But I kept goin' straight at a curve, and it seemed like I fell for hours."

"When I come back up to the house all cleaned up—*now* look at me—your momma begged me to track Lone down. She's gonna spit in my face when she sees what I drug back."

"She's still at the funeral home. They just all went off and left me."

"Well, hell with them people. Me and Boyd's been havin' a goddamn good time, ain't we, Boyd? Ain't we, Boyd? Ain't we, by God?"

"I want to bless you! And we said, let's go see Cassie and tell her all about it."

"Where'd you get all this loot?"

"You know that ol' deserted commissary store in the ol' company town?"

"You finally broke in?"

"Now didn't we?"

"*Raided* the fool thing! Boyd said he needed a good buddy —a cigarette, good buddy, and I said, 'They got good cigarettes in the commissary, man,' and he said—"

" 'An' the best ol' flyswatters!' "

"So we went up to the door and it had a yellow X on it for where they gonna come through with the highway, so we said, 'Knock, knock, who's there?' 'It's the new highway,' says Boyd, 'Come in,' says me, and we made a run at it, and the door come off like we's invited."

"Then what?"

"Then we crept around in the dark." Lone crawled around and around in a tight circle. "And guess what we found in that ol' deserted store?"

"What?"

Lone suddenly put his nose to Cassie's: "A green-eyed mockin'bird with her loot—her lap full of loot."

"OOooooo! Sounds scary as that old song."

"Hell, sing it, Cassie." Boyd bounced on the cot.

"You all, too. But quiet." Lone handed her the guitar.

"Qui-ut."

"Qui-ut-ly," Boyd raised his edge of the quilt. "Let's make us a tent."

They scrambled around on the cot until the quilt was spread over them, Lone on his knees, his head the center pole, keeping it up.

As Cassie began to strum, Boyd shined the flashlight in her face.

"There was an old woman all skin and bones."

Together they sang, "OOO–OOO–OOooooo!"

"She lived down by the old churchyard," Lone sang, the light on his face.

"OOO–OOO–OOoooooooo!"

Boyd turned the light up into his own face. "One night she thought she'd take a walk."

"OOO–OOO–OOooooo!"

The light hit Cassie again. "She walked down by the old churchyard."

"OOO–OOO–OOooooo!"

The light on Lone again.

"She saw the bones a-layin' around."

"OOO–OOO–OOoooooo!"

The light showed Boyd's face again. "She thought she'd sweep the old church house."

"OOO–OOO–OOoooooo!"

"She went to the closet to git her a broom," Cassie sang.

"OOO–OOO–OOoooooo!"

Lone sang as Boyd snapped off the light.

"She opened the door an'—"

"Boooo!"

They laughed, then shushed each other.

"I sure love to hear you sing those ol'-timey songs, Cassie." Boyd flicked the light off and on, rapidly, on her face.

"Gimme that bottle, good buddy."

"Take it easy, buddy-row. That stuff's gonna lift the top off your head."

Lone felt in the black dark until his hands touched curved glass.

"Save Cassie a swaller."

"She don't need it," said Lone. "She can get higher than a kite just by shuttin' her eyes."

Boyd took back the bottle. "Take a sip, Cassie."

"No." Lone pushed it with the back of his hand.

"You all tell me ever'thing that happened."

"Man, those old shelves was loaded." As Boyd spread his arms, Lone felt the quilt move.

"So warped they was about to tip and spill that stuff right in our arms," said Lone.

"Meat case was empty except for the carcass of a jarfly on *dis*play."

"Shoooo-law!" said Cassie. "Tastes like ol' sour butter-milk!"

"I said, 'No!' " Lone felt for the bottle, his hand grazing Cassie's breasts.

"Just a drop or two left." Boyd took the bottle from Lone.

"It's steamin' up in here." Fighting the quilt off his head, Lone stood up in the middle of the cot.

"Hey, did you all hear that big explosion while ago? It shook the cot like a earthquake."

"Did we *hear* it?"

"Hell, honey, we *made* it." Boyd pulled a stick of dynamite out from under his jacket. "Care for a stick of dynamite?"

"Where in blazes you get hold a *this?*"

"You know them strikers that's been rovin' around the mountains in them long lines of cars?"

"They was out agin tonight," said Cassie.

"Me and Boyd was thinkin', tonight would be a good time for 'em to blow one of them coal tipples sky high. We kept followin' 'em around, waitin' for 'em to blow somethin' up, but they never did—so we . . ."

"Hell, I know where they keep their dynamite hid, see, so me and Lone borrowed a few sticks, and had us a little explosion all our own."

"Gypsy's been after us to move our hideout."

"We sure as hell *moved* it, didn't we, good buddy?"

"I'uz afraid Kyle'd or somebody'd be layin' for us in the bedroom."

"Folks, I innerrupt this program to bring you a special news bulletin. The whiskey is shot."

"No need to cry when you got 7-Up in your saddlebag," said Lone.

"You got 7-Up in *your* saddlebag? Well, hell, son, I got Royal Crown in *mine*. Where's a nailhead?" Boyd got up. Cassie flicked on the flashlight and followed the movement of his head as Boyd walked around in a circle, looking at the dark walls. "Bull's-eye, Cassie." Boyd pried off the cap and the foam shot short of the ceiling.

Lone scooted off the cot and clawed at the nail with the cap, until the 7-Up spurted out on the wall.

"I bet you my dope can do a longer fizz than yours." Spotlighted by Cassie, Boyd shook the bottle violently.

"It's a duel." Lone pressed his thumb over the mouth of his bottle.

Cassie moved the light over them.

Boyd squirted Royal Crown at Lone.

"Got me in the damn eye!"

Boyd ran from Lone, his back hunched up. Lone aimed and released his finger. The foam drooled down Boyd's neck.

"My damn pants are sticky."

"Looks like you peed in 'em."

"I won."

"The hell you did."

"It's a tie," said Cassie.

"*You* lose." Boyd squirted Cassie. Lone saw her nightgown cling darkly to her breasts before she dropped the flashlight and the room got dark.

"Okay, you all asked for it." Lone heard Cassie stir around inside the saddlebags. "Have some three-year-old peanut butter."

"Hey, all over my jacket!"

Then Lone felt her hands on *him*, wiping, and he smelled the stale peanut butter. He felt around on the bed and found a jar of mayonnaise, dipped his fingers into it, and felt around in the dark for Cassie.

"Gangin' up on me, huh?" said Boyd.

"I thought you was Cassie."

"Who threw *sug*-ar on me?"

"That wasn't sugar. Don't you know coffee when you wear it?"

"You gonna wish you'd stayed in Brazil," said Boyd.

"Who's that pourin' jelly beans down my back?"

"Boyd," said Cassie.

"Tell lies, you get Bull Durham tobacco in your hair."

"Wheeee! Feels like we're on a rolly-coaster," said Cassie.

"Hey, if we don't be quiet, we gonna wake up your Uncle Virgil," said Boyd.

"Why you reckon we set off that blast while ago?" said Lone. "Wake the son of a bitch *up!*"

"Don't you cry, don't you weep, I just dropped off to sleep."

"Ah-haaaaaaa, praise Jesus!" yelled Lone.

"Come all ye sinners!"

"God's got you on the roll call!"

"Step up, step up, step right up, folks!"

Boyd held the flashlight: "First in line is Cassie McDaniel, then Lone McDaniel, then Charlotte McDaniel, then Coot Mc-Daniel, then Kyle Stonecipher, then Mavis Weaver, then Boyd Weaver, and—"

"Praise God, amen, hallaluyer!"

"Get up and preach us a sermon, Brother Lone. Give us the word from above."

"We dyin' to hear, brother!" yelled Cassie.

"Hey brother, hey brother, hey brother, hey!"

"Heal us, Saint Lone!" Boyd tapped his foot, and Cassie clapped her hands.

"We hear the call!"

"We want the word!"

Lone jumped up on his cot and spread his arms. "Peace, brothers and sistern, peace!"

"Hallaluyer!"

"I come with the word! The word according to Saint Lone! No long sermon tonight, folks, no rantin' and ravin' and stompin' and hollerin' and rollin' in the sawdust and wakin' up the neighborhood with the loudspeakers of God. Only the word, brothers and sistern."

"Give us the word, Lone!"

"We dyin' to hear!"

"Precious Jesus!"

"I come with the word and the healin' will commence."

"Oh, give us the word, Saint Lone, then heal the flesh!"

"The blind and the bug-eyed and the lame and the lame-brained and the spastic and the bowlegged and the left-handed and the pigeon-toed and the snaggle-toothed and the dog-bit and the knocked-up, and the I-don't-know-what-all, all you that whine and groan, come unto me, and by the hand of the al-mighty God, be *healed!* But first, the word—"

"Oh, oh, oh, oh!"

"The word is—The word—Let's ride, Boyd."

"Finish the service, Lone. You were goin' good."

"It *is* finished."

"Let me *try* it. I bet I'd make a good faith-healer, son. To hell with the word, brothers and sisters, let's get to the healin'! Raise up them arms, girl, and take a hold on high! Oh, the holy ghost is in you tonight!" Lone heard a slap and felt around on the bed for the flashlight. "Fever, fever, come out a this girl's body, devil, devil, devil turn loose a this girl's body!"

Lone snapped the light on Boyd. Balanced on the edge of the cot on one knee, he held Cassie by one arm, his other hand pressed against her forehead the way Virgil had done. Lone slugged him with his forearm across the chest. Boyd fell back on the floor. Lone shined the light on him.

"I told you, Boyd, not to ever touch my sister!"

"Don't get your bowels in a uproar, I'uz just kiddin' around."

"Git out a our room, Boyd! I shouldn't ever let you come in here!"

"I'm too low-down? Am I as low as your Uncle Virgil? They just a damn counterfeit nickel—Kyle on one side, and Virgil on the other."

"Please go home, Boyd." Cassie's voice was calm, as if she knew how to handle him.

"Reckon that white lightnin' finally hit him."

"No, it ain't that. It's Uncle Virgil."

"Hell, we been makin' fun of him all night."

"That's just what hit him. Go on now."

"Well, don't you think it hit me, too? He had *me* fooled same as you all. Never nobody could work on *me* like *he* done."

"I shouldn't even let you *in* our room," said Lone.

"Okay, I know when I ain't wanted." Boyd raised the window. "But just tell me somethin', will you? Why you afraid of me and Cassie, little brother?"

"You son of a bitch. You ain't as drunk as you act, are you?"

Boyd slipped through the window onto the porch, laughing. He gave the swing a violent shove and it clattered against the side of the house. He revved his motor until Lone's head began to throb, then he shot down the hollow.

"Oh, me, oh, my," said Lone. "I'm bone-weary . . . of ridin' and crawlin' around . . . so blind on white lightnin' I cain't hardly see my cot."

Angry for sleep, he jerked off his clothes and boots and slung them aimlessly, as if, when he got down to his skin, he'd be able to lay his hands on what was keeping him awake. "God, I'm cold. . . ." He crawled under the covers. "I wish it'd snow. Snow all over creation, from pole to pole, from sea to shinin' sea! I don't care if Kyle and them *do* come for me."

"Don't worry, Lone," said Cassie, "we'll run away to India together." She was pulling on the covers at the foot of the cot.

"What you doin' down there?"

"I'm gettin' under the covers."

"Get in your *own* bed."

"I *cain't*."

"Then get in Momma's."

"I want a be next to you, Lone. It's gonna rain agin, and I'm gonna hurt, I'm gonna hurt. The pain's gonna ramble, and I'm gonna wake up stiff as a dead mule."

"I'll prob'bly have nightmares and kick you in the face."

"Next to *my* nightmares, that's not so bad."

"Way I feel right now, I wouldn't care if the judge said, 'Lone McDaniel, I sentence you to eternity.' I'd just say, 'Thanks, Judge. It fits the crime.' I could sleep till doomsday." He sighed and blinked and settled for sleep. "Cassie, why did he do it? He had ever'thing on earth a man needs that loves God. . . . He said he had somethin' to tell me. Then he shot himself. All he said was my name. 'Lone . . . Lone!' " He clenched his teeth so Cassie wouldn't know he was crying.

"The snow's fallin' on my mountain bed, my high Himalaya," Cassie murmured. The rhythm of a lullaby. "And the mountain climber is comin' up to look for me, to find the legendary tiger's hide. But it's so cold, it'll freeze him up, like that giant elephant they found in a iceberg up in Siberia."

"Please, Cassie . . . please . . . please don't. . . ."

Turning on her side, Cassie snuggled up against Lone's legs. Lone turned and moved over on the narrow cot, flattened himself on his side against the cold wall, under the sill. Thinking of the tiny space he had put between himself and Cassie made him even more aware of her body. He still felt as though she was clinging to him. Her foot leaned sideways and—cold, clammy—touched the small of his back.

> The mountains are high and old,
> Look down on the town below.
> The mountains are high and cold,
> The town is warm below.
> But to the cold mountains I'll go.
> But to Big Black Mountain I'll go.

Suddenly, rain struck the window like a jet from a fire hose.

CHAPTER

12

LONE WAS HARD ASLEEP WHEN HE HIT THE FLOOR.

"Momma!" The iron frame cut into his ankle, but it was his head that hurt.

A big black balloon, the air hissing out, Kyle stood over Lone. "I said, 'Pick yourself up.'"

"Who pitched me here?" Wearing only his jock shorts, Lone felt defenseless.

"You better git out a here, Kyle." The unfamiliar rage blazing down on Kyle from Cassie's eyes as she stood in the middle of the brass bed, her toes curled around the bare springs, bewildered Lone.

"And I don't want one squeak out a *you*." Kyle shot out his arm, pointing at her. "Sleepin' with your own brother! You ain't little kids no more."

"Shut up, Kyle, by God! She was sleepin' at the foot of the cot. She was scared to sleep on that mattress or in Momma's room by herself." Kyle's holster was still empty.

"I ought to put *her* in the reform school, too. She was hugged up to your back like a Siamese twin."

"You might have hurt her, dumpin' that cot like that."

"Okay, Lone, I pitched you on the floor, I'll pick you up."

When Lone hit the wall, a pillar of Cassie's boxes and crates full of magazines, papers, and junk spilled out on the floor. Kyle held Lone up and kicked at a well-water bucket and rope and a mailbox as they both slipped and slid on the magazines. Groggy, Lone felt each jolt like a blackjack. Finally, Kyle got him turned around and shoved him into the rocking chair. "Move again and I'll hurt you, Lone."

Doubled up in the rocking chair, Lone stared at him, his head throbbing like a toothache. He saw Cassie pull a brass horse out of a basket. "Don't, Cassie!"

It rolled out of her hand and clattered on the floor, and Kyle did a dance step backward into a streak of peanut butter that made him slip off balance again. "Was you about to *throw* that thing at me?"

"You just *touch* him again."

"Goddamn you little hellions. Your momma cryin' her eyes out in the funeral home, no children nor husband to comfort her—just me, *I'm* all she's got left—Virgil's deserted us all—and you two *sleepin'* together. You get your duds on, Lone." He scraped his foot under Lone's brown corduroys, scooped them up and dumped them with the toe of his shoe into Lone's lap. Having set the cot straight, he sank on it, reached for Lone's boots and slung them at him. "Get that stuff on in less time than it would take me to break all your bones. And, Cassie, you stand still in the middle of that bed or I *will* hurt him. I mean get *off* that damned bed. Ain't you got no respect?"

Lone got dressed.

"I was *tryin'* to take care of your momma. She wouldn't leave the buildin', but she wanted me to go look for you. Talked of *both* of you like you was *both* dead. She's sittin' over there now, Lone, certain you've run yourself off a mountainside. Then the captain come in and told me to *arrest* your ass. Some civic-minded neighbor called *in* on you. He blames *me* for not bein' able to handle my own nephew. Hell, I disown you, here and now." Very slowly, Kyle unwrapped a King Edward cigar, each noise etched upon Lone's aching brain. "And God, look at this crap. Just because you a cheap hoodlum, no sign you gotta be a idiot to boot. You left a trail broad as a highway from that store right up to the tipple—spilled sugar, broken bottles, little cans of deviled ham, jar lids, Tootsie Rolls. Good Lord, what a senseless mess!" The cellophane wrapper seemed a foot long. "What the hell's *that?*"

"A stick of dynamite," said Cassie, her hair brushing against the alarm clocks dangling from the ceiling. "Stick *that* in your mouth and smoke it."

Kyle threw the cigar band into Lone's lap while Lone pulled on his boots. "Don't say I never *give* you nothin'."

"I remember when you used to give both of us those bands from your cigars," said Cassie, stepping backward, bouncing lightly, like a trapeze artist in the net, onto the rolled mattress. She leaned against the head of the bed and the wall behind, crossing her ankles, stretching her arms along the curving top railing. "You weren't such a son of a bitch then, were you?"

Kyle half rose, blotches of red rising in his fat cheeks. "You think I *want* a hit a sick hellion?"

"Hit, hit, hit, hit, shit!"

Lone yelled, "Shut up, Cassie!" It hurt her. "Honey, I just don't like to hear you cuss."

"Where *you* preachin' tonight, Saint Lone?" Kyle blew smoke across the room at Lone.

"I'd 'preciate it if you'd shut up."

"Go ahead, *let* your mouth run. I'll have *my* say when I get you down there."

"Down where?"

"You dressed?"

"What's it look like?"

"Then git up and get a damned move on."

"I want to see Momma."

"You should have thought of her last night, before you and Virgil broke her heart."

"Ain't you gonna let him drink a cup of coffee, at least?" Cassie glared at Kyle.

"He's gonna be on cold cornbread and tap water till he turns twenty-one. You can crawl back in this cot now, and hug up to nothin'."

When Kyle reached for him, Lone jumped up out of the rocking chair and ambled toward the door, with Boyd's cockiness. Cassie got quickly down off the bed and ran to his side in the doorway, holding on to his sleeve. "Cassie, don't snag at me like that. He ain't gonna hurt me."

"Oh, God, why cain't they leave you alone?"

"They?" asked Kyle. "They? Who the hell is this 'they' ever'body's always talkin' about?"

"If I knew, I'd poison 'em all." Cassie spoke so viciously a fine spray of spittle settled across the front of Kyle's white uniform shirt, and then her nose began to bleed down the front of her mauve gown.

The room was dark. In the moment before Kyle snapped on the light, Lone heard a tremulous, mournful sound, pigeons under the eaves, settling.

"How does it feel to be cut off from Boyd and Cassie?"

"You don't see me bleedin', do you?"

"Not yet."

"What's *that* supposed to mean?"

"I mean they'll sweat blood out of you in those fields at La Grange."

"What about Boyd?"

"What about him?"

"Nothin'. I thought—"

"That friendly neighbor that called in didn't identify anybody but Lone McDaniel. Described him right down to a T. You're the only one. The evidence points to you and nobody else. I'm glad you *weren't* with Boyd last night. Then you'd still be together—in a cell."

"You got to try me."

"You won't want a trial. You'll plead guilty and go before the judge and you'll git three years, because I'm gonna lay it *on.* Till you've been deprived of your freedom a few years, you won't be nothin' but trouble and a burden on people that loves you. You and Virgil owe 'em a few years of peace. As long as you're runnin' loose, ain't none of 'em free to live no kind of normal life. Your momma used to worry you wouldn't foller Virgil, but Lord God, you're just like him. I only wish I could git you inside La Grange before Virgil's in the ground and your momma can git to you."

"I wish you could, too. I cain't face her."

In the room there was only a table and a chair. The walls were dark green halfway up, light green to the gray ceiling.

"Hell, you're a coward, just like him."

"I know how you feel, Kyle. But let's don't talk about him."

"All the time, just like you, he wasn't thinkin' of nobody but hisself. And all of you thought he was *better* than anybody else."

"Okay, Kyle. Okay. Just don't turn that pistol on *me*."

"What you mean? This holster's empty."

"You know what I mean."

"I reckon it's public knowledge I ain't as lovable as Virgil was, if that's what you mean."

"I mean, you can go to hell."

"Don't provoke me."

"You know the *way*, don't you?"

"Shut up!"

"Go to hell."

"Say that again."

"Go to hell."

"Louder."

"Go to hell!"

"So they can hear you in the hall!"

"Go to hell, you big, fat bas—!"

Lone didn't know how many times Kyle hit him. He just felt the first one. The one in the mouth.

CHAPTER

13

LONE WOKE, SHIVERING.

A red glow showed a long, foot-high, barred window just under the ceiling. He crawled to the foot of the cot, stood up, and looked out: the red neon lights of the Harmon Hotel, the Gold Sun Café, and the Majestic Theater. Dizzy, he almost lost his balance on the sagging cot. He sat on the edge and tried to wake up. Above his head, he heard wings flutter. He waited for the mournful coo of pigeons. He heard a car horn, then numb silence in the cell.

Lone swung his legs over the side of the cot to get up, but fell—feeling for a moment as though he was back on the motorcycle, going over the cliff again. He hit the floor, and it was like yesterday morning when Kyle dumped him. His head rang with the shock.

The floor chilled his feet. He wondered whether Kyle had stolen his boots. He moved slowly in the dark, his bare feet scraping the cement floor. His hands blundered into a cold washbowl. He stubbed his toe against the toilet. Groggy, swaying, he missed and it splattered his feet. Then he felt along the wall, found the bunks again and sat on the edge of the bottom one. He put his hand back for support and felt a leg under a thin wool blanket.

He screamed, thinking for a moment that the foot was Virgil's.

A flashlight made him shut his eyes tightly. "Hey, Lone, shut up in there."

"Who's that?"

"Poteat." Lone couldn't get used to the idea of Poteat, the football hero of Harmon County, as a jailor. "Keep still, Lone. You'll wake him up."

"Who's in here with me?"

"That little boy that shot his momma and daddy."

"*What* little boy that shot his momma and daddy?"

"Didn't you read about it in tonight's paper? Climbed up on the roof and called his momma and daddy out into the yard and shot 'em down with a .38. He said they was mean to him. Reckon they lost track of just how mean they were?"

"Where's he from?"

"What difference does *that* make?"

Lone climbed up onto the top bunk and fell back, hard.

"Let him sleep, Lone."

"Just turn off that damned flashlight."

Across the hall, somebody started coughing. He coughed for a long time. Then he was quiet. Lone strained to pull sleep over him like a hood. The cough started up again. Lone listened for the little boy to start crying. Wings fluttered at the window. A motorcycle went by in the square below. "Hey, Boyd," somebody yelled. "Give me a few whirls on that thing!" Then he heard rain on the roof and the window ledge. The little boy below made no sound. Not even in his sleep. It was a lie, then. Because how could he sleep? The coughing across the hall stopped.

In the silence, Lone felt for a moment as though he were lying in the bedroom on his own cot across from Cassie. He pulled the blanket up and it flapped over his face, the wool making his lips and nostrils itch.

He was on the roof of the house. He kept sliding on the tar-paper roofing in the moonlight, calling for help. Cassie and Momma and Coot and Uncle Virgil and Kyle and Gran'paw McDaniel, and Gran'daddy and Gypsy and Boyd, and others he couldn't see, stood in the yard with their arms open and extended. But their arms were not shaped to catch. The way they looked bewildered him, so he did not jump. And slowly the dark came on and soaked them up.

A bucket raised a racket that opened his eyes. Someone in the cell across the hall bent over a mop, in a down-slant of light that honeyed smooth back muscles and a knobby spine. Lone leaned over the edge of his cot and looked down: the blanket was flung back and an Almond Joy candy wrapper lay twisted on the bare mattress.

Poteat came into the cell and looked at Lone. "What *you* looking at?" He stuck his face, raw with acne, up to Lone's.

Lone turned over and faced the wall. Poteat shook him. He remained inert.

"Hell, let him lay," said the man across the hall.

"You want a shut up?"

"No, but I will."

"Okay." Poteat peeled down the blanket and caught Lone at the back of his trousers. "Do I have to drag you out?"

"Why's he have to git up?"

"To clean his cell and eat his breakfast."

"I don't think he wants no breakfast."

"You ain't the world's daddy. First candy for the kid, now stickin' up for *him*. . . . Okay, McDaniel, cut out the horse-crap and hit the deck."

"Poteat, can I say somethin'?"

"No." Lone heard the man sit hard on his bunk. "What?" asked Poteat, begrudgingly.

"I think you got a case a shock up there."

"A what?"

"A case a shock. I've toured jails all over the U.S.A., and I've seen it before."

"First we got a case a T.B. with *you*."

"It's a ticklin' cough."

"Now a case a shock."

"It hits some kids that way. Let him lay a while. It wears off. Then they git up and they're fine. Otherwise . . ."

"Otherwise, what?"

"Well, you can be tough as hell on 'em, but it don't do no good and they might snap."

"Snap?"

"Yeah."

"And you seen it before?"

"Yeah. All over. Ain't you?"

"What? Shock?"

"Yeah."

"Sure, I seen shock. Hell, I work here, don't I?"

"I thought you had." The man sloshed the mop up and down in the bucket once. "Reckon it's bad?"

"It don't look *too* bad. He'll be all right by mornin'."

"I hope so. It scares me to be in the same jail with a shocker."

"Yeah. . . . Well, you eat your chow."

Poteat unlocked the door. "Say, Lone," he said gently, "you want a git up now? Your momma's in the visitin' room."

Lone didn't speak. Staring at the ceiling, he listened to the pigeons cooing outside where the sun was bright on the windowsill.

"You'd think the shock would wear off by now," said the man across the hall.

"I knew he'd be this way. I told her. I said, 'Mrs. McDaniel, don't let it worry you if he don't come out. He's in a mild state of shock.' Aw, he'll snap out of it by mornin'."

Lone stayed on the cot all day. He didn't utter a word. About noon, he tried to sit up to go to the john in the corner but realized that he couldn't. He couldn't move. He didn't care. He didn't think about it. Lone slept while daylight crossed over to dark. Then he swung off the cot and landed on his bare feet on the cement. He felt around till he touched the wall and till his toes touched the cold sweating toilet. Swaying, he missed, but most of it hit the water hard and loud. He thought it would go on and on. When he quit, he was weaker, but not so stiff. Walking back to the cot, staggering and swaying, he felt as if he were on a ship that slanted and shoved.

On his cot again, Lone pulled the blanket over his feet, chilled from the floor, and listened to the wings and the cooing. Then no sounds at all. Quiet as it was dark. Then Lone broke into a coughing fit. So loud and hard he heard the metal in the room ring when he stopped to catch is breath.

A flood of early morning sunlight—fluttering wings along the edges of the window frame. Lone listened to the crisp rustling of dying leaves in the sycamore outside.

"You got visitors," said Poteat, unlocking the door. "She brought Kyle *this* time so you better show your ass in the visitin' room."

Poteat led him to the doorway. Kyle leaned against the wall between the door and a glossy painting of Jesus. Momma sat in a big, dull red, stuffed chair, in front of a barred window where yellow drapes with blue irises hung. She wore her green coat and her best dress and held her pocketbook in her lap, her hand stroking the smooth imitation leather. Lone wondered if she wore the new slip.

"Hello, Lone."

"Hello, Momma."

"Kiss your momma," said Kyle.

Lone leaned over, his eyes shut, to kiss her cheek, but felt her quick mouth. He reached behind for a straight chair and sat down. She looked at every feature of his face, returning again and again to his eyes. Hands in his pockets, Kyle leaned between the door and the picture, looking at Lone.

"Honey, what happened to your face?"

"Does *he* have to stay in here?"

"Charlotte, I told you I wasn't gonna take—"

"Please try, Kyle, please. Just keep still and let us talk. Now, Lone, Kyle just wants to help."

"He's just hangin' around for his thirty pieces of silver."

"Yes, I know, but he wants to help me. Boyd said you wrecked on Black Mountain." They were quiet, Lone staring at Kyle, who finally looked away.

"When you gonna kiss him, Kyle?"

Kyle stared at Lone, trying to figure what he meant.

When Lone turned to speak to Momma, Kyle asked, "Kiss who?"

"Him." Lone pointed at the picture.

Kyle uncrossed his feet, pushed off heavily from the wall, and looked at the picture. He didn't get it. "Maybe they won't send him to La Grange, Charlotte. Maybe they'll put him in the asylum at Frankfort with that little kid."

"Kyle, please. Please, Kyle. I've got to go to work. I walk out of the cemetery and into the jail and right into the *hotel*—to clean up *other* people's messes. Please don't send me off all tore . . . you promised you'd help me talk to him."

"Okay."

"Will you tell him?"

"Okay. Lone, you go before Judge Gentry tomorrow for a hearin'. If you plead guilty, he won't make it too hard. I'll do what little I can."

"See, Lone, Kyle can make it light. He might git you off. We're all doin' ever'thing we can."

"What difference does it make? This or the army, and you all will be shut of me."

"Oh, Lone . . ." Momma stifled an impulse to cry.

"See? See?" said Kyle, taking his hands out of his pockets. Standing there, clenching his fists.

"What'd you take your hands out a your pockets for?"

"Lone!" Momma gripped his wrist and held it.

Kyle, disgusted, glanced at the picture, then went over into a corner and, when he sat down and tipped his hat over his face, was partly hidden by Momma.

"Momma, forgive me—for not bein' with you."

"It wasn't Virgil. The man that would do that wasn't my brother."

"It *was* him, all the time," said Kyle.

"Momma. . . . Momma, what can I do?"

"Lone, I'm gonna do ever'thing a human *can*. If you go, they ain't no use for me to care about nothin'. The world and all that's in it can shrivel and die. You're the only one in this world I look to."

"Cassie. . . ."

Momma looked Lone full in the face and sucked in her upper lip. "She don't matter."

"Momma!"

"Forget I said that." Tipping a corner of her handkerchief with her tongue, she wiped at the corner of his mouth. "Soot." Then she combed his hair with her fingers. "Why, Lone! Your head is hot as fire! You got a fever?"

"It's hot in the—cell." He looked at her through a film of tears and fever. A blue vein pulsed in her neck. Vaguely, he remembered a blue vein in her breast when she had suckled Cassie. They were quiet. Lone's heart pounded. He looked at Jesus forgiving the woman taken in adultery.

"You're the only one."

"She's talkin' to *you*, Lone."

"I know she is."

"Hush, Kyle. . . . It cain't end here, Lone. Or in La Grange, hundreds of miles away. To sit here with you in this place. . . . Oh, Lone!" Momma put her hand on his shoulder.

He swallowed several times, hard, and shut his eyes, tight. In the darkness, he reached to wipe a tear, but she flicked it away.

"I brung you a fresh orange." He felt it rock and settle in his lap.

"Is he actually cryin'?" asked Kyle.

"Shut up, Kyle," Momma said.

To avoid answering more questions, Lone started to peel the orange. But he couldn't. Only claw at it and make the acid spew into his eyes and nostrils.

"Here. Let me." Momma peeled with her fingernails. "Lone, honey, it's just that so many people's put so much stock in you. You don't realize. I don't think you ever realized. Fully. Today, I stopped hopin' for the life Virgil saw for you. All I want is for you to graduate, git a good job, marry, settle down. And git along. Do well in the end and be respected. I don't dream of too much for you. I know what we are. I know we ain't got much in us to be anything. But one of us, at least one of us. I have my heart behind you, Lone, to be the one who *will* graduate, *will* make a place for himself in Harmon and count. Just a normal, average, ever'day life. But one that folks will say, 'My, Mrs. McDaniel, that Lone sure turned out to be somebody, didn't he?' And I could say, 'Well, we always knew he would.' " Her face tensed, then she began to weep, sitting very still, not moving her head.

Lone took a piece of orange from Momma's lap and ate it. The smell soothed the ache.

Lone looked at the picture on the wall. Momma used the heels of her hands to wipe away the tears that had calmed her.

"We're gonna git you out, honey. It's not too late. I pray and I pray, and I feel it, oh, so strong, Lone, that it ain't too late. That Judge Gentry knows me. He used to follow me around when I was runnin' free—before the restaurants and the *hotel* got me. Honey, do you know that I would walk across the fires of hell for my boy, the only one in the world?"

He looked up, his mouth full of juice that seeped at the corners. The look in her eyes made him choke. She slapped him on the back while he coughed and when he settled down, she suddenly took hold of him with both her hands and hugged him till he had to catch his breath. Then she got up quickly and ran out the door and slammed it behind her.

Lone looked at the pieces of orange that had tumbled out of her lap onto the floor.

He stared at his hands. Then he laced them over his face. When he opened his eyes, the picture looked at him across the room.

"She just wants a normal life for you, Lone."

"I heard her."

" 'I heard her'!" Kyle jumped up and came over to Lone, his face red, his mouth quivering. He didn't look the way he did when he got mad enough to hit somebody. He was mad in a way that came from deep inside him. "You heard her, huh? Well, goddamn you, now you hear *me*, you hear what *I* say to you. You think I'm a mean son-of-a-bitch, don't you? You think I'm out to git you. All right. All right. I beat you up, I run you down and run you down ever since I come back from Sicily. I admit it. But do you know the hell why? Do you? Hell no, you don't! And maybe it's been so long since I thought of you as worth a damn that I don't know why no more, either. When I sat there and heard Charlotte tell you the same thing that stands for me, too, it hit me agin that that's all *I* ever wanted. You think I wanted to see you ride yourself to hell? I didn't want 'em to call me on the shortwave and tell me to git out on the highway to help pick up my nephew in a basket, because *her* plans, her hopes were the very ones I had in Sicily, when I laid in mud for forty days and forty nights, with death in iron helmets starin' at me from the windows in that white farmhouse. Not just then, when I thought they were gonna get me, but all through the war, Lone, all through that gut-spillin' war. I guess you forgot, too, how I used to send money to Charlotte to put in the bank in my name—in my name so Coot couldn't touch it, so even Charlotte couldn't if he drove her so far down in the ground she had to draw on it. Ever' month, month after month, from the start to the finish of that war, it come to Harmon and went in that bank, so if they got me, the folks back home would have *you*. To send you, not just through high school, but maybe straight on through college and be ahead a the rest, because by that time I didn't give a damn for me or my hopes if I got back. I knew what I was, and after a while I was killin' to stay alive, and then livin' just to kill. But before I went to that war, I was a good cop, and you can ask even some a the guys I arrested if I wasn't a good cop, and with a future, doin' in my way, in one kind of life, what Virgil set out to do when he got back from the South Pacific. But somewhere over there it got hold of me. I won't say they took me and made me a killer. They just brought out the lowest in me, and there I was to be used, and they used me to the limit, and decorated me. Now I got a badge, too, a permit to kill. But long ago, I lost hope in you, son, even before this summer, and it turned me inside out. 'Cause by the time I got back, Virgil had already got to you—to *all* a you. So now all I got is nothin'. I ain't nothin' to nobody—you even turned Cassie against me—and ain't nobody nothin' to me. And worst of all, you keepin' Charlotte from what she deserves out a life, too. My sister's gonna be happy. You'll not drag her down in front of me. She's gonna get rid a that drunk and remarry and have a kid maybe, and *it*'ll be the one, not *you;* you *had* your chance. That money's still there in the bank. I ain't touched it. It's blood money. I killed for it. But I'm gonna try to buy you out of this. Not for *you*, for Charlotte. You're done with. As far as I give a damn in hell, they can shoot you before supper. *I* won't cry."

He hung his head and his body shook once as though his elbow had touched a radiator. When he bent down and picked up the piece of orange that lay between his feet, his hat tipped off. Lone picked up the hat while Kyle straightened up with the orange slice. Offering him his hat, Lone saw that Kyle's eyes were wet and red. He looked at Lone like a man just told he hadn't long to live. He turned his back on the hat and walked out, the orange slice in his hand.

Lone looked at the picture in the empty room. It wasn't *Kyle's* place to kiss Him.

CHAPTER

14

LONE WOKE UP WITH A STUFFED HEAD, FEELING SMOTHERED, HEAT pouring into the cell that stank of urine and sweat that Lysol hadn't eradicated. His fingertips felt sticky and his bare feet made a sound like ripping adhesive tape as he walked from the toilet back to his bunk. He opened the window and let in cold air, tainted with the odor of slag heaps, some of which had started burning before he was born.

From the window, he looked down on Harmon. Among the rooftops and on the mountains above the town, the red leaves of fall had turned brown, and were beginning to turn loose. If the wind kept blowing, in a few days he would be able to see the house through the trees. Yesterday Poteat had brought him something to read: last Sunday's Louisville *Courier-Journal*. It lay now on the floor, fanned out. Lone gazed down from the top bunk at an aerial view of what would have looked like the photo in one of Cassie's *Life* magazines of the atomic bomb after it fell on Hiroshima, if he hadn't known that it was Harmon by the way the pines rose on the slopes above the ruins. "Freeway Open to Traffic Next Thanksgiving." Lone saw again the ruins of his house as he had seen it in a dream the night before. When he returned from La Grange there would be a spread of asphalt where his life had been.

On the sill, a snail had made a track of silver on the sooty cement. The snail did not move. End of the line. Lone stuck his finger through the diamond opening in the mesh and gently prodded the snail. A tiny black ant ran out from under it, darted into a crack. He pushed the snail over the edge of the sill toward which it had been moving when its silver ran out. But the ant, or other insects like him, would get him down there, too.

"Okay, lonesome stranger," said Poteat, unlocking the door. "Let's go have a little powwow with the judge."

Lone followed Poteat's bouncy athletic stride down the stairs.

"Wouldn't mind bein' a orphan right now."

"You got no cause to gripe. You got all kinds a people pullin' for you." Lone suddenly felt weak in the stomach. He tried to get in focus the picture of a lot of people pulling for him. He had an odd, but clear, feeling of being pushed.

Poteat opened a door marked Juvenile Judge, and behind a desk with sunlight at his back sat Judge Gentry. Momma and Kyle turned around. Momma smiled, but Kyle just turned back. Nobody was smoking, so Lone didn't hope to be offered a cigarette. He stood just inside, on the floral rug. With the sun in Lone's eyes, the judge was just a dark shape, but light glanced off the metal reinforcements in his special crutches. Coming back from Buckhorn Lake in the rain one summer at twilight, a car wreck—his wife and little girl and two little boys killed. But that didn't seem part of the way he sat there without moving in the center of what was going to be Momma and Kyle on the right and Lone on the left.

"Come in, Wayne."

"My name is Lone, sir."

"Lone . . ." pleaded Momma.

"Shut the door," Judge Gentry said curtly. Lone shut it. "Sit down." Lone went over and sat down and looked at him. The light hurt. "I don't think you need remain, Stonecipher."

Kyle shifted in his chair. "Well, sir, I *am* his uncle."

"You are the arrestin' officer and as such you are no longer needed. Excused."

"Yes, sir." Kyle hauled himself up and turned to go, then half turned back. "I'll be outside, Charlotte, if you need me."

Kyle went out. White papers moved in front of the judge's dark shape. Momma didn't look at Lone. This wasn't a trial, but maybe she thought a glance would prejudice the judge.

"Wayne McDaniel. Wayne McDaniel."

"Yes, sir."

"You are charged with dynamitin' a coal tipple and with illegally enterin' the premises of a commissary store, both owned by the R. C. Luttrell Company, and with illegally removin' from said premises the followin' items: one case of Royal Crown Cola, four bottles of 7-Up, six bottles of Nehi Orange, three bottles of Grapette, five tins of deviled ham, a bag of coffee, four tins of sardines, two jars of chipped beef, one jar of mayonnaise, four bars of Lifebuoy, ten bars of Camay, two bars of P&G, and two bars of Ivory; three boxes of—oh, my God—Kotex, four rolls of toilet tissue; six five-pound bags of granulated sugar; four packs of Lucky Strikes, two cartons of Camels, and seven packs of Old Gold cigarettes; three plugs and two braided ropes of chewing tobacco; two boxes of King Edward and four boxes of White Owl cigars; six Mars bars, seven Butterfingers, ten Baby Ruths, ten Milky Ways, fourteen Tootsie Rolls, two Log Cabin pecan logs, six packs of Dentyne gum; four cans of diced pineapple."

Lone looked at Momma. Her face was sober as a church window. He wondered how the judge could read all that with a straight face. To keep from laughing, Lone gritted his teeth.

"Seven jars of peanut butter; ten packages of animal crackers, two boxes of Hi-Ho crackers, four packs of brown shoelaces; a box of thumbtacks, ten Eveready flashlight batteries, three flashlights; eighteen packets of yeast, four bags of potato chips, seven jars of—" The papers rattled and Lone stiffened. He hadn't expected him to get angry so soon. "Seven jars of—" Then Lone realized that Judge Gentry hadn't had a straight face all that time. He slapped the papers down on the desk and made a sound as though he were crying. Under the desk his braces clinked like spurs. In the dark by himself—Lone and Momma in the bright light from the window—the judge seemed to be out riding the range at night, remembering a joke he once heard in a cathouse.

Lone laughed, too, and then Momma broke into a smile that she covered with one hand, smoothing her black hair with the other.

"Now isn't that somethin' to be goin' to reform school for?" said the judge. "Mrs. McDaniel, don't you think that's ridiculous?"

"Yes, sir, I do. But is it certain Lone will have—"

"Wayne, wouldn't you call that list ludicrous?"

"I'm guilty, sir."

"How did you transport all those—groceries? Go on. Figure out how you got it all out a there by yourself." He waited. Lone didn't say anything. "I have been tryin' to do that very thing, and I am left with the problem of determinin' how one boy could transport so much on a motorcycle."

They were quiet.

"Sir?"

"Yes, Wayne?"

"Isn't that all I have to do?"

"What?"

"Confess."

"Yes."

"Then, could I go back to my cell? The sun's hurtin' my eyes."

"You want a go where it's good and dark? It could be arranged at La Grange, if you give 'em trouble. And you won't even have to worry about what day or month it is, because you won't care. Or maybe it will get to the point where that's *all* you think about. And when that happens . . . Wayne, have you ever tried to climb a slippery bank and get right to the top but keep slidin' backward?"

"Yes, sir."

"What do you suppose it means when your mind starts doin' that in the dark?" Lone imagined Judge Gentry lying half out of a ditch beside a steep mountain road, answering a park ranger's questions.

Lone stared at him against the light. "You got it all figured out, ain't you?"

"You may go."

"Please, Judge," said Momma.

"I'm sorry, Momma," Lone said, standing up.

"I can see what you've had to endure, Mrs. McDaniel. I've studied enough psychology to recognize a person entirely cut off from any understandin' of guilt and remorse, moral compunction."

"He just gits these moods, Judge Gentry." Momma stood up. She was going to cry. Lone hadn't wanted her to go over to the high school and beg Mr. Deaderick, but now he had put her lower on her knees than that.

"Judge," Lone said, "I'm sorry."

"I accept your apology. One thing, Wayne."

"Yes, sir."

"Are you sorry about the store?"

"I haven't thought about it, sir."

"Well, just what *have* you thought about these past few days?"

"My mind has been a blank." Lone felt the lucidity of the simple fact.

The judge's braces clashed.

"He didn't mean it in that tone, sir." Momma touched the scar on his cheek.

"You're tryin' my patience, Wayne."

"I'm sorry, sir."

"I think that's all for today. I'll have a few words with you, Charlotte, alone, and then— You may go, Wayne."

"Thank you, sir."

"Your mother will be out in a moment."

In the courtroom, Kyle and Poteat sat on the front bench, smoking Kyle's cigars.

"When you due to be shot?" asked Poteat, snickering, smoke spewing through his nose.

"Not shot," said Lone. "They gonna dark me to death. Too bad they can't do my mind like they do land after they tear down some old buildin'—blacktop it."

"We'll git you out, Lone," said Kyle. "I throw a little weight around this town." He bumped Poteat with his hips, and Poteat laughed with him, getting up, bent over waltzing in a small circle, holding his cigar delicately.

They waited for Momma to come out. When she finally did, her eyes were red. "Sit tight, son. They ain't got us licked yet. I got to get on to work, Kyle. I'm pullin' overtime to scratch together some money to fight this thing."

"Momma, you go home and get your rest at five o'clock. Don't you linger on for *my* sake."

"Don't worry, honey, I'll live."

"Don't let her work at night, Kyle."

"Try stoppin' her."

"Well, listen, Momma, you gonna bring Cassie to see me before I go?"

"Go where?"

"Are you?"

"I'll bring her with me when I come Saturday."

"Coot, too?"

"Why, honey, you know Coot."

"Does he know about it?"

"Well, I guess so."

"You *guess* so?"

"Ever since he moved lock, stock, and barrel up to the attic, we ain't seen too much of the poor soul. Keeps up there like a mangy old owl."

"Why hasn't Gypsy been to see me?"

"Now, honey, when would I see Gypsy Travis? Besides, how come Boyd's girl would be comin' to see *you?*"

"Didn't she come and ask about me?"

"Cassie's comin' tomorrow. Oh, Lone!" Momma began to cry. Poteat looked away, dusting the ash off his cigar.

Her crying was put on, partly, but if he kept at her it would become honest. She kissed him, gave him a pack of Juicy Fruit gum to chew out the day, and went.

CHAPTER

15

THINKING OF MOMMA'S AND KYLE'S HOPES AND THEIR SLOW END in him, Lone mopped backward, toward the pool of noon light that fell through the window. When he backed into the pointed leg of a chair laid on a table, he stuck up his hands like a cowboy in a movie, and looking up, discovered he had mopped himself into the corner of the visiting room instead of out the door.

"I'd like to come over there and shake your hand, but I cain't git over this wet floor." Boyd stood spread-legged in the door. A girl hid behind him, only her legs visible.

"Well, you're welcome to walk on the water, you son of a bitch."

"After you, son."

Lone walked toward them, wiping his hands on his pants, but they still smelled sour of the mop, of the filth of the visiting room. "Who's behind you?"

"None other than—" As Boyd stepped forward and then sideways, Lone feared it would be Cassie.

Gypsy, in blue, smiled. "They like to not let us in. We told 'em we'uz your cousins. They didn't believe us, but they didn't know any better, either. Who *ain't* cousins in Harmon County?"

Lone and Boyd got some chairs and set them on the gleaming floor in the middle of the room.

"I need to find a rest room." Boyd swaggered out into the hall, hiking his cods.

"Boy, he never takes that rig *off*, does he?"

"You miss me, Lone? You miss us in the silo?"

"What do you think, honey?" In dreams, they *were* in the silo, and he woke up wet. He was a little ashamed of it now that she sat across from him, bouncing her black hair back with her wrists.

"I think about it all the time," she said. "Ridin' that motor-sickle brings it back on me. Then to have to come in a place like this and just sit down across from you and—" Spreading her legs in the red chair, showing a flash of red panties, she got up impulsively and stood beside him as he bent back his head and opened his bruised mouth for her tongue.

"Boyd might bust in on us." Lone hugged her around the waist.

"I'd be ashamed if I was him." The palms of her hands slid down the front of his body, and she smiled with delighted surprise when her fingertips touched it, stiff, hot against his leg. "Law, law!" And as she backed toward the chair again, he let his hands glide down her hips and legs.

Suddenly, Lone realized that what speed did for him, *this* did for her. She followed the speed to get it, and the riding, the speed made her want it. And now that he had gotten himself locked in, Lone was afraid she might turn to Boyd. "I'm sorry."

"What for?"

"For bein' in here."

"When I first saw you at school on that track, outrunnin' the whole pack, I knew I wanted to marry you."

"What makes you say that?"

"It's the truth."

"I mean just now."

"Seein' you fresh after so long, I guess, reminded me of it. Remember where it was we first spoke? I was in the *libary* writin' a theme on Longfellow. And you was starin' at me when my pencil broke and you offered to sharpen it for me."

"Because I had seen you before. Comin' out the front door of your house, and the day the truant officer drug you in with the dirt still on you."

"Anyway I high-hatted you and sharpened it myself. Then I got to studyin' about it and broke the lead again on purpose and looked at you and smiled. And you saw right through me, but you sharpened it, and every day we met in the *li*brary. Well, I always knew that if a girl wanted a real good husband, you'd be it."

"Why?"

"I don't know. I don't know *that*, anymore than you know some things about yourself. Well, shoot, Lone, people love you, they love you and throw off on you somethin' awful in the same breath. . . . You wiggle out of *this* mess, and we can git married and settle down."

"What about Boyd? You're *supposed* to be his girl."

"Let's tell him right now 'bout me and *you*."

"No. Wait."

"That's all I ever wanted in my life. Peace. To be away from my folks and that shack. To be in a place of my own, with you, and live decent. Not grand. Just decent and regular. We'll go to Chicago or *De*troit to work, and have us a good car and a radio-phonograph combination. Move *out* a that holler. You know where I want a live?"

"Where?"

"In one a them nice duplexes in the housin' project like they put up in Hazard."

"Is that really the kind a place you want to live in?"

"Why not? They're brand-new and modern and pretty. They come with a automatic washer in the basement a every buildin' and a new refrigerator and a electric stove. No more scrubbin' Momma's and Daddy's nasty laundry in a tin tub or cookin' over a hot damn cookstove. And I want kids all over the place, yellin' and fightin' up a storm. They's all kinds of neighbors around them project houses. Come next spring I'd like to sit out on my little concrete porch and look up and down the row and see all my neighbors takin' it easy in the evenin'. And they ain't no better or no worse than us, because we all got the same, except for differences in the makes of our cars. And won't you be glad to see that house of *yours* tore down?"

"How come you think *that?*"

"And we won't have to have anything more to do with our folks. We can cut ourselves plumb off from *them*. You don't care nothin' about 'em anyhow, do you?" Lone looked at her. "Well, it's obvious to ever'body that knows you."

"To who? To who?"

"Ever'body. Me. Well, ain't it the truth?"

Lone let that soak in awhile. "What if I did git out and ran smack into a notice to go in the army?"

After a few moments, she said, "Well, you'll be back." It didn't seem to bother her a hell of a lot. "The baby and me'll be okay. Now, you gotta leave me a baby behind. We can move on to Chicago in some project, and it'll all be waitin' for you when you git out."

"What'll you live on?"

"Love. And they send money home to your wife, don't they?"

"You have to be a prisoner to take a leak around here?" Coming in from the hallway, Boyd did an exaggerated, tight-legged waddle across the floor. "We better be goin'. I saw Kyle drive up in a squad car with your momma and Cassie."

"How come you ain't been to see me sooner, Boyd?"

"I ain't been doing much a nothin', son. Been feelin' low."

"It's the truth, Lone. Some days you can see his motorsickle parked from daylight to dark in front a his house."

"What they say about me around Harmon, Boyd?"

"I don't listen to gossip, son. Too many people's screwed *me*, runnin' their mouths."

He *did* seem different. His dark face sullen. Almost a trace of resentment about something. Let down. His old mannerisms fuzzy around the edges.

They paused just inside the door.

Lone heard Momma's voice in the hall. "In the visitin' room?"

"Yes, ma'am," said Poteat.

"Hello, Lone," said Momma, unable to see Boyd and Gypsy from where she stood.

"Hello, Momma."

"Just a second, honey," she said, inching sideways into the room as she spoke to Cassie in the hall. "You wait there. Mr. Poteat said the floor was wet in here."

"Momma . . ." Lone said, moving closer to her, until he and Boyd stood side by side behind her.

"Wait on the bench, Cassie," Momma said, and reached behind her and took Boyd's hand, and asking "What, honey?" turned and looked into Boyd's face. She jerked her hand loose. "Boyd Weaver!" Gypsy giggled. Boyd smiled and looked at his gloved hand. Lone looked at Momma and then at Boyd, a little bewildered. "Ain't they caught you yet?"

"Far as I know they ain't lookin' for me, Mrs. McDaniel. I'm safe as the angels in heaven, long as Lone's the only one that could tell."

"If you ever showed up at church, you'd learn about the angel they kicked out."

"Well, it wouldn't help Lone none if we was both crowded in the same cell, would it?"

"Least he's away from you and her for awhile. They told me nothin' but kin was allowed."

"I just come in out of the cold for a minute to see Lone," said Boyd.

"It wouldn't thaw no tears out of me if you froze to death."

"Well, I just stopped by to give you this, Lone." Boyd held out a five-dollar bill. "You have to pay for your own cigarettes at La Grange."

"They ain't sendin' my boy to no reform school, Boyd Weaver. That's prob'ly money you made off his own daddy. How much did you deliver to Coot today?"

"Mrs. McDaniel, he begged me for it, but I didn't have it. I ain't made no pickups, and I ain't about to. I'm gettin' shut of that way of livin'. I reckon I been the cause of a lot of drunken misery around you."

"Well, eager as I am to nail the blame to one place, the cause was here ever before you come."

"I confess the blame's mine for the way Lone's turned out."

"I won't argue with you about that. Thanks to you, he's rottin' in this blamed jail."

"Now if *I* was in that cell instead a Lone, my momma'd broadcast it all over Harmon County that I'd found a home. She always said I'uz born to spend my life in solitary—that is, if they didn't shoot me at dawn instead."

"If she'd throwed you in the Cumberland River before you opened your eyes, nobody'd been surprised to hear it."

"No, she had to hold onto me for that GI check, then the welfare check—then she just checked me off the list. You know, them evenin's me and Lone was fixin' his 'sickle and you all let me eat with you, I felt kinda like part of the family, and I felt kindly what it was like to be *in* a family, where they might not git along all the time, but where it's possible a bunch of people can feel good together. You know the family *I've* had. A daddy that went away to war when I'uz too little even to play soldier, that just stayed gone when the war was over. And that *mother* a mine."

Momma sat down in the red chair and looked up at Boyd. "Boyd, you can help me if you just will."

"At your service, ma'am." He swept off his cap and spread his black arms.

"And don't act smart."

"Boyd wasn't actin' smart, Momma," said Lone.

"I'm goin' out and talk to Cassie," said Gypsy, and ambled into the hall.

"How long till they take him before the judge?" asked Boyd, sitting astraddle the straight chair in front of Momma.

"Might be weeks, but I brung him a fresh clean shirt in case it's in the mornin'."

"I got a tie he can wear."

"All I need from you is the exact truth. He won't hardly tell *me* a *thing*."

Momma and Boyd looked at Lone where he stood on the wet floor, tracked with mud now, blinking his eyes.

"How I know it wouldn't go out a *your* ear and in Kyle's?"

"I ain't like the dirty somebody that turned Lone in."

"Yeah, I been tryin' to find out who that was."

"*You* must a been invisible."

"It was dark, black as coal, Mrs. McDaniel. Wasn't it, Lone?"

"Yeah. Pretty dark."

"I want you to tell me exactly what happened, because I'm gonna see a certain somebody first thing in the mornin', and I need to be able to give him the full story!"

"Son, you beat ever'thing I ever saw!"

"What you mean by that?"

"If I had a momma that cared half as much about *me!* Well, I reckon *you* wish she *had* drownded me. Least I wouldn't have growed up to turn so many people aginst me. And *you* 'specially, that would kill me with a look if you could."

"Now, Boyd, if I had that kind a hate in me, the Lord would shut me out, wouldn't he?"

"Seems like all you women around here dump the blame on me for ever'thing bad."

"Boyd, them that cain't forgive on earth cain't expect forgiveness in heaven."

"I never thought I'd see the day," said Lone.

Momma and Boyd looked at him, wondering what he meant.

"You know, I ain't really talked to Boyd since he was little," said Momma. "All I've had to go on is what I hear."

"Well, if I was bad as folks say, I'd been struck by lightnin' *long* ago. All I know is, Lone's lucky to have the kind of momma that'd stand up for him the way you do . . ."

"Oh, I swear, Boyd, I just don't know where to turn. Even if he don't get stuck with the whole blame of that raid, what's he got to come home to? More aimless wanderin' with *you?* No wonder he turned to trouble. Ever since he could walk, he's been pushed and pulled ever' which way. His daddy hung over him with all that talk of Black Mountain and farmin', and then me and—Virgil—held religion over him. And, Boyd, you and Cassie was another pull. You tempted him into that motorsickle foolishness, and Cassie pushed him into it with the way she acted about it. Half the thrill was tellin' *her*."

"I promise you, Mrs. McDaniel, I'll do ever'thing *I* can. Lone's my buddy."

Momma began to cry. "*Be* his friend, and come around the house if you want to when he gets out, but stop pullin' that boy down with the way you live. He looks up to you like he done Virgil. For a while he couldn't open his mouth without Boyd Weaver and them motorsickles comin' out, so now you work him toward the good. Talk him into junkin' that motorsickle. Hear? Say!"

"Yes, ma'am. I'll do anything you say."

"You ready, Boyd?" Gypsy stood in the doorway. Her eagerness to be on the move seemed odd, for the blue dress looked delicate compared with the riding slacks she usually wore.

"If you are," said Boyd.

Cassie appeared at Gypsy's side in the hall, pushing her long blond hair back out of her eyes, having forgotten that Momma had already pulled it back and tied it with a red band.

Boyd reached to shake Lone's hand. Behind Boyd Gypsy blew Lone a kiss, and said, "Good-bye," and just as Boyd turned loose, Cassie kissed Lone's cut cheek and, moving her lips along his jaw, whispered in his ear, "Don't let the bastards git you down." The secret smile as she drew away and Boyd's and Gypsy's backs as they turned and went down the hall disturbed Lone.

"I've got to see the chief of *po*lice, honey," said Momma. "Wanna get permission to leave this shirt and bring you some black walnut ice cream. Your favorite."

God, how they all loved to say that about the least thing.

You'd think he never lived in anything but a world of favorites.

"Okay," he said, already tasting, slightly gagging on the black walnut.

In the rig she wore, Cassie looked awful, but the healthy glow in her face startled Lone. She wore things Momma had probably plucked on the run off a pile of clothes donated to the Salvation Army: a thin, black rayon dress too large for her frail body, white-and-black oxfords, and boy's blue socks. Cassie sat on the polished wooden bench against the wall and looked up at him. Lone sat down. She looked at him intently.

"How do I look to you, Lone?" she said, putting her fingertips on his wrist.

When he reached for a cigarillo, she had to take her hand away. "Okay. I'm glad to see you, honey."

"I thought she'd *never* let me out. I threw a triple conniption fit. You ought to see the wreck I made a the room."

"I'll bet!" Lone lit the cigarillo and stared at it, to keep from swapping looks with Cassie.

"Momma said I was too sick, but I heard what she didn't say out loud: 'I don't want you around him.' "

"Well, you ain't exactly well, are you? What you doin' out a bed?"

"But we was walkin' across the bridge and I got the feelin' she was glad I finally did take up my bed and walk. Maybe she already sees me gettin' on a Trailways for Louisville."

He avoided Cassie's eyes, expecting her to plague him with questions about the jail. But she didn't seem interested. All she had to do was look over the foot of her bed at his cot and see him on the bunk in the cell, not much smaller than their room, but cleaned out, bare except for the very basic things. Even in the cell, he often woke feeling her eyes on him. Not until he lay in the cell later did he see it clearly: her awe of what he had done each night, her look, the way you'd look at a horse in its stable the morning after it had won. But there was no race last night, and there would be none today. Looking at her sitting on the bench, he missed something. The listlessness. Maybe she was thinking she'd run the race herself this time.

"Are they really makin' you go?"

"They'd love to."

"Will you miss me?"

She acted as if he were just passing through, as if he were in jail just long enough to be tried, sentenced, and shipped out.

"I never expected *you* to ask me a question like *that* . . . Two or three years—I'll be almost two hundred miles on the other side of the mountains and won't be able to look after you."

"Don't think I won't write you."

He tried to understand, but it was coming too fast. It had been too long since he'd seen her out of the house. He always thought of her in the junk-cluttered room, in the bed. "Promise me you'll stay in the room. Promise me you'll not go to the window if Boyd comes by."

"Don't worry, Lone. I'll write and tell you ever'thing that happens."

"Happens? When? You gonna try to go out in spite of me?"

"Not in spite, Lone. *For. For* you." As if that ought to satisfy him, she smiled.

He didn't know how to take it in. Cassie sat quietly on the bench, against the dirty green wall, hardly moving, taking little sharp swallows of air. He wanted to believe that the trip had wearied her, and he wanted to get her back home to their room and shut the door. He heard the key turn in the lock. Was that what he wanted?

"The Gold Sun didn't have no black walnut," said Momma, "so I got you two packs of Luckies instead." She had a special way of giving them to him as though she gave him an injection they both knew would ease the pain. She sat down and stuffed the cigarettes into his shirt pockets, and with Cassie close on the other side, he was locked between their bony hips. "Lone, I wish you'd say somethin' to Cassie about Boyd."

He turned abruptly on the bench and looked Cassie in the face. "Cassie—"

"Don't boil up at me, Lone. He won't stop comin' by. He'll

rip up that holler on that black Harley-Davidson and sit out
there and rev it and rev it till I come to the window, and he'll
beg me to come out. But honey, he don't never do nothin'
wrong. We have a good time talkin'. He listens to me till I talk
myself to death, and it gits so cold I cain't stand it."

"Cassie . . ." Lone looked at the floor, shaking his head.
"Cassie . . ."

"Well, she ain't her old self, Lone," said Momma, "and if
you ask me, it's probably for the best. God didn't *plant* her in
that bed, you know. Potted plants ain't part of God's scheme."

"Cain't Kyle stop Boyd?"

"Kyle's been acting kinda peculiar lately. Since you been in
here, seems like ever'body's down so. Now, I shouldn't a even
mentioned Boyd. The way he whips around Harmon with that
Travis girl stuck to him on the seat like a Siamese twin, no need
to fear him coming around a sickly child like Cassie."

"You tell him I'll kill his rotten soul!"

"Won't hurt to *tell* him," Momma said.

"And you." He glared at Cassie. "Look at you. Look at
your eyes. You can hardly sit up, you're so weak."

"I feel strong as a bull. Just like Doctor Boatwright said.
'Girl, you can break loose from that bed any time you set your
mind to it.' Well, I *have* set my mind to it."

Cassie's hair clung damply to her forehead and her cheeks.
"You runnin' a fever."

"That's energy seepin' out," said Cassie, wiping her forehead.

"Blamed if *you* ain't, too," said Momma, putting her palm
on Lone's forehead. "And they got you workin' up a sweat
that'll chill you to the bone."

"I need to git out, Lone. I've got to git out. Even if it's just
to see you. I had to see you before—I cain't stay in bed all my
life. Not now."

"Not now?"

"With you gone—with you shut in. What'll I look forward
to? When you went ridin', I could lay on my back and shut my
eyes and go with you. But now—if I go on layin' there I'll take

root and grow like a stinkweed. Lone, they's energy in me, way, way deep down, that wants to flare up, like in a engine that's damp and rusty. Now I can get out in the open air and—"

"Now?" Lone stared at her.

"Well, you know what I mean, don't you, Lone? It got so ever'where you looked, you saw what you was comin' to. So you did like *me*—backed away from it. Only it's a cell and a cot, instead of a room and a bed. And that's why now, *I* got to get out. We cain't both—"

"Goddamn it, take her home!" Lone jumped up, feeling Cassie's and Momma's hips as he rose. As they talked, they had moved in on him like a vise of flesh and bone, love and accusation. "Git Kyle to take her home!"

"Lone, what's took holt a you?" Momma looked up at him.

Cassie was hurt and bewildered. She had expected him to understand, even to want it that way. "Are you gonna take her home?" he asked gently.

"She's goin' with me to the *ho*tel till I'm off work. You ought a be glad." Momma put her hand gently on his arm. "Well, we better go, Cassie." Cassie rose slowly, her hand almost gripping her stomach as if to calm a surging excitement.

"Cassie, I'm beggin' you to go home."

"I cain't."

"Why cain't you?"

"Could you stop when they all told you to?"

"Stop what?"

"Goin'. Just goin'."

Lone turned and leaned forward with both hands against the wall. "Please, Lone, I cain't leave you without—I got to have your blessin'." Lone felt Cassie close at his side. "Turn around, Lone." Her voice was strong with command.

"What do you want?" He turned, and she kissed him, hard, full, hot, and trembling, then whispered as she drew away, "Good-bye, Lone," and for the first time in his life, he saw her run. At the end of the dim corridor, she stood straight in the afternoon sunlight, the red and brown tops of the trees before her, the town below.

"I've got to git out!"

"I think she's gone a little crazy to act that way. I better go look after her."

"You got a git me out a here, Momma!"

"Well, ain't that what I been tryin' with every ounce of fight and sweat in my body to do?"

"Cassie. Cassie. I've gotta—"

"For God's sake, let *her* alone. They's other people to worry about, for a change." She kissed Lone's cheek and patted it and let the palm of her hand slide down his naked arm. "Look for me agin Monday."

"Good-bye, Momma."

Lone watched her go. Poteat unlocked the cell-block door. "What's the matter? Cain't you walk?"

"Huh?" Lone realized that he had tried to move. "No. No. I cain't."

"Cut the clownin'." Poteat grabbed him by the shoulders and pushed him through the door.

Slowly, Lone began to move, his body began to obey again. The immobility of that moment frightened him. On his lips was the taste of Cassie's frantic mouth.

CHAPTER

16

"WHAT YOU DOIN', LONE?"

"Playin' hide-and-go-seek with God."

"Who's *it?*"

"*I* am."

He opened his eyes and Cassie was climbing up on the foot of the high cot. Facing him in the pale light, like candlelight in a pumpkin, she shucked off Lone's old brown mackinaw. "I run off."

"He won't stir a limb," said the infirmary nurse, shooting him in the arm. "Rots the will."

"Well, *I'm* here now . . ."

"That little feller that shot his momma and daddy sprinkled germs like fertilizer all over that cell. If we don't all come down with the flu, it'll be a miracle."

"I didn't know jails had little hospitals inside 'em."

"They don't need no hot barbed wire to keep *him* in," said the nurse. "Pneumonia beats any jail." Her needle sticking up in the air, the nurse went out.

"How you feel, honey?"

"Light as a kite."

"Lone, honey, you remember . . . ?" Whether he did or not, he wanted to. ". . . how when we'uz both sick, we'd sleep with Momma sometimes, you on one side and me on the other, and she'd talk to us real low, and Coot, when we called him Daddy, was workin' on the railroad—or was that when he worked the night shift in the mines?—and he'd come home at dawn, dressed in black all over, and Momma would be fixin' breakfast? But no, that wasn't it, that's what *you* used to tell *me*—and I wasn't born then, and you could remember even when you was three years old how it was. Oh, and I remember . . . we'd go down to the tracks to meet him and come up the path swingin' on his arms and Momma would look up from the stove and say, 'Found your father, I see.' And remember the sirens screamin' from down in Harmon, and me and you huddled in the dark in the middle of the bed and Momma and Coot sittin' around, and we all held our breath, listenin' for gunshots, and a voice on the radio sayin', 'The Shadow knows. . . .'" *And the lockin' of coal gondolas echoed up the holler from under the swingin' bridge.* "And you, that fall before the other kids let you run with them, swingin' in the porch swing, painted and dressed to run in the scary dark with them, then walkin' in the yard by the steps with the pumpkin swingin' beside you, the raw insides and the candle smellin' strong, the porch light dim in the black dark. . . ." *And Cassie sittin' in the middle of the big brass bed in my fuzzy blue sweater, wearin' a wolf mask, Momma ironin' in the kitchen, and Coot up on the ridge feelin' around in the black under the trees for wood to burn in the grate to take the chill off Cassie's sickroom. . . .* "And we'd look out the window together and watch airplanes go over and you'd say, 'If you yell to him loud enough, Cassie, he'll drop you a Milky Way,' and I'd scream till the window-pane rattled, but nothin' ever dropped, and—"

"Then the night one crashed on the ridge and set the dry trees ablaze and the smell of char got in the blankets even. . . . And, honey, you remember," Lone said, as though he were in a delirium, as he knew, from old times, *she* was, "that time you had a good spell and you—one evenin'—and I still don't know whether it was real or somethin' I dreamed—but I was up on a ladder changin' the movie marquee and I saw you on the swingin' bridge, and the soot made the rim a the sun all smudged and you was pullin' a wobbly old wagon with a statue a somebody in it—looked like Jesus layin' down with one broken leg stickin' up and one arm with no hand hangin' down. And when I got home, it *was*—leanin' on the front porch."

"All busted up and the gold all chipped off, and it was sittin' up inside a restaurant-size rusty Frigidaire in Gran'daddy's junkyard. Up in Coot's barn now . . ."

"Couldn't hail, rain, snow, nor March wind run you off the streets when a real good spell come over you."

"I can see me sittin' on the wide steps of General Hospital, shakin' gravel from my shoes, and I scoot over for a cripple on crutches. . . . I'm layin' in the grass in the empty ball park, tryin' to find a four-leaf clover, then I git up and pitch imaginary strikeouts from home plate. . . . I'm standin' in the alley gulpin' up the hamburger smell that the fan blows out of the Gold Sun Café, and watchin' a man and his little boy pick boxes from the trash and flatten 'em and load 'em on a cart. . . ."

"And I'm standin' at the window sharpenin' my pencil," said Lone, and the American flag's flutterin' at half-mast and when it blows one way, I see you sittin' on the down end of a seesaw on the school playground. . . . And honey, it's October, remember, when I was eleven and you was eight and we ride my scooter all over Harmon, pickin' up Coke bottles to sell till we git enough to go to the show."

"Yeah, and we see *The Return of the Werewolf*."

"Remember, Cassie, when we'd cry in the night, our bones hurt so bad, and Momma'd git up and stir up the fire and heat some bricks, wrap 'em in towels and snuggle 'em up to us?"

"And sometimes it seemed like the pain left my backbone and leaped over to your fingers, and when you cried, I'd say, 'Touch me, Lone, and maybe it'll shoot into me for a while.'"

"And it come a big rain, and we all think the Cumberland River's gonna flood the holler."

"And Coot teaches us that old song to keep our mind off the thunder and lightnin'."

"Wish't you'd brought the guitar."

"Reach down. It's leanin' aginst the bed."

She struck up and they sang:

> "Killy Kranky is my song,
> Sing and dance it all day long,
> From my elbow to my wrist
> Then we do the double twist.
>
> Broke my arm, I broke my arm
> A-swingin' pretty Nancy,
> Broke my, leg, I broke my leg
> A-dancin' Killy Kranky!
>
> Killy Kranky is my song,
> Sing and dance it all day long,
> From my elbow to my knee,
> Now we'll wind the grapevine tree."

The nurse came in and said it sounded like fun but to knock it off.

"Hey, Lone," said Cassie, sitting statue-still.

"What?"

"I think somebody was here just now."

"How can you tell?"

"They's fresh hoofprints in the mud. See 'em fill up with water?"

"You know I cain't see. Ever since I bombed Hiroshima without my dark goggles on, I been blind as a mole. You supposed to be blind, too—you been lyin' to me all these years?"

"I *am* blind. I hear ever' sound in the world at once, and I can *feel* the water rise in a hoofprint."

Cassie came to the jail's sickroom every day that week, and sat cross-legged like the picture of Buddha in *Life,* talking faster than a carnival barker. Images welled up in Lone out of a place that had long been dry. Remembering was like giving himself a slow injection of Novocain. To make a point or stress a comment or rouse a memory, Cassie would grab one of his ankles and jiggle it.

On Thursday they forgot the time, and Momma caught her.

"I swa'an, with you two shut in together, *I* mize well be in Asia."

Lone let Momma take his hand, and, as she leaned over to kiss him, he picked a wisp of lint from her hair with his other hand.

"I saw in the *National Geographic*s one time," said Cassie, "a picture of two old black women, sittin' on the bank of the Congo, pickin' lice out a each other's hair and eatin' what they caught."

When Momma tried to slap her, Cassie jumped up on the other cot and onto the windowsill and pressed herself against the pane, laughing. "What good's it do to go to church if it don't make you *act* no different?"

"Well, I'm goin' agin tonight to get juiced up on good will toward men and peace on earth." Cassie's eyes looked a brighter green.

"You go just to mock religion."

"Well, if I can fool God, how come I cain't fool *you?*"

"Girl, I don't want to hear another word a spite out of you."

"I don't either. It gits so monotonous, it even makes *me* sick."

"If it wasn't for Lone bein' sick, I'd jerk you down from there and . . ."

"Cassie, I can see ever'thing in our room. When you ain't here, I shut my eyes and lay here and see— Shut your eyes, honey, and see if you don't see what I see. That highway sign, DEER CROSSING, nailed to the wall behind your bed, and the well-water bucket that tripped up Kyle, and three broken guitars and that autoharp hangin' from the wall, and a scrub board, made of wavy tin in a gray pine frame, and a coffeepot, blue and white speckled enamel, and a banjo, and dolls—oh, Lord, them dolls— some with heads off, some no eyes, some of 'em bald-headed, and one a those hollow heads full a old green keys we got out a wrecked cars in the junkyard, and—"

"Don't forgit that—"

"Hush! Let *me*. . . . And that busted tennis racket, and that chair with no bottom, and a spittoon, and a 'lectric fan, and a car radio, and aerials, and old radios, a music stand, and that cane some old man must've carved, and a thermos bottle full a washers, and license plates, that one goin' back to 19 and 36, and boxin' gloves, and cowbells, and black miners' helmets and one new silver kind, and a empty holster, and a toilet lid, and a rotten saddle, and umbrellas, and rollers from ol' washin' machines, and a flour sifter, razor strop, and a old movie camera, and pay telephone box, and headlight from a T-model Ford, and huntin' knives, and some vases washed down out a the cemetery, and a tin cup like the one I use in my cell, and them hundreds of books, some with leather bindin's, datin' back to 18 and 15, and slews of magazines, and that Coca-Cola sign, with the giant bottle that used to be taller than we was, and them mailboxes with Bill Abshire, Route 4, Hindman, and the red one with Majel Bright painted in white, Route 1, Cumberland, Kentucky, and that big green glass jar, dead flies in the bottom, and them framed pictures a strangers, some of 'em too brown to tell any of the features—family reunion in one, and all you can see is the white tablecloth under the trees, and Civil War soldiers gittin' their pictures took in Louisville and Knoxville. And the old gas pump leanin' against the outhouse, and under the house, our little green scooter, and. . . ." He talked until the sickroom had become the brass bed in their room, and he and Cassie had shut out everything else.

Why in the name of hell and all the fallen did he want that? he wondered, after she had gone. It didn't look like a picture that would stay permanently in focus. At night, it kept trying to fade. A clear black, like black marble, smooth and bright black, stayed on the ceiling.

"Heavy, heavy hangs over thy head," said Lone.

"Fine or superfine?"

"*Damned* fine!" said Lone, and wrapped the sickroom blanket around Cassie's shoulders, hugging her.

Opening her eyes, looking at the brown wool blanket, she said, "Oh, Lone, did Gran'paw McDaniel send it to *me?*"

"No. It's for me. Gran'maw and some old Indian woman wove it the winter Coot commenced to walk. But Gran'paw sent that dulcimer to *you*. You'll have to string it yourself." Lone held out Cassie's own guitar and she looked at it as if it were one of those old-timey dulcimers she'd heard about from Coot all her life but had never seen, not even in a photograph.

"Tell me *ever'thing* about it." All the green in the mountains turning brown, while the fever ebbed in Cassie's eyes.

"Well, he's got a long white beard, just like in that picture over your bed," said Lone, trying to get the pretense started, knowing she would bring it alive, "and gold teeth that sparkle when he looks up at the sun, and a pack a hounds foller him around like Coot's do."

"No. From the start. Let's start where you left me when you went. Tell just what it's like sailin' around Black Mountain on that motorsickle."

"I didn't feel a thing till that cold wind cut into me on those steep drops. Then it was the *world*."

"Well, let's get *on* the blamed thing first." Cassie slipped on the goggles and crawled around and knelt behind him as Lone grabbed the bottom rail of the sickroom bed. "Okay, we're on! Then you kick it off!" Cassie grabbed him around the waist so suddenly she startled him. Excited, he pretended to kick off as she made motorcycle sounds with her mouth. "And suck in a lungful of gas and smoke, and see the sparks fly and flicker and feel the power pump up, tremblin' through the steel and iron and rubber—goin' right up your spine and into your hands on the grips!"

"And a soft snow startin' to come down."

"And we go down the path and swoop over the swingin' bridge."

They shook the cot till they hit, and held, a steady rhythm.

"Over the railroad where the coal gondolas are slammin' on the tracks."

"And on across Harmon."

"Don't waste your breath on Harmon," said Cassie. "Let's hit the highway."

"And on through Coxton and Ages and Evarts and Kenvir and Dizney and up—"

"—and on up into Black Mountain."

"And we park the 'sickle and strike up a path among the pines and the dead chestnuts the blight hit—and there's his house in a cove of white poplars, sky-high."

The cot swayed and got still, and they didn't move, seeing the house clearly together.

"He's gittin' old," said Cassie.

"He sure is a forlorn somebody."

"What'd he say about Coot?"

"Said for me to tell him to come on back home. 'Why, I don't hold it agin' him,' he says."

"And what else?"

"He just about begged me to come up there and live with him and help him keep that farm up."

"Let's go, Lone!" said Cassie, breaking out of the dream voice. "Let's *really* go, me and—"

"How many miles to the gallon it git?" They turned toward Boyd's voice. He stood in the doorway, fiddling with the tassels on his white silk scarf.

"What?"

"That bed you all ridin'."

"What *you* doin' here, Boyd?"

"Why, I come to see you, good buddy. Heard you was dyin'. Sure wish I could run *my* motorsickle on imagination."

Boyd scraped his boots back and forth on the doorsill. The dry hissing irritated Lone.

"Did you ride over here with *him?*"

"He offered," said Cassie, "but I walked it."

"You lyin' to me?"

"The livin' truth, son," said Boyd, sawing the back of his neck with his scarf. "Thought I'd ask your permission to take her back, though."

"She's already out the door—by herself. Ain't you, Cassie?"

She looked at Lone a moment, then kissed him and went out, huddling into Lone's mackinaw, still wearing the goggles.

Clean as he looked, Boyd had a strange odor about him that Lone had never smelled on anyone else.

Drowsy from the pills, Lone listened to Boyd tell about his adventure with a married woman in Bledsoe.

"I hope you *git* a dose," Lone said, sleepily, hearing the pigeons under the eaves.

"Sometimes I fear your love for me is fadin', Lone."

When Lone opened his eyes, Boyd was gone.

His head hurt, his eyes stung, his throat was raw, he felt on the verge of vomiting. He knew the moment he woke up that the fever had ebbed, that he was going to get well, but the air was full of the gas of burning leaves, kudzu vines, dead chestnut trees, young saplings. The fall fires had started. Through the window, he saw a bright metallic haze. The last three days had been suddenly hot and dry. Every fall, the fires came, and boys, idle men, started a few themselves just to watch the spectacle, and some of the same helped fight it when it got out of hand. Everybody followed the reports in the papers. All eastern Kentucky coughed and cried for weeks.

"Better kick that fever, boy. Judge's gonna try and sentence you in the mornin'," said Poteat, tossing a stack of comic books on the infirmary bed. "If we don't all go up in smoke."

"I think I've got it sweated out. . . . Turn on the radio as you go out." His eyes red, Poteat looked at him. "Please."

Poteat turned on the radio as he went out. Catching the tail end of some church singing, Lone reached out to switch over to another station.

" 'That Old Gospel Ship' sung by Mizriz Edna McIlroy and Tama Lee Norton. And now for the first time on the Gospel Hour we're gonna hear from a girl that we think has a ministry to sing for Jesus. For all the shut-ins and for her brother, Lone, 'specially, here is Cassie McDaniel to sing 'The Wayfarin' Stranger.' "

A steel whang made Lone see Cassie kick the microphone as she stepped up to it. Faintly, a string twanged on her guitar as if of itself.

"I am a poor wayfarin' stranger,
Wand'rin' through this world of woe,
But there's no sorrow, toil nor danger
In that bright land to which I go.
I'm goin' there to see my father,
I'm goin' there no more to roam;
I'm just a-goin' over Jordan,
I'm only goin' over home.

I know dark clouds will gather 'round me,
I know my way is rough and steep,
But golden fields lie out before me,
Where all the saints their vigils keep:
I'm goin' there to see my brother;
He said he'd meet me when I come;
I'm just a-goin' over Jordan,
I'm only goin' over home.

I'll soon be free from every trial,
My body rest beneath the sod,
I'll drop the cross of self-denial
And stand before the throne of God:
I'm goin' there to see my Saviour,
To sing his praise forevermore;
I'm just a-goin' over Jordan,
I'm only goin' over home."

She was standing by his bed in the infirmary when he woke from a doze a few hours after supper. Like a glass of beer filled too quick, she needed somebody to take a sip before it spilled over. Lone did. "You were pretty on the radio, Cassie."

"See! See, I told you," Cassie said to Momma, then flashed her eyes at Lone. "I told her you'd hear it."

"Take her back home, Momma. She's too sick to be racin' all over Harmon, singin' from dawn to dark."

"She sang one song this mornin' and she's got one more to go tonight. Now that ain't no strain, and she looks fine."

"Don't you want to hear about it, Lone?"

"About what?"

"This mornin'!"

Lone looked at Momma. "Don't think I don't know what you're doin'."

"All I done was arrange for her to sing."

"Take her home and put her to bed."

"Now, Lone, she's a willful girl when she gets a notion in her head."

"Reckon who *put* it there?"

"We cain't stay long."

"Just long enough to torment me?"

"You look like you've done come through it."

"I'm well enough to be sentenced tomorrow."

"Well, let's don't talk about *that*. Your momma's gonna fix it."

"I'm La Grange bound."

"I'll write and tell you ever'thing about it, Lone," said Cassie.

"What?"

"What I *do*. They might let me sing regular on the radio."

"You hear that, Momma? If she starts roamin' Harmon, it won't be no time till she . . ."

"Why, Kyle will skin her alive if he catches her on Boyd's 'sickle," said Momma, flopping her purse on her lap.

"Nobody said nothin' about Boyd," said Lone. "Has he been comin' around the—?"

"What's the use of bein' on the radio if I cain't tell you about it!" Cassie slammed the guitar on the foot of the bed. They listened to it until the strings stopped humming.

"I'm listenin'," he said. "Momma, would you go down to the Gold Sun and get me some Robert Burns cigarillos?"

When Momma went out, Lone closed his eyes, darkened himself for Cassie's voice.

She had brought in on her clothes the smell of smoke that drifted over the narrow valley from the fires smoldering on the mountain slopes in Harmon County.

"Way it happened, this mornin' Momma said let's go over to the radio station and attend the Gospel Hour. So we did, and she knew some a the folks that was waitin' to go on 'the wind.' She told 'em, 'This child's tongue's been dipped in Jordan,' and that it was too bad I wasn't lined up to go on. So they said sing one, and I sung four hymns before that red light turned on and the program even come on the air.

"And they said it'd be a sin not to squeeze me in somewhere on the program, so they did, and when I got done, the announcer said I was the best thing he'd heard in a month of Sundays, that if they was more girls like me, the country music field wouldn't be so overgrown with men. And I said, but that was a hymn, and he said, you got the voice. And so he asked me to sing one like the Carter Sisters, and when I finished, he said if I ever got a break, I'd be cuttin' records in Nashville—country-music capital of the world.

"Anyway, they want me to sing on the Morning Gospel program again, 'cause the phone calls they got before I left the studio showed that a *lot* of people hadn't switched over to the news."

The tone of her voice made Lone feel cold. Knowing that people would go to their radios just to turn on her voice made her feel she was something big to somebody. And if she could know her own family heard her sing and was proud, especially if Lone listened, if her voice became something he needed, lying on a cot in La Grange, she would feel as though she had been reborn. Radio put her way up on top of the mountain where the radio tower's red light blinked and shot the essence of her in a web of wires over the county.

"Well, this whole week, we had us a time," said Lone. "Just like it *used* to be. Like we were shut off in our room on the big bed from the whole damned city of Harmon. The last couple of years while I was out deliverin' papers or usherin' at the show, I'd come home and you'd have a new door, ever' time, standin' wide open in your mansion of dreams, and your voice would echo out to me from some room inside, beggin' me to come in and shut the door behind me. Well, for a week I was *in*side, wanderin', not just in body but finally in spirit, and now you've deserted it. I wish we could shut ourselves in and live only on what we could dream up. I always wanted, honey, I always wanted to give myself over to you and let you take me way inside from everything, and let it all be what we could create between us. I always did. I reckon I was scared."

Cassie raised her head. "I wanted it more than you did. And don't you think I know better than you what would happen if we ever shut that door against all the others? Lone, them three days before I first come to visit you, I almost *went*." She began to tremble. "They almost sent me, I got so bad. I heard 'em talkin' about the asylum in Frankfort, even. You was gone, and I was on our bed." She flinched, seeing it, and turned a little aside, as though it might rise up and pull her down on it. "You go so far inside yourself, and it gits to where all you meet are monsters and landscapes that almost thrill you to death, they're so everlastin'ly the end of the world, and the things you see are just as clear as they say you see things when you're drowndin'." She leaned her head back and made the nape of her neck snug along the bottom rail of the bed, legs straight, ankles locked tight. "And I always was pulled farther, sure that deeper still it would be beautiful and peaceful. But then I felt it, I felt it in a way I never felt nothin' before—that if I got past the horror and reached the beautiful, I would be *in*sane." Rising, she said, "If sufferin's what you got to take at *this* end, I'll take it." Looking into Lone's eyes she seemed to be trying to see how far *he* had gone.

"That's when I turned back. Comin' back is when I almost died, because I had to cut myself loose from that bed and git out, and here—" she slapped the guitar—"is my salvation, praise Jesus. Momma held that out to me, like a rope to somebody in quicksand, and I took holt and pulled myself up with singin' and makin' music on the timbrels, like the old tribes used to say. And you know somethin'? This mornin', I think I got as close as I *ever* did to what must be God—not because of all that stompin' down hell. But comin' back to life is like risin' up to touch God, who put it in you." She reached for the guitar and hugged it tight, then let it rest gently, and strummed softly. "Cain't you *see* I'm different now, Lone?"

"Sometimes I wish I'uz blind."

"Godamighty, honey, don't you know that dreams, just dreams, can stifle a body? I'm still weak, but I don't think I'll ever be sick agin. I won't *let* it happen."

"Cassie." He took hold of her hands, held them tight. "You stopped writin' in the margins, too?"

"Ain't you stopped ridin' in the streets? I shipped it all back to God," she said, pointing at the ceiling with the toe of her slipper, jabbing upward.

"The attic?"

"Yes. And I'm itchin' to burn it all, ever' livin' scrap."

"Maybe if somehow we could go live on Black Mountain with Gran'paw . . ."

"Well, let's dream about that *tomorrow*. I gotta ring the rafters tonight with 'Power in the Blood.'"

Lone looked down and stared at a streak of banana pudding on his white hospital gown. He grew sullen and quiet. Then he looked up at her, and without speaking, stared reproachfully into her eyes.

"Lone, if you're gonna set there and say things to me, you mize well say 'em out loud." He looked at the wall. "Lone, I tried! I tried! I pretended as long as I could. I played like we was little again. But, Lone, I ain't no little girl no more. *I* know it, if *you don't*." She got off the bed and walked around in the two-bed sickroom. "I had to git out of that room and see me some people, even if it meant singin' with them soul-snatchers. I'm tired to death of just *witnessin'* people's misery. You know what, Lone? Turn over, damn it, and look at me." He didn't move. He heard her feet on the floor and felt her knee sink into the edge of the mattress. "Sometimes I think I'd like to *cause* some of it."

"Don't—good God, Cassie, don't talk that way!"

"Look at *you*. Look at all the misery *you* cause." Her other knee sank into the mattress and the springs seemed to float as she balanced, kneeling, on the edge. "And yet, look at how you're loved." She let that sink in. "Now just stop and think, Lone. Name the people who love me."

He looked at her over his shoulder, a vivid black shape eclipsing the lamp. "What do you mean?"

"Start namin'." He turned his head away from her again. "Don't turn your head. Start." She lost her balance and fell on her side behind him. Raising herself on one elbow, she said, her breath on his neck, "Don't feel guilty."

"Cass—"

"No. Don't lie. Just don't lie."

"Momma . . ."

"She don't care a spark in hell for me. She ain't got no love left over from *you* to squander on *me*." She got off the bed again. "Listen, I knew about myself. That I laid on that bed all these years on the edge of bein' crazy. Don't cringe so. I knew it and I lived with it, but I'm *not* gonna give *in* to it." She slapped the mattress behind him. "When you go, Lone take the old guitar." She laid the guitar in his lap. "Why don't you learn to play this and sing the songs I know?"

"I know by heart ever'thing you used to say and sing." He slammed the guitar on the bed beside him and Cassie watched it bounce until it was still.

"Them songs I used to sing when I'uz sick that Daddy and various ones taught me here and around, sometimes they was just a way to talk to you all, mostly you, Lone, and sometimes to

try and tell you all what I felt in my very skin, that somethin'
like what the song said was about to come over us, or was some
way *about* us. Did you ever know that?"

"I tried every way *not* to."

"That's what I know, *now*. . . . Take it for the times
when you cain't stand it another minute. You ain't forgot the
old songs, and listen, honey, I'll be here in Harmon the way you
were. I mean, I'll go uptown and I'll see interestin' things by the
truckload, and soon I'm gonna get work. I'll come home at night
and tell it all in a letter, airmail to La Grange, describe it just as
clear as you used to tell things to me. . . . It's like we been
playin' hide-and-go-seek all our life and that bed in our room
was home-free. Play like your bunk at La Grange is our big
brass bed. *Some*body's got to be *it*."

Suddenly, he fell on the guitar with both hands, jerking at
the strings. One snapped and lashed him under the eye. Cassie
tried to stop him but he kept pulling, and the nurse and Momma
were in the room when he jerked the last one off and flung it up
and it twanged against the railing at the foot of the bed. Cassie
caught his hand and kissed it. When Cassie drew away, Momma
screamed at the blood on her lips.

That night, on the razor edge between waking and sleeping,
Lone heard a motorcycle. His nostrils, even with the window
closed, quivered with the sharp smell that he could almost taste
of gasoline and sparks and hot rubber. But when he looked out
the window, crouching at the foot of the bed, he saw a quiet
street aglow with the red neon of the Gold Sun Café that flared,
then faded off as he lay back.

CHAPTER

17

"THREE YEARS IN THE STATE REFORMATORY AT LA GRANGE."
Momma looked at Judge Gentry a second, her head tilted,
as though she were about to ask him to repeat it. He got up and
mechanically attached himself to his special crutches and got
himself down the steps from the bench, trying to give the impression he had *everything* under control, while the look of rage
and hate Momma gave him would have curdled sweet cream.
Like a wrestler trying to see an opening, a way to pin his
shoulders to the mat, she stared at Judge Gentry. And as he
dragged and hobbled into his office, his back toward the small
courtroom where only Kyle sat, far in the back, Lone blinked at
the certainty that Momma *saw* the opening.

"You ain't goin' to no La Grange, Lone." She took hold of
his arm just as Poteat stepped toward him.

"I'm sentenced."

Kyle came up the aisle. "Hold it a minute, Poteat. Well,
Charlotte . . ."

"You got him into this, Kyle. Now you march in there and
beg that man off some way."

199

"Charlotte, I cain't—"

"Cain't, hell." Lone flinched. "My boy is *not* goin' to no La Grange."

"But the judge has sentenced—"

"He's human. He can change his mind, cain't he?"

"It's too late, honey." Kyle looked down, shoved his hands into his pockets, and shook his head. "Lord knows I'm sorry for it *now*."

"Sorry!"

"I was just tryin' to make him see, Charlotte. What he'd be without Boyd. Reckon I let it git too far, plumb out of my hands. I didn't think he would give him that much. Six months at La Grange *can* make a boy *see*. But three *years*. I was just tryin' to watch over him like you kept at me to." He looked at Lone, his face soft and sad. "Lone, you think I really . . . ?"

"I don't blame *you*, Kyle."

" 'Fore I forget, here's some money for cigarettes." Kyle felt around in his pockets. "You'll need some up there." He handed Lone a palmful of change.

Momma slapped it out of his hand. "He's not goin'!"

Lone sat beside Momma on the bench in front. Poteat picked up Kyle's change, then walked around, and ended up in the judge's chair.

"It's not that we lack money," Momma said. "Did you know that your Gran'daddy offered—?"

"Yes, Momma."

"We're gonna do ever'thing we can."

"I know, Momma."

"And more, if we have to."

"I appreciate it, Momma."

If money wouldn't fix it, what would? In Momma's light hand on his knee, Lone felt the weight of her hopes, of Kyle's, of Gran'daddy's. Under that load, the possibility of being free scared him. Looking at the gavel on the judge's desk, he felt guilty and ashamed, though not of the official crime on the books. It would have been good to open the door and step right into a train to La Grange and be there for supper. He wished he carried their hate and damnation, rather than their love and high hopes with him.

Momma wiped her nose, took a deep breath and tossed her head to get her hair back from her eyes.

"Didn't nobody really want it to happen, Charlotte," said Kyle.

"Let's go, Lone." Poteat took his arm.

"I've slaved and I've slaved, and so long as I've a breath in my body, ain't no man. . . . I'll see you—*soon*, Lone." She kissed his mouth.

Lone lay on his bunk that night, inhaling the fumes from the mountain fires, listening to the radio music that drifted down the corridor. The announcer introduced Cassie as the Nightingale of Harmon County. As she sang "Fair and Tender Ladies," Lone saw her buck-naked in the kitchen, taking a bath in the huge washtub they had used since they were little, when they popped their bellies out, hip to hip, to see which was the biggest. Momma, sitting at the round table, said, "Law, law, how you've filled out!"

A few days after the sentencing, Kyle brought him a note from Cassie. "Dear Lone, Sorry I ain't been to see you but I been singing. Don't worry. I won't go near Boyd's motorsickle. But don't think it's not a temptation. Stay tuned to WKPL. Love. Your sister, Cassandra McDaniel." Lone tore up the note and lay down on his cot and ate the pieces and her handwriting.

That night, up on his toes, looking out the cell window down the slope, he saw the dim figure of a man standing under the Gold Sun Café neon sign, staring up at the eaves where the pigeons were asleep. As Lone lay down to sleep, he wished it were Coot. At the end of a long, struggling, smothering dream, he stood, his voice a garble of murmurs, stifled gasps, and whimpering, in the valley of ten thousand smokes, interlocking and unlocking his fingers.

For a week, while he waited for them to put him on a train to La Grange, getting up only to step over to the toilet, groggy, inhaling the smoke of the forest fires like opium, Lone lay on his cot, seeing Black Mountain and Gran'paw McDaniel, until he had dredged up everything Coot ever told him, and saw more vividly than ever the images Cassie had forged in fever, until one night it came to him not in fragments but in sequence, and the cot began to move, it became the motorcycle, and he climbed into the mountains. . . .

Keys jangled Lone out of a deep sleep. Poteat stood by the cot, looking young and beefy like Kyle before the war. "Up, McDaniel, pick up your ass and follow me. Your daddy's in the visitin' room."

"What's the joke?"

"No joke."

Lone sat up on the edge of the bunk, lit a "duck," and took a puff, looking at Poteat. He tried to figure it out. As a joke it had a lot of rough edges, aside from falling flat. A man who lived as though the world had died yesterday wasn't liable to give a damn about a kid being shipped to the reform school. Taking the last drag, the cigarette down hot, Lone tried to picture it: Coot in filthy overalls, muddy brogans, a railroadman's cap, the hounds curled around his feet, white lightnin' fumes rising around him, standing in the visiting room by the picture of Jesus and the Woman Taken in Adultery, rooted to the spot.

"Okay, Poteat, I'll fall for it." Lone got up and followed him to the waiting room. *My daddy, he had said. Daddy.*

Lone stood in the doorway and looked at him. Coot didn't see him at first. It was like looking at a photograph blown up to life size: the picture of Coot the year he married Momma, taken at the Studio on the Square. He wore a soft brown hat, blue-and-white striped shirt with white collar attached, and a blue suit that fit him snugly. It had hung in the attic for years. Cobwebs hooked up from the chimney to the sleeve, and Coot had scraped a mud dauber's nest off the breast pocket, leaving a cigar-shaped stain of yellow dirt. "Suit I'uz married in," Coot had told Lone.

His shoes were pointed and perforated, and his silky socks glistened in the light. He sat motionless in the red chair before the barred window, where Momma had sat.

Coot looked up and Lone got a full impression of his face, clean-shaven, deep brown, the features distinct. Only the eyes were Coot's. The rest was David McDaniel, a Black Mountain boy, trying to behave in Harmon as though he had never left home.

Coot didn't speak. Poteat seemed to sense that something unusual was going on and that the awkwardness was not between Lone and his daddy. After Poteat went out, the long silence before either spoke was natural. Two mutes, they were getting acquainted without sign language, sensing in each other a kinship based not on a triumph over the deformity but on the deformity itself.

Suddenly Coot remembered he'd brought Lone something. From beside his chair, he picked up a brown bag and handed it to Lone. The first thing Lone pulled out was a packet of Robert Burns cigarillos. Even in his drunken stupors, he had noticed more than Lone realized. Since Coot was smoking a cigarette, Lone unwrapped a Burns and felt for a match. Coot shoved his face up to Lone's and Lone lit the cigarillo off Coot's half-smoked cigarette. Then Lone unwrapped another cigarillo and handed it to Coot, and he used Lone's to light it. He coughed. Though white lightnin' was as much at home in his system as blood, he wasn't prepared for strong tobacco.

Coot motioned for him to dig into the bag again. He watched every move he made, but Lone wasn't embarrassed. Coot seemed just as curious as Lone was. Lone fished out a Milky Way. Then some Dentyne gum. And Coot had brought him a *True*. He had not thought Coot knew the things he liked. The last thing was a white bag of banana candy. Coming home from the mines, he used to bring it to Lone and Cassie in a white bag. Lone ate a piece and offered Coot some. He ate one.

Coot slowly wiped the yellow-orange powder off his mouth. As his hand came away, Lone caught what he had mumbled, "Three year. . . ." A tone of awe, as though somebody had told him how long it takes the light from a star to reach the earth, and he had repeated it. "Lone, ain't they no *way?*"

Coot's voice startled Lone. Low and mellow, it asked a question he had obviously pondered for days.

"I'm sentenced."

"They wouldn't tell *me* nothin'. I heard 'em say three year in the kitchen, and I didn't believe it. Not from them. When I passed by the house in these clothes, she come out on the porch. 'What's come over you?' 'The valley of the shadow of death,' I says. 'Didn't it ever come over you?' So I come to see you. And you *are* sentenced?"

"Leavin' tomorrow."

"Leavin'."

They were quiet.

"Lone, we could still yet do it. The land's still yet layin' there. Hit's gone to the bad a little, but—Lone, a man and his son, why, they could take that mistaken property and make it show. A man had him a good mule or workhorse and that plow honed up and a place for chickens and hogs and plenty of hay stored up for a cow—maybe, why, no tellin'. Hit wouldn't be only once in three years that a man would clean up and put on a suit, if him and his boy was behind the wheel, day by day, together, the way they ought a be." Lone nodded. He nodded emphatically to everything Coot said. He had said it before. In different words. Words that struck. Words that cut. Words that tried for tears. But *these* words were of another time. Long before. Lone listened to him as though Coot had the answer. "He'd give up what's killin' him. He'd never go near that pop-skull whiskey agin, because he wouldn't have to." They were quiet. "Lone, sure to God they's some way."

"It's on the books. And that highway's about to hit us head on."

"Hit just come over me—how good it would be—that I forgot the highway. Even with them orange caterpillars, the first thing you see when you step out on the back porch. I keep forgittin'. . . . You tell me what to do, Lone. You just tell me.

Whatever I have to do, I'll do it. But this cain't be the end of it. Lone, somethin' got started long time ago when I left Black Mountain, and hit cain't be allowed to end in a cell."

"That's what I been thinkin' the last few days—nothin' else. But it's—I reckon—too late."

"I've done forgot the mornin' that hit didn't seem to me the daylight I woke up to would be the last. But all that time, all that dead-drunk time, Lone, I never give up. I always thought 'fore dark that hit would change, or start to. Never fear, son, I got my eye on a piece of land."

"That's good."

"But cain't nobody tell me it's too late."

"Nothin' I can *do*."

"Then I mize well go home, hadn't I?"

"Do you have to go now?"

"Have to? No, I don't have to. What's they to go home to that I'd *have* to? Home. It was home with you there, but—"

"You mean that?"

"But now the last hope's gone."

"You got Cassie."

"I always had Cassie, boy, exceptin' when she took *your* part aginst *me*. But I never had *you*, Lone. If only he'd *come*."

"Gran'paw?"

"He could at least of done that."

"I'm gonna tell you somethin' that nobody, not even Cassie, knows." Lone wanted to give him something. Coot looked at him. "I been to see Gran'paw McDaniel."

A glimmer of the old resentment glazed Coot's eyes. "You never told me. When?"

"Right after Virgil—pulled that trigger, I went ridin' in the country and ended up at Black Mountain."

Coot nodded. Then he stared. "Hit was just you and him—in the Cove? Did you mention my name? What did he say about me? What did you tell him?"

Lone was trying to see it, to imagine how it was and what it meant to Coot. "You just walked right in? And he took you right in?"

Something broke between them. Then Lone saw it. Coot was left out of it. Lone had done what Coot had grieved so many years over failing to do. Gone back. Climbed back up to paradise. And it made Coot's failure darker in his eyes, and put a greater distance between them. He was in the overalls and brogans again, unshaven and stoned.

"It was just like you always told it, Coot. But he's gittin' old, and the farm's goin' down. He needs help."

"I god, I god, I god, Lone, you finally went, didn't you? Did you ask him why he never come to my farm? Did you tell him I only got it to show him I hadn't turned my back on farmin' and huntin' and—? Did you ask him if he forgive me, Lone?"

"Well, now I tell you, Coot, he told me to tell you that—"

"Don't lie."

"No lie, Coot. He said you needn't lay around Harmon worryin' 'bout what's done and buried."

"And you needn't lie neither. I know. . . . I'm dead to him. I always been dead to . . ."

"Let me finish tellin' you," said Lone, finishing the lie that welled up in him at the prospect of what it might do to Coot. Well, it wouldn't make a new man of him—nothing would do that as completely as whiskey. . . . "He said, 'You tell David, I've overcome my hardness toward him and that I forgive him.'"

Coot sat there, looking inside himself at something, shutting Lone out. Then he looked at Lone, and the look drew Lone in, and he stuck out his hand and they shook hands. Coot squeezed Lone's hand hard, tight, till it hurt, to confirm the fact that after all these years he really did exist. "Then the reason for livin' is belief," said Coot.

"You ain't about to pull any church stuff on me, are you?"

"God's God and Coot's Coot, and maybe once in a lifetime the twain do meet, and as far as I'm concerned, that says it all. No, it's belief in people."

"Who? Momma? Kyle? Gran'paw?"

"You."

"Oh. Then that makes another one."

"You gittin' up some kind of club?"

"No, but someday, it might just about be a family."

Returning to the cell, holding on to what he had felt with Coot, Lone didn't notice that he was on his way back. When Poteat turned off the light from outside, it hit Lone where he was and what he had done and where he was going and how long it was going to be. Funny thing. To get next to your father you had to go far away. Just as a jar of white lightnin' often took Coot far away from what he had thought was Lone's hate.

He lay down on the cot and tried to let the dark drink him in and the fumes of the fires drug him to sleep, but after a while he began to tremble and couldn't stop. A fly on flypaper, he had no choice but to stick in one spot and think about the fix he was in. He had become, he noticed, a goddamned little thinker. One who looked through a keyhole and saw only himself.

Cassie, a moth pinned to the bed, her mind always on the wing, had known how to live without people, except for Lone. But after the long orgy of talk in the jail infirmary, Cassie was dropping the junk-bag of the past, breaking loose. With Lone gone, she could begin to fly. And nobody could set the pace better than Boyd. Boyd had set it for Lone. Looking at Cassie's image a moment, it seemed to Lone that somehow the foulness of his life since spring would seep into *her*, as though he were a membrane through which filth would pass into her body.

His nightmares had anticipated the moment when everything he had forgotten would rush upon him, a smothering blanket of wool soaked in ether. But behind terror, joy surged. Joy in the love he had for people who came to him contaminated, who contaminated him, and whom he contaminated. He wondered why he had not seen this before he had come to this cell. Out in Harmon, he had raced fitfully in dark ignorance. Now he was beginning to see clearly images he had always known were there, images Cassie had sung and talked about, images that had always hovered behind him somewhere.

Now these people had cornered him in a cell and told him

what would end when he went away. Love seemed to explain everything. Then he thought it might even be hate. Or both love and hate. Now he began to wonder about guilt. A sense of guilt. At the root of every flowering act and blighted act, every act of love and hate: some kind of guilt. He was surprised that such an answer, though only probable, didn't depress him. It made a bright light that put them all in sharper focus: pictures in an album, spread out on the black ceiling of the cell:

Her fingers crooked on the strings over the black mouth, one small breast resting in the curve of the guitar, her long blond hair slung over one shoulder, her mouth open, her tongue curled behind her bottom teeth, Cassie sat on her heels in the middle of the big brass bed, the quilts swirled around her. When Lone stepped over the threshold into their room, her lips closed on the first syllable of a song.

Momma stood beside the hotel bed, her legs pressed against the mattress, facing the open window, sunlight flooding into the room. She bent slightly, the half-folded sheet in her hands, then threw up her arms and bowed her body backward. The sheet popped like a sail above the bed, bellied full of the breeze that brought the odor of forest fires through the sooty screen. Then the sheet drifted down and clung to the filthy mattress, Momma's green uniform clinging to her weary body.

Under the broken bronze statue of Jesus lying across the rafters, sat Coot on a log, his ankles crossed, his hands limp in his lap, his head bowed, sun motes whirling slowly on the crown of his striped railroad cap, a Mason jar at his feet, the lid on his knee. When Lone stopped just outside the stall, Coot looked up, waved Lone in.

Standing spread-eagle on a smooth covering of pine needles, ringed with tall pine trunks, the straps of his overalls pulled taut against his back, the ax raised over his head, Gran'paw McDaniel kept steady with his eyes the spot where he wanted the blade to sink. When he heard him step into the clearing behind him, Gran'paw turned and handed the ax to Lone.

Standing on a bench in the middle of a hot tent, the center pole at his back, Uncle Virgil, at the height of a preaching fervor that already had ten women and three men full of the Holy Ghost lying on their backs in the sawdust, took an orange from the cupped hands of a sleeping baby and tossed it to a woman witnessing the blood. She caught it and tossed it high over her head, and even before it fell into the lap of an old woman clapping, eyes shut, the woman jerked, shot through with a current that connected everyone in the tent. And the orange moved on until everyone had handled it and everyone had gone down.

Gypsy lay on the blanket in a pool of moonlight that poured through the broken roof of the silo, her hair spread out, her hands crossed over her breasts, legs apart, eyes closed. Mouth, eyes opened at once as Lone knelt on one knee at the edge of the blanket.

Braced with his back against a smooth telephone pole, one foot on the bumper of his black and white cruiser, one hand in his pants pocket, his coattail flung back, the other hand holding a cold cigar, Kyle stared over the hood ornament, the *Gold Sun Café* behind him. Lone stepped up to the curb and Kyle pushed off from the pole and handed him a cigar band.

In his protective skin of grease and grit, resting on Lone's promise to help him salvage Harmon County, Gran'daddy Stonecipher stepped out of the shack into the junk garden.

And maybe a few others he didn't even know about. The fact that to get such a row of pictures, all it took was for him to blow up a tipple and loot a condemned grocery store made Lone sit up in a cold sweat. Looking down between his dangling bare feet into the black below, Lone saw a motorcycle and a rider dressed in black hit the swinging bridge. Flashes of sunlight seemed to buzz around him like wasps, glancing off the steel and glass and the white leather seat and handlegrips and tasseled trimmings and the goggles under the white-billed cap. The first sun after days of spring rain. And it passed the revival tent and came up the hill path and was lost for a moment, the steady throb of the motor tuned down a little. Then he was suddenly up over the rise and pressing to a stop right in front of Lone,

*who stepped aside, afraid he would be run down. With one
smooth movement, the rider slipped his goggles up over the bill
of the cap, and in that moment, he was a stranger. Now Lone
wondered how much of a stranger Boyd had always been. He
wondered where Boyd's place was in the album of images.
Somewhere in the back, beyond blank black pages? The picture
of Boyd persisted in focus so long that Lone began to doubt.
Maybe Boyd belonged in the front of the album.*

He tried to see a picture of himself. But all he saw was a
hub stabbed full of spokes, and each spoke was a person who
needed the hub if the wheel was to turn. Not the wheels of his
motorcycle, locked and frozen in a drift of snow down some
road in his mind. Another wheel inside him stood still. But right
now, as he lay on the edge of sleep, there was only a hub. Racing
on those other wheels, questions had never come up. It was Lone
racing that made Cassie, impaled on the bed, turn. As Boyd
moved over the streets of Harmon on wheels, did he, too, move
on the turning axis of himself toward a future he hoped he could
lay his hands on?

As Lone drifted to sleep, the hub began to vibrate and
sprout spokes, the wheel began to move, and Uncle Virgil, no
longer screaming, spoke his name.

CHAPTER

18

"UP, MCDANIEL, UP." POTEAT BANGED A MOP PAIL AGAINST THE bars. "Today's the day, trooper. La Grange Special at your service." Lone didn't make a move. "You cain't pull that stuff today. Yesterday and the day before, layin' on your can all day and all night—that's one thing. But this mornin', trooper, you mop up your mess, you eat, you shit, shower, and shave, put on a starched suit of prison rags, and you kiss me the hell good-bye. Good-bye Harmon, hello La Grange." He stood beside the cot, looking at Lone, his hands on his hips, his glossy, pimply face cocked sideways. Lone didn't make a move. He had lain there two days, and with only one meal in him, he was weak. Too weak to try.

"If we have to pick you up with a crane and shovel you into the squad car, we will." He looked at Lone, and Lone looked at him, hardly listening. "Okay, between now and when the train arrives at two o'clock, you better lift ass."

Lone did not want them to touch him. But not until noon could he haul himself all the way up and off the cot. He called for the mop. He accepted lunch. At one o'clock, he climbed up on the top bunk and looked out through fluttering pigeon wings at Harmon. Wind had stripped the trees in the Square. He saw the ruins of the tipple, a black clutter of tin and lumber. Over the tops of the buildings, he saw the house, surrounded, above and below, by yellow caterpillars, moving the earth. He was trying to locate the silo when Poteat said, "The last mile, Dillinger."

Lone followed him to the showers. As Lone undressed, Poteat said, "Say, did you know Dillinger come through Harmon one time?"

"No, I didn't." Lone turned the nozzle. "I was just a dishrag in heaven, then." The water hesitated, then gushed out full force against his tense chest, ice-cold.

Lone got scalding water going.

Just when he was beginning to see that his life was not a complete waste, that hope had been there even while he was racing away from what he thought was hopelessness, they were cutting him off, locking him up. He could blame the way the country was, the way he knew the world must be, if Harmon was any indication. There were certain ways of thinking that encouraged him to blame everything and everybody but himself. He might even follow Momma's directions and blame Boyd. But standing in a cloud of steam, the only way he could see it was that he alone was to blame. Instead of making him want to go ahead and cry, that made him feel good, as though he were going to La Grange on his own steam, out of his own free will. It didn't take away the pain of waste, but crying didn't seem to express what he felt. He scoured his body almost raw with cheap soap. Glistening clean, he still felt dirty. The water made him sleepy, the soap stung his eyes. After he had rinsed the suds from his eyes, he saw that Poteat was gone. An image from an old newsreel flashed across his mind: a GI outside the door of a shower room, pointing inside with his rifle where the Jews were *gassed* through shower nozzles.

"You look like a newborn baby," Kyle, behind him, said, and popped him with a towel. "Right on the ass! Brings you into the world screamin'."

"Don't git your hopes up."

"Your Momma sent me by the house to get you some decent clothes, but I couldn't find anything but this pair of pants."

"Bought 'em with my paper-route money. Too tight for me now."

"Jerk 'em on. And here's you a present from your Uncle Kyle."

Lone caught a department store bag and pulled out a blue-and-white-striped polo shirt.

"Poteat said they had some regular prison rig I was supposed to put on."

"La Grange's been postponed. I'm takin' you to meet the person who got you out a this."

"You mean they turnin' me loose?"

"Oh, shut up."

"Well, where's my motorsickle clothes?"

"When I asked the chief for 'em he said Cassie come by about two weeks ago and claimed her mother sent her for Lone's stuff. Charlotte says it's a lie. That sister of yours is achin' to ride herself straight into the fires of hell quicker'n you all can get free of that house."

The old pants were tight, the legs too short.

"Here's you some old beat-up shoes, too."

They were too tight. Lone pulled on the polo, inhaling the smell of new cotton. "You always have to have the last word, don't you?" Lone felt the stripes across his chest.

Kyle chuckled. "You look like you excaped."

Lone stepped over the police station threshold onto the sidewalk, and inhaled his first fresh air in a month, though still laden with woodsmoke. He looked back at Kyle, who stood in the doorway, his legs apart, his fists on his hips. In one glance, Lone saw the clean, white, starched, short-sleeved shirt, the gold badge over his heart, his bill-cap down to his eyebrows, the wide black belt, the shiny holster, the black pants and polished black shoes, and the resemblance to his and Boyd's motorcycle outfits struck him. Light-headed anyway, he almost laughed. Luther, who had quit the mines with black lung and was now about to retire from the police force, sat in front of the window, his feet on the sill. Two old men from the mountains lounged on the bench under the awning, watching traffic—people they'd known since birth, and machines. Lone saw the high school football field and the track.

"Summer in October," said Kyle behind him.

"I know what you mean," said Luther in the window, but Lone felt it was meant for him.

"They's somebody waitin' for you in the Gold Sun."

Lone looked at the blinking neon sign. Then he started across the street.

"Hobart Jenkins," said Kyle, "I been a-lookin' for you."

A thin man in a torn purple cowboy shirt stepped off the curb and passed Lone, crossing over to Kyle, trying not to look worried.

Lone pulled open the sooty wide-screened door to the Gold Sun Café and stepped into the cavelike coolness and dim light. The row of counter stools, almost all the plastic seats split, was empty. Behind the cigar and candy case, surrounded by rubber plants and a green-scummed aquarium, sat the Greek, as he had sat the first day Lone ever saw him, when Momma had come back to work for him for a few months, behind the cash register on a high stool, his feet jacked up, one hand stuffed in his filthy white jacket, the other resting lightly on the cracked marble shelf above his register drawer, a cigar butt dead in a corner of his clenched teeth. Like a man tending a still, he sat at the register waiting for the bead. He didn't move. Lone usually spoke, but the Greek never answered, though Momma used to report good things he said about Lone in the days before he began to run with Boyd. The three fans, hanging from the ceiling, moved slowly. Empty of people, the place seemed occupied by its various sources of light: the Pet Milk clock over the swinging doors to the kitchen, the advertising gadgets for beer and Royal Crown, the jukebox, the windows of the refrigerators, the high-mounted television, quietly snowing.

Jessie, the cook, backed out of the narrow men's room

door, lugging a bucket full of water, dragging a mop. Turning, she butted open the swinging door to the kitchen, and saw Lone. "Do I see who I *think* I see?"

"You *better* git to *work*, Jessie," said Lone, with mock severity, to the crazy old woman who had named him. One summer she had come up the hollow almost every day, hunting for wild berries with a Jewel lard bucket dangling from her wrist. "You 'lone, little boy, you 'lone allatime?" she'd say, and Cassie, in the sickbed, the window open, picked it up, and Wayne had become Lone years ago.

"Lone, honey, I ain't never *quit*." She was still laughing when the swinging doors, whopping back and forth, stopped, and someone caught hold of Lone's little finger as he passed a booth.

"Lone, honey." Momma. In a yellow dress with a raw look of newness, the old green coat with the fox collar draped over her shoulders. Smiling, her wrist bent, a straw between her fingers. The malt half down. Her brown eyes were bright and moist, as though an hour ago she had cried for joy. She sat straight on the stool and bent back a little to see him better. "Surprised?"

"I reckon I *am*." As she slid over to let him sit down, her coat slipped off her shoulders into his hands. Sitting down, he draped the coat over her shoulders again, her black hair brushing his hands as she fluffed it up over the fur collar. "What you doing?"

"Waitin' for my son to come meet me."

"You don't want to be seen with a somethin' dressed like me."

"You know somethin', Lone?"

"No."

"Fix that boy a malt, Charlotte," said the Greek, unseen behind the aquarium.

"Thanks, Max, but we're about to git up." Momma shoved the malt in front of Lone. "Finish it up, honey."

"What were you fixin' to say?" He took a deep, soothing-good swallow.

"That if you want to know the truth, tonight I don't give a damn."

About to drop the tall glass, Lone set it down and looked at her. Her head bowed, she dug in her purse to pay the check. She had said it so brightly, with a little toss of her voice, that it did something to the striped polo shirt and to the tight pants. But the misshapen shoes still looked run over by a coal truck.

He started to ask her how she had gotten him released, but he didn't want to spoil the magic of the mood. That could wait.

"I'm gonna see P.O. and Mr. Deaderick first thing in the mornin'," said Lone. "It don't hurt to beg."

"If the stores were only open, I'd march you down to Conway's and outfit you to beat the band, but it's early closin'." She took hold of the lapels of her coat and stood up, bent over in the narrow space. Lone slipped out, and as she passed him, she did a little swirling turn, and smiled. "Today's the day of days, Lone. We're gonna turn over a new leaf—together."

At the cigar counter, she placed a fifty-cent piece on the marble shelf. The Greek rang it up and handed her back two quarters. "Change."

"Well, thanks, Max, but I wanted to pay for a *ci*gar, too."

"Pick one."

"Lone. . . ."

He bent over and looked at the cigars, and Momma bent over in the yellow dress, holding her coat by the lapels. Lone pointed at the Robert Burns panatela box.

The Greek reached in and held the box in front of Lone. As Lone took one, the Greek said, "I got 'ducks' on that one."

Momma reached out and slapped the Greek on his hairy forearm. "You're the berries, Max."

"That's the truth, too," said Lone, and Momma and Lone went out laughing, but the Greek just sat there, a cigar clenched in his teeth so far smoked down it wasn't even a "duck."

At the corner drugstore, they stopped and read all the headlines of the papers from Louisville, Lexington, and Knoxville. Lone spat over the curb nonchalantly. Between the bank and the drugstore, the sun smoked red, going down the mountains, and when he inhaled, the October air was raw. He felt what wasn't quite a chill on his bare arms. Even with the dirt and coal dust and gasoline fumes and wood smoke, and the café and drugstore and department store odors that drifted back and forth across the street, the night scent was sweet. Even the newspapers in the rack smelled good.

"Oh, Lone, look!" Four pigeons perched on the helmet of the World War I soldier statue in front of the courthouse. As if on signal, they flew into the trees.

Lone and Momma ambled along the streets of Harmon until all the lights had come on. Then, in front of the finest restaurant in town, Momma put her hand on the nape of his neck, and said, "You 'bout ready for a feast?"

When Lone told her to let him have her coat, she slipped gracefully out of it, and the coat he hung up didn't seem to be the same coat she had worn for ten years, a coat some rich woman in Louisville had cast off, donated to the fire department the year of the big flood. Light gleaming on the dishes and silverware and steam from the food made Momma's yellow dress look warmer, softer. She seemed so natural. Here they were, where she wanted them always to be: in a place like this, following a strutting hostess who swayed and swung, in and among the tables, and placed the menus on the white tablecloth as though they were scripture.

They studied the menu leisurely, they awaited the food tranquilly, they ate slowly. The waitress seemed to understand and care about them, as though she had seen Lone racing through Harmon on a motorcycle and watched Momma trudge back and forth from the hotel to the house up the hollow, and now here they were. They had finally found a time to sit down somewhere off from the house and just quietly eat and listen and look together. And not even have to talk. Still. As though the waitress looked forward to such a time in her own life.

"If God would just stop ever'thing right here—let this be His picture of us—for eternity." Lone looked into her eyes without flinching as she spoke.

Past the dark stores, they strolled back toward the Square.

Momma stopped and bent her knees slightly and moved her head to squint through the trees at the Majestic marquee. "Reckon that's any count?"

"Rerun of *Call of the Wild.*"

"Law, Clark Gable!"

As they entered the lobby, she said, "I loved you in that usher's suit."

Lone smiled at his former boss. "Where you all *been?*" Fred Morgan asked, tearing up their tickets.

Lone and Momma passed the popcorn bag during *Call of the Wild* and when the news came on, Lone went for a Mars bar, and then they saw the feature again up to the rescue. Passing through the lobby, they yawned, and stepping out onto the sidewalk, they inhaled the cool air as he helped her get her coat on. "Good ol' Jack Okie," she said, buttoning the coat up to her neck. "He was with Charlie Chaplin one time where they ate a shoe."

As they passed a parked car, one shape in the front seat became a man and a woman. Lone took Momma's hand and they crossed the highway to the swinging bridge. The tracks below were full of coal gondolas. Still. But they seemed alive. The semaphore was red, but they heard no sound. Frogs down by the river thought it was still summer. High against the sky, the radio tower blinked. They stopped in the middle of the bridge to listen to the river run in the dark under the bridge.

Remembering the rotten plank too late, Momma awkwardly skipped to miss it, dropped her purse, and the contents spilled. On their hands and knees in the dark, Lone and Momma felt around on the boards, the bridge swaying. Their hands touched in the dark as they groped for pennies, and a light breeze started in the sycamores at the end of the bridge. The breeze worked up a wind that turned cold and bent the trees and rattled the dead leaves and made Momma's coat flap against her legs and hips as she rose and snapped her pocketbook shut. He took her hand, and they walked on across the bridge and climbed the path up into the hollow.

Suddenly, the yard lit up, and by a strange, glowing orange light, Lone saw the wind blow at the fur collar, exposing the white skin, and saw a purple vein under Momma's eye, and when the wind lifted and held her hair above her shoulders, he saw strands of gray. Looking toward the house, he saw his motorcycle braced between the persimmon trees, stripped now to black limbs and twigs, the bark on the trunk looking, just as Cassie often said, like alligator skins.

CHAPTER

19

A BONFIRE ROARED AT THE DEAD END OF THE PATH BESIDE THE outhouse under the catalpa tree. It lit up somebody in black, who fed papers and magazines into the fire.

"Who in the world?" Fearfully, Momma took Lone's hand.

Lone thought it might be Boyd, burning Cassie's books and magazines and pictures. But then he recognized the bill-cap, the goggles, brown leather jacket, the brown corduroy trousers, and the black engineer boots as his own.

"She's all right," said Momma. "Just burnin' some of her old junk from out of the attic. We'll all have to be moved out, ever' hair, in a few days. They're workin' on what they call a crash schedule, with earth-movin' machines big as locomotives."

"Don't talk about it, Momma. They's bound to be some way."

"A body's *got* to talk about it, if it's hangin' right over their head! Between home and wherever we're goin', we're holin' up at your Gran'daddy Stonecipher's a few weeks. He's already moved a few sticks a furniture and stuff over there."

Close enough to the fire to feel the heat, Lone saw vivid red lipstick on Cassie's mouth and rouge and powder on her cheeks.

"Where did *you* come from?" Cassie looked as if a mean joke had been played on her.

"I never thought I'd see the day . . ." said Momma.

"Well, you *have*, so take a *good* look!"

"You just puttin' on a tantrum that'll land you flat a your back again," said Momma. "Well, she's *your* sister, Lone. See what *you* can do with her. I ain't about to let her ruin my good night."

Momma went into the house by the kitchen door. A light flashed out over the yard, and Lone began to recognize the objects in the yard: the T-model Ford headlight, the giant Coca-Cola sign, the mailboxes, the music stand, license plates.

"While you got that fire goin' good," said Lone, speaking through the flames, "you just peel off that costume, and we'll git rid of *my* part, too."

"What good is it to you, if you're goin' to La Grange?" She sailed a *National Geographic* into the blaze. It fell open on color photographs of Hawaiian beaches. "Who else would *need* them?"

"Didn't Kyle tell you?"

"He ignored me."

"They turned me loose."

"You mean you ain't goin'?" He couldn't tell by her voice whether she was glad or disappointed.

"No."

"You're free?"

"Yeah. . . . Don't break a leg dancin'."

"I thought you was on the train."

"So you was pourin' on the fuel, huh?"

The wooden crates and bushel baskets that held her junk burned in the bonfire, and he saw dolls' heads, the boat paddle Coot had brought in, the miners' helmets, the tennis racket.

"And now you're back," said Cassie.

"And now you start unzippin' that jacket. If I knew Gran'daddy had as good a fire goin' at the junkyard, I'd ride over there tonight and deliver that motorsickle to him."

"Don't say that. You're just tryin' to torment me."

Lone looked at Cassie through the flames, trying to see what she was up to that went beyond the costume and the fire. They avoided talking. She kept swooping down to pick something up and pitch it on. Over their heads, the crackling and sputter of burning leaves, dead and alive, seemed for a moment to speak for them both. The Indian cigars of the catalpa tree began to smoke, upside down.

"Looks like the valley of ten thousand smokes in Alaska, turned upside down, don't it? Remember?" Lone tried to see her eyes through the goggles.

"No," said Cassie. "Ever'thing I remember's goin' up in smoke. Cain't you see?"

"See? Yeah, oh, hell, yeah, I can see all right. If you could see your*self*, you'd laugh."

"Don't you laugh at me."

"*I'm* not laughin'. I just said *you* would laugh. Hell, no. *I'm* not laughin'. . . . What got into you?"

"I got inspired. Look behind you."

Lone turned around. Across the path, he saw bulldozers in the firelight. Sparks fanned by the wind wafted down over them.

"Watchin' 'em all day long gets into you. Come daylight, you'll see what they done to the ridge behind the barn."

Turning around, Lone looked down the yard at the motorcycle where it set between the persimmon trees. He walked over to it, and even over the odor of burning trash, and magazines and paper, he smelled a burnt ignition. She had tried to start it. Rings of trampled dead grass and crushed leaves. Around and around the tree she had pushed it, just to feel it move. The wind coming down the hollow turned cold.

Turning toward the fire again, he didn't see her. Then she came out the back door, the mauve nightgown fluttering in the wind behind her as she carried it at her side, a sullen half-attempt to hide it.

When she saw him running toward the fire to block her, she began to run. But before either of them reached the flames, the medicine bottles began to explode. Shielding his eyes, Lone moved around the bonfire, his back to it, and caught the nightgown just as Cassie gave it one long fling toward the flames.

"Throw ever'thing away, huh?" He kicked viciously at the smoking magazines.

"We're all headed for the trash can, sooner or later."

"Git in the house, Cassie, and jerk on this nightgown."

"I wasn't expectin' to see you agin for three years. They're gonna tear the house down in a few days, anyway. Now, Lone, listen . . ."

"What you talkin' about?"

She ran across the yard, up the front steps, and into the house. When he reached the door, he heard the shriek of the bolt on the door to the bedroom. They reached the window at the same moment. He slammed it up before she could lock it. Above his head, the wind jiggled the swing that had been pulled up to the ceiling for the winter. He climbed over the sill, the nightgown looped over his arm.

She tried to block him as he moved in the dark to the light string, but he walked her backward to the railing where it was tied and pulled it. In a moment of panic, he thought that if he turned, he might see a bulldozer aimed at him from the corner behind him, for while he had been in jail, the wreckers had leaped ahead to the place toward which they had aimed since the first house fell on the east end of Harmon: this room. He ran his hand along the rail, and though the mattress was still rolled, the solid feel of the brass bedstead comforted him as he turned. Directly under the light bulb, in the exact center of the room, like a hub, sat the cot, made up with military tightness. The big bed, its rusty springs exposed like a network of veins, had been shoved into the corner. The rest of the room was bare, as neat and clean as an old room with faded and torn wallpaper and worn floors could look. She'd picked it clean—to the bone.

"My God," he whispered, but she took a step backward, putting her hands over her ears as though he had shouted. "Why didn't you just mount one a them bulldozers and work on *me* with it?"

"It's for *me*, not *you*. They said you'uz sentenced."

"Stop sayin' that!"

"You cain't just rise from the dead and expect me to yawn like it was ever' day." A new, sullen tone in her voice made her seem strange.

"If you ain't out of that rig in one minute, I'm gonna rip it off you."

As she did a graceful little dance to keep out of his way, he pushed her toward the cot. She didn't fall but staggered away from him to keep her balance, and one foot, bare and white, came out of a boot. As she knelt to grab the boot, he kicked it across the room. Reaching for the sleeve of the jacket, he felt the smooth leather slip through his fingertips as she dodged, whirled around, and bumped up against the wall by the door, clutching the jacket at the zipper under her chin. Pinning her against the wall with his shoulder, he tried to pry her fingers loose. "Don't, Lone! Don't! Leave—it—alone!"

"Turn loose! Turn loose! Damn it to hell!"

He plucked the cap from her head and slung it. The bill pecked viciously once at the windowpane and flopped on the floor, and her yellow hair swung down around her shoulders. When he jerked the goggles down over her nose, her green eyes flared at him. The goggles swung around her neck by the band as her legs worked around like an eggbeater against his. On his feet, he felt the hard heel of the one boot and her other naked, soft heel. He got her hand loose and had unzipped the jacket halfway when she rammed him with her knee. He staggered back against the bottom rail of the big bed, his stomach whirled, then coiled tight, and a red streak flared in the darkness of his tightly closed eyes.

When he got her into focus again, she was zipping the jacket back up, covering the white flesh between her small breasts. The brown pants hung low, twisted, on her hips, showing her navel. The wide black belt lacked holes enough for her to pull it tight, and between her knees and the top of the boot, the corduroy pants bulged. She looked like a little girl dressed up in her big brother's clothes for the hell of it, and Lone sensed painfully how true that was: she wore them for the *hell* of it. She smiled uncertainly and then started giggling, as if she hoped he would fall in with her.

"I'm not kiddin', Cassie. Don't stand there gigglin' at me. Now, please take my stuff off or I'll jerk it off, naked or not."

Reaching for her, he hooked a finger in one of the pants loops and pulled her to him and caught her wrist.

"Listen, Lone, I cain't stand for anybody to squeeze my arm like that. It drives me crazy. Please let go 'fore I lose my temper, 'fore I hit—"

"You cain't hurt me any worse—"

She started slapping his hand with her free hand. "Please, Lone, don't make me. I cain't stand— That hurts!"

When Lone tightened his grip, she swung and her fist scraped his ear. Lone slapped her. Fingernails that had grown out for the first time in years scraped down his face and along his arms. Struggling backward to break his grip, she fell on the bedsprings and kicked her feet, one booted, the other bare, at him, striking him on the chest, and arms, and face. Sweat on the palm of his hand allowed her to slip her wrist out of his grasp.

When he looked at her again, she was on the other side of the bed on her knees on the rolled mattress at the foot where the light glared on her bleeding mouth.

Panting and swallowing, he tried to get his breath.

"Lone," Momma said, through the locked door. "You all—" She tried it, found it locked.

"Go to bed, Momma. It's okay."

"If you reach for me again, Lone, like that, I'll—" She sensed he wasn't going to, seemed relieved she didn't have to say it. "A few months before they arrested you, you wasn't nothin' but a human cyclone, hittin' and hurtin' ever'body. It's about time it come to this."

Standing at the railing, he thought he caught the smell of Boyd.

He backed across the bare room onto the cot, his leg looped over the bottom rail, and looked at her as she turned toward the wall and unzipped the brown jacket, slipped out of it very gracefully, and threw it backward at him. The whiteness and narrowness of her back, the deep groove that went down below her waist, and the way her hair hung down and clung to her white damp skin almost to her hips made him look away. Then she slung the pants and they wrapped around his neck, slapping his ear. The boot hit the wall over his head.

He lay on the cot and shut his eyes against the glare of the new hundred-watt bulb that dangled from the ceiling on the hairy, gray-black, twisted cord.

"I just wanted to feel that leather on my bare skin, so I could try to imagine what you ain't been here to tell me."

"The goggles were enough before." He paused, then laughed. "Where'd you git all that energy?" Not that it was funny. But it was exhilarating to feel the pouring out of that unfamiliar power in this musky room where her body had been as damp and soft as the quilts after a rain.

"I been collectin' it drop by drop since they took you off. I still ain't strong enough to be up all the time. But I *would* a been."

He turned to speak to her, to let her know that his anger was fading.

She faced him, wearing only panties, leaning against the wall, her fists pressed into her hips, staring at him.

He jerked his head away from her. "Put some clothes on!" He stared at the window. She giggled. "Are you doin' it?"

"Yesssss. Back into the old mummy wrap."

"You know damn well you ain't no little girl no more."

"That's right. I'm not. And I mean to prove it."

"Cassie, what's come over you since I been gone?"

"*Nothin'*. Since you been gone, I had *nothin'* to look forward to. All I did was lay in that bed, tryin' and tryin' to figure some way."

"To what?"

"Git out." He heard her bare feet on the floor, but he wasn't going to turn until he was sure. "And come night no Lone. Nothin' to even *lis*ten to. I was left with just layin' there."

He heard the flop of the mattress as she broke the string

that bound it in a roll. He looked. No blood stains. A different mattress—from Gran'daddy's probably.

"What about your songs, and them books, and the talks we had in the infirmary? And you could write and dream up stuff."

"How you think I could sing or write anything? You can look at me now." Lone turned and she was in the nightgown that fit her like air, kneeling on the mattress. "So I went out ever' chance I got, and I sang a time or two on the radio. I'm Nashville-bound one of these days—move over, Kitty Wells!"

"Good God."

"You needn't 'good God' me, Lone. What do you want me to do?"

Lone couldn't say, so he got to his feet and picked up his boots.

Sitting bolt upright in bed, she asked, "Lone, do you hate me?"

With a boot in each hand, he looked at the floor. "No. If you'll just git settled and let me tell it . . ."

"Momma knows what's stirrin' in me. She knows I'm comin' into a good spell that won't quit, and that I'm not gonna just wander *this* time. *This* time I'm really goin' out into Harmon County and try to be a human with other people."

Lone set the boots neatly at the foot of the cot and sat tensely on the iron edge. "You ready to listen?"

"That don't work no more, Lone."

"No, I mean something new. That blamed motorsickle outsyonder's doomed. It don't spark a thing in me no more. No, I mean a new life, honey. Listen, this last week I been like I was up on Big Black Mountain with Gran'paw, and I had time, almost a month, and peace, to think things out, and I decided I couldn't just disappear and let ever'body's hopes go in the ground like Coot's pissed-out whiskey. I want to *deserve* the people that care for me. I'm gonna beg P. O. Fletcher and the principal to take me back in school. Might be he'll even let me go out for track this spring. One time he said he might could get me a sports scholarship to some college—if I'd just get serious about runnin'. *Maybe* preachin' after that. But I gotta start buildin' from the quicksand up. That's what Virgil wanted me to *see*."

"Lone, will you help me to git well, so I can git out and go? I tried it alone, but I cain't *do* it without help."

"You wasn't even listenin'."

"I don't want that. It won't do *me*—"

"You're sorry they let me go."

"No, Lone, no, honey, it's just I was caught up in the way that outfit made me feel. Listen, now I got the *will* for it, help me before I git to dependin' on *you* so much agin."

"Not if it means you're gonna follow in *my* tracks."

"Take me, take me after all this time, for just one ride—"

"I'd rather see you—"

"Dead? I'd rather *be* dead than lay *here* the rest of my life."

"You tryin' to torment me to death, the way you're actin'?"

"Why cain't you understand? All I want to do is ride down the highway, Lone. That's all in the world. You never would—"

"You ain't leavin' this room! You ain't gonna start runnin' wild in that outfit, stuck like a wart on the back of Boyd Weaver's motorsickle!"

"*N*obody's stoppin' me when I really do abandon this rock," she said, pounding the bare mattress with her fists.

"He's not gonna *touch* my sister!"

"He promised me this morning he would teach me to ride sometime. It's a way to git out."

"You gonna let him hug you?"

"Shut that up! I just want to ride the way you used to."

"You're fifteen years old and ignorant of—"

"It ain't that, Lone. It's just he's been like a—"

"Like a what? Say it!" Lone stood up and looked down at her.

"Nothin'."

"Has he been comin' in this—"

"No. Hell, no!"

"Stop cussin' ever' word."

"Stop, stop, stop stoppin' me, Lone!" They got very still, looking at each other. "When you parked that 'sickle, the ground turned to quicksand for me. Don't blame *me* if I sink."

The force of it made him go limp: he was still the cause. While he had lain on a cot in a cell, Boyd was out here in Harmon, where his sister was trying to create some kind of life for herself from scratch. And whose scratch marks did she follow as a guide? His own.

He rolled the boots up in the pants and wrapped them in the jacket and tucked the cap under his arm and went out into the yard. But the fire was too low now to burn the motorcycle outfit. The roll of movie tickets was black, but had not burned, and the violin case smoked. He wondered if the green scooter lay among the dark objects scattered over the yard. Walking around the black circle in the moonlight, poking it with a stick to make all the papers burn, he watched the ashes turn black. One last page flared up like the start of a new bonfire, and he kicked dirt on it, and when it went out, picked it up and tried to read it by moonlight, but all he could make out was "Me and Boyd dynamited the tipple . . ." and it seemed like something dug up from Egyptian ruins and pondered a lifetime.

Coot came into the circle of light, holding aloft the naked ribs of a kite, with a tail of colored rags lagging, curved behind him on the ground. "Nice wind up. Good for flyin' a kite. Hangin' in the barn where I found me a jar of white lightnin', bless the Lord."

"I'm home, Daddy—for good."

"Kyle told me." In the glow from the fading embers, Lone saw that Coot had lost a tooth. It lay beside some railroad track where he had stumbled in the dark, full of white lightning. Coot's missing tooth seemed to go with the empty room and the new highway coming through.

"It's gonna be different now, Coot."

"Hit already is. If it wasn't so dark, you could see up behind the barn. Hit's just one smooth slope. They cut the road and pushed the dirt down the hill and even swamped the trees over. And look where the wind tore up my willa tree—like wringin' a chicken's neck."

"It's too dark."

"Wait till mornin'."

"Come set on the porch with me."

Coot dropped the kite in the hot ashes and one strip of pale red paper caught.

They sat on the back porch.

"You and me all alone. Father and son—two unholy ghosts. No fire and brimstone—just a puny wiggle of smoke ever' once in awhile."

"I'm goin' back to school, Daddy."

Coot pulled a blue Mason jar from behind his bib and took a swallow. "Lone . . . Lone . . . I—I—don't want—to live— no more. Do you care? You don't care, do you? Does Charlotte care? Does my daddy care?"

"I told you what he said . . ."

"Hit come too late, son. . . . Nobody cares. Why should I care? Always hated this place. Never belonged here. I belong on Black Mountain with my daddy, near my momma's grave. She was pure."

The door opened behind them. "You comin' in, Lone?" said Momma. "Who's that on the porch with you?"

"It's Daddy."

"Coot, you let him git to bed now. He's goin' to school in the morning."

Coot got up and started for the path.

"Where you goin'?" Lone wished Coot would come in and sleep in Momma's bed.

"I'm nestin' in the barn where the manure is sweet and warm."

Lone went into the kitchen, while Momma held open the door. "Better take my hand. I got the hall full a boxes."

"Boxes?"

"I have to pack little by little. It'd kill me to pack twenty years in one night after a day at the *hotel*."

She took his hand and led him. His hips scraped against the sharp edges of boxes. "Night, night, honey," she said, tapping the back of his hand with her fingertips as they parted.

"Good night, Momma. When we wake up tomorrow. . . ."

Lone tossed the bundled boots and jacket and cap and pants on the floor. Moonlight came into the room, and the stars were out strong, every one.

Momma had brought her some quilts, and Cassie lay in the big bed, her eyes wide open. But the room no longer existed for her. Stripping to his undershirt and shorts and crawling in under the covers on the cot, Lone wondered what that change did to *him*. She had not destroyed anything with the fire. She had merely transferred it to him, forced it on him.

"I don't *want* to remember," he used to say, and she'd smile. He saw now that she had been *keeping* it all for him, waiting for the day. Every scrap. Now all those scraps had gone up in smoke that drifted down and settled in fine ash on Harmon and Harmon's slag heaps. Maybe that daily effort to keep the past alive in her imagination had stretched the fever over the years. It wasn't for herself that she had written it down. It was a reminder to *him* of what he was doing. All she had needed for herself was to see him walk into the room, carrying the lingering smell of the present—the sharp smell of the motorcycle and the freshness of the wind that filtered into her own hair.

The wind in the buckeye tree moved the moonlight in the room as though a headlight swooped through the window. He had watched that movement all his life, and one dark night Boyd had made it himself. For a moment, he listened for the sound of Boyd's 'cycle. He heard only the echo of lone truck tires in the frost on the highway.

Had she really changed? Was there something in her now that responded to the makeup and the outfit, or were those trappings a way of stirring up a change she desired? No, she was ignorant. She'd heard talk about lovemaking, and she'd read about it, no doubt, but dressing up and putting on lipstick was just disguise so they would let her into the damned world. She didn't know what sex was. Not in her blood. A lack of feeling for it? If what he had heard was true, that sometimes such energy gets drained off somewhere else, then Cassie, he hoped, was dry. But what hurt was that he couldn't be certain. It was horrible, he suddenly realized, to *want* your sister to be that way: hollow inside like a lissome statue, with a smooth place, like marble, between her legs.

The window frosted over. Cassie's eyes were closed. Down on the highway a dog barked, then screamed in agony for five minutes when a truck hit it without braking. Cassie's arm twitched and her bare foot, thrust out over the edge of the bed, jerked at the sound. He sensed that the terror he seemed to swallow in the dark air itself seeped into her, too. He wanted to speak to her, but his heart beat too close to his mouth. As he lay in the moving moonlight with her, the flood of possibilities came over him, of this doomed room as a place where they could begin over.

Chapter

20

LONE OPENED HIS EYES. AN EARTH-MOVER COUGHED IN THE KEEN air. As if on signal, others cranked up. Then he felt a rumble in the cot frame, and the windowpane began to tremble. A thin powder of plaster sifted down from the ceiling. It made a little pile, like sand in an hourglass, on the brass rail of the big bed, but then the bed itself shivered and the dust dripped off as fast as it built up. The covers up to her eyes, Cassie slept soundly.

Then Momma came to wake him.

"Honey, I'm sorry as I can be, but you'll have to wear that motorsickle rig to school. They let you go so sudden, and your other clothes are dirty—not that you got so many decent clothes to start with."

"Today's my last day on that 'sickle, so I mize well get the good out of it and ride over there."

"Oh, bless Jesus, the end of it!"

She went out, and Lone picked up a boot and stared into it. It was as if he had been in the hospital three years and was trying to come back to what he had put down the day he left. Things had changed that wouldn't let him just stroll back in.

The air in the room was chilly on his back, and the floor was cold on his bare feet. He dressed and, pulling the cot over to the window, sat on it, legs crossed, and leaned on the sill, looking out. Working behind and above the house out of sight, the machines were stirring up dust, but he could see that it was a blue haze day. Then as he watched, the haze became the smoke of brush fires. As the machines creaked and roared, he imagined them as giant yellow grasshoppers. Cassie had lain in a bed full of monsters for years. *Maybe these are some kin.*

Pulling back from the sill, he saw marks his elbows had made in the dust. As he backed out of the room slowly, he watched footprints emerge from under his feet. "Cassie?" She didn't stir. He streaked his finger across the boxes in the hall as he passed and wiped the crumbs of dust and dirt on the sides of his corduroys.

Momma put a good breakfast before him. Then she sat down and took a sip of black coffee. "We're *all* gonna be together Sunday," said Lone. "One last time in this house, at this table. Me and you and Cassie and Kyle and Gran'daddy and Coot."

The motors outside were so loud she couldn't hear. He told her again, and she smiled as she had smiled last night in the Gold Sun Café.

He was surprised at how smoothly he was able to return to the motorcycle. To avoid a bulldozer that blocked the path, Lone had to weave among the trees. Going over the swinging bridge, he decided that with the money Gran'daddy would pay him for the motorcycle—for the thrill of wrecking it—he would buy Momma a necklace and Cassie a new dress. In the neat little oasis in the middle of the sprawling junkyard, they would live a few weeks while looking for a new life.

The ruins of the tipple still stood on the leveled slag heap above the river. Where R. L. Luttrell's Commissary had stood under a high oak, the ground was smooth, and signs said DETOUR.

He didn't want to go roaring into the high school parking

lot on the motorcycle. In a place cleared for the new highway, he kicked down the stand.

In his homeroom, P. O. Fletcher read the morning bulletin as though it were a list of duties to be performed during man's last day on earth. Lone stood in the hall outside the open door. Finished, P.O. looked up, saw him, and walking toward him, said, "I thought we got rid a you?"

"Mr. Fletcher, I'd like to talk with you."

"Why aren't you in the reform school?"

"The judge changed his mind."

"We all make mistakes. . . . I see you're still wearing that hoodlum's uniform."

"Well, yes, sir, but my momma didn't have anything fixed so—I almost burnt up it last night. And tonight I'm ridin' that motorsickle into my gran'daddy's junkyard and *walkin'* out. Well, the thing is, I'm—well, beggin' you to let me back in."

"Beggin'? Don't beg," said P.O., caught off balance by Lone's attitude. "Just tell me *why* I should help you, that's all."

"I can still run."

"You *want* a run?"

"Yes, sir."

"Like a bat out a hell?"

"Yes, sir. All I need's a little what you call moral support, I reckon."

"Hell, *I'm* just as moral as the next one." Lone watched a slow smile break on P.O.'s face. "But you've gotta convince Mr. Deaderick that you *have* reformed."

"How about you?"

"All it takes is your word."

"Will *he* take it? 'Cause right this minute that's all I got. Ever'thing else depends on gittin' back in school and startin' fresh."

"Well, you out of shape, boy, or you could offer to run. But if Mr. Deaderick *will* let you back in, it would be a good thing if you started tryin' to catch up on all the time you lost. . . . I'll git somebody on the Bible and the bulletin, and we'll go see Mr. Deaderick." He stepped into his classroom. "Okay, which one a you deadbeats knows how to read?"

The principal listened to Fletcher, rocking in his swivel chair, fingertips pressed together, and then he listened to Lone.

"Even though I finally turned your momma down . . ."

"My momma was here?"

"Yesterday. Didn't she tell you? Hum. . . . Well, maybe she wanted to see what you could do on your own."

"Pardon me, sir," said P.O., "I might also add that Lone's parkin' his motorsickle in the junkyard."

Surprised, Mr. Deaderick stopped rocking and pit-patting his fingertips. "In view of all you've said and the fact that he's abandoning the motorcycle, which seems to be at the heart of the trouble . . ." *Well*, that's *simple enough*, thought Lone. "And also there's the fact that Judge Gentry saw fit to change his decision—I don't see why Lone shouldn't be granted another chance. A kind of reprieve. Welcome back." He offered his hand.

As Lone shook it, Mr. Deaderick said, "Frankly, I hated to see you go. I love to watch you run."

"Let's stop off at the gym," Lone said, as he and P.O. entered the hall.

P.O. held the watch on him, as Lone ran three times around the gym, stripped to his corduroy pants.

"How was it?"

"How did it feel?"

"Awful."

"That's how it looked. You got a lot of catchin' up to do, but it isn't a rat race, Lone, unless you *make* it one. Tomorrow, we'll ease into it. Come spring, you'll sail off like the wind."

Bouncing over the swinging bridge, Lone looked up the hollow over the roof of his house and saw the caterpillars and bulldozers moving the earth. In the hard, cold air, each noise reached him separately, and the barn was so vivid in the light that if he stood still long enough, he could see the grain in the wood.

He rolled the motorcycle between the dust-skinned persimmon trees. Birds sang as though winter weren't threatening to swoop down any minute.

What he was going to tell them was certain to soak up some of the stain he had put on their lives. But as he stumbled in the frozen tire marks, moving toward the house to commit his life into their hands, he felt a sense of loss, and doubt made him shiver. He was going to walk up to a bunch of people and offer each the same gift to answer to different wants.

Pausing, the ball of his foot on the edge of the bottom step, he felt the place all around him, and tried to get some picture on the spur of the moment of what his life had been. When he saw the little swipes of dirty white paint that time had stained green along the bottom boards of the house, the rest of it the gray of old wood that Coot had never painted, he got it. A picture of what "unfinished" meant. And as he raised his foot to climb, he felt joy rise in him at last. The swing hung like something drawn on the wall of a cave in one of the books Cassie burned last night. When he reached for the screen door handle, it would be flat, as though the whole house were a picture on a billboard that would stand long after the last highway had crumbled and run to weeds again. From the porch, he looked down at the obsolete highway—that stretch where he had made time outrun itself—and saw it cracked, crumbled, and crawling with honeysuckle, and he felt the kiss of truth in what Cassie had said and Gran'daddy Stonecipher had echoed: that there's something about junk, and that meant ruin, too, that thrills a body's soul. Then joy stopped in him again, and he felt just like the swing: flat, immobile, hanging high in immortal lines of black and rust-red on the wall of a cave.

He shut the front door on the image outside, and called to Momma, but when she didn't answer, he guessed he'd beat her home. Cassie didn't call to him from the bedroom. Then he realized that what had caused the sense of loss was the absence of the face at the window. The door to the room was shut. Suddenly, he wanted to go in and root through those piles of boxes of hers and read some of that stuff she had written in the margins of magazines she'd found in empty houses or spilled around trash cans in the alleys of Harmon. He wanted to see himself through her eyes, as he had the day he just happened to pick up her Tarzan nickel notebook.

But as he opened the door, he remembered the smell of burning magazines on the wind in the raw night air, then saw the bare room and her: lying in the bed, covered up to her eyes, her flat, thin body lost in the shape of the mattress under the quilts. Her eyes were on him, but she didn't blink. The shades were drawn on Harmon and the grate was gray with ashes that had turned to powder. Under the quilts, her foot jerked the least bit. Standing in the doorway, he looked down into her trance-like gaze. Months ago, it wouldn't have thrown him. Somewhere way down in a cold well, her mind was full of pictures, some frozen, like photographs or paintings or sculpture, some moving. She was feeding on the whole oncoming swarm of them, like a fevered and famished animal devouring carrion left by a hunter who kills for sport: himself, framed in the door.

His hands in his pockets, his feet ice-cold, he sat on the edge of the cot and watched his breath become smoke in the cold room. Then he went to the kitchen and brought back some newspapers, kindling, coal, and kerosene, and got a fire roaring in the grate to thaw them out: Cassie down in the well, himself on the cot. Raising the shade, he let the afternoon light in. He wanted her to rise to the top, underground water in her eyes.

But when she turned over enough to make the springs cry, the look he turned to shocked him: for the first time in his life hate showed in Cassie's eyes.

"What time is it? What day? What country? What a goddamn stupid way to live."

"Honey. . . . Honey, let's have *one* day. At least one day, all of us together, before this house comes down."

"I burnt the heart out of it last night."

"That had nothing to do with it."

"You always promised me. We'd ride to Gran'paw Mc-Daniel's at least. But I never got to ride it two feet."

He blinked, hung his head, and gazed into the fire, realizing that she had discovered that the well was dry. If *he* didn't replenish it, somebody else would. He poked the fire and stared deep into it, until the skin of soot fluttered in the down-draft, and he couldn't feel the hole she was burning into his back. He hoped that someday she would see that he was not betraying her. That, like everything else she could see at a glance, would dawn on her someday. He listened to the coal gondolas jointing up down in the yards, until he was unable to bear the strain of Cassie's silence on his nerves. Walking out, avoiding her eyes, he thought, *Maybe it's too long overdue. Easter in October.*

Lone went into Momma's bedroom where the hawk spread its wings on the bed. He felt Momma's presence more in her empty bedroom—though it was now more crowded with boxes than Cassie's had ever been—than when she stood before him, her large brown eyes gazing somewhere over his shoulder. And he used to wonder what she gazed at. Now he knew. A picture of the future, which now was possible.

Hearing something stir in the attic, Lone went into the hall, squeezing through more stacked boxes, and climbed the narrow stairs to talk to Coot. Claws scurried away as he reached the top. A litter of blue fruit jars, whiskey bottles without labels, Krispy Kreme doughnut boxes, old bologna rinds, apple cores. On the army cot were a few messy blankets and one filthy sock like something twisted in agony at the head. Coot's shotgun leaned against the cot.

Something that felt like a book was wrapped in a tow sack under the cot. Lone sat down and reached inside the sack. Through slivers of space in the roof a little light fell on a Bible with cherrywood covers, the thick pages bound with leather thongs. It was heavy. Printed in Glasgow, Scotland, in 1706. Trembling, hardly able to keep it on his knees, he opened it at the family record, starting in 1710 in Scotland.

He had seen it once before, when he was too little to understand that the smell, the thing that lingered, wasn't important. It

was like coming across a picture of himself he never knew
existed but that someone had treasured for years. In a way, he
felt like an intruder. But he had come onto something that
seemed to have been denied him. He read the names, the births,
the marriages, the deaths. In the different handwritings, the
different colors of ink and shades of pencil, they said more than
if the whole book were about the people named. Then what hit
him was that, in a way, it *was* all about *them*, because to them, it
was their book. Where was *his* book? Where was Cassie's and
Boyd's and Harmon's and Lone's book?

He opened it at random and read:

And God remembered Noah, and every living thing, and all
the cattle that was with him in the ark: and God made a
wind to pass over the earth, and the waters assuaged. The
fountains also of the deep, and the windows of heaven were
stopped, and the rain from heaven was restrained; And the
waters returned from off the earth continually: and after
the end of the hundred and fifty days the waters were
abated.

"My daddy used to say," Coot had once told Lone, "that a
man could come to the Bible in any trouble, open it any place,
and there where his eyes fell, he would find counsel, peace, and
understandin'." Lone could imagine, since he wanted to believe
Gran'paw, that if he studied and studied about Noah and the
rain from heaven, he would find some meaning in it for himself.
But he didn't have time. He didn't have time to sit there in the
pale light and worry about the rain.

He looked at the shotgun that leaned against the cot.
Remembering Kyle's revolver on the windowsill, he began to
sweat and feel sick. Another gun laid casually aside, waiting for
someone to pick it up.

When he left the Cove in Black Mountain, knowing he
wouldn't be allowed to come back, Coot had taken the Bible.
Lone opened the cherrywood covers and read the names and
dates and places again. Back and on back through the genera-

tions in Greenock, Scotland, to 1710. Sometime, in a better light, he would decipher *all* the names. He wrapped it back as he had found it and shoved it under the bed.

He wandered up to the barn, as though it were natural to stroll up there in the evening. Wind had shattered the willow. The plow, cut down, lay across the path with its sharp nose pointed toward the highway. Stepping over it, he remembered Coot's spell of optimism when he roped it clear of the ground to keep it from rusting rotten since it was already rusted badly. The silo was gone.

He turned and looked down over Harmon. The aroma of burning leaves, coal and slag and trees hung on the air. He felt like a child, his head light, but the ache of nostalgia was in his chest. The leaves burned everywhere below and in the gutters and on the hillsides that afternoon when he was eleven, the first fall after Virgil freed him of the bed, when he realized for the first time that he, like people he had heard about, would have to die. In the chill of the October afternoon now, Lone was aware of two selves—one innocent, the other corrupt, one living the past, the other breathing fitfully in the present. The two blending. Becoming confused.

In the barn, the smell of whiskey and filth was thick. He hadn't walked in there since spring. In a corner of one of the stalls the statue of Jesus that Cassie had salvaged from Gran'daddy Stonecipher's junkyard lay, the face sunk in the soft ground, dry pigeon droppings all over the shoulders. Safe in a cell brimming with filth lay Coot, the hounds asleep around him. With the noise of the bulldozer behind the barn, Lone's footsteps didn't stir them.

Then his father opened his eyes.

"Set with us, Lone, and be real quiet and be real still, and won't nobody even know we're alive."

The book of Genesis. Did a man have to go back that far? Lone didn't know. He was just asking himself, with his father in a drunken stupor at his feet and Jesus' face toward the ground behind him in the corner of the next stall.

"Better lay low. Them clouds festerin' up for a snowstorm," muttered Coot, and passed out, just as one hound opened the eye above his paw. Lone didn't move. The hound's eye shut, as if on a dream image.

"See you after while, Coot . . ." said Lone, backing off.

Running down the path toward the motorcycle, Lone said aloud, "I'll junk the motorsickle, and I'll surprise Cassie with the dress, and tomorrow. . . ."

CHAPTER

21

CROSSING THE SWINGING BRIDGE, LONE PASSED BOYD IN A SPACE SO cramped their elbows struck. As he sped down the highway, Lone caught Boyd in the rearview mirror, turning around at the other end of the bridge. Lone slowed down to let him catch up.

Boyd followed a few feet behind as Lone wove in and out of the traffic through downtown Harmon past the Gold Sun Café, the Majestic Theater, the jail, the hotel.

The gates to Gran'daddy Stonecipher's junkyard were locked. Smoke poured out of the chimney of his house.

"What happened to La Grange, good buddy?"

Lone climbed over the top of the gate, not answering.

Under one window, where Gran'daddy still let the Gold Star Mother banner hang beside the ice card, a striped cat was curled up on a green cushion in the corner of a white glider. A wooden woodpecker hung beside the door, over a place for notes if nobody was home. Lone wrote: "It's later than you think, but not *too* late. Love, Lone." Then he used the wood-pecker on Gran'daddy Stonecipher. Listening to his rumbling charge through the house from far in the back, muffled by closed doors that clashed open, Lone waited for him to appear at the oval window of the door, the beard of lace sagging, as it always had, off its tacks. The sun about to sink below the hills hit Gran'daddy full in the face, forcing him to make horse blinders with his hands. Gran'daddy got him in focus just when Lone grinned. As Gran'daddy opened the door, wearing his coveralls, Lone gave the glider and the cat a swing, causing a creak that Boyd might have heard all the way to the gate.

"You excape?"

"Remember what you said?"

"It's a Christian's dinnertime. Mine's pipin' hot on the table, waiting."

"You said you'd git me, you'd have to haul me in off the side a the highway. Well, if you can call this junkyard a highway. . . ."

Gran'daddy opened the screen to see Lone better. Then he looked down the path through the junk where Boyd's and Lone's motorcycles were parked outside the gate, by a fireplug sunk in the weeds. "That Boyd waitin' to laugh at a boy that would drag his Gran'daddy away from the supper table to play a joke on him?"

"You come on out, and in less than three minutes, I'll be beggin' a cup of coffee off you."

He looked straight at Gran'daddy, and despite the light behind Lone, Gran'daddy began to see the way Lone looked. "What's come over you?"

"*You*. All of you. . . . I come to give myself up. I'm startin' with you, Gran'daddy."

It had been so long since he had heard Lone use that tone with him that Gran'daddy stroked the screen door.

"You git yourself in here and let me pour you a cup of coffee and tell me what—"

"Nothin' to tell, Gran'daddy. I'm turnin' the blamed thing over to you. You lead the way."

Gran'daddy came out, and the sunlight hit him full in the face again. "Hadn't you better put on a jacket?"

"A sight like that'll warm me aplenty. After Virgil, I'd about give up."

"Unlock the gate and let him in. I want him to see me do it."

"*Do it?*"

"Please. . . ."

Gran'daddy went ahead of Lone, unlocked the gate, and, with a mock welcome, waved Boyd in. Boyd pushed his 'cycle into the junkyard, as though that was what the occasion, whatever it would prove to be, called for. The only sound was the one Lone made as he walked out the gate past him and started up his motorcycle.

Lone pulled up directly under the crane. The hook knocked his cap off as he swung down. Boyd stood off to the side, trying not to believe what he was watching. Gran'daddy stood in front of the block-long stack of old batteries, amazed, his arms dangling at his sides.

Lone felt them watch him snag the hook in the spokes. No one said a word. Then he got up in the cab of the crane. For a moment, there was only the sound of a flock of starlings passing over, then the motor.

The crane lifted the red motorcycle off the ground, the tires dripping dust. Suddenly Boyd began to cheer. Even through the glass of the cab, bleared like goggles, he saw that Boyd didn't realize what he was doing, that at first he was dubious and now he was certain: Lone was just joking, and Boyd thought it was damned funny and deserved a cheer.

Lone dropped the motorcycle on a bread truck, getting it right the first try. Something sparked it, and smoke, then fire, rose from the heap.

Lone shut off the motor and got down from the cab and looked at him, but Gran'daddy didn't budge, leaning against the batteries, stacked three times his own height, watching it burn, the light licking up his chest and over his face.

"Gran'daddy, let's have a cup of coffee and set by the window while we watch it burn." Lone put his arm around his grandfather's shoulders, and they turned their backs on Boyd and started up the path toward the house. He turned for a moment to catch the look on Boyd's face, but Boyd had turned toward his own motorcycle.

Lone saw Virgil's white Cadillac convertible, the wheels stripped off, the hood up where somebody had been at the usable parts. "That Boyd," said Gran'daddy, "keeps after me to sell it to him."

As Lone and Gran'daddy reached the porch, the motorcycle gas tank exploded. Flames shooshed up, curled above the pile of truck tires. A ball of black smoke thinned.

During the two hours with Gran'daddy, Lone began to feel that his life was, as he intended, going to be different. Walking home, he knew that the life he had lived with Boyd had ended the life he had lived before Boyd appeared on the path, riding that black 'cycle. As he strolled across the bridge, carrying presents for Momma and Cassie, he saw Boyd on his motorcycle go through the arch of vines that led to his shack, with what looked at a hazy distance like the butt end of a sandwich in his mouth.

When Lone opened the door, Cassie was sitting on the edge of the big bed, wearing only a pair of red panties and Gypsy's blue blouse, unbuttoned, both too large for her, the mauve nightgown tangled at her feet.

"I got a present for you, Cassie—new dress, and Momma a necklace."

Her eyes blazing at him, Cassie said, "Goddamn you."

She bumped against him as she walked swiftly to the cot, and when he turned, he saw Gypsy sitting there. Cassie grabbed something in a paper bag from the foot of the cot and ran out of the room, slamming the door.

"I'm tickled to death to see you again, Lone."

"What did you tell Cassie?"

"What Boyd just told *me*. That you just got done murderin' your poor ol' motorsickle."

"What *you* doin' around Cassie?"

"She's my buddy. Just like Boyd's *your* buddy. Or *was*. He won't be, after we tell him."

"Tell him what?"

Gypsy stood up and looped her arms around his neck. "That, by God, me and you're going before the justice."

She sat on the big bed and opened her arms. He let her hug him around the waist. The smell of her blue dress and of her flesh, freshened by the cool night air, made him ache for the scent between her breasts. She took his hand and placed it under one of them. He gripped the bone of her hip tightly to keep his other hand from moving down to the moistness between her legs.

"Not in this room, honey." He went over and sat on the cot and pulled the shade. "What did you want to tell me?"

"Lone, why're you like this?"

"Like what?"

She sighed, annoyed. "Is it that old purity idea?"

"I guess so."

"It's not fair."

"What's not?"

"They's nothin' wrong with me, but I'm still not a angel." She pulled the light string and walked over to him. He heard her undoing the buttons that ran from her throat to the hem of her dress.

"Gypsy, would it hurt your feelin's if I said I'd rather not see you for a while? I mean until I git things—?"

"Hurt my feelin's? Oh, no. I'd just love it." She stopped unbuttoning the dress.

"Just for a while . . ."

"I'm gonna be your wife and have your kids, ain't I?"

"Listen, you saw what Uncle Virgil did, didn't you? Before he—"

"I *felt* it. I didn't *see any*thing."

"That's what I want to do. Bring people into harmony."

"Be a preacher?"

"One way or another. I don't know. But I gotta finish school at least, and might even go to college, if I can. Virgil wanted me to have it all backin' me up. And I owe things to my family—I owe them time and consideration and—I've worried my mother long enough."

"What's so special about your mother?"

"Watch it, Gypsy . . ."

"You talk allatime about how pure *I* am. She any purer than me?"

"What you mean?"

"Nothin', honey. I guess I'm just tryin' to be mean. I'm selfish. I want you to put it in me, right now. Quick!" He heard and felt her spread the wings of her dress. "I slipped my panties off before you got here." The tone of her voice was like flesh, and he felt it on his cheek, the curve of her hip hard against his shoulder, as she sat down. "Lone, just put your head on my belly." He knelt and laid his head on her stomach, one hand on her knee, the other on her breast. "Play like you got your head on a train rail." He chuckled and dipped his tongue into her navel. "Hear anything comin'?" He thought she was being silly until he heard her take in her breath and felt a slight shudder in her body. As he lifted his head, coal gondolas coupled and creaked down in the yards. "I should a had the rag on two weeks ago."

The dark pulsed black before his eyes. She reached for his hand and held it very softly in her warm lap. For a moment, he saw the creek by the church where he had cleansed himself of her a month ago and where Virgil had baptized him when he was eleven, and he felt an impulse to sink himself and his new hopes into it.

Lone got up and walked around the room, going up against the wall and pushing himself off with his hands and his shoulders, as he had moved after lights out in his cell. "Goddamn!" She lay still, silent about five minutes, and he sensed her listening to him move in the dark. "Goddamn!" A coal truck slammed on its brakes down on the highway and screeched. Lone imagined the long black tire mark. Then the truck horn, deep and long, and a few barps of cars. "Blow, damn you, blow!"

"Lone?" He let her be afraid. "Lone?" She sucked in her

breath, shuddering again, sitting on the edge of the cot. Trembling, he too shuddered when he breathed, aching in the dark alone, aching with regret. "Lone, is it all right? Is it all right?" she whimpered, reaching for him in the dark. "Lone, what's the matter? Say somethin' to me."

"That one night with you, that first night when I got my gun, I blew my brains out!" He was sorry even as he said it. He hugged her and let her rub against his body as she stood up.

"Oh, Lone, don't worry, honey. You'll make a good father. You don't *have* to go to college. You can git work, and preach different places on Sundays. Round *here* they's a lot of men like that. Let's find some place now, where we can do it. Up in the barn."

"No. Let's wait till we git married, Gypsy."

"Oh, shut up, shut up! I want you, I need you, Lone. Now. Tonight. I'm not a damned virgin. I won't keep."

Her wetness soaked through his pants and turned cold on his leg. He tried to hug her, to make her be still, but she kept at him, trying to get his pants unzipped, making it worse, until he retched at her touch. The thought that he had put a living creature in her without loving her suddenly hit him. Horrified and afraid, he opened his mouth and tightened the muscles in his throat to keep from screaming. He had to stop her, he wanted to hit her, hard, slap her until she wouldn't even want to touch him, but slowly she quieted down and sat on the cot and lay back, her hand pulling hard at his pants pocket.

Maybe if he were married to her he could do it and not have the painful pounding of blood against his forehead, and the way she acted would not disgust and burn him in the same breath.

"Button your dress."

"You want a git married?"

"You sure you're—"

"I can really have you, Lone. The way I want you. You're all bound up by somethin', this idea you got in your head, I reckon, but —"

"It's not just in my head. If it was, I could explain—"

"Well, wherever it is. But after we're good and married, you'll be okay. Will you kiss me, at least?"

Lone kissed her a long time and her hands went all over him. When she hovered over him, her black hair brushed his cheeks like cobwebs.

"In a way, I'm glad."

"About what?"

"That you're that way about it. Puttin' so much weight on marriage first—on the ring. And I'll bet carryin' me over the threshold will be the thing that will really cut it loose in you."

"It's more than that."

"We're different from Boyd. I loved runnin' around with him, but I know where girls like that end up."

"Button your dress before we git started agin."

"Once is enough."

"Once what?"

"I already come."

"How?"

"Rubbin' up against you. Sometimes it happens just when I'm ridin' behind Boyd on the 'sickle." He heard her buttoning her dress, her elbows buffeting his arm as she moved. "You know, Lone, I been thinkin' about havin' this baby, and sometimes I wake up scared in the night and I go in the bathroom and turn on the light and lock the door and read the Gospel of St. John. Ever read it?"

"Yeah."

"It comforts me. Your Uncle Virgil's words didn't fall on deaf ears." She pulled the light string. "It's wonderful to be alive tonight, Lone. To know that 'fore too long I'll be Mrs. Wayne McDaniel, with a baby in my belly, and you the way you ought to be in bed." She squeezed his hand. "I *am* glad you're so odd, Lone. Know how it makes me feel?"

"How?"

She stood up and did a little turning dance and kicked her leg into the air as she grabbed the rail of the brass bed. "Just like I really was a virgin."

"Listen, honey, you better go on 'fore Momma gets home. She's way late as it is."

"Well, when the hell you gonna *tell* her 'bout us?"

"Okay, tonight, but right now—"

"Then why not let both of us be here?"

"If she caught us by ourselves in the house, she'd wonder . . ."

"Oh, hell. Okay. You tell *her*, and I'll tell Boyd." She stopped in the doorway. "He might come lookin' for you."

"Nobody would blame him, if he did."

She looked at him as though she couldn't begin to understand how he felt about *any*thing. Then she went out the front door.

"Cassie. Come and look at your new dress, honey." Lone listened to the silence. He went down the hall to the kitchen. In the center of the round table sat a jar of peanut butter with a table knife sticking up out of it.

Momma's room was freezing cold. A little bottle of fingernail polish had spilled and hardened on the cracked-veneer face of the chest of drawers. The hard smell of ether, as in an operating room. On her bed lay a wadded paper bag.

Lone smelled Coot's hounds in the hallway, and heard Coot's voice raving. "Lone! Lone! Where the hell are you, boy? You mangy bitches, git up and go find Lone! Bring him back, drag him back! I want a see my boy. They got him locked up, a hundred feet below ground."

The hounds began to bark and growl. Lone rehearsed what he would say: "Now, Coot, tonight I want you all to be here in one room, together, sober, because it's all come true." He would worry about Gypsy tomorrow. But as he turned to go into the hall, he glanced out Momma's window and saw Gypsy crossing the swinging bridge with her arm around some girl's shoulder. The girl wore Gypsy's blue blouse and yellow slacks. Lone opened the paper bag and Gypsy's perfume made him catch his breath.

"He told me, Lone. He leaned right at the foot of that bed

and laughed at me, the cocky little son of a bitch!" Coot's tone suggested that he didn't know Lone was in the house. "All right, Charlotte, all right, don't try to lie out of it! 'Down in the valley, the valley so low, Hang your head over, hear the wind blow. . . .' No more, no more, bitch! That's all she wrote, good God, ain't it now?"

Lone crossed the hall. Blood jumped in one eyelid and his heart pumped hard. He stood in the doorway to his bedroom. Afraid to move.

CHAPTER

22

COOT SAT ON LONE'S COT, THE THREE HOUNDS CURLED AROUND him. Between his feet sat a blue Mason jar, empty, and a bottle of whiskey, the seal unbroken, and between his legs was the shotgun, the two black eyes staring up into his face as though pleading. "We see eye to eye, we know a thing or two, don't we? Virgil done the only thing a man *can* do, but I ain't got the guts even for that."

Seeing Lone, the dogs began to growl.

"What you mumblin' about, Coot, what you sayin' about Momma?"

"Shut up, you mangy bitches!" Coot kicked at the hounds. "I God, Lone, I just want you to tell me one thing, son."

"You seen Momma?"

"Stand still, boy, I got somethin' to ask you."

"Momma ought a be home by now. After dark . . ."

"To hell with your momma!"

"You better watch it, Coot!"

"This is your daddy talkin' to you, boy, and I want you to answer me."

"I sure don't want to fight with you tonight, Coot."

"Lone, no lie now. . . . Did my daddy forgive me? Huh? Huh? Say!"

"I told you . . ."

"Tell the truth!"

"He did, he did, Coot."

"And that's the God's truth?"

"Yes." *Is a lie the only thing I can give him?*

"That's all, that's all we need to know. You see this room?"

"Yeah. I see it."

"How would you like to shut the door on it—walk away—never come back?"

"It'll be *c*emented over by next month."

"Listen, Lone, what I'm tryin' to say is, let's you and me hit that trail to Black Mountain, tonight, right now, without nothin' but the clothes on our backs."

"Don't tempt me, Coot. I cain't just walk away. Why don't you go on by yourself and see. Gran'paw might not even be alive after all this time."

Coot backed off from the possibility. "You *want* me to go?"

"Ain't you dyin' to? Finally?"

"I hardly know whether a man can go back that far, son. Hit seems like a dream—the kind a sober man that had nothing weighin' on his soul might dream with the hope of bein' able to go back where he left off. I would die peaceful on Black Mountain, but. . . ." Afraid he'd say the wrong thing, Lone let him think and see and feel the altitude. "You want me to go, Lone, and leave you to them?"

"No, but I cain't go now. I got things to do *here*."

"Well, I god, now, Lone, well, I god. . . ." The shotgun still in both his hands, his head dipping down to it and raring back from it, he rocked, back and forth on the cot as if it would take him to Black Mountain. "But I'm a-beggin' you to go with me." He looked up at Lone, on his face a scared look, as though he were about to do something that would horrify the whole county. Not scared for himself. Terrified of something he saw happening inside his head.

"I owe it to her to stay and *be* somebody."

"You owe it to your momma! Well, I'll be damned. Set down, Lone. I got somethin' to tell you about your angel of a momma."

"Don't you trifle with me, Coot. I heard you growlin' about somethin' a while ago. Don't pile more meanness on top of the misery you've done caused already."

"You don't have to worry no more about the meanness in me, Lone. For I'm pullin' out. I'm goin' home, son. Me and my daddy's gonna bring back the *old* times together. When I'm done tellin' it, you *stay* with your momma, if you want to. Now set on the bed and listen."

"All right, just for a few d'recklies." Lone sat on the big bed.

"You just don't know, Lone." He sounded almost sober. "You *never* knowed. I should a knowed it when she caught me lookin' up her dress at the Gold Sun Café and give me that look. Listen, I took that woman up the mountain to the Cove, where God started when he *made* the world. But no, but no, she had to have more'n nasty ol' beauty all around her, had to have soot and *ce*ment and— And even when she runned off, didn't I take her back? Watched her go down on her knees in the Square and confess to the Lord how she laid out with that barker from the carnival, and . . ."

"Just stop right there, Coot. I ain't about to listen . . ."

"Don't you come in here and throw up her purity in my face after what Boyd told me . . ."

"*What* did Boyd tell you?"

"Just set still. . . . So her soul was warshed pure. And you didn't know you had a brother, did you? I named it after me to show her I forgive her. But the Lord brought down on your momma the punishment he saves for women like her. Your brother's buried in the Cove. I said, 'We'll start fresh,' cause I loved her. Then *you* come; you was the new start. But them dogs'll testify she turned black as soot as the years trudged by. And now—and now . . ."

"Don't tell me no lies, Coot! Don't stir me up over nothin'."

"That bed you settin' on, in this room that you love so much. Your momma was borned in it. Your Uncle Virgil was borned in it and laid down on it to shoot hisself. And when your great-grandmother Stonecipher died, she give it to us, and you and your sister was borned in it—that weren't the first bloody mattress it's knowed—and Cassie's spent half her life right there." He waited a long time, swaying on the edge of the cot, the two black eyes of the shotgun swaying with him, the jar slopping over on his bare feet. "We see eye to eye—we know a thing or two, don't we?" he said, staring into the barrel. "More than you, you mangy bitches!" The dogs got up and stood still. The stillness of a photograph. Coot got still as though he were in a photograph in an old, yellowed detective magazine, transfixed in time and space. His head down, he stared into the barrels of the shotgun: "Look into your eyes and I see Cassie, and Charlotte, and me, and Lone, all of us—shot to hell. Now, Lone, you tell me what kind of a mother would lay down on that bed and fuck Boyd Weaver?" Saliva dropped from the dogs' mouths as slow as mercury upon the bare floor where the fumes from the empty blue Mason jar rose.

Lone jerked the shotgun from between Coot's legs and aimed the two black holes into his face. "I'll shoot your damn head off!"

"Pull it, Lone, good God, I'd just as soon. . . . I won't testify against you. Except to say you *aimed* it the wrong way. While ago, I pulled it myself. Empty. But it's live now."

"Don't—don't—please, Coot, don't tell me that!"

"Ain't it all your fault, didn't you bring it all on, Lone? You and your buddy, Boyd? He delivered me some bottle whiskey up in the attic where I'uz finishin' this jar a rotgut, and he said, 'Keep your money, your wife's done paid for it in trade.' And in a few minutes I heard him talkin' to Cassie, and I come down, and Cassie was at the kitchen table, fixin' that son of a bitch a peanut-butter sandwich, and I come on in *here*, and

Boyd follered me in and said, 'Right there, Coot, in Cassie's bed. It's been a whorehouse from the start.'

"Lone, I ain't got the guts God give a flea. So pull—hit's way past the goddamn deadline. . . . Break this bottle open, Lone. Hit's paid for. Boyd'd love to see me and you drink it down together, and stagger off the swingin' bridge into the river."

Lone lowered the shotgun, and stood statue-still as Coot rose from the chair.

"I gotta—go see my daddy. . . . He's lookin' out the winder down the path, lookin' out to see me coming up along the creek. He's gittin' old." He took the shotgun gently from Lone's hand and started out. "He needs me. Needs his boy to help him git in the crops. Hit's cold. Got a long way to walk. Hit's gonna come one long, stickin' snowstorm. . . . Cassie! Come in h'yere, honey! . . . Where's Cassie?"

"Gone."

"Wanted to hug her 'bye."

Coot's voice was low and warm and good. "Lone, I god, son, I god. . . ." He let Coot hug him. "I hate to go and not say good-bye to Cassie. . . . But once I git up yonder and git back in good with Daddy, I'll write, and then I'll look for you and her to come up the path, and then all these years'll be over." Coot went out, the dogs following him.

Lone reached down, picked up the whiskey bottle, broke the seal, and took a long drink. It had the effect he craved.

Letting the whiskey soak into him, Lone stood awhile in the middle of the room, the emptiness making it seem bright, then he went out.

As he ran down the path, the speed of the plunge was strange on foot. At the arch of kudzu vines, he picked up some rocks and threw them against Boyd's shack, but he didn't come out, and his motorcycle was nowhere in sight. On the swinging bridge, Lone looked out over Harmon, scanned the streets on the hillside for a sign of Boyd's 'cycle. In the middle of the bridge, he stopped, and, feeling the sway of the boards under his feet, listened for the sound of Boyd's motor, knowing he could recognize it in the general roar of traffic. Below, on the railroad tracks, Coot had struck up a steady walk, the hounds trotting behind him. Up and down the banks, scrawny sycamores still bent under the weight of the vines, though the heavy, lush leaves had shriveled. As if casting them off his own body, Lone thrashed the air with his arms, began to run again, and the swinging, swaying motion of the bridge catapulted him into the highway where the pounding of his own feet on the pavement made him aware of his body and its speed, and, with a coal truck blaring its horn behind him, flooding him with its lights, he felt free, even though he was looking for trouble.

CHAPTER

23

PASSING LONE ON THE HIGHWAY, THREE EMPTY TRUCKS STIRRED A wind that chilled him. He closed his eyes tightly against the whirling coal dust. When he opened his eyes, a light suddenly flashed out of the dark hillside where the coal tipple hideout once stood. Turning off the highway, he walked over the plank bridge and up onto the slag heap to the area the blast had cleared.

Boyd revved his motorcycle as he swung around the clearing, the headlight swooping over the charred frame of the tipple. The blast had blown the wall planks off the frame and shattered the ramp and wrapped a sheet of corrugated roofing around a little sycamore tree fifty feet away. The headlight stopped when it caught Lone, blinding him. The light followed him in a half-arc as he tried to circle around behind the motorcycle.

Lone almost tripped on an empty beer can. The light flashed off several other cans. He couldn't see who sat on Boyd's buddy seat, making him look humpbacked in the dark. Nobody else stood nearby, unless Cassie was hiding behind the sycamore. But then the figure behind Boyd leaned back, one hand holding onto Boyd's jacket, the other holding a can of beer, and Lone saw Cassie's long blond hair as she threw back her head to drink.

"Cassie, I told you, damn it, I ain't gonna let the filth of Harmon rub off on my sister!"

Boyd turned his 'cycle around, and the headlights glared at Lone. A grin cocked off to one side of his face, he half-saluted Lone. "Well, if it ain't our little brother the firebug. You ain't gittin' near *my* 'sickle, son. You a damn dangerous character."

Cassie held onto a strap on Boyd's jacket as Lone knocked the beer can from her hand and pulled on her arm. "Git home!"

"What home? It'll be just like this tipple tomorrow."

"Turn her loose, Boyd!"

Boyd raised his arms. "I ain't touched her, son!"

"Who you think made me want to *be* out in this goddamn world?" Cassie broke loose and hugged Boyd's waist with both arms, and beer foam from her lip streaked his jacket.

"Shut up! If I told you what's happened, you'd never want to see his face again! Shut off that damned motor, Boyd!"

"Sorry, Lone! The shutoff's out of commission!"

"Git home, Cassie! Please, honey, I don't want you here when I ask him!"

"Ask him what?"

"You stold my girl off me, Lone, so I got room for my little sister now."

Lone pulled at her narrow waist, but she clung to Boyd's back. He dug his fingers into her hair and pulled until she screamed.

"Go on, Cassie!" Boyd turned his head and yelled at her over his shoulder. "Me and Lone's got some things to talk over! Brother to brother!"

"Shut off the damn motor, Boyd!"

"When you burnt your motorsickle," Cassie yelled, as Lone relaxed his grip on her hair, "you burnt the last bridge between me and you, Lone! You gotta suffer for that! You promised me all summer, and then you burnt it up! Out of pure meanness! Goddamn! Let loose a my hair!"

"Git off, Cassie!" yelled Boyd. Cassie turned loose of Boyd's waist and Lone pulled her off the buddy seat. "We'll ride tomorrow night!" Boyd pulled off his goggles, and Cassie broke free of Lone's grip and caught them. "Just you and me!"

"Give him back his damn goggles!" Cassie didn't hear Lone as Boyd revved his motor, deliberately trying to drown him out. But she saw him coming toward her and turned and ran out of the light and into a thicket of little trees on the bank of the railroad.

"I like a little sister that'll mind!" Smoke from his cigarillo moving to a standstill in front of his face, Boyd sat in the saddle, one hand poised on the rearview mirror, the other shoved cockily into his back pocket.

"I just want to ask you one thing, Boyd!" Boyd revved the motor. "Cut that damn motor!"

"I *love* the sound of a motorsickle, son! If *you* don't like it, you can kiss ass!" Taking the cigarillo out of his mouth, he spat between his teeth, raking his crotch with his other hand.

"Boyd, I got somethin' to ask you!"

"Louder! I cain't hear you!"

"Coot told me somethin' tonight, and—"

"You gonna have to scream it, son!"

Trying to drown the sound of the motor, Lone screamed painfully, "Have you been near my mother, Boyd?"

Boyd spewed smoke out his nose and mouth, letting the motor idle. "Near as you can git without bein' a baby inside her!"

"You lyin' son of a whorin' bitch!" Aiming under his eye, Lone rammed his fist into Boyd's face and jumped over the rear wheel before the motorcycle had finished falling on top of him. One leg free, Boyd kicked the motorcycle off him and struggled out from under Lone. As they rose, Boyd caught Lone in a bear hug. Clutched together, they fell and rolled in the mud and coal dust, rocks and chunks of charred wood cutting into Lone's legs and back. He flailed Boyd's ribs with his fists until the strong arms relaxed, sloughed away from him. Lone jumped up, and Boyd rolled and sprang to his feet.

In a dancing, circling pause, they stared at each other, waiting for a chance to lunge, the motor sputtering fitfully.

"How was it in jail, Lone? Did the rats cuddle up to you? Did the cockroaches nibble at your ears? How's that Harmon County cornbread?" The motor coughed and stopped. The headlight shot at a low angle across the clearing, seeming to be the source of silence as well as light on the hillside. "Did you ever find out who it was sicked the cops on you, Lone?" Boyd whispered, his face in the light now, but his voice so low Lone read his lips.

Swinging, Lone ran at Boyd. Black, then flashes of red burst in his head, and he felt Boyd's knee jab his crotch, but he staggered a few moments before the nausea doubled him up and he fell to his knees.

"No need to go to your knees to ask forgiveness, son, 'cause it was me sicked Gypsy on you in the first place. I talked her into lettin' you have a little, and she done it for a joke. Then the little bitch comes here and tells me she's goin' to marry you. But we was gittin' it all the time."

The ground heaved and sank and turned and seemed to slur like a fast merry-go-round. Lone tasted coal dust and felt rocks against his cheekbone.

"Ever' time you all went to that silo, with that silly-ass X mark on your boot, I watched you all. Best show ever I saw. 'Oh, Gypsy, always be pure and good and don't never leave me!'"

Lone rolled over on his back. Boyd stood over him, his face in a darkness streaked red by the ringing shock the blow caused in his head. Lone thought the snow falling behind Boyd was in his own head, then he felt it on his lips and his eyelids.

"You only got it off her once, and even then she had to put it in for you, and I was 'bout to die laughin'. Then me and her got it that same night after you took her home, in that same damned silo. She says it made you feel guilty, double-crossin' your ol' buddy. Son, you just too delicate to *live* in this world. You need somebody to put you out a your misery."

Lone didn't see Boyd's boot coming at him.

"If you live to marry the little whore, I'll let you name the kid after ol' Boyd. And couldn't nobody be a better choice for the best man than me, since the kid she's carryin' right now is mine."

Lone got to his knees again and finally to his feet and staggered in the light that shot up from Boyd's fallen motorcycle, glaring on the leather and nickel trimmings of Boyd's jacket, making the snow flit like moths.

"And maybe I'll sometime even cut that holy little sister of yours, too. But the ol'-timey way to do is to ask somebody's permission."

"You're not fit—"

"Shut up till I'm done askin'. Sir, I would like your goddamn permission," said Boyd, taking off his hat, holding it over his heart, "to marry your sister."

"You're not fit to even look at—"

"Ever' dog must have his day, and mine's overdue. Git over here in the light where I can see you!" Boyd lifted the motorcycle, kicked down the stand, and turned the handlebars, aiming the light directly into Lone's eyes. Lone saw Boyd as a shape of black in the dark behind a burst of light. "Because I'm gonna marry that girl. Too bad you ain't man enough to stop me."

Lone picked up a can of pineapple that they had looted from the commissary. It bounced off the handlebars. Through his tears he saw blood on the coal dust and glass and rocks and the thin layer of snow. He saw a flash of white. Then Boyd jerked him backward by his neck. On his stomach in the dirt again, he felt Boyd's knee in his back, and the silk scarf around his neck pulled his head back.

When Boyd relaxed his grip a little, Lone said, "If you ever *touch* her"—he spat blood into the coal dust—"I'll jump you with a knife, Boyd."

"Don't hurt to try, little brother. 'Cause you *are* gonna be my little brother." He put his mouth close to Lone's ear, jerking on the scarf. "Listen, damn you, I *like* Cassie. That's the best I can do, and I'm stickin' to it. I want to see her git well and give her some kind a life out in the open, even if I have to play like she's just a kid that craves ridin'. It could a been *you* takin' her for her first ride. It ain't that she didn't beg."

Lone heard trucks on the highways slush the snow.

"I'd even go to work for that girl. Somebody's got to protect her from bastards like *me* and saints like you. Hell, she might even make a famous singer, and we'll travel this country together. I went along with your momma, playin' like I was helpin' *you*, just so I could see Cassie."

His eyes blurred with tears and pain, Lone stared at the motorcycle, the fast snow lying over it a skin of white.

"At first, Charlotte just treated me like a son, for I *am* your big brother. I wasn't *playin'* that night Virgil swooped down on us in his white-assed Cadillac convertible. That was one of the cleanest times in my life. And that goddamn Virgil had to put a bloody end to it. Charlotte told me it was the mean-heartest thing a man ever did. Drove across the Cumberland Mountains with his mind set, come home to people who lived their whole life by what he preached, played with us, made fools of us, and then he laid down and put a hole in his head. Deliberately, to ruin your life like he ruined his own.

"And you ain't no better—if we could just see you clear enough. I won't feel clean till I've shit all *over* you, son. Then I'll be fit for Cassie. And you'll be my brother."

"Yeah, you're my brother, when you ain't tryin' to corrupt my mother!"

"Nobody corrupted her."

"Yeah, I know. A whore from the start. You don't have to say it." Lone tried to keep Boyd from knowing that he was crying. He strained his neck against the scarf to make his body rigid.

"You was in jail, Virgil was buried, she didn't *have* nobody. So one fine night while Cassie was singin' on the radio, she let me git in the bed with her. Then she turned on me, and called me names, like nothin' had happened, and her a whore like my momma."

"She always played like she was pure and good—"

"Yeah, what kind a mother would do that to you? Just go home and look at her, look at your mother, close."

"You son of a bitch," said Lone, struggling to break loose, "I ain't takin' no torment from you!"

"Torment?" Boyd pushed Lone's face into the coal dust and snow. "Why, I wouldn't torment you!" He dug his knee into Lone's back, then jerked him to his feet, pulling tightly on the scarf with both hands, dragging him by the neck. Boyd jerked back, and Lone's head struck wood. The silk dug more deeply into his neck as he clawed at the scarf, drawing blood with his own fingernails. "Torment you? Now when I ever torment you?"

Lone smelled charred wood. Around and above him in the shifting veils of snow stood the black frame of the tipple. Behind Lone, behind the post, Boyd pulled at the scarf. Then Boyd was in front of him, but he still couldn't move his head. He reached back and his fingers, aching and cold, touched the silk knot and the tassels. His fingers fumbled at the tight knot. He kicked at Boyd. The light behind Boyd flashed on a knife in his hand.

"Better stop kicking, Lone. Knives cut. See?"

Lone felt the polo shirt break across his chest as a cold blade ran up and nicked his chin. The shirt fluttered like a vest. As Lone started kicking again, Boyd got behind the post, and Lone heard the knife stab into the wood above his head.

"Did I torment you when I fixed up that junked motor-sickle for you? You think I didn't know what runnin' with me would do to you? And it sure did."

Boyd's arms were around the post, around Lone's waist, his hands unbuckling Lone's belt. Lone jerked at the silk knot behind his head, behind the post.

"I wouldn't dream of tellin' you that ever'thing's turned out just like I hoped it would. Hell, I don't want to torment my own brother."

As the wide leather belt slipped through the loops around Lone's waist, Boyd jumped in front of him again, swinging in the same swooping motion the belt across his hips. The buckle stung. Then Boyd whirled it around above his head and let it go into the dark beyond the circle of light where the snow fell.

"That's it. Go ahead and kick." Boyd grabbed one of his feet and pulled at the boot. "Kick now and you'll choke yourself to death. Go ahead, you got my permission." Boyd jerked off the boot and flung it into the dark. Staring at Lone, standing still, he let the silence seal them off from the rest of Harmon.

"I sure ain't gonna tell you about your family," Boyd said, whispering. "The whole sorry pack a bastards—rotten, skin to core. Calm down. . . . Why, nobody wants to torment you. They ain't nothin' wrong for you to feel tormented."

Boyd lifted Lone's other leg and struggled with the boot, as Lone clawed at the silk knot. "It ain't your fault your daddy is the filthiest, sorriest drunkard within fifty thousand miles. And your Uncle Kyle—you cain't help it if he cain't sleep at night 'less he's got a little blood on him. And it ain't your fault your little sister wants to take up with the lowest trash in Harmon quick as she can break out of that prison. And it ain't *your* fault your Uncle Virgil turned out not to have one ounce a faith to heal a chigger bite. And that your Momma'd go to bed with the devil, if he'd chance it. What you think she works in a *ho*tel for? What you think that crippled judge was doin' draggin' himself in there this evenin'?

"Ain't you gonna say somethin'? Ain't gonna give me the satisfaction, huh? Well, don't you reckon that's what she's givin' *him*? Ain't he already paid for it? How you think you walked out of that jail free? She hinted to me she'd do it if she had to. I'll stick that knife in you, if you beg me hard enough, Saint Lone."

Boyd yanked at the waist of Lone's trousers until the snap broke, then he jerked one leg up and pulled on the cuff, then on the other, the glare from the headlight breaking his movements into sharp black fragments, until he had shucked them off.

"But don't let it torment you. Try not to think about it." He threw the trousers into Lone's face, letting them fall to his feet. "It cain't none of it be any your fault, so what is they for me to torment you about, even if I wanted to?"

Shivering, dressed only in the ripped polo, his jacket, and

his shorts, Lone looked at Boyd, a black mass, the snow a veil, fluttering behind him in the headlight.

"Please, Boyd, stay away from Cassie. She'll end up just like her momma!"

"Cassie's not like *any* of you!"

"She's foul if she goes anywhere near *you!*"

"Foul! You! You! Don't you know anything about *you?* Are *you* so pure? God, ever-lovin' God *damn* it! Ain't none of it *your* fault? That's right, disown her, disown *all* your sins! She wants to be like you were, and I'm gonna help her, and I'll hate ever' move that reminds me of you, but I will, just to be *with* her. But don't ever forget—*you started* it. I'm guilty. I don't deny it. But *you!* You're *pure.* That's it. Keep pullin' at that knot. Break loose and run—*run* from filth like me!

"But people that don't know us could look at us and not see no difference, though. Turn yourself inside out, Lone, so ever'body can see how pure you are! You need some way for ever'body to see the difference between me and you. This'll show how lily-white you are." Boyd scooped up snow and coal dust and threw them against Lone's chest. He scraped a huge handful off the seat of his 'cycle and dumped it over Lone's head. "You look like a monument. But we need to christen you."

Blinded by dust and snow, Lone heard a loud pop and a long hiss and felt cold beer on his head, running down his back and his chest. "I christen you Saint Lone, loved by all!"

Boyd stopped. He let the silence enclose Lone. Lone couldn't see. He didn't know where Boyd was. Then he felt his breath on his face.

"But if I was a statue, I wouldn't want to stand around with my pecker hanging out. I'd want some little boy to come along and chisel the son-of-a-bitch *off.*"

Boyd's cold, gloved hand fumbled around Lone's groin and grabbed his penis viciously. At the touch of the blade against his skin, Lone shuddered throughout his body and screamed and raked his fingernails into the knot behind his head.

"Naw, naw, naw," said Boyd, behind him now, pulling on

the scarf, "if I did that, you couldn't have no kids. I want you to have kids, Lone. So maybe they'll all grow up to be like *me*."

The scarf, like a dull knife, slipped across his throat. Boyd put his foot against Lone's back and shoved him away from the post. "Don't ever forgive her, Lone! Hate her! Hate Virgil! Hate Kyle! Hate Coot! Don't forgive 'em, damn your soul! All the hate I ever felt, I put into you, son. But tonight, I'm gittin' shut of you! I always wanted to see you go down so I could spit on you." Lone staggered in the clearing, unable to see Boyd. Then Boyd tripped him, and Lone heard him hawk and felt spit strike his face.

"Now you lay there till you putrefy. And don't you *ever* forgive *me!*"

Through a wavering blur of snow and darkness, Lone saw Boyd standing above him, the scarf dangling around his neck, wiping tears from his eyes with the back of his gloved hand.

The motor revved again, the headlight came straight at Lone, the tires spewed dirt and snow on Lone's legs as Boyd swerved, and the motorcycle roared out of the clearing. Lone tensed his body, trying to stop shivering.

CHAPTER

24

MOMMA'S BEDROOM WINDOW WAS DARK. OVER THE SNOW UNDER the bare buckeye tree stretched a swath of light from the kitchen.

In the dark hall, light exploded as Cassie threw a lump of coal on red ashes in their bedroom. The trembling light from the grate showed his face in the mirror over Momma's dresser: snow melted in his blond hair, and through the dirt streaks of blood showed on his face. Snow, coal grit, and gravel clung to his wet corduroys. In the mirror shadows of the flames in the grate leaped against him.

When he turned, Cassie stood in the doorway of their room, wearing Gypsy's blue blouse and yellow slacks, bracing herself with both hands against the doorjamb. "Lone. . . ." Smoke thickened in the grate, the odor drifted across the room and Lone inhaled it in the hall, acrid, almost suffocating. "He—beat you up—didn't he?" said Cassie, her face black with dark, shadows of flames licking her shoulder. "Come in and go to bed."

"I'm glad that boy's finally home." Momma's voice, coming down the hall from the kitchen, startled him, made him shudder.

"It's all over. You can sleep in the big bed tonight," Cassie said, quickly, her voice throbbing, "and I'll sleep on the cot."

"It's awful cold tonight," said Momma, "and we need some coal to bank these fires."

"Play like you don't hear her. I told her you and Boyd was fightin'. She's afraid of somethin'."

"Lord, I don't know what I would a done if they'd took him off to La Grange—and me with no man about the house at a time like this."

"She's hopin' you won't come in there." Lone walked among the stacks of boxes in the hall. "Leave her alone, honey."

He walked along the narrow winding space among the boxes, his shoulders scraping against cardboard on each side.

Wearing a pair of his old, yellowed white socks, Momma stood on some newspapers spread over the floor under the padded plank that rested on the back of a straight chair and the oak table. A cup of steaming coffee sat on the curve of the table, within reach from where she stood, ironing, wearing the new slip. She stood behind her maid's uniform that hung, stiff, on a hanger hooked into one of the links in the light chain, casting a shadow over Lone. Lying wrinkled and damp on top and hanging limply over the edge of the board, the yellow dress she had worn last night steamed as the iron hissed over it.

"How can you stand to be out in this hurtin' cold?" When she bent slightly to thump the beak of the iron into an arm hole of the dress, he saw her head, but she did not look up, a hank of her black hair concealing her face. "Kyle brung me home. I been walkin' Harmon, looking for us another home. . . . Listen, honey, would you do your momma one last favor and bring us in some coal? It's freezin' fast outsyonder."

Lone stood in the doorway, staying in the shadow her green uniform cast, and stared at her.

"Well, don't shiver over there in the dark. Come over by the stove and thaw out." She ironed very carefully around the neck, under the yellow collar. Then she propped the iron back and picked up the lopsided coal bucket. "Here's the bucket."

Looking at the dress as she handled it with one hand, she held the bucket out to him with the other.

Not moving, Lone stared at her.

"Cassie, I said stay in your room." Momma looked past Lone at Cassie. He sensed her behind him, among the boxes. "See, Lone, I got on those socks you used to wear on your early mornin' paper route that kept your feet so nice and warm. Found 'em when I'uz packin'. Now, honey, will you take this bucket and go out to the coal pile?"

Lone didn't move.

Momma set the bucket beside the stove and opened the oven door. "That ought a take some of this chill off." She started on the collar, stopped, feeling his eyes on her, and went to the stove again. "What you need is a nice, steamin' cup a coffee before you go back out in that blowin' snow and— Set down." The fresh coffee smoked beside her own cup, where the steam had stopped rising.

Slowly, he walked toward her.

"Don't, Lone," Cassie whispered.

He wished Cassie had the strength to stop him.

Momma thumped the board with the beak of the iron. "Drink that coffee, honey." She glanced in his direction, keeping her head down, letting her hair screen her eyes from his. "You're shiverin' somethin' awful." The iron passed, steaming, over the dull wrinkles, leaving a smooth yellow sheen. "Will you please git me that coal so I can bank these fires to keep us from freezin' to death, and we can git settled in bed? I gotta git up and git *your* clothes ready for school, then git myself off to work in the mornin'."

She stopped, looked into his face, and flinched. When she looked away from his dirty, bloody face and down at her ironing again, he knew she was guilty. She thumped the iron harder and faster, but he saw that her body shuddered. "Lone, please stop that starin'."

"You ironin' that thing," said Cassie, behind him, "or beatin' it to death?"

"Cassie," said Momma, looking over Lone's shoulder, "you're just beggin' for a good slap in the face."

"What's a *good* slap?" Lone knew that she was deliberately provoking Momma.

Momma edged between the coned end of the ironing board and the stove, bumping the plank slightly, sloshing the coffee, and walked across the linoleum to the hall doorway, slipping an inch on one of the newspapers in the cotton socks as Lone turned, saw Boyd's goggles over Cassie's eyes.

"You think I won't slap a little hellion like you?"

Cassie turned toward the boxes and the shadows of flames on the wall.

As Momma walked back toward Lone, the table, and the ironing board, her head down, the papers rustling under her feet, Lone stared at her, the fingers of one hand pressing into the padded board, coffee dripping over the edge of the table down the back of the other hand.

She stopped. "Lone, stop it! Stop starin' at me!"

Lone realized that he *couldn't* stop. If only she would stand still and let him turn her into a statue with a stare.

Covering her confusion, Momma reached for Lone's cup quickly, her teeth clashing on the rim, and the coffee scalded her mouth. She swallowed painfully, her face pinched in toward her mouth and nose, to keep from spewing it in Lone's face.

"Look at me, Momma. Momma, I said look at me." Lone walked around the ironing board and stood very close to her. The hanging uniform lay stiffly against the back of his head. "I want to see your face when I ask you." Slowly, she turned and looked at him. Her eyes showed the pain she felt at seeing his cut face, but she stifled a cry. "Boyd was here, Momma, while—while you were—uptown. He stood by Cassie's bed and delivered Coot some information and some whiskey to wash it down with. Coot couldn't stomach either one. He's gone home—to Black Mountain. Is what Boyd told him true, Momma?"

"He was lyin', Lone. I mean, I don't know what he said,

but— You know a body cain't believe a word Boyd Weaver says . . ."

"I don't believe a damn thing *yet*, Momma. All I got to do is look in your eyes."

"Cassie, please don't listen to him."

Cassie stood beside the table, a few steps behind him, wearing the goggles.

"She's gonna hear every word. I want her to know, so's she can git the hell outa here, and away from Boyd, and never come back. She don't need *me* to tell her. All she has to do is look in your eyes. Remember how I'd tell you I wasn't with Boyd last summer and you'd hold my head and look in my eyes and catch me in a lie?" Lone pressed both palms on her cheeks and forced her to look at him. "Right in there in that bed, while I'uz locked up, Momma. . . . And again tonight in the *hotel* with Gentry. . . . Was Boyd lyin'?" Momma tried to turn her head. "Turn your head and look at *me*. Look at her, Cassie. Open your eyes, Momma."

Behind him, Lone heard the rubbery sound of goggles and turned and saw them dangle around Cassie's neck and saw Momma's guilt in Cassie's eyes. Turning, yelling, "You whore!" Lone slapped Momma.

The blow forced her eyes open wide, but they seemed not to blink. As the print of his hand inflamed her cheek like a stain, her eyes stared at him—a look of confessed guilt so frank he stepped back, pushing against the ironing board. The yellow dress slid down to the floor and buckled over his feet. The look that stayed in her eyes seemed to make him a gift of her absolute guilt. As he bent to pick up the dress, concealing his shame, she began to walk slowly past him. Holding the dress against his chest, smelling the dampness and the freshly ironed cotton, he listened to her leave the room.

"Come on now, Lone," said Cassie, taking his hand. "Let's go in our room."

"Why did I have to grow up thinkin' you and her was the only good in Harmon County?" He let her take his hand, and as he turned he saw Momma's door close and the shadows of flames in the grate lap gently against the panels.

Cassie led him among the stacked boxes in the hall. In the doorway to his own room, he stopped and looked at Momma's closed door. "Cassie, did you see . . . ?"

"Come on, Lone."

"Listen."

"Let her cry. Then she'll go to sleep."

"She'll never be like she . . ."

"No, she won't."

"You neither, after tonight . . ."

"Tomorrow night, we'll sleep at Gran'daddy's. And it will all be over. Come on in."

"I'm so tired. . . . I feel—dead. . . ." Cassie pulled him onto the big bed. The coal smoked in the grate, small blue flames sputtered.

As she lay down beside him, snow spat against the windowpane over his cot across the room. He felt the empty space between. He felt her fingers gently digging into his fist until he uncurled the fingers of one hand and felt her palm, moist and cold, slide against his.

"You're shiverin', you're tremblin'."

"I cain't stop," Lone said. Snow fluttered on the glass and stuck. "I put a present on her bed. A necklace—pearls."

"She found it, and hid it. She was ashamed."

"And a new dress for you."

"I'll put it on when I wake up."

She pulled the quilts over them, and as her body warmed, his trembling subsided. He hugged her bony body to him. He was back in that time when they slept together before the cot separated them. The hands that caressed him were gentle, soft, slow, and grew warmer as they moved over the brown corduroy on his legs and over his bare chest.

"Why did Virgil do it, Cassie?"

"I couldn't hide it. He saw it in my eyes—that I was fakin', and that I knew *he* was fakin' it, too. That triggered it. He come home to do it, I reckon, and that triggered it. I wasn't gonna tell you. But we've got to start." Her fingers stroked his aching ribs. "Lone, it's been like all my life, watching a spider start in a sunshiny corner of the buckeye tree . . ." Her fingers slid over the curve of his bare stomach. ". . . and spin a cobweb till it gets dark—but I never could tell nobody and—that's the awfullest thing in the world."

So weary that he was hardly able to move, he turned his head and felt her small breasts along his jaw through Gypsy's silky blue blouse. He felt her breath on his neck, the shuddering beat of her heart. Her warm tears fell on the blouse and turned cold on his cheek. She writhed under him, kissing his neck. As though trying to soak up all the warmth of his body, suck all his energy with kisses, she moaned, "Boyd!"

Pushing her away from him, Lone jumped up and swayed over her. "Virgil! Virgil called *my* name that way, that night! Then he shot himself, he shot his brains out, Cassie!"

She lay in the pallid light from the snow and the fire, her blouse darkly wet over one breast.

"Look at me! *I'm* not gonna die! You want me to die, Cassie? You want me to die, don't you? Say it. I *know* it! But I ain't gonna kill myself, *no*body has to kill himself. Boyd stripped me down tonight, like just bein' naked would be enough to kill me. You git Gypsy's clothes off your back, girl!"

Cassie cringed on the bed. Grabbing the tail of the blouse with both hands, Lone pulled her off the bed, ripping the blouse as she hit the floor, hard enough to hurt. He threw it into the air and it floated down like a tent, sliding against his shoulders. As he reached for her feet, Cassie rolled around and around on the floor, trying to keep out of his reach. "Stick 'em up here!" He yanked one boot off and flung it against the wall. Cassie crawled on her hands and knees toward the bed. Lone grabbed her other foot, jerked off the boot and flung it.

When he turned again, Cassie stood, bouncing, in the middle of the bed, trying to strike a balance. Lone jerked her feet out from under her. The way she landed flat on her back and bounced, making a little uhuhuh sound, made him feel sorry for her. He pulled hard on the cuffs of the yellow slacks until they slipped over her ankles, and he lost his balance and staggered backward onto his cot, then rolled to his feet again and, laughing, flung the slacks behind him.

Cassie stood in the middle of the room, naked, holding Gypsy's red panties out to him, trying to keep from giggling. Taking the panties, he tossed them over his shoulder.

"All right, goddamn it, you're my sister and you're buck naked, and I can see you, and I ain't about to blink or blush."

But he half turned aside as he shucked off his leather jacket, as if getting ready for bed, but feeling her eyes upon him. He slung the jacket into a dark corner of the room. When Cassie took hold of the tail of his polo shirt that Boyd had ripped up the front, he plunged away from her so it would come off. She turned to him again, and he handed her his trousers, and she flung them into a corner, and when she looked up again, he was naked.

"Now look, damn it, *I'm* naked, too, see?"

"Yeah, I see."

"Well, so what?"

"Nothin'."

"That's right. Nothin'."

"I'm cold, though."

"Huddle close to the fire."

"It died down."

Seeing nothing to poke it with, Lone reached for a flap of torn wallpaper, ripped it off, and fanned the fire with it until the coal began to flare up. Then he fed the flames with the strip of wallpaper.

"Now we've had a good look at each other, reckon I could huddle up to that new dress you got me?"

"To sleep in?"

"Any law says I cain't?"

"Go ahead."

Lone crawled under the covers. From his cot, he looked across the room at Cassie. She wiggled into the soft blue dress that had tiny white flowers sprinkled over it.

"How do I look, now?"

"I'll worry about that tomorrow."

Lone closed his eyes, burning from the coal smoke. Listening to Cassie crawl into the big bed, he hoped Momma had stopped crying.

"Night, night, Lone."

"Cassie, listen."

"What?"

"Can you still hear her?"

"No."

"Night, night, Cassie. Sleep tight."